Shepherd of the Kingdom

By: S.L. Kotar and J.E. Gessler

Ahead of the Press
St. Louis, MO

Library of Congress Cataloguing-in-Publication Data

Shepherd of the Kingdom   /
S.L. Kotar and J.E. Gessler

ISBN   KINDLE   978-1-945594-74-8   (ebook)
ISBN   PAPERBACK   978-1-945594-73-1

Ahead of The Press Publishing
St. Louis, Missouri

DEDICATION

"Shepherd of the Kingdom"

This novel is dedicated with reverence to all the classic monsters, the men who brought them to life and the individuals who created them. To Dracula and Frankenstein's monster, the Wolf Man and the Invisible Man; to Lugosi and Karloff and Lon Chaney, Jr. and Claude Rains; to Bram Stoker and Mary Shelley, Curt Siodmak, H. G. Wells and R. C. Sherriff and to all who terrified us and inspired us and touched both our fear and our hearts, we thank you.

SLK

And JEG, always

Table of Contents

"SHEPHERD OF THE KINGDOM"

To the naked eye, the dark heavens were lit with a billion stars, twinkling from afar. They were the celestial orbs upon which lovers dreamed, poets derived inspiration and astronomers coveted.

Greater even than these, due to its closer proximity to Earth, shone the moon. Full, bright and nearly within touching distance of wide-eyed children, the satellite had withstood the test of time, absorbing the strikes of falling asteroids, defying the gravitational pull of its closest neighbor and even resisting the incessant gnawing of mice which desired the surface, reputedly made of green cheese.

The expression, "God is in His heaven and all is right with the world" seemed particularly apt this night. No clouds marred the view and the sky seemed particularly amenable for late night gazing. Sitting on a bench in Central Park or leaning back against the wall of a high-rise apartment complex with a bit of breeze drifting in from the east, a solitary human might dare believe in universal brotherhood and goodwill toward Men.

The night, with the distant blessing of the stars, covered ghettos, areas of famine, pestilence and plague. It hid war zones, smoothed out mountains, filled in valleys. The night gave rise to Pegasus, the flying horse; it titillated the ancient gods, prompting some to mercy and others to mischief.

The known and the unknown merged in a fluidity of time past and time future, making the "now" both yesterday and tomorrow.

Hundreds of millions of *homo sapiens* prayed to their deities, whether in thanksgiving or supplication, but all with hope, if not outright faith, that some sentient All Powerful being would hear their thoughts.

In that, they were correct. Whether their hearts would be gladdened to know exactly who eavesdropped on their private transmissions remained the Great Unanswered question, for in the Beyond there existed much that religion, science and superstition omitted.

For lack of a better word, call it a void.

CHAPTER 1

"If you don't step back, you'll get your toes run over. And you're likely to ruin a lot more than your Gucci shoes."

Stinging from the rebuke, meant neither to be kind nor friendly, the youth stepped off the curb and into the street, positioning himself between the speaker and the approaching object of attention. As the speeding black limousine passed, greasy black water from standing runoff, pooled at the side of the road, doused his K-Mart footwear.

Behind him, he heard snickers from the assemblage and burned with shame.

"Shit!" he cursed, more to sound like an "old boy," which he could not be considered by any stretch of the imagination, than from any acute distress. While the shoes and suit were the best he had, they were hardly a ticket to the eclipse.

Wiping the obvious wet spots from his cuffs, then swiping his foot on the back of his trouser legs, Shepherd Kingston raised the camera to his eye. A half dozen other flashbulbs lit the night in accompaniment as he snapped off his picture.

"There goes your exclusive," a woman's voice jeered. "Go down the street to the Roxy. I heard they were showing a rerun of *A Hard Day's Night*. Maybe Paul McCartney will show up and you can take a few 'pix' for the local tip sheet."

While common wisdom held competition to be the soul of inspiration, in the world of freelance photography, it represented the kiss of death. Those outsiders attempting to break into an already bloated profession were considered less than the scum of the earth.

"If Paul did," Shepherd hissed, wounded because of his youth, inexperience and unemployed status, three strikes against him before he ever came to bat, "I'd damn sure get an interview."

No one listened. They had heard it all before. Thirty-odd years ago, someone might even have told them the same thing. They did not want to be reminded of past failures. Their lives existed only for the moment, which happened to be 6 May, 1989. What transpired in the dark regions of yesteryear counted only at 3 A.M., when the battle-scarred gathered in the recesses of cheap bars to brag about snaps taken of long-dead celebrities.

Normally, Shepherd would have rushed alongside the desultory group, clicking off pictures as he went, with as much discretion as an amateur at a friend's wedding. Being desperately low on film, however, the option of wasting half a dozen rolls in the hope of getting one saleable print did not present an option.

Waiting until the mob dispersed, their "safety in numbers" metamorphing into "every man for himself," he sauntered toward the entrance of the SoHo Grand. The subterfuge of hiding his camera behind his back fooled no one.

As a tactic, it had existed since the dawn of Thomas Edison.

Shepherd acted on errant hope, nothing more. In the world of high finance he attempted to capture for fleeting posterity, the freelance photographer was as common as interest rate fluctuations. Nothing he could do or say would make an impression on anyone.

He stood, in the eyes of the world, a nobody. A "less than nobody," his friend and mentor, Abraham Trent, had pointed out to him more times than he could remember. Unlike the professional's comments, his advice had not meant to hurt, but rather to educate. Like other warnings Shepherd received, it had gone unheeded.

"One great shot will establish me," he repeated for the one hundredth time. "Just one big sale and I'll have my foot in the door."

Feet, he learned, were notoriously susceptible to being run over, slammed in elevators, or implanted on his posterior.

"Good evening, sir," he respectfully addressed the doorman. He might have been speaking in pig-Latin for all the response he received. "A lot of excitement going on inside."

The liveried servant finally reacted by shooing him away.

"Bug off."

"I can make it worth your while," Shepherd suggested. Unlike a Buckingham Palace guard, the doorman rolled his eyes, unlikely he had even heard of those illustrious icons of un-emotion and "stiff upper lip." They did not travel with the Queen and the only royalty this American acknowledged walked on red carpets leading to hotel foyers.

"How? With what – Monopoly money?"

Shepherd bristled at the copyrighted insult and the generic slur. While a fact he did not have a dime to his name, he fancied himself enough of a dandy to inspire respect, if not bows. For all the doorman knew, he might have been the star of his own television series.

He should have remembered his locale: Manhattan. It took more than a pretty face to impress the natives. It took money.

"I can write a check," he offered, feeling the fool. All he could think of to say, the statement assuaged pride if nothing else.

"I know that kind of check," the employee grimaced. "My brother-in-law works for an *Avant guard* theatre couple blocks down from the Great White Way. They call it 'off off Broadway.' The producer pays him with checks that bounce higher than a basketball."

"I freelance for the *Times,*" Shepherd tried, without much heart.

"Yeah, I know. And in my spare time I fly James Bond's jet airplane. Beat it before The Quality calls for an exterminator."

Unsure whether the doorman referred to an actual person, or lumped those inside under one umbrella, he smiled and wandered away.

"The Quality," he muttered under his breath. "Well, they all started out in diapers, just like everyone else."

As a parting shot, it fell short of a three-pointer at the buzzer.

Crossing the street against the light, Shepherd positioned himself directly opposite the hotel. Craning his neck upward, he stared with hunger at the brightly-colored windows, sparkling like jewels in the night.

"A reliable informant" had told him three ballrooms had been reserved for the shindig of Wall Street Wizards. Live bands, with names he could recognize, played in each one. Supplementing food provided by the hotel's Five Star chef, catered dishes were brought in from "Tony's," a trendy eatery where a cup of expresso started at ten dollars.

Not only party rooms, his friend and paid stringer had reported, but the top five floors had been reserved for "dalliances," should any of the Rich and Famous care to powder their noses, or exchange hot tips under silk sheets.

Shepherd wistfully ran his eyes over the heights he aspired to climb. Had he been a jock or a super hero, he might have considered scaling those walls, then slipping through an open window. But he lacked the strength, as any number of women observing him on the beach, could attest. Although tall and lanky, the youth bore no more muscle than that which he earned by right of gender.

His claim to earning those stares came not from physique, but boyish good looks, sentient blue eyes and blond hair, worn unstylishly long. Had he wished, he might have conquered those sunbathers with a wink and an invitation for dinner, but he did not. Like him, they were just wannabes, hoping for a part in a play, a chance at a modeling job, or marriage to a wealthy playboy. Were he going to shell out fifty dollars on an intimate supper, he would need more incentive than a quick jump with a girl as anonymous as he.

Not that baser emotions failed to stir his blood. While he could not claim to be the most experienced of lovers, he imagined himself a stud, capable of pleasing even the most demanding of ladies. He simply did not have the time – or the money – to waste.

Dreams of "making it" in the field of photography occupied his waking and sleeping hours. To be someone: to have a recognized style and a portfolio including the top newspapers and journals in the world mattered more than anything.

Everything else would come later.

If wishes were horses, Shepherd Kingston would have ridden to the penthouse suite of the hotel, slipped through the door of a boudoir and snapped photographs to his heart's content. But wishes were not horses, and his feet were as planted to the ground as though he were a weed, growing wild between cracks in the sidewalk.

"Damn!" And then, just as suddenly, "I'll be damned!" as his acute eyesight detected a figure at the uppermost window. While he could not make out the face, the body contours gave the impression of breasts and slim hips. A woman. A strikingly beautiful creature of the night.

In a moment of pure madness, Shepherd raised his left hand and waved. A gesture, no more. He could not even be certain the woman looked his way; more likely, she contemplated the heavens, disinterested in so humble a personage as himself.

No matter the direction of her gaze, the moment he waved she disappeared. Gone as suddenly as though she had never existed. Perhaps, he mused, he had been mistaken. There had been no one at the window.

Yet such rationale did not explain why he had broken out into a cold sweat. She had been there; she had seen him wave.

Ego, Trent would have chided him. *Pure, unadulterated ego.*

And so it seemed.

At that moment, an idea struck. Nothing new; nothing which had not been tried before, by ten score of nameless photographers. But a hope. Sprinting back across the street, Shepherd once more approached the canopied, red-carpeted entranceway.

He caught the doorman helping an elderly couple from their black Rolls Royce. No request to see an invitation, merely a sycophantic, "Have a pleasant evening," before escorting the pair toward the door, bowing behind their backs as they entered. Neither acknowledged his service.

Waiting until the expensive motorcar rolled away, Shepherd approached his erstwhile acquaintance. Seeing him, the doorman curled his lip.

"If you're looking for a job, they take applications at the rear door," he joked. "During regular business hours. Pay starts at five dollars an hour, which includes the uniform. I think they have several openings for busboys."

"Too heady for me," Shepherd confessed, almost giddy. "Say: I was thinking."

"Good for you."

"You have an interesting face."

"Everyone tells me that."

"I'm serious," he persisted, stepping aside as the front doors opened. Two men appeared, one Shepherd recognized as belonging to his own humble crowd of freelance photographers. A "bouncer" unceremoniously held the back of his suit collar.

"I catch you in here again without a pass, I'll break your neck," the well-muscled guardian advised. His voice sounded smooth, educated, singsong. Well-rehearsed. Shepherd decided the bouncer to be yet another wannabe, a Midwesterner who had come to the Big Apple hoping for a career on the stage.

Just working to keep a roof over my head until that call from my agent comes, he might have explained, had anyone asked. No one ever would.

The photographer angrily straightened his collar, shot Shepherd a hateful look, then sauntered away to smooth his feathers.

"It's men like that who keep the speakeasies in business," the youth remarked to the doorman as the discharged cameraman disappeared into the darkness.

"We haven't had speakeasies in New York since they retracted Prohibition," the doorman laughed. "You're either older than you look, or watch too many late-late movies."

"It's my friend," Shepherd agreed with a beguiling smile. "He's a professor. From the Dark Ages. He talks like that all the time. I guess some of his antiquated expressions rubbed off on me."

"If I were to hang around with a guy like that, he'd have to pay my rent," the doorman teased.

"He does," the youth replied, returning the unexpected grin. "But he's taught me a lot."

"I bet."

Ignoring the innuendo, Shepherd hurried on.

"About faces. 'Characters,' he calls them. You have a character actor's face."

"That just misses being a compliment."

"I mean it. You don't look like the run-of-the-mill New Yorker. You have something... special."

"I'm not your type."

"Not my type." Shepherd dismissed the comment with a wave. "That's not what I mean. I was thinking if you had some decent photographs of yourself – not a portfolio, I don't do that sort of work," he hastened to add. "But some snaps of yourself, standing beside a couple of big shots. You know what I mean –"

"John Wayne is dead."

"O.K., so he's dead. But what about the movers and shakers here tonight? The Wall Street Bigwigs. In New York, they're just as important as recording artists. More so," he added with emphasis. "These people run the world. Without financing, even John Wayne would have been nothing more than a lounge lizard."

"What's your point?"

"You can do better than this. Or at least make some serious money on the side."

"Doing what? I already told you, acting doesn't pay."

"That couple that just went in; you knew who they were, but they didn't know who you were. For all of them, you're just the doorman. A nameless, faceless flunky." The truth hurt, as Shepherd knew it would. He babbled on before the man could dwell on his lowly position and dismiss him as a fellow failure. "But if those people knew you – recognized you as someone with a name – they'd be more polite. More inclined to drop a little in your hand as you opened the car door for them. You understand what I'm saying. What's your name?"

"James Parkins," the man gave, though he could not, for the life of him, comprehend why he bothered to give away anything so intimate to a mere photographer.

"So this is how it goes," Shepherd continued, warming to his task. "Mr. and Mrs. High Finance roll up to this big hoopla. You open the door for them. They recognize you. They've seen your face around. You're not just a nobody to them, anymore. Maybe they've seen a picture of you with Paul McCartney's arm around your shoulder. It behooves them to be polite. They slip fifty bucks in your hand as a 'thank you' for your attention."

Parkins appeared thoughtful.

"Maybe," he decided.

"How long have you worked here?"

"Three years."

"That's a long time. You should be established. But you're not. That couple's probably been to parties here lots of times, but to them, you're just a fly-by-nighter. Not worthy of a kind word, much less a few bucks. Am I right?"

"So?"

"So, they see your picture in the *Times,* maybe. Standing beside someone they do recognize. That makes you a celebrity by association. Next time they see you, they say 'hello. 'The time after that, they tip you. Pretty soon, you're *Mister* Perkins and everyone knows you."

"You're gonna make me famous?"

"There's fame and there's fame," Shepherd reassured. "Do you want to stand here another three years, making minimum wage? Or do you want to go home with some real cash in your pocket?"

"You couldn't get a pic published in the *Times* to save your life."

"O.K., so I'm dreaming. But I have had photographs published in some of the trades. I sell another to the society column, this one with you and Mr. So-and-So and you've got a start. Maybe even you name in the caption. It's better than what you have now."

"What's the deal?"

"I hang around, snapping your picture with the next five or six arrivals. Who knows? Maybe one of them will be good enough to get published. At any rate, I'll give you copies. Ten of each," he bragged, hoping the lie did not reflect in his voice. "You show them around – maybe to your boss. He sees how you get along with the dignitaries and maybe you get a better job."

"That's all you want? To stand over there in the shadows taking pictures of me?"

"I want to get inside."

"You saw what happened to the last guy who sneaked in. You think Mr. Marks didn't mean it when he threatened to break that guy's neck?"

"I think he meant it," Shepherd avowed sincerely, and with meaning. "I take my chances – and if I'm caught, I tell 'Mr. Marks' I got in the back, through the serving entrance. How about it?"

He might have added "please" to the end of his sentence, but pride got the better of him.

"Ten copies, each? And you don't squeal on me when you're caught?"

"Cross my heart."

"And hope to die," Perkins finished for him. The sentiment went unappreciated. "All right But if you're stiffing me –"

"And hope to die," Shepherd reiterated.

Which happened to be the furthest thing from his mind.

CHAPTER 2

Shepherd saw the hotel employee coming toward him and avoided her "like the plague." She would know in an instant he did not belong. And he doubted very seriously he could entice her to fall for the line he had given the doorman.

Squirting through a narrow opening between a man's shoulder's and a woman's breasts, he muttered suitable apology.

"Sorry. Just got a hot tip. Gotta make it to my broker's before the closing bell." The woman's puzzled interrogative to the man, "I didn't know Wall Street was open on Saturday" went unanswered.

But then, she had not been invited for her brains.

Scampering up the sweeping staircase to the second level of the magnificent mezzanine, Shepherd ducked behind an elaborate floral arrangement to conceal his presence. Catching his breath, he glanced furtively around. So far, so good. No one had spotted him as an interloper.

A fellow photographer suffered a more inglorious fate. Hearing a commotion to his left, Shepherd inconspicuously glanced in that direction. There, to his amusement, he saw the gal who had advised him to stand outside the Roxy in the hope of taking the Pretty Beatle's picture, being unceremoniously escorted out. The woman, Shepherd noted, lacked her camera.

And would likely miss her dinner.

Suppressing a shudder more superficial than real, for he wished his competition no mercy, the youth unobtrusively turned away as they passed. The idea of inquiring where the expensive Canon had been deposited briefly crossed his mind, before being reluctantly discarded.

His motives were purely crass. First, his question would not go unnoticed by the bouncer, who would, after dumping his friend in the nearest dust bin, be back for him. Second, even if he located the camera, he would never be able to take it home. Abraham Trent, being a card-carrying member of the Moral Generation, would demand he return it.

More to the point, were he ever caught using purloined equipment around other photographers, he would surely find it inserted where the sun don't shine.

Lovingly tapping his own camera, Shepherd straightened his tie, brushed back his hair, then stepped into the open. Like a pigeon at a target shoot, he waited for the firing to commence. When no literal or figurative bullets went zinging his way, he smiled at his cleverness, walked casually down the stairs, and mingled.

Had he been ten years older or a generation wiser, Shepherd would have realized no amount of preening would make him anything other than one of the Great Unwashed. A man with money exuded poise, confidence, an Armani suit and wore cologne imported from Barbados. His suit came off the rack from J.C. Penney's, his after-shave smelled suspiciously like Old Spice and whatever *savoir faire* he assumed had been copied from watching Clifton Webb go down on the *Titanic.*

His confidence on the other hand, more correctly styled arrogance, fell in the category of unbounded.

Being a successful photographer, he had learned, required more than snapping impromptu pictures. One also had to know whose photograph to peddle. While building a portfolio of the merely wealthy impressed the uninitiated, editors only paid for candid shots of the influential and the famous.

Skirting a group of men he did not recognize and thus dismissed, Shepherd glided into the main floor, stopping occasionally to listen to snatches of conversation. Having no money of his own to invest, he found the topic of money necessarily foreign. But in his role of Casey, *Crime Photographer,* he suffered from acute awareness that he must appear to fit in.

Grabbing a glass of champagne from a passing waiter, he sipped the bubbly liquid, then smiled at the first woman who caught his eye.

"A good vintage, but over-chilled," he observed. "It always is, at such functions."

She turned away, as though he had insulted her wine selection. Promising himself never to use that line again, Shepherd drifted toward another group, where the speaker energetically gesticulated with one hand, while unsuccessfully balancing a glass in the other.

"I don't care what Edwards at the *Journal* reports," he snapped. "I say it's a bull market. Anyone investing in stocks at this time is –"

"Edwards has Greenspan's confidence," a man at his side retorted. His voice expressed weariness, as though giving advice, no matter how bland, ran contrary to his nature. "The Market is whatever Greenspan makes it."

"Greenspan is an old cow!" the other sniffed, sloshing red wine onto the carpet. The others in the group took a step back, fearful least they suffer the same fate.

Spinning on his heels, Shepherd ducked behind a caterer wheeling a cart of *hors d'oeuvres* and snapped the speaker's picture. With a caption like, "Greenspan is an old cow," he ought to be able to sell it for the equivalent of next month's rent.

Grinning to himself that he had gotten at least one saleable photo, Shepherd recommenced mingling. Having done his homework, he resumed the quest for other celebrities, discretely hiding the camera behind his back.

Spotting whom he thought to be John Thomas James, the pseudonym for the CEO of Baxter Investments, International, a man notoriously camera-shy, Shepherd made his way through the crowd, discretely looking for a place where he could take a snapshot in private. Unfortunately, Mr. James had positioned himself in the center of the floor, making stealth impossible.

Making a quick decision, Shepherd returned to the sweeping staircase. Going up them one at a time, as befit a man of commerce, he paused by his former hiding place. Bringing the camera to his eye, he refocused the lens when the sound of heavy footsteps alerted him to the fact his "friend," the bouncer, had returned.

Slipping the camera in his pocket, Shepherd sauntered away, crossing around the semicircular overhang until he had positioned himself behind another large floral arrangement. Unfortunately, he could see nothing but Mr. James' back from that angle. Hissing through his teeth, Shepherd determined to wait him out. Sooner or later, the great man would have to move away. When he did, he would have him.

Ten minutes passed without the worthy altering his position more than an inch. Couples came and went, but he had apparently decided to hold court exactly where he stood. Shepherd had almost decided to chance a reappearance by Mr. Marks and resume a place opposite, when a snatch of conversation drifted his way. Without knowing why, he paused to listen.

"I hear she's present tonight," a man remarked in hushed tones, obviously fearful of being overheard. Peering out through green leaves, the photographer absorbed the small gathering.

Beside the speaker, distinguished by an obvious toupee, a bald-headed man and a platinum blonde were huddled together by the curve of the stairwell. Shepherd identified the woman as being a high-ranking officer for one of the English banking houses. He did not think her picture worth taking, as she frequently appeared in the society columns, but his interest had been stirred by the mysterious "she" to whom the three dignitaries referred.

"I don't believe it," the woman, whose name, he remembered as Allison Breem, remarked. "She never makes public appearances."

"Nevertheless, I have it on good authority that she is here. My informant advised me she reserved the penthouse for the evening."

"My God," gasped the other, truly shocked. "How does one get an introduction to her?"

"I wish I knew." Both men turned to Ms. Breem. "You've met her, haven't you?"

"Me? No. I had an appointment once, but I never got in."

"But she's a foreigner, and you run the most prestigious British bank in New York."

The woman appreciated the compliment, but had little with which to enlighten her listeners. "She is not British."

"I heard she has a trace of an English accent and presumed..."

"Then you thought wrong. She is not English. Nor Scottish, Irish or Welsh. My sources tell me she represents the monarchy of a small Eastern European country."

"What country?"

"I... don't know," Ms. Breem admitted with more than a trace of puzzlement.

"What bank does she use?"

"I don't know that, either. I wish I did."

"This appointment you had with her. Why didn't she keep it?" The speaker failed to conceal his dire curiosity.

The banker hesitated, then pursed her lips. Her expression displayed more distaste than her words.

"I had the impression she thought I was a man."

"A man?"

"The name Allison; it can be used by either males or females. When I arrived at her office, I was told to wait. After several minutes, the secretary informed me 'Miss Elvina' had left the country that morning, on a matter of State."

"Queer business. Rude of her staff not to tell you immediately."

"That's just what I mean. When they discovered my gender, Ms. Elvina saw no reason to consult with me."

"But surely any of her advance men could have told her –"

"This was several years ago. She was just making her mark in the investment field. Since then, I have never heard of her dealing with any woman."

"Maybe she's looking for a husband," joked the man to her left.

"I don't know that she is unmarried. In fact," Ms. Breem continued, "I don't know anything about her at all."

"Except she's turned into the highest-risk speculator on Wall Street. An occupation, I might add, which has brought her astonishing success."

"Astonishing is hardly the word for it. From what I've learned – which isn't much – she has anticipated every fluctuation in the Market. And used it to her advantage."

"But surely someone must know something about her. In this day and age, no one can remain anonymous. She works for some Eastern European monarchy, indeed. God, how many are there?"

"I rather think she works for the devil," the lady remarked, raising her eyebrows before eliciting chuckles from her companions.

"Because she doesn't use your bank?"

"Because she's never wrong." The words, lightly spoken, were as serious as though accompanied by a funeral dirge.

Without any apparent cause, all three investors shivered. Both men glanced uncomfortably around the room.

"What caused that draft?"

"One of those damned porters probably left the front door open too long."

A poor excuse at best. Their discomfiture did have an unanticipated result, however, as they spotted Shepherd lurking nearby.

"Who's he?" hissed one of the men. Three pair of coldly calculating eyes trained on the youth, rendering him naked to their appraisals.

"He's nobody," Ms. Breem contemptuously diagnosed. Whether she made her decision from the cut of his cheap suit, the general lack of a moneyed aura around his head, or from some other, more subtle clue, mercifully went un-elucidated.

Without further conversation, the triumvirate dissipated, going their separate ways. They had touched on dangerous ground. Safety now came in the form of forgetfulness.

A desire to know more overcame hurt pride and Shepherd shadowed the banker. Biding his time until she stepped over to the appetizer table, he sidled up alongside.

"Excuse me, Ms. Breem," he began, swallowing his nervousness. "I couldn't help overhearing your conversation about Ms. Elvina. I'm doing a piece on her for the *Times* and I'd appreciate a moment of your time."

Allison Breem's expression turned blank. "I beg your pardon?"

"I'm doing a piece on –"

"I heard what you said," she replied in a chipped London accent, sounding broader and more distinct than previously. "But I do not understand your reference."

"You were speaking of Miss Elvina – the investor?" he cautiously trolled. The banker shook her head.

"I know of no person by that name."

Suppressing an irascible temper, Shepherd edged closer, implying by body language his capacity for keeping her confidence. The tactic only served to make the woman uncomfortable.

"I realize she does not bank with your institution, but –"

"I know of no person by that name," Breem repeated.

Finally irritated, Shepherd pressed the point.

"Miss Elvina; the European stock market genius," he added, anointing the enigmatic figure with an accolade of reverence. The look of puzzlement on his companion's face deepened. "I overheard your conversation with two gentlemen. Over there," he indicated with a toss of his long hair. "Just a moment ago."

Ms. Breem's brows knit as she riffled her fingers, less in denial than concern over failing memory.

"I – I have spoken to many people here," she tried. Had she been less controlled, Shepherd guessed she might have wrung her hands. "But I do not recall speaking of... this person."

"The investor who is never wrong," he prompted. "You went to see her, but she denied you access."

"Excuse me," came the lame apology. "You have mistaken me for someone else."

"You are Allison Breem?"

"Yes.... And you? Did I catch your name?"

Before Shepherd could answer, she spotted an acquaintance in the crowd. Abandoning any desire for food, she hurried away, forgetting, in her consternation, to make a farewell.

Normally he would have blown off her ignorance as subterfuge, but in this instance it proved more complex. As good an actor as she might be, her expression of forgetfulness could not be taken for anything but genuine.

Who was "Miss Elvina," and why did the mere mention of her name frighten people? How could she emerge as one of New York's most successful stock market investors and succeed in keeping her anonymity?

Why did she refuse to speak to women? More to the point, for whom did she work, and how did it come to pass she never erred?

Stifling an urge to follow Allison Breem, Shepherd scanned the room for the other two participants in the overheard conversation. Neither seemed to be present. As the keynote speakers had not yet addressed the audience, it did not stand to reason they had departed. He decided to search the men's rooms, hoping to corner one or both there, when a sensation of cold nearly overwhelmed him. Not until he drew the lapels of his coat closer did he realize the same phenomenon had occurred before.

Abruptly terminating the original conversation about Miss Elvina.

While hardly a student of the occult, Shepherd knew enough about unseen forces to attribute a sudden chill to one possessing extraordinary powers. Did Miss Elvina keep curious New Yorkers at bay by witchcraft?

Preposterous. Yet he knew someone who would disagree.

Never, ever disregard the supernatural, Trent often lectured. *Because* you *do not believe does not mean it does not exist.*

You're only saying that because you're an educator, Professor, Shepherd had argued.

I am saying it because I am older than you, and wiser. I know better than to disregard what I cannot explain as 'nonsense.' You would do well to emulate my example.

Shepherd used the word "nonsense" to dismiss all of Trent's studies. While such fascinations were enough to fill classrooms, they had no place in the real world.

If "Miss Elvina" existed, then she were flesh and blood. If she were "never wrong," then she had inside information. As simple as that.

"Simple" was also Trent's word for Shepherd.

Dismissing the sensation of cold with the same idea suggested by the two men who had now disappeared, the photographer checked his camera, nervously adjusted his tie, then went in search of rational explanations.

He had come seeking a break, a foot in the door, his chance at fame and fortune. A photograph of the elusive investor could portend a voyage to Lucky Town.

CHAPTER 3

Shepherd Kingston had a problem. He did not know what Miss Elvina looked like. The fact that no one in the room knew either hardly pacified. Ignorance was not bliss but rather the missed opportunity of a lifetime.

Had he been pressed, he might have argued that his very soul depended upon the outcome.

The soul of his career, certainly. Fame and fortune could not be achieved by hawking photographs of nobility. Not when royalty hid in the wings.

Shepherd smiled at the comparison. Trent would appreciate it. A devout Anglophile, anything having to do with the British Isles or the Queen immediately caught his attention. To that list his young protégée might have added trolls, faeries, leprechauns and the evil "sidhee," but only if he wished to subject himself to a long lecture, inevitably beginning with the old chestnut, "There are more things in heaven and earth, Horatio, than are dreamt of in your philosophy...."

He had once sarcastically remarked Hamlet's line constituted the last refuge of poor script writers and tired professors, and had promptly gotten himself thrown out of Trent's "flat." Without supper, a far worse punishment than being banished to the corner, it had taken an hour to contemplate his sins before composing an apology.

What history did Miss Elvina, no first name given, hide, and more importantly, when did she plan her grand entrance? Surely she would not stay in her penthouse all night. If she had taken the trouble to come, a grand entrance would be in the offing. Or would it? Perhaps her plan comprised nothing greater than slipping in the back entrance and circulating among those who were not her peers.

Scanning the room, Shepherd tried to guess. There were any number of attractive women present. Most he dismissed as "fluff," premiere members of the Greater New York Escort Service. Dowdy wives were never invited to such gatherings. While they suited admirably at formal dinner tables, or posing for Christmas cards with their proud offspring, they made a poor impression for the husband/banker/investor wishing to move up the exclusive corporate ladder.

He counted sixty women and wrote off forty-five, including Ms. Breem, who would not have been flattered by his dismissal. That left fifteen possibles. Making himself look agreeable by clutching a glass of sparkling wine, Shepherd began his exploration.

Three glasses of champagne and one turn around the room later, he parked himself in the corner of the ballroom to reassess. If Mystery Woman truly were present, then she had to be as dull as dishwater, for he had found no one extraordinary. Including snatches of conversations concerning the bond market and investments in *Sud Arrow,* which were "sure to quadruple within the next five years," he remained sorely unimpressed.

Not having any money of his own, portfolios were as alien and as useless as tax shelters. Surely Ms. Elvina would have more to comment on than those.

Such as the wonders of working for a monarch, and how she divined inspiration from the stars.

Lack of success only served to whet Shepherd's appetite. Not only would he manage to photograph this extraordinary lady, he would interview her, as well. An exclusive. Byline material. His head swam, which had nothing to do, he assured himself, with the fact he had consumed copious amounts of alcohol.

Passing up innumerable changes to photograph the Suddenly Unimportant, Shepherd resumed his mingling, praying for a lucky encounter. It never occurred to him Ms. Breem and her gentleman companions had been in error. Good authority promised Miss Elvina's presence and so it must be true. Doubt constituted failure.

The party was excruciatingly dull. Minutes dragged like hours. Shepherd drank more champagne. The wine sharpened his wit, giving him an exulted sense of his own worth. No longer did he shrink into the wallpaper when the tuxedo-clad bouncers drew near. He had entered as an invited guest.

Or the next best thing.

Strangely, this newly acquired confidence kept the thugs at bay, for whenever one suspected him of being a party crasher, he would get only so far before being diverted by a more obvious suspect. Shepherd counted three of his brotherhood shown the door, while he remained unmolested.

The gods, it seemed, were on his side.

The itinerary called for sit-down banquet at 10:00 P.M.. Coinciding with dinner, an ensemble the size of the New York Yankees roster began playing in an adjacent ballroom. Without the brass to bluff his way into the feed, the youth drifted into the dance hall. It stood to reason that when Miss Elvina finally made her appearance, it would not be to partake of the jet set's version of rubber chicken. With all her money, she could afford surf and turf. Therefore, her grand entrance would come during the recital of "Here Comes the Queen."

Ordinarily, Shepherd would not know the difference between "Rule Britannia" and "Hail to the Chief," but for Trent's penchant for England. Most of the classical music he played on his antique gramophone originated from Britain, or were derived from Celtic influences. Shepherd therefore readied himself to stand at attention when the orchestra struck the first notes of anything remotely familiar.

He need not have bothered, for the band played nothing but what Trent would have styled "contemporary pop," his euphemism for "crap." Trent never swore, never even used slang in his vocabulary. It made their conversations off kilter. Shepherd had once accused the older man of being a throwback to "The Dying Gaul," a statue his friend displayed on his coffee table. Meant as an insult, it had been taken as a compliment.

Two hours of excruciatingly boring Muzak later, Shepard prepared to consign Ms. Breem and her cronies to the round file, abandoning the idea of genius financiers altogether. It was then, scarcely a moment before the last, lingering hope died in his breast, that the pendulous chimes of midnight rang through the great hall.

No grandfather clock, no Big Ben to sound the passing of one day into the next. Had he his wiles about him, Shepherd would have presumed the tolling came piped in over the loudspeaker as a dramatic salute to the Holy Dollar. He erred, but would have excused himself on the grounds he laid no claim to being a reporter.

There were many things Shepherd Kingston was not; and an equal number of things he was, beginning with Alexander Pope's admonition that "fools rush in where angels fear to tread."

Feeling suddenly lightheaded, he swayed backward, nearly falling. Awkwardly catching his balance, his head jerked toward the left. At that moment, he saw her. And forgot how to breathe, augmenting his dizziness.

The object of his rapt attention stood in the middle of the dance floor, a drink in her right hand. With the opposite, she made a sort of chopping gesture. All eyes obediently dropped, searching the linoleum for the metaphysical head she severed.

The act apparently coincided with an amusing comment, for her male audience smiled or made low noises denoting good humor. Although he had been "casing the joint" the better part of the evening, Shepherd could not have identified a single individual in her group. Were it Times Square on New Year's Eve, the youth would have, could have, seen no one but Ms. Elvina.

That it were she, he had no doubt. He would have sworn to it on his deathbed.

Had he acknowledged possession of such, Shepherd Kingston would have staked his soul on her identity.

Only the near proximity of a bouncer, staring directly at him, prohibited Shepherd from bringing the camera to his eye. Heart fluttering in his throat, reality came crashing. Without doubt, the man recognized him for slime.

"You," he began, taking a step nearer. "Let me see your invitation."

Shepherd feigned innocence. Reaching into his jacket pocket, he withdrew the first object his fingers encountered: a parking ticket.

Not even an understudy for Quasimodo could mistake that for a gold embossed license to swill booze with the High and Mighty.

Please, the youth willed, closing his eyes in concentration. He did not pray to God, but oddly begged himself. *Make him see what I want him to. Just this once. I won't ask again. I promise.*

Shaking from an all too familiar inner fear, Shepherd extended his hand. The enforcer glanced at the paper, then mumbled what might have been an apology and lost himself in the crowd. Shepherd fell back against a potted plant, the ticket dropping from numb fingers.

Thank you.

Had the occasion been less momentous, the summoning of what Trent called "his powers" would have rendered the boy-photographer into green Jell-O. The fact he possessed "power" at all was a subject of contention. One which brought with it the spectre of horror.

"I must be a better actor than I thought," he reasoned aloud, consciously pushing the incident from his mind. What he did not dwell on now, he could later deny.

Swallowing more than the lump in his throat, the hopeful in the J.C. Penney's suit jacket hopped away, up the ballroom stairs. Safely hidden behind the lush Rent-a-Plant, his trembling hands searched for the camera.

Rekindled faith restored self-confidence. Dissipated with his fear of a supernatural power were his doubts of the moment before. The blessed Ms. Breem had been right, after all. The Wall Street genius had arrived. Fool, he, to have doubted. Were he to find himself in possession of an extra twenty, he would surely send the lady banker a box of Hershey's kisses.

Elvina. The woman's name rang with magical overtones. If love truly came at first sight, then Shepherd fell to Cupid's arrow. The overhead lights seemed brighter, the music almost melancholy in its brilliance. Even the fake shrubbery behind which he hid assumed a life it never had.

Miss Elvina.

His gateway to heaven.

Raising the camera, Shepherd prepared to photograph the incarnation of Cleopatra. Without bothering to adjust the focus, he got off three shots before realizing, to his mortification, he had failed to remove the lens cap.

Frowning at his own inexcusable inattention, he slipped the black plastic disc into his pocket. Hands shaking from emotion, he drew in a deep breath and tried again, forcing his mind to concentrate. He must act the professional, rather than a virginal boy on his first date.

Twirling the multiple adjustments, Shepherd attempted to bring the female icon into focus. For some peculiar reason, he could not.

"Jesus! What's the matter with me?"

Rechecking the camera, he confirmed that all settings were appropriate. Trying again, he had no better luck.

"The devil take me," he hissed through gritted teeth. The invocation worked. Immediately Miss Elvina's features jumped into sharp focus. Just as he clicked off a photograph, a broad-shouldered man blocked his view. Angrily, he snapped off half a dozen more pictures, on the off chance she would move. His chance came and went. Before his finger depressed the lever, the object of his desire disappeared.

"Hells bells!" he cursed, shuddering under the weight of Trent's omnipresent reprimand. A devoutly religious man, the professor tolerated no expressions of pagan sentiment. "Sorry, old friend," the boy whispered, mustering a weak apology. Time for atonement later.

Thus confirming Trent's observation of his penchant for putting off today what might be forgotten tomorrow.

Falling in behind a group of nondescripts, Shepherd worked the room, absolutely certain Miss Elvina could not have gone far. Pleading with the gods for a second chance, he pushed and shoved with abandon, unable to quell the premonition that his life hung in the balance

Eyes failing to aid the quest, Shepherd employed his auditory sense, absorbing snippets of conversation, assured that the appearance of so great a lady would occasion all to speak only of her. The assumption proved correct, although what he gleaned could hardly have been said to be informative.

"... made a killing on Thomson Microchips, I believe...."

"... divined the fall of Swiss National and sold her shares at top dollar before the bottom dropped out. Or so I've heard ...."

"... Shocked everyone by buying those worthless shares. Then, when the company announced a new diamond discovery, she sold them for an ungodly profit."

As background, it might have proved fascinating, but Shepherd's interest lay solely in taking the woman's picture. Everything else served as gravy.

A man needed meat before worrying about side dishes.

A flash of silver, the sound of a laugh, the tone of command. Shepherd spun to his left, discovering she had somehow gotten behind him. Disconcerted, he jerked abruptly, inadvertently knocking the hand of a woman standing next to him. A drop of blood red wine spilled over her hand.

"I beg your pardon," he mumbled, not from good breeding, but from Trent's constant instruction in manners. "Do forgive me."

Forgetting the bow he had been taught to make, Shepherd moved on, oblivious to the stares he received.

One photograph; God please, one decent shot.

By the time he reached her last known address, he discovered a circle of men with no one in the center. Forgetting his invocation to God, he swore aloud. The men parted and stood back, fearing contagion.

Abandoning the habitual caution of the lower orders, Shepherd ran pell-mell up the stairs, searching the room from an eagle's eye view. Sweating profusely, a phenomenon attributed to exertion, he scanned the crowded room through the camera lens. A second before his aching arms gave out, her visage slipped into frame.

Knees buckling, he leaned over the railing, bringing the financier into sharp focus. The second before he took her photograph, Miss Elvina turned in his direction, meeting his eyes through the medium of the lens. Locking his gaze, she smiled. His immobility remained past the count of ten before locomotion returned.

He clicked the camera. His finger did not stop moving until he had taken forty, fifty snaps on a thirty-six count roll.

"How did you get in here?" demanded a gruff voice. Shepherd's perspiration turned cold faster than if hell had frozen over. Before he could hope to protect himself, a fist grabbed the back of his collar. "Out you go, you sewer rat." Behind the words lay the latent threat of violence Shepherd knew all too well.

Being young and proud, however, he squirmed against destiny, growling, "Get your hands off me! This is a free country."

"A free country? There's no such thing as 'free,' boy. Everyone pays the ferryman."

Unfettered by whatever power Shepherd had found and lost, the tuxedoed thug lifted him off his feet, shoved him one-hundred-and-eighty degrees in the air and carried down the stairs. Bypassing those dignitaries either late in arriving or early to depart, he deposited the interloper into the street.

Falling hard, Shepherd used his body to shield the camera. Broken arms would mend, but a smashed camera meant the end of life as he knew it.

"Son of a bitch!"

As a curse, it proved as impotent as he.

CHAPTER 4

The smell of the darkroom stimulated him. Hands trembling with excitement born of witnessing a dream come true, Shepherd worked the photographic paper in and out of the tartly-scented chemicals. Knocking the red overhead light, elongated shadows danced around the room, making the most common items appear alien, frightening.

Had Shepherd been a superstitious man, such deformed objects might have portended evil, or at the very least, a radical alteration of life. Without knowing how or why, his actions simulated turning over the key card in a deck of Tarot and discovering XVI, *La Masion De Dieu,* or lightning-struck tower.

Otherwise known as "The House of God."

Described as *the breaking down of existing forms to make way for new ones.*

With a shudder to which he gave no credence, the youth with a past which bore no deep introspection brushed aside the mental hauntings of the Gypsy fortune-teller, affectionately known as Trent.

"Mine. Mine. Mine." A chant, with a cadence as old as bearskin-clad cavemen.

Mine.

His future emerged from the murky liquid of the Martian laboratory. The Big One. The break he had been seeking for as long as he could remember.

Ambition had been part and parcel of his existence since childhood. Counting the hard labor he had executed in high school learning the art of photography, he had logged one thousand, ten thousand hours learning his craft. Time now to collect on the dues he had paid, the lumps sustained. At twenty-four years of age, and ten times that many rejections, he had earned this exclusive.

"Mine."

Dreams of Pulitzer prizes, covers of *Time* and *Newsweek* shuffled through his brain like so many slides in a projector, clicking, one after another, on the screen of his imagination.

Job offers, invitations, exclusive photo ops. A corner office with his name on the door. Trent's respect. And vindication, perhaps for the death of his parents. He had succeeded on his own terms, without aid of what the uninitiated commonly referred to as "the supernatural."

Vanished from memory the incident of the parking ticket. It had never happened. Or, if it had, the bouncer had made a mistake, misread the printing. Nothing odd in that. Happens all the time.

Earth existed as a three-dimensional place. Shepherd Kingston's achievement would prove that to even the most devout believer in "things are not what they appear to be."

As fast as jubilation awoke in his soul, it melted away. Something had gone terribly awry. Frowning, Shepherd adjusted the crimson illumination, then stepped sideways, thinking, perhaps, his own shadow interfered with the development of the picture. No improvement.

"That's odd," he remarked. Two words, stemming off uncontrolled panic.

Clucking his tongue, he used a pair of tongs to elevate the dripping-wet photographic paper. Even in the otherworldly light he could see the image of Miss Elvina was blurry. In any dimension, that constituted the Kiss of Death.

"All right," came the well-rehearsed lecture. "She was moving."

Putting the shot aside, Shepherd went to the next in sequence. It, too, depicted a fuzzy image. Thoughts of homicide replaced acceptance speeches. Liberally punctuated with invocations against merciless gods.

"I'm sure she wasn't moving in this one."

Or thought he remembered. In the heat of battle, he found memory surprisingly muddled.

Pausing to control his raging temper, Shepherd wiped sweat from his brow. He erred. Surely so. The photographs only appeared blurry because he squinted from anticipation. He did not stop to rationalize that narrowing one's line of vision sharpened, rather than softened the image under scrutiny.

Without the courage to go forward, Shepherd retreated. Examining the series he had shot of James Parkins, doorman, and the financier who had called Greenspan an "old cow," all appeared sharp and in focus. That indicated the camera functioned properly.

Logically, therefore, the rest of the photographs were perfect. It stood to reason. Trent was a methodical man. He had taught Shepherd well.

One thing at a time.

Everything in its place, and a place for everything.

Where men fail, trust in God

Of Trent's three homilies, Shepherd believed none and followed two.

Wasting no time on the idle speculation of holy numbers, he finished the developing without pausing to scrutinize any other images. No sense pushing his luck. The first six were perfect. Rationally, therefore, the last were equally good.

The law of averages.

Another of Trent's sayings. Or was it? He found he could not recall exactly what Trent harped on. No matter. With even one perfect shot of Miss Elvina, he stood to be a made man.

With a dozen, he could reach the penthouse.

"Son of a –!!"

Switching on the halogen desk lamp, Shepherd examined the entire series of photographs. Being stingy with his film, he had managed to get thirty-eight complete pictures. Five were of the doorman and one of the cow-caller. These he discarded into the trash can. The next ten were of luminaries no editor in his right mind would pay half a tuppence for.

"Tuppence" being an English word. Shepherd had once accused Trent of picking it up from a perusal of Dickens. His friend had not been amused. His annoyance, however, had not prevented him from advising Shepherd to read more classic literature.

Twenty-two remaining photographs were of Miss Elvina. The early attempts contained no more than the back of her head, or were ones in which men partially obscured her. Only the later shots, when they had made eye contact, revealed her face.

Not one single photograph displayed crystal clarity. Even tweaking and professional tricks would not improve them enough for sale. They were simply unacceptable. In this era of digital quality, no newspaper or magazine would consider publishing an inferior photograph. The editors would reject his effort as poor workmanship. Worse, of being amateurish.

If there were anything a man hated to hear, it centered around the word "amateur."

Shepherd's world imploded.

He had gotten his big break and blown it.

"No," he declared to the omnipresent demons. "No! I won't accept it."

To accept defeat was to be defeated. Another of Trent's sayings.

Trent. He would take the photographs to Trent. Trent would help him.

The old man went through the photographic collection one-by-one. He might have been examining newly discovered works by Matthew Brady, rather than the contemporary images of a Wall Street wizard.

"Are you doing this to annoy me?" Shepherd demanded, finally throwing up his hands in a theatrical gesture. On impulse, he reached out and snapped one of Trent's suspenders. For as long as he had known him, Trent had never worn anything more stylish than a starched white shirt, braces, a vest and a tweed jacket. His students at the university thought him eccentric.

Shepherd had a less flattering description.

Queer.

Pushing his reading glasses down his nose, Trent stared at the impatient youth.

"What do you want me to say?"

"That you're not as slow as an elephant, you're just being thorough."

"No. That isn't it, at all. What you really want is for me to wave a magic wand and make these pictures saleable."

"O.K.," Shepherd agreed, bouncing on the balls of his feet. "Can you?"

Had there been less credulity in Shepherd's voice, Trent would have been tempted to give him a flippant reply. As it stood, he did not have the heart.

"No."

"Oh, good God, I'm ruined."

Slumping down in an ancient rocker, a spot normally reserved for the owner alone, Shepherd hung his head in a picture of abject dejection.

"It can't be as bad as all that," Trent prompted, ignoring, for the moment, the fact his private space had been violated. "There will be other opportunities." Shepherd miserably shook his head. "Who is she, anyway?"

"Miss Somebody-or-Other Elvina," came the mumbled reply. With no elucidation forthcoming, the sage felt compelled to prod further. But his inquiry fell along unexpected lines.

"Miss Somebody-or-Other Elvina? What kind of a name is that?"

"How do I know? You're the genealogy expect. You tell me."

"I am not a genealogy expert," Trent snapped. His reaction, out of keeping with the situation, finally compelled Shepherd to raise his head.

"I'm the one who's mad at the world; not you. What's the matter?"

"I... don't know." Rather than attempt to rationalize his sudden edginess, Trent returned to the photographs. Shepherd sunk further down into the old oak chair, rocking back and forth in a vain effort to comfort himself.

"What kind of film were you using?"

"K-Mart's best."

"Why did you change lenses?"

"I didn't."

"Surely you did."

Something in the tone finally roused Shepherd from his self-castigation. Lifting himself up by his arms, he joined his friend at the desk.

"I tell you I didn't. I was shooting with a long range lens; there was no reason to change it."

"No special filters? No – journalistic license with the focus?"

"I wasn't shooting stills for *Star Wars,*" Shepherd groused. "Just taking snaps for the dailies. Why would I use a filter?"

"You did something, then. Altered the settings; got the lens wet? You didn't spill a drink on it, by chance? Anything to cloud the image artificially? Now think: this is important."

"You're damn right it's important. So I ought to remember, shouldn't I? No, Trent, I didn't get the camera wet. I did nothing more than change the focus."

"You weren't drunk?"

"Never touched a drop. Honest Injun."

"I don't like that expression."

"Swear to God."

"And I like even less your evoking the Lord's name without due respect."

Shepherd rolled his eyes. "Cross my heart and hope to die."

"One day you'll say that to the wrong person, and won't live to regret it," came the stern rebuke.

"Nothing I say pleases you," came the whined protest. "Besides, I don't believe in god. Not Jehovah, not Jesus, not all those innumerable deities you know so much about," he concluded, turning to indicate numerous charts and esoteric paintings covering the walls of Trent's apartment.

"If you knew more, you would scoff less."

"What I know is that I've just blown a chance to make a mint. Anything else is irrelevant."

"Who is Ms. Elvina?" While enunciated in the form of a question, the statement had the tone of demand.

"A Wall Street wizard; a genius with stocks and bonds. A recluse in an Ivory Tower."

"For whom does she work?"

Shepherd suggestively raised his eyebrows. "No one knows. From what I gathered, she's supposed to work for some unnamed European. A king."

"A king? What king?"

"I don't know. An Eastern European monarch."

"You're joking."

"I'm only telling you what I heard."

"Someone was being factitious with you."

"No."

"What country?"

"They didn't say."

Trent gave his un-adopted ward an exasperated look. "You don't know anything about her, but you tell me you've just missed the opportunity of a lifetime?"

"No one knows anything about her. She's a recluse. She's never had her photograph published. People get – nervous – talking about her."

"This is what you overheard at the banquet?"

"Yes."

"And someone wasn't kidding you?"

"They weren't speaking to me; I was eavesdropping. I don't imagine they'd lie to one another. Why? What do you know about her?"

"Nothing."

"But –?"

"She has a very unusual name."

"So did Gypsy Rose Lee."

"Elvina. That's not an Eastern European surname."

"So she changed it from Ludovic. What do I know?"

"Have you looked closely at these photographs?" Trent asked, returning to the group of thirty-two Shepherd had brought.

"Enough to know I wasted a roll of film."

"Take a close look at them now."

Grabbing the photographs, Shepherd went through them with the disdain worthy of an editor.

"So?"

"Sit down and look again. Carefully, this time. And not in my chair." Shepherd took the photographs and settled on the couch. When finished, he shot his friend a quizzical expression. "What do you see?" Trent pursued.

"The first shots are all right. Perfectly clear. Utterly undistinguished."

"Put those aside for now. Examine the others."

"All right. There are twenty-two shots of Miss Elvina." Feeling, rather than seeing Trent stiffen, Shepherd glanced up. "What's wrong? Did I make a mistake in the count?"

"Where are the other four photographs? Assuming you were using a thirty-six shot roll."

"I got thirty-eight out of it. Six were wasted. I threw them out."

"From the beginning or the end?"

"The beginning."

"Were any of them blurry?"

Shepherd thought a moment before shaking his head. "No."

"So only the last twenty-two were –"

"Defective," Shepherd supplied. "The *damn* film was defective."

"I do not appreciate you using that word here," Trent warned. "It is not a sentiment to be used lightly."

"And may God take my soul if I don't wake," Shepherd retorted, quoting from a common child's prayer. Trent scowled.

"Yes," he agreed. "You had better pray for that."

"Oh, come on. I'm a big boy." And then finally making the connection, "Oh, shit! It's that stupid number bothering you. Twenty-two. You don't like that number. There's nothing to numerology, Trent. No one believes that anymore. It went out with phrenology and voodoo dolls."

Instead of arguing the point, Trent's turned back to the photographs. "What else can you tell me about them?"

"I feel like I'm in photojournalism 101."

"Do as I say. You were the one who brought them to me, not the other way around."

"Not so you could lay some mumbo-jumbo on me."

"I'm not going to ask you again. If you don't want to continue this discussion, you know where the door is. It works both ways. You came in: you can go out in like manner."

"What's for dinner?"

"You're not going to get any at this rate."

With that palpable threat hanging over his head, Shepherd reexamined the pictures.

"In these *twenty-two,* all are blurry."

"Be more specific, please."

"If you already know the answer, why don't you just tell me and make it easier on both of us?"

"Because I want you to see for yourself."

Responding less to the ominous enunciation than the potential loss of dinner, the youth shrugged. Returning his concentration to the task at hand,

Shepherd went through the entire stack. When finished, he nervously licked his lips.

"All right. I see what you mean."

"Say it, please. So I'll be sure you know."

"The men standing by Miss Elvina –"

The *men,"* Trent elucidated. "All men. There are no women in any of the shots."

"That's right. The men are all clear; no distortion. Perfectly focused. Only she is blurry."

"As a photographer, what do you make of that?"

"Well... it's not because she's in the foreground or the background. She's standing alongside them."

"So?"

"I don't know." His puzzlement showed. "There is no explanation."

"No rational explanation."

"Now, wait a minute! You're not trying to suggest there's something supernatural about her, are you? Because if you are, I'm outta here. What is it with you, that everything has to have some weird cause?"

"I gave you the opportunity to tell me."

"You're nuts. All that research you do on mysticism has gone to your head. You're like one of those monks who squats in a cave for years on end, trying to divine the meaning of life. After a while, he finally goes insane."

"Thank you," came the droll acknowledgment.

"All those degrees and titles after your name mean nothing to me!" Shepherd screamed, standing to face the seated man. "I don't believe in hocus pocus. I don't believe in the devil. I don't believe stupid numbers hold the meaning of fate. You can't make gold out of lead. Crystals don't heal. I hate that shit!"

"Then you hate me, for I do believe."

"So I hate you! I don't know why I came here. I should have known you'd turn this on me. You were right in the first place. I manipulated the focus. Or got the lens wet. Pure and simple. A rational explanation for a rational world."

"I wish it were that simple."

"It is, Trent. It's just that simple and you can't see it. Because if you did, then all your life's work is down the toilet."

Clutching the pictures to his chest, Shepherd shuffled toward the door.

"Where are you going?"

"Out. Home. Anywhere. Away from you and your stupid theories. Bela Lugosi is dead and so are all the vampires. Dead and gone. 'It was *reality* killed the beast,'" he misquoted from *King Kong.*

"Stay," Trent relented, feeling the loneliness creep in before the actuality. "I'll make dinner. Steak and mushrooms. Whatever you like."

Too late for Shepherd to retract his harsh words.

"I don't want any. I'm not hungry."

He was half way out the door before Trent spoke again.

"Then leave the photographs."

"Why?"

"So I can study them."

Torn between anger and regret, Shepherd hurled them at the old man, then hurried away, without bothering to close the door.

The chill he had brought with him did not dissipate with his absence. It lingered behind with the photographs.

A superstitious man would have believed it foretold things to come.

CHAPTER 5

"No double exposure, no flaw in the film. I went to a lot of trouble over this," Trent added, looking up over his fork.

"I appreciate it, Trent. I really do," Shepherd avowed, wolfing down another swallow of steak before wiping his hands on his trousers. Only when assured his fingers were clean did he take the photographs his friend had been studying.

"The images of Ms. Elvina – I took them to the lab at the university and had my friend make copies. I wanted her image separated, so I wouldn't be distracted by extraneous background."

"I hope he can be trusted."

Trent ignored the comment. "Some of them I had reduced, hoping to bring out more detail."

"Did they?"

"I also had them enlarged. As large as he could make them. Poster size."

"She's a pin-up," Shepherd agreed, which had not been Trent's point.

"I was looking for somcthing."

The question took longer this time.

"What?"

"I don't know. Some latent idea, hiding in the back of my mind. Some... remembrance. Or an association with the past." Shepherd made a disparaging noise under his breath. "With someone I've known – or seen a picture of, perhaps."

"Well, it sure can't be of an old girlfriend." The anger generated from his friend sealed Shepherd's lips, forcing him to try a different track. "A movie star perhaps? From the silents?"

"I thought that," Trent admitted. "When I couldn't find her in any of my scrapbooks, I went to the library; searched through the old stills they have on file. I came close, but not close enough. Not a film star," he added. "It was just a try."

"You sound disappointed."

"I am."

Shepherd ate more of his steak before realizing the obvious. "How could she be a silent movie star, anyway? She can't be more than twenty-five, if that."

"Hard to tell from a blurry photograph, but you're probably right," Trent replied, avoiding the larger issue. "What did you find out at the morgue?"

"Not a hell of a – not a lot. No published photographs. I did find one, printed two years ago, with a caption mentioning her name, but she wasn't in the picture. Pretty damned careless of the editor."

"Please don't use profanity. You know it upsets me. Particularly under present circumstances. We have a mystery here. Until it's solved – to both our satisfactions – I abjure you to take care."

Shepherd rolled his eyes toward the ceiling. "Are you afraid we're being watched?"

A blunt "Yes" sufficed.

"By what – or by whom?"

"If I knew that, I'd have an answer about the photographs, wouldn't I?"

The photographer shrugged, then carelessly waved the sign of the cross in the air. Trent grimaced, then repeated the symbolism with piety.

"Did the caption give you her first name?"

Shepherd brightened. "Ericka."

Trent wiped his mouth with a linen napkin. "Who was in the picture?"

"I didn't take note."

"I mean, was it a picture of several men and women, or were there just men?"

"Just men."

"What were they doing?"

"I didn't ask them," Shepherd retorted, then regretted his casualness. "They were standing around talking, I suppose. It was some fancy 'doings'; they were dressed to their eye teeth."

"Talking to themselves – or speaking to someone who should have been in the photograph, but wasn't?"

Adding more sour cream to his baked potato, Shepherd scanned his mind. "Now that you mention it, the snap was rather... odd. It did look as though they were talking to... no one. I guess I chalked it up to a lousy centering job. What I mean is, the photographer meant to get more in the frame but didn't."

"How was the picture cropped?"

"You mean, was there a space for another person, or was it cut around the men?" Trent did not have to answer, for Shepherd grasped the point without further elucidation. "Yes, you're right. There was room for another person. Dead center."

"Who took the photograph?"

Retrieving his pocket notebook, Shepherd consulted his notes.

"Someone called Joe Warren."

"Do you know him?"

"No."

"Are you familiar with his work?"

"Sure. He gets around."

"You might get a copy from the newspaper and ask him about it."

"Yeah. I might."

"What else did you unearth while I was working so diligently on your behalf?"

"Nothing came up on a name search, so I went through the newspapers manually. Sunday supplements, mostly."

"Why?"

"Because most society shots are printed on Sundays. Parties are held Friday nights or Saturdays. Anything interesting gets printed on Sunday."

"How far back did you go?"

"Nine years, before my eyes gave out."

"What did you find?"

"In that time, I found her name mentioned seven times. The earliest was five years ago; a reference to a new tenet taking up offices in the penthouse of a newly renovated building."

"What was the name of the building?"

Shepherd checked his notes. "The Stone Gate."

"Stone Gate? I don't know of any older building in Manhattan called the Stone Gate. Did they rename the building after they renovated it?"

"It was called the 'Miles Building," if I remember right."

Trent frowned. "I thought they tore that place down. Years ago."

Shepherd shrugged. "Apparently not."

"The article didn't happen to say which floor the penthouse was numbered, did it?"

"The twenty-third floor," Shepherd replied smugly. "You're one off. I do pay attention, you know."

"I know nothing of the sort. And you know nothing about human nature. Or numerology."

"What do you mean?"

"You said a renovated building. They may have redecorated the inside, but they probably didn't re-number the floors."

"So?"

"So, take a tour of any old building. I dare you to find one with a floor numbered thirteen. They always go from twelve to fourteen."

"Shit."

"Subtract one, and you get twenty-two," Trent overlapped. "I bet she had to look long and hard to find exactly what she wanted. What were the other references?"

Shepherd flipped a page of his notebook, reading from his scrawled notes.

"One mentioned she had bought a large quantity of oil stock, wondering why, since the oil market at that time was unstable. Three blurbs mentioned vast sell-offs of stock at unexpectedly large profits. One of the three was in the context of her as an 'up and comer,' in the market. Another speculated she was a 'high flyer,' someone who took wild chances in the hopes of a big pay out."

"That's six."

"The most recent was dated six months ago. It merely listed her name as having attended a big social gathering."

"Check the gossip columns next; or better yet, call the local rag-mouths. If they'll talk to you, ask if her name has ever been romantically associated with any one man. Or any man, at all, for that matter. Find out who escorts her to those big 'doings,' as you put it."

"I'm not looking for a date," Shepherd protested, choking a bite of food before continuing. "Although I wouldn't mind one. She's a honey."

Trent ground his foot into the floor. "She's out of your league – honey."

"I've never broken any mirrors," the youth protested, turning his profile to best advantage. "Why? Are you jealous?"

"Worried is more like it."

"I can hold my own."

"I'm sure you think so. And therein lies the danger."

"I've never had any complaints."

Slapping his hand down against the white damask tablecloth, Trent pushed back from the table. "I'm not sure this woman is worth... pursuing."

"You *are* jealous," Shepherd accused, following the older man into the living room.

"There's something not right about all this. It doesn't ring true."

"If she invites me to her penthouse, I'll show her a good time."

Trent ignored the blatant insinuation. "If she's really a high flyer, and as successful as your limited information seems to indicate, then why hasn't more been written about her? New Yorkers love a mystery. 'Foreign beauty captivates Wall Street.' 'Long-legged wizard outshines the establishment.' '*Femme fatale* makes a killing.' Whatever."

"She doesn't grant interviews."

"When has that ever stopped a reporter from filing a story? Surely she's Sunday supplement material. You implied as much, yourself. Fodder for the gossip columns. Come on, Shepherd – no one remains anonymous in the Big Apple."

"What's your point?"

Trent finally sagged his shoulders, sitting down on the couch. Shepherd understood that as his cue to sit beside him, but his blood had risen.

"Does not equate," Trent tried, smiling for the sake of his company. "Does not compute. On one hand you have a beautiful woman, a stocks and bonds genius, raking in big money. On the other, no one knows anything about her. She just goes about her business. If nothing else, you'd think there'd be a dozen men trying to emulate her moves.

"Success breeds interest, Shepherd. If I were a wheeler-and-dealer and I saw someone buying blocks of shares in some obscure company, I'd follow suit. I'd watch the ticker tape. She must have a recognizable name she trades under, whether it's her own, or that of her employer."

"But no one knows who her employer is."

"Or that she really has one?"

"What do you mean?"

"If no one knows anything about her, then they can't really be certain she's working for anyone, can they? The story about an unknown royal from an unnamed country just doesn't make sense."

Shepherd frowned, biting off the end of a hangnail as an excuse not to make eye contact with his mentor.

"That's what you say. But that's not what you mean."

This time Trent turned be obtuse.

"Explain, please."

"I know the tone of your voice. You believe it," Shepherd sniffed.

"Believe what?"

"That she is working for a king or a prince or somebody. That she comes from some little podunk country in the Balkans, or from Transylvania."

"Yes. I do."

"How can you, when you just debunked it?" Trent made no reply. "Because no one has ever managed to take a decent snapshot of her? That's pretty thin evidence."

"Take another look at your photographs. The ones we left in the dining room."

Obeying his suggestion, Shepherd retrieved the glossy stills. Placing himself by Trent's reading chair, he snapped on the goose-neck lamp and re-examined his work. Discarding the close-ups, he concentrated on those which were enlarged.

"This glow around her – it's a double-exposure," he decided finally.

"No. It's not. It looks like it, I agree, but photographically, there's no way she could be double-exposed when everyone else in the shot is perfectly normal."

"I can't see anyone else," Shepherd protested petulantly. "You cropped them out."

"You don't have to take my word for it; you already know. Look closely."

Bringing one of the photographs nearer his face, Shepherd scrutinized the female image.

"I still the see the glow around her head, if that's what you mean."

"But what is it?"

"Double exposure. I thought we decided that."

"No. We hadn't. And presuming you're not trying to deceive me with trick photography, I think you may have captured something quite special here."

"Such as?"

"It's just possible this may be Ms. Elvina's aura."

"Her aura?"

"Life force, if you will. The band of energy around every living thing." Noting Shepherd's skeptical expression, Trent reverted to his teacher's mode. "There's nothing supernatural about a life force, Shepherd. Other photographers have captured such energy on film. Although not, I confess, using regular methods on inexpensive K-Mart film."

The youthful photographer winced at the reference to his lack of money, then returned to the images.

"You're talking about some religious phenomenon, like what Tibetan monks see?"

"No, although some Buddhist monks are gifted to see auras. They read them the way Western physicians interpret CT scans. They can tell a person's mood, or his wellness, or ill heath by the colors of their aura. But generally, it's used to determine the status of a person's spiritual advancement; the golden aura representing the most advanced state of development."

"But I'm not religious. And you're not a Buddhist," Shepherd accused.

"That doesn't mean I reject their beliefs. In fact, I happen to hold more than a few of them, myself."

"I know where you're leading. This is going to devolve into some lecture on the supernatural. I told you; I don't believe in that crap. You know what I think?" He hurried on before Trent could answer. "I think all that book learning and research you've done has affected you; gone to your head. You profess not to believe in witches and demons, but you do."

"I never said I didn't believe. That's your line."

"I don't have any faith. I never have and I never will."

"Me thinks those who protest most are the greatest believers. They're just afraid to admit it."

"I'm not afraid of anything!" Shepherd cried, flinging the photographs from him as though the paper had suddenly caught on fire.

"Be afraid, Shepherd," Trent warned. "For God's sake."

"Don't lay your doubts on me, old man! Just because you bend the knee to Zeus, don't expect me to! Thunder bolts went out with the Enlightenment."

"I am a Christian, son. But that doesn't mean I disregard the old religion."

"Good for you. And don't call me 'son.' I'm not your son! I'm not anyone's son!"

Emotion clouding his better judgment, Shepherd stomped to the door. Unlike his previous exit, however, he did not want this one to be done in anger. He knew the old man had meant no ill, and actually quite the contrary. Forcing himself to calm, he wiped his brow with the back of his hand, then nervously held it out as a peace offering.

"I'm sorry, Trent. You know how sensitive I am on that point."

Peace offering accepted, but not without conditions.

"For your sake, if not God's, hold your tongue, Shepherd. You did have parents – a mother and father who loved you very much."

"You don't know that; you didn't know them," came the harsh accusation.

"No... but I've seen their photographs. There was no evil in them, boy."

"No evil? Yes, well I've just had an example of your photo-journalistic-mumbo-jumbo interpretation and I'm not impressed. You think Ericka Elvina is evil, don't you?"

"Evil is not a word I use lightly."

"Don't change the subject."

"I don't know enough about her."

"But you consider the possibility?"

Trent tugged nervously at a strand of his unruly white locks. Shepherd had put him in an awkward position, well aware he must answer guardedly or turn the young man away. Painful as though it might be to temporarily lose Shepherd's affection, worse the fear he would push him too far. Rebelling against the idea of Ericka Elvina being evil, Shepherd would blind himself to the truth, should such present itself.

"I have an open mind on the subject."

"Which means?"

Had Shepherd let it go, they could have arrived at the proverbial Mexican standoff. His further request demanded a specific answer. Trent's nature did not permit him to lie, and therein lay his failing.

"Yes. I consider it a possibility."

"I knew it. You're just like my parents. You can't let anything go. You've got to keep probing and poking around, always looking at the dark side of perfectly ordinary situations. My mother and father's obsession with the so-called supernatural got them killed."

"For which you blame them. I understand –"

"You don't understand. They didn't understand. They had a responsibility to me; first and foremost. I didn't ask to get born. But once I was, my father should have relinquished his morbid fascination with all things ancient and unexplained."

Stomping back into the room, Shepherd absently picked up a crude, hand-carved stone idol. Unlike others in the professor's collection, this image did not originate from Eastern Europe and looked oddly out of place. He shook it at Trent as the older man spoke.

"He was an anthropologist."

"Then why didn't he teach in a university like you do? Why did he have to go trudging around Central America, with those little shovels and brushes? Why did he have to bring her with him?"

"They died in a landslide."

Replacing the idol, Shepherd went to the sink and washed his hands. He then rubbed the damp towel over the stone to wipe away any lingering impressions he might have left on it.

"Yes. I know. I told you all about it. A landslide which the natives say was caused by angry gods, who didn't want them digging up their bones and artifacts."

"A perfectly normal landslide... as you've told me two dozen times."

"But they wouldn't have been there in the first place if they hadn't spent their summers in the field. Doing their own research," he added bitterly, "so my father's publisher wasn't even held responsible for their deaths. And the life insurance company didn't have to pay off."

"People die, Shepherd."

"They die in car accidents and they have heart attacks. But *normal* people don't perish in landslides in Central America, leaving behind a fifteen-year old son, who gets shuffled off to a state boarding home."

"I'm sorry."

Moving the ancient deity to a spot other than where he found it, Shepherd stood back and waited for a lecture. Normally hypersensitive about the placement of his artifacts, Trent appeared not to notice, for which Shepherd belatedly gave thanks.

"You should take care," he continued, feeling bolder. "Maybe now that you've seen the photographs I took, a half dozen of those heavy tomes will fall off the top shelf of your bookcase and crush you."

"And you? Shouldn't you take care, as well?"

"No," came the scornful reply.

"Why not?"

"Because *I* don't believe in the supernatural. Evil powers can't hurt me because I don't acknowledge their existence. There is no evil in the world, Trent. There may be bad people and there may be stupid, preventable accidents, but there is no malevolence."

Before answering, Trent's eyes snaked toward the shelf, as if willing the books to stay put.

"Evil is a concept as old as Mankind. Evil is the opposite of good."

"Are you implying there cannot be good without evil?"

Trent left the challenge unanswered.

At the moment, he felt unequal to the task of saying "Yes."

CHAPTER 6

"Come back and sit down. Have some coffee. Stay the night," Trent invited. The awkward repetition stemmed from the fact he knew Shepherd would refuse and did not want to hear it.

Shepherd followed true to form. He always did. "No, thank you."

"What are you going to do?"

"I don't know. Call a girl; call Deborah and shack up with her. Go to a movie. What do you care? You've got your books and your spirits to keep you company."

The seconds dragged out. Trent wished he had not asked him to stay. His regret did not prevent him from compounding the error.

"Call me in the morning? Come over and have breakfast?"

"I think it's about time I started fending for myself. I mean, really earning a living, so I don't have to mooch off you."

"I'm not complaining. I never have."

Trent had known Shepherd six years, but at times like this – times when stressed or worried – it seemed as though their relationship transcended spatial age.

Staring up at the tall, almost stately youth, the older man took stock of his ward. "Ward" being Trent's word, for it conferred rights of protection, as well as permission to love. Shepherd never used it, preferring to think of Trent as his mentor. Although spoken respectfully, "mentor" implied a technical relationship, constituting no attachment, legal or emotional.

The professor would have had it otherwise.

Studying the smooth face, bright eyes and long, carelessly brushed, straw-colored hair, Trent marveled at how little Shepherd Kingston had altered over the years. A casual glance from a disinterested observer could easily put Shepherd's age at eighteen or nineteen for he carried about him the innocence of a teenager; that quality of effervescence reserved for those who knew they could change the world.

Time had not yet marked Shepherd with the wisdom of age, with brought with it the wrinkles of Truth. The blame for that, Trent mused, lay at his feet. Rather than abandon the boy he had met in the halls of the New York State Museum of Art, staring wistfully at an exhibition of photographs, he had taken him under his wing. This protection had kept harsh reality and starvation at bay.

Their relationship began with a conversation. Nothing Shepherd said about the display had marked him for a keen observer of his chosen profession. Instead of critiquing the style, or admiring the use of texture and subject, he opted for a far lower level of evolution. One, which in another, would have caused the teacher to turn away in disgust.

"If I had taken these photographs, no one would have bought them, much less given me a private exhibit."

Perhaps it had been the pique in his voice, or the haughtiness, tinged with hurt which struck a chord in Trent's subconscious. More likely, his own loneliness prompted a second look.

"Why not?"

"Because I'm considered a nobody, and this guy," Shepherd contemptuously continued, "is considered a somebody."

The word "considered" elicited a sad, longing smile from the listener.

"I'd like to see your portfolio – for comparison."

"Are you a publisher?" The question, so quick and hopeful, forced Trent to retreat a step from the nearness of the boy's body.

"No."

"Oh."

Which would have terminated the discussion, had not Trent pursued it.

"Does that disqualify me to judge?"

"Everyone's a critic," Shepherd retorted with a dismissive wave. Offering an apologetic European bow, Trent shuffled away before a plaintive offer accosted his forward movement. "But I'll show it to you, if you wish."

With a hitch in his shoulder bespeaking age, more worldly than chronological, Trent agreed.

Although fifty-six years old, he might have passed for a Medicare recipient. His naturally dark hair had greyed in graduate school, while his smooth countenance had given way to crow's feet and jowls in his forties.

The wardrobe he habitually wore nobly aided a descent into his golden years. Nothing more modern than suspenders, which were currently in fashion, graced his stocky Scottish-Irish frame. Coupled with a pair of half-moon glasses suspended by a black cord around his neck, he represented the epitome of a time traveler, lost in the future he neither understood nor cared to influence.

"I would like."

Shepherd hesitated, then nodded outside. For the first time, a flush of shame crept into his cheeks.

"I don't have a place. I mean a studio, or anything like that. Just a... room. It's not very neat."

"My name is Abraham Trent. I'm a professor at SUNY. You can come to my – place – if you want. I'm not very neat, either."

He meant to put the photographer at his ease and succeeded beyond his wildest expectations. The gratitude which flashed in the bright orbs told him a tale out of Dickens, or Hugo. In their works, hopeless runaways always identified with like creatures.

"Over dinner?" Trent suggested. "Or would you like to eat out?"

Glancing down at his shabby jacket, Shepherd demurred.

"Your place sounds great. Is it far?"

"No. Not very. Within walking distance. If you've got stamina," the older man added with a wink.

"Stamina comes with the territory. My feet are my best friends. Shall we go?"

Trent had not meant for the invitation to be accepted on the spot, but with more excitement than he had experienced in many years, he nodded.

"Certainly."

Once outside, Trent shot his new friend a look.

"Don't you have to go home and get your pictures?"

With a grin, Shepherd retrieved a faux leather case from behind a bush.

"I'm never without it," he explained. "You don't know when you might run into an editor."

"Is it safe to leave it outside?"

"The museum police wouldn't let me in with it, for fear I'd steal something of 'quality,' and conceal it inside," came the contemptuous retort. "And as far as it being valuable, I'm told it's worthless."

"I'm sorry."

"It's not, you know."

Trent did not know the value of the photography, but he sensed the worth of the boy.

"Come along."

Because he did not think Shepherd would agree to his hailing a cab, they walked the twelve blocks to Trent's apartment. While the trip proved time-consuming, neither, as befit their actual ages, were winded as they arrived.

Abraham Trent lived in an old brownstone, from the heyday of the Roaring Twenties. Little had been done to modernize the exterior, and less the interior. He appreciated that fact, but the building was hardly the showplace he unexpectedly wished he owned. It did not take a Ph.D. to interpret the fact his new friend appreciated money and Trent seriously wished to impress.

"This is my flat – where I live," he advised after they climbed the steps to the top floor. Inserting an old-fashioned key more appropriate for opening a jail cell in Dodge City, Trent stepped back, allowing Shepherd to enter before him.

"Wow! This looks like someplace out of the movies!" And then accusingly, "I thought you said you were sloppy. This place is as neat as a pin."

"I have a housekeeper."

"You must make pretty good money to afford that. What kind of professor are you?"

"I specialize in the Ancient World. Literature and the arts, mostly, but I teach summer classes in religion and mysticism."

Had he guessed Shepherd's reaction, Trent would have omitted the latter.

"You're not a religious freak, are you? You're not going to try and convert me, or anything like that?"

"No," he hastened to reassure, as his guest spoke over him.

"Mysticism means mumbo jumbo. A faith in old gods. Dead civilizations. Burnt offerings; blood sacrifice. I hate all that damn shit!"

Before Trent could stop him, Shepherd backtracked out the door. In desperation, highly uncharacteristic of his usual calm demeanor, Trent grabbed him by the arm, literally dragging him back inside.

"I'm sorry. I didn't mean to offend. There's nothing here that can hurt you."

"You're damn right there isn't, because none of it is worth a damn!"

"Come in. Please. I really would like to see your photographs. I might even know someone who can help – at the University," he stressed.

Clearly torn, Shepherd took another step back before slowly reconsidering.

"If I had known, I wouldn't have come."

"We won't speak of it. I promise. Really. You can sit at the dining room table and set out your work while I fix dinner."

"What are you making?" A cry of the starving, to which Trent appropriately responded, "Steak and mushrooms."

While the boy arranged his photographs, Trent busied himself in the kitchen. Between the two, a nervous tension filled the air.

Shepherd's fears were obvious: a dislike and distrust of the supernatural and the conjectural, coupled with a craving for praise. Trent's concerns were latent and conflicting.

Never before had he invited a total stranger to his dwelling. In fact, aside from the requisite holiday parties, when tenured professors were expected to open their homes to colleagues and select students, he had never extended that privilege to an outsider.

Not that he was an unsociable man. In his own environment, he exuded the epitome of Old World charm and wit. More accurately, such nostalgia segregated him from society. Those who brought Modern Ideology within his cloistered walls were intruders.

Trent ached from loneliness. Shepherd's presence proved that, even as he tried to dismiss the idea. Aside from a worldwide association with individuals of like mind, conducted over the telephone or through the medium of the written word, he called no one friend.

He needed someone – a flesh and blood body – with whom to communicate. And perhaps more. But those were thoughts best left unexplored, even from himself.

From what he rapidly and correctly ascertained of the youth, Shepherd fit entirely into that class commonly referred to as undesirable. His guest fairly reeked of New Age music, contemporary morals and a total lack of appreciation for anything pertaining to the millennium.

That referencing the 15th Century. For the professor, anything as late as the 1700's constituted "new."

"What's this?" Shepherd called, breaking into his thoughts. Glancing up, he experienced a wave of shock to see the youth had wandered into the living room. A finger pointed to an odd-looking machine.

Trent joined him, wiping his hands on a towel to keep them from touching the boy on the shoulder.

"A gramophone. For playing records."

"Does it work?"

He smiled, grateful for the interest, no matter how casual.

"Everything here works." Noting the tremor rippling head to toe through the questioner, he regretted his statement, no matter how accurate. "Let me demonstrate."

Cranking up the well-loved player, he set the needle into a groove. The chamber instantly filled with the soft sounds of *Swan Lake*.

"Dracula," Shepherd smugly identified. Trent rolled his eyes and let it pass.

"I don't even know your name," he tried instead.

"Shepherd Kingston. Never 'Shep,'" came the admonition. Offering his hand, he completed, "Pleased to meet you."

"Likewise," Trent acknowledged, copying his students' typical response. "Where's the TV?"

Trent scurried over to a large wooden cabinet, carefully drawing back the sliding doors to reveal an old RCA model.

"An antique," Shepherd whistled. Then, with a twinkle, added, "Does it have sound, too? Or does it only play silent movies?"

"It has sound."

"If I had your money, I'd fill my place with a big TV and a speaker system loud enough to blow away my neighbors."

"We're mostly old people in this building."

Shepherd missed, or chose to ignore the point.

"Want to look at my photographs, now?"

Trent did. They moved eagerly into the dining room.

The work revealed more than expected. While lacking the overall quality of a professional, the compositions displayed unique style.

"This is especially good," he judged, picking one which garnered attention. The black and white study highlighted a decrepit brick building, long shadows and filtered sunlight augmenting a sense of timelessness.

"I did that for a class," the photographer dismissed. "What about these?"

The series indicated were portraits, standard head and shoulder shots. Nothing about them came close to capturing the artistic soul of their subjects.

"What makes you ask?" Trent queried in his professor's voice.

"That's where the money is," Shepherd firmly retorted. "They're newspaper quality. Sharp. Clean."

Trent pursed his lips with equal firmness. "But undistinguished."

"That's because I was using a cheap camera."

The answer proved as unrewarding as revealing.

"What would you have done differently with an expensive one?"

The interrogative seemed to leave Shepherd at a loss.

"I'm a freelance – that means I take shots of famous people, in the hope of selling them to the society editors. Or being the first on the scene of a fire, earthquake. Something like that."

"Is that enough for a career?"

Crossing the room, Shepherd picked up a copy of the New York *Times* and indicated several photographs. Trent indicated he understood the reference.

"No," the youth pouted. "But if I'm lucky, I'll latch onto a newspaper. Then, they'll send me out on assignments."

"How likely is that to happen?"

"That's what I want."

"Nothing else?"

"I want the whole world eating out of my hand." Shepherd demonstrated by thrusting his empty fingers toward his listener. "Does that answer your question?"

"What about your sense of the artistic?"

"Artsy-fartsy doesn't sell."

"Is that all that's important to you?"

Shepherd startled him by jutting out his chin, nearly touching his host.

"I want to be someone. I want money. Fame. Is that so wrong?"

"I like the photo of the building," Trent carefully reiterated, retreating from the physical presence of his guest.

"I suppose you can afford to."

The begrudged reply ended the review and the pair went into dinner. Afterwards, they retired to the den, where Shepherd returned to his portfolio, laying the portraits on top.

"I'm afraid I have nothing but sherry. Will that do?"

"Do I have to hold the glass with my pinkie sticking out?"

Trent chuckled, pleasing Shepherd.

"No. But you don't mind if I do?"

For this, he elicited a like response and felt like crying.

After bandying around some banal conversation, the lonely, frightened old man blurted out, "I would like to buy you a camera. An expensive one."

Shepherd was neither offended nor frightened. Picking up his sherry glass, he held it to the light as though examining it for alcoholic content.

"Why?"

"Because you have talent."

"No one else thinks so. What do I have to do for it? Take photos of old buildings?"

"Do what you please. To further your career," he awkwardly offered.

"What's in it for you?"

Shepherd sipped the wine without once thinking he ought to offer a toast. His nose wrinkled which a worried Trent ascribed to "distaste," before more correctly deciding on "unfamiliarity."

"I thought perhaps...." The pause became uncomfortable. "You would show me your work. So I could follow your progress."

"No big deal. What else?"

Trent nervously wrung his hands. He felt like a boy on his first date, which, for all the world, he might have been.

His eyes focused on a stone idol perched at the edge of his desk. He did not mean to stare, yet felt compelled to do so as if heeding some silent command.

The object, although authentic, held no special significance. It did not even originate from his theatre of interest. Trent's specialty lay in "the Continent," and for him, only one existed. Europe. This piece was undoubtedly Central American.

Frowning, he could not, for the life of him, remember exactly where he had obtained it. He would not have purchased such an item, and none of his learned colleagues would have offered it as a gift, knowing his line of research.

Rising from his rocking chair, Trent crossed the room. The action required no more than a few steps, yet he panted heavily by the time he reached the desk.

Taking a moment to compose himself, he attempted to pick up the little deity and found he could not. It felt inordinately heavy. Stooping at the waist, he examined it more closely. A minute inspection brought two startling realizations: the first, that the object had blue, semi-precious gems for eyes, and second, he had never seen it before.

With goose bumps popping out across his arms, the professor glanced sideways at Shepherd, puzzlement commingling with doubt and suspicion.

His guest could not be that which he purported. Astutely observing him pour more sweet wine into his glass, Shepherd's limbs gave the impression of being grotesquely elongated, his face almost lupine.

Trent blinked, refocusing his vision. Instead of dissipating, the impression grew more acute.

Welsh devil flashed from his subconscious.

"No!"

The boy reacted, assuming Trent addressed him. He smiled sheepishly.

"Sorry. I didn't mean to help myself. I should have asked. I guess it's expensive."

He presumed Trent were admonishing him for taking more sherry. The wolfish image disappeared, or more accurately, retreated into the shadows. Trent's heart rate lowered back to normal.

"My fault," he quickly apologized. "I was talking to myself. The habit of solitary people."

"That's O.K. I talk to myself, too." Shepherd grinned. "They only say you're crazy when you answer back."

"I do that, too," Trent admitted, rubbing his eyelids. "I'm afraid I'm the archetypical absent-minded professor."

That had to be the answer, he decided, willing himself to look again at the stone idol. He had owned the trinket for years. Received it as a birthday present. Purchased it at a bazaar. More than likely, it had been pawned as a paperweight; nothing more than a cheap reproduction.

Prodding it with a finger, the god symbol moved easily. Lifting it, Trent decided it weighed no more than ten ounces.

Odd, how it had seemed so heavy a moment ago.

Replacing it on the desk, Trent returned to his chair. If only he could convince himself those blue-gem eyes were not following his every movement, he might have dismissed the entire incident as a fantasy, the work of an overwrought imagination.

But he could not.

Nor could he rationally explain the next words which tumbled from his lips.

"You need a place to stay? A decent roof over your head? I don't mean to imply you can't support yourself," he hastened to add. "Just until you get yourself established. To further the Arts," he concluded lamely, feeling utterly foolish.

The irrationality of the offer added to Trent's confusion. He had known Shepherd Kingston less than three hours, yet in that short time, he had fallen under a spell.

Or, more accurately, an enchantment.

The boy transfixed him, evoked fascination. Without rational explanation, he knew their lives had been drawn together for a purpose.

In God's Universe, they were playing out the roles prescribed by destiny.

Being a man deeply imbued in the occult sciences, this idea took precedence over closer, more physical reasons why Trent's interest had been stirred. Not only had he been given permission to keep Shepherd, the gods absolutely commanded him to do so.

Logic, therefore, held more sway than emotion.

Or at least presented a more acceptable solution to a very solitary soul.

They had lived together for nearly five years. During that time, their relationship grew more familiar, but hardly more physical. The times when Trent longed to deepen it, he restrained himself, though his desires were clearly evident. At first, Shepherd had been repulsed by the obvious affection, then gradually grew accustomed to it, accepting the emotions as the price he paid for room and board.

Occasionally, he would let the older man stroke his arm or snuggle beside him, rarely returning the gestures with similar ones. He felt no guilt in remaining aloof, nor any pressure to accept the unspoken request for love. How Trent dwelt with his sexual urges did not concern him.

The day Shepherd fledged himself nearly broke Trent's heart. Having saved enough of his "allowance" and the small stipends he made hawking his "gossip column pics," Shepard rented an efficiency apartment. Knowing such separation as inevitable as necessary, Trent had purchased linens, dishes and necessities, leaving open the invitation to "come home" often.

That, Shepherd had done and their relationship continued along the same lines as previously. Trent critiqued his work, praised his successes, commiserated with his failures. He listened to the abbreviated stories of the youth's casual associations with women, offered fatherly advice and cried himself to sleep.

Never once did he go back and further examine the mysterious stone idol. The man of occult sciences simply did not wish to delve further into what may or may not have been a psychic premonition.

Eventually, he forgot about it altogether, until one night, when tidying up his room, he discovered the god missing. Trent dismissed the fact with casual indifference.

His housekeeper, he presumed, had stolen it.

Reverting to the present, Trent started, then hastened to restructure the thread of the conversation only registered on a subliminal level.

"... I have to make it on my own, Trent. This story of Miss Elvina is my big chance. I don't know how or why she's managed to keep herself hidden from 'inquiring minds,' but I intend to get to her." Trent raised an eyebrow, asking for further elucidation. "Interview her; take a few hundred snapshots – enough to satisfy the society pages and the rags for months."

"What makes you think you can reach her, when grown men – professional newspaper reporters and photographers – haven't?"

Shepherd flushed at the reference to his tender years and lack of success.

"Maybe because I am young; because I've never learned the rules. Refuse to play the game. Because I won't take 'no' for an answer. Come on, Trent. You were young once. Don't you remember what it was like when you were hungry for fame and fortune?"

"Yes," he admitted, the force of the argument finally reaching him. Smiling sadly, he crossed to a lawyer's bookcase. Drawing back the glass door, Trent spread his legs, equalizing his balance while inadvertently assuming the stance a lawman took before a life and death face-off.

Sixteen books were arrayed on the top shelf. Beneath vertical titles imprinted on dust jackets ran the horizontal name "Abraham Trent." Two-thirds of a cross, lacking only the bottom portion.

"I remember the first time I ever saw my name on the spine of a book; running my hands over the cover; cradling it to my breast as though it were a child." Withdrawing the first in the series, he opened to the title page, lips silently forming the words of the dedication.

To my mother and father, who permitted me to utilize my greatest gift: the ability to see beyond the commonplace.

Reverently replacing it, Trent chose the last tome, a thick, one-thousand page thesis entitled *God in the Eye of the Beholder: A Study of Ancient and Modern Theology.*

He did not have to refresh his memory of this dedication, but did so for the comfort it afforded.

"For Shepherd Kingston," he whispered aloud. "Who reinstalled in me a sense of divine goodness." Wiping away moisture from his eyes, he uplifted them to stare into the boy's orbs. "You, Shepherd, are my true life's work. The reason I was born. Whatever it is you were meant to achieve, I was placed here to help you."

"You have helped me," Shepherd freely acknowledged, gently removing the book from his mentor's grasp. "That's just my point. I'm right on the verge of a great transition. I can feel it."

Setting the work beside the others, he gently appraised his friend. In contrast to the image he had grown accustomed to seeing, he experienced a wave of shock at how old Trent appeared. For the first time he saw that his beloved, absent-minded professor, had not withstood the test of time.

Where he remembered crow's feet, deep gorges lay; Trent's hair, once full and wildly erratic, had thinned and plastered to his skull. Bluish circles under the still-sharp eyes had deepened and darkened, making his countenance appear sunken and lost.

When had this happened? Why had he not seen? The answer, even to his skeptical mind, tolled with obvious clarity. He beheld not the passage of years but of days. Since his first encounter with Ericka Elvina, his friend had aged considerably.

Not without help.

The blame lay at his feet. In Shepherd's pursuit of fame and fortune, he had overlooked the toll his quest had on another. Yet the cost could neither be prevented nor pursued. The time for that must come later. His leg shook in nervous anxiety.

"I want to grasp the brass ring, Trent. I want to see my name in lights. I want you to be proud. Don't condemn me for what I seek."

The odd expression ill-suited the conversation. Trent straightened as his head slowly moved in the negative. He felt his moment fade.

"*I* won't condemn you, Shepherd. But for God's sake, be certain no one else does, either."

Anger flashed behind Shepherd's blue eyes, stirring an unpleasant association with the missing Central American idol. Although alone with the boy, Trent had the uncanny impression they were being watched. Not by God, of whom he wrote so elegantly, but by a far darker power. For the first time, the professor of the occult wished he had never met Shepherd Kingston. Despite the fact he so recently declared his own dedication to aid the boy in achieving some lofty goal, he doubted now whether that statement reflected Divine Providence, or originated from God's counterpart.

Blasphemy in the extreme, the idea rendered his heart to shreds.

Damning him to hell.

Unwilling or unable to read Trent's conflicting emotions, Shepherd brought his face closer. He saw the argument on only one level. He chose that place to make a stand and fight his battle.

"You can't lose what you don't have. I don't have a soul, so I can't lose it."

Trent's jaw quivered from the blow. His eyelids narrowed in mortal combat.

"Whether or not you have a soul I leave to a higher power." He hesitated, confused. He had meant to say *I will leave to God*. But it had not come out that way. "But you do have a life. That, you can lose," he lamely concluded.

"My life is my own. What I do with it is my *affair*."

While not precisely true, Trent did not pursue the argument solely because Shepherd purposely chose to end his protestation with an inflammatory word, meant to inflict pain. In that, he succeeded beyond his wildest expectations.

The ensuing silence gave Shepherd the impetus to continue.

"I refer you to your ancient books, old friend," he replied, rocking gently on the balls of his feet. "The Greeks, the Romans. They worshipped beauty."

Springing away, the wannabe photographer pointed to a woodcut of Athena, the daughter of Zeus; the woman whom no mother bore, springing to life from her father's head. Athena's arms were spread outward, the city of Athens in the far distance. At her feet knelt a worshiper, eyes transfixed on her expression of haughty domination.

"Beauty is pure and good" Shepherd ranted, purposely choosing to ignore Athena's history as a fierce and ruthless goddess. "Miss Elvina is a beautiful woman – even you can see that. I have no fear of her. Through her is my destiny. I swear to you, I know this." He placed a hand to his heart. "I feel it, Trent. In my bones; my very makeup."

Behind them, a grandfather clock struck the hour. Neither spoke until the chimes faded into obscurity.

"And if behind her there is ugliness?"

One last try. From her place on the wall, Athena's smile seemed to grow. As a god, she had access to secrets withheld from mere mortals.

"There isn't."

Gliding to the door, Shepard waved a fond farewell.

"Call me in the morning?" Trent repeated, ignoring the ache in his soul.

"Yeah. Sure. Good night."

"Good night." Not until the lock clicked shut did Trent finished his thought. "And God bless."

Behind him, Athena laughed. Even a religious man understood mockery when he heard it.

CHAPTER 7

Shepherd did none of the things he told Trent he would. Instead, he returned to his apartment and went to bed, "doing nothing" being the better part of valor.

In the morning, he performed a quick brush up of his rather mangy appearance, then made a few phone calls. Numerous dead ends, sundry lies, evasive promises of "rewards" and profuse "thank yous" finally obtained for him the address where Joe Warren worked. As the photographer credited with taking Ericka Elvina's picture, Shepherd deemed him a good place to start. Although the lady in question had not actually been in the shot, he knew of no better option.

The mighty steel and glass, 50-floor building nearly took Shepherd's breath away. Here was success; corner offices, phones ringing off the hook, assignments to exotic locales. Life in the fast lane, where salaries reached six figures and assistants delivered aged Scotch like bottled water.

Mister Warren had done well for himself. Without the slightest regard to morality, Shepherd wished himself in Joe's shoes. Surely, he had the talent to achieve such heights. If only someone – or something – would give him a break.

Glancing upward toward the penthouse, the youth stubbed his toe on the curb. Losing balance, he plunged unceremoniously to the sidewalk, scraping his palms. Lips curling in irritation, he sarcastically remarked, "Thank you, God."

What was the expression? If he didn't have bad luck, he wouldn't have any luck at all. Muttering an invocation against trite familiarisms, he brushed past a motley solicitor standing by a red kettle. Because he did not stuff a dollar through the narrow, locked lid, the charity-seeker did not jingle his bell in appreciation.

"No angel will get its wings on my account," the hopeful youth, looking for his own handout, dryly observed. Licking a drop of blood off his hand, Shepherd squared his shoulders and marched into the lobby on his less than holy quest.

He found Joe Warren listed on the directory. Several dots separated name from title: Professional Photographer. Shepherd's heart swelled with pride. Not for Joe, but from the idea that someday his name would be as prominently displayed.

Admiring the original artwork on the walls which Trent, in his old-fashioned, out-of-touch way would dismiss as a display of modernistic soullessness, Shepherd took the elevator to the thirty-third floor.

Following the signs, no more useful than the non-sequential suite numbers, he eventually arrived at the Successful Man's office.

With a shudder akin to reverence, Shepherd drew back the glass door and slipped into his vision of Valhalla.

A secretary, dressed in fashionable business attire from Sax Fifth Avenue greeted him with cold, detached formality. The petitioner explained the nature of his business.

"Mr. Warren," she summarily retorted, "is not available."

Cranking up the charm, he politely inquired, "Could you be more specific?"

"He is out." Meaning, *He wouldn't give you the time of day.* Shepherd immediately took offense.

"Out, where? Out on assignment? Out to lunch? Out taking a shit?"

For his trouble, she escorted him to the door.

Promising himself that when he achieved success he would always make himself available to young, talented photographers looking for a break, Shepherd hit the pavement. If he could not get in to see the exulted Joe Warren, he would start at the bottom and work his way up.

Beginning first with those cohorts to whom he did not owe money, Shepherd selected Sam Greeley.

Sammy was a down-and-out-er. Always had been, always would be. But he kept his ear to the ground and might know the odd tidbit that Shepherd could fit along the edges of his jigsaw puzzle.

He had not seen Sammy in ages. As the man turned to him, his appearance elicited an uncomfortable impression. The type of feeling one occasionally got when flipping through pages of old high school yearbooks.

This one has a glow around his head.

He isn't going to make it out of college.

Sammy would not have been flattered.

Listening him out, the informant gave a disinterested shrug.

"Never heard of the lady. Queer sort of name, though, isn't it?"

"She's foreign."

"Sounds like a stage name. Doesn't work at the Bottoms Up, does she?"

"No, she doesn't," Shepherd snapped. "She's a Wall Street wizard."

"Ticket tape types don't talk to the likes of me. And they sure as hell don't talk to the likes of you," he unnecessarily interjected.

Sammy received a "Go jump in a lake," for his trouble. Shepherd hoped his impression of high school yearbooks was correct.

He tried Bill Ford next. Ford was a drunk who had once worked for the tabloids. These days, he supplemented his income by dabbling in dirty pictures hawked over the Internet.

"Showed up on the scene five years ago, you say?" Bill asked while pocketing Shepherd's ten dollar bill. "Five years ago I was still getting around. Seems to me I remember something of her."

A short man with light brown hair, tinged with grey, the photographer had once been handsome, with a flair for the ladies.

"Tell me anything you can think of. No matter how insignificant."

"I wasn't writing copy by that time, but I still make a buck here and there with a good pic. Refresh my memory. She's tall, dark and shapely?"

"That's right."

Bill scratched under his arm, eyes distant.

"I did see Ericka Elvina once. Camped outside her office. You know, they had just renovated the building. I think she was the only tenant. I was hoping for a decent shot. I bet I waited two weeks and never saw her go in or come out. Then, one evening, just at sunset, there she was. Walked right out the lobby door, pretty as you please. Not ten feet away from me. Dressed in this – outfit, I guess you'd call it. A sort of dark, shimmering green. Looking right at me."

"What happened?"

Bill shook his head, then interlocked his fingers, snapping them back until his knuckles cracked.

"I froze, you know? Got caught off guard. I mean, I'd been casing the joint for two weeks and never seen her."

"So you said."

"She never went in, so I wasn't expecting her to come out."

"O.K.," Shepherd urged. "So she took the back entrance."

"No. No, she didn't. I had money then, you know? I was paying the guard. He would have told me. She never went in the rear."

"All right; she flew up to the twenty-second floor but decided to take the stairs down. Did you get her picture?"

"No."

"No? No! Why not?"

Incredulously, Shepherd dismissed the man from the land of the living with a wave of his hand.

"Because she surprised me, see? One minute she wasn't there and the next minute she was."

"But you were a pro – you were waiting for her. Maybe you were surprised, but you couldn't have been knocked off your feet."

"She was looking at me – right into my eyes. She did something to me."

"Yeah; I know. You got a hard on."

Bill grinned. He had a front tooth missing. Five years ago women considered him handsome, but time and booze had been cruel.

"Yeah. I probably did at that. But that's not what I mean. She... did something to me."

"You said that. What 'something'? Put a spell on you?" Shepherd taunted.

"Funny you should say that."

"I'm not laughing."

"O.K. Call it what you want. But once I looked into her eyes, I forget everything. Forgot to take her picture."

"You were on the sauce."

"No. Not then. Not much. I just... forgot what I was doing there. She was damned beautiful. A woman in her prime. Twenty-three, twenty-five. Not a day older."

"She looks that now," Shepherd protested. "Younger, five years ago, surely."

Boy, I know ladies. I was at the top of my profession, once. I took a lot of snaps. I know faces. Skin. Wrinkle lines. She was perfect."

Shepherd's shoulders sagged. The description Ford gave fit Ericka Elvina to a 'T,' yet it could not be possible she remained unchanged.

Twenty-three, twenty-five. Not a day older.

"Black eyes. She had the blackest eyes I've ever seen. No trace of color. I've never seen truly black orbs before. But she had 'em. Startling."

"Are you saying you were so taken by her black eyes you forgot to take her picture?"

"I'm saying... I don't know what I'm saying. I wasted two weeks. That much I do remember."

"What happened after that? After you saw her, I mean?"

"A limo came up and she got in. It drove away."

"What kind of limo? Did you get the license plate?"

"I don't think my eyes left the place where she had been standing for a full minute. Maybe longer. For all I know, I could have been standing there, staring into empty space for an hour."

"You don't know much." He meant to stab the man into a further elaboration, but got nothing more for his money.

"No," Bill Ford slowly remarked. "I don't know much."

"Did you go back after that – to the office building, I mean? Try again?"

"No. I didn't."

"Why not?"

"It... didn't seem worth it."

"But you had been so close."

"Too close."

"What does that mean?"

"I don't know."

Frustrated, Shepherd prodded the man by tapping him on the shoulder.

"Look. I've got to get to her. I mean it. Tell me what to do."

"Leave her alone. She likes her privacy." As a friendly warning, it came across as a dire threat.

"So did J. Edgar Hoover. And look what he did behind closed doors."

"Sorry. I can't help you anymore."

"You haven't helped me at all."

Shepherd was ten feet away before the prematurely aged photographer called after him.

"You might try Danny Poole."

"Who's he?"

"A photographer. He works out of a studio on 54th Street. He might be able to tell you something."

"Thanks."

Daniel Poole was busy shooting a spread for a soup commercial. When told he would be occupied all day, Shepherd waited until the receptionist answered the telephone, then casually strolled onto the private set. A small portion of the room has been transformed into a sandy beach. Three scantily-clad women were posing with an oversized can.

"That's right," the photographer encouraged. "Turn the product toward me. Another half inch. Good. Say cheese."

That was the second oldest line in the world after, "Come on up and see me sometime." Shepherd winced.

Heat from the lights made the room intolerable. A huge fan, used to blow the women's hair, only made the air stuffy.

After what seemed like several thousand pictures were snapped off, Mr. Poole called a halt to the proceedings. As the women relaxed, two of them directed withering invectives his way.

Oblivious to their displeasure, Danny caught a glimpse of the interloper out of the corner of his eye.

"Closed set," he warned.

"I won't tell Campbell's, I promise."

"What else is it you promise? Poole suggestively asked. Retreating a step, Shepherd smiled endearingly.

"My name is Kingston. Bill Ford sent me to see you."

"Like to do him a favor, but I'm not hiring."

"I'm not looking for a job. I'm on assignment. I was hoping you could help me."

Taller than Ford, younger and with lighter hair, which in a man universally characterized him as "blond," the photographer cracked open a bottle of water.

"You've got five minutes."

"I'm putting together a piece on women in business," Shepherd lied with good intentions. "Specifically, women who work in the stock market."

"Good God. Who died to get out of that?"

"Most women like to have their picture taken," Shepherd grinned. "But there's one in particular I haven't been able to approach."

"Send flowers," Danny suggested.

"A wizard on Wall Street."

"Send bonds."

"Ericka Elvina."

Poole stopped drinking, replaced the top on his bottle and turned a blank stare on his visitor.

"Who?"

"Ericka Elvina."

Although clear from his expression he perfectly understood the name, he forced out a question.

"Why come to me?"

"I was told you used to take a lot of pictures; might have taken a few of her."

"No. I never did."

"You do know who I mean?"

"Yes.... I know."

"How can I get close to her?"

"You can't."

"I have to. You did. Didn't you?"

"Close to her? No."

"But you wanted to?"

"Sure. She's beautiful. She's got the body of a god. If she weren't so good at what she does, I'd say it was a damned waste she wasn't a model."

"You shadowed her, maybe? Hoping for a candid?"

"Hoping for anything," Danny agreed. The grin appeared lopsided and effected. "If I'd gotten a shot of her, I'd have retired to Hawaii."

"How come you didn't?"

"Never had the chance." The answer sounded less than convincing.

"Why not? Did you hang out at her office? Maybe her apartment?"

"I think she lives in the office building. Upper floor; works out of one or two suites on the lower levels."

"Did you ever get up there?"

"No chance."

"What about parties? Ever see her at one of those society events?"

Poole searched his memory by dissecting the beach set. The palm fronds had withered under the kliegs, the life sapped out of them.

"Once or twice."

"And you didn't take her picture?"

"No."

"Why not?"

"Well, I thought I did. But it turned out I hadn't."

Shepherd followed his gaze, thinking that if someone took a torch to the place, no one would ever miss the occupants or the work produced there.

"What does that mean?"

"The film I used was... corrupted."

"What does that mean?"

"Listen, I don't want to talk about this."

Danny drank more water. All the Perrier in the world would not put out the blaze Shepherd contemplated.

"Please, I don't mean to bother you, but –"

"Yeah. You're bothering me. Go away."

"Can't you help?"

"No. Leave me alone."

"You were young, once. There was a time you needed a break. I bet someone gave it to you. Repay that debt now – with me."

Daniel Poole hesitated, torn and confused. Behind him a timer sounded, its shrill beep causing him to shiver. Looking more like a spy imparting classified secrets than one professional doing another a good turn, he whispered, "Try Paul Delgado."

"Why? Who is he? Where do I find him?"

"He works out of the South End Building. He interviewed her once. I think. Now get out of here."

When Shepherd reached into his pocket to pay the man for his information, Danny held up his hands. Without making contact, he went through the motions of pushing Shepherd back.

"I don't want you to touch me; I don't want anything you've handled."

For a man who did not know where his next meal would come from, such a refusal equated to sacrilege.

"Why not?"

Poole shivered in the sweltering room. His orbs assumed a wild, almost canine expression.

"She'll trace me through you. If you get that far. Even if you don't, you're just as likely to end up in the East River."

"Why? For God's sake, tell me what you mean."

"God," Danny retorted, "had nothing to do with Ericka Elvina."

"It's just an expression," Shepherd mumbled, but Mr. Poole had turned a deaf ear. The young photographer watched as the models repositioned themselves in front of the super-sized can, then smiled to himself as Poole's words escorted him off the set.

"Turn the product around this way, sweeties. That's right. Thank you. Smile. Say cheese."

Shepherd mouthed the words in perfect sync with the older man, feeling relieved to know there were still some constants left in the world.

It took the rest of the morning to locate Paul Delgado. He worked out of a building reserved for those with enough money to rent an office, but not enough to impress. A sign taped on the cheap wooden door advised, "No appointment necessary. Knock and Enter." Opposing him to right and left were two other operators: a private investigator and a person DBA a "Divinator of Tarot." Beneath the occupation were the words, "Always Open." Shepherd's nose wrinkled in disgust.

Heeding the first sign, the youth knocked and found himself confronting the Mildly Successful Man.

Tall, with sandy hair, cut in a style which went out with the Beach Boys, Paul Delgado had a pert, freckled nose and neatly sculptured eyebrows which would have made Dick Gephardt president. In age, he appeared to be about thirty.

"I appreciate you taking the time to meet with me," Shepherd began. The journalist dismissed the opening line which he had already heard over the phone.

"I owe Danny," he replied abruptly, although by no means unfriendly. "He stood in for me once at a convention and gave a nice speech. Wouldn't even take the honorarium. What can I do for you, kid?"

"I understand you once interviewed Ericka Elvina."

The friendliness vanished like a burst balloon. "Who told you a thing like that?"

"Your old pal, Danny Poole. Remember him – the guy who stood in for you once?"

"No. I – I never interviewed her."

"Think carefully," Shepherd urged. "She seems to have a sort of amnesic effect on people."

Rather than replying, Paul got up from behind his desk, walked to his file cabinet, then abandoned the effort before opening a window.

"I thought you were looking for a job," he slowly remarked. "Isn't that what you said?"

"No. I never said that. I want to talk to you about Miss Elvina."

"She's a recluse."

"So I've heard. But you did interview her?" No answer. "Danny said so."

"Did he? That's odd. When... when did he say this interview took place?"

"Within the last two years," Shepherd guessed. "Why don't you check your files? Maybe you still have your notes. A good reporter never throws anything out, right?"

"Right...." Returning to the cabinet, Mr. Delgado randomly selected a file, checked it, then put it back, out of alphabetical order. "Nothing here."

"Look under 'E,'" Shepherd suggested. "For Elvina. Right?"

Without waiting for the journalist to follow his suggestion, Shepherd crossed the room and joined the man. Running his gaze over the manila folders, he immediately spotted one marked "Elvina, Ericka."

"It's right there," he indicated. "Mind if I take a look?"

"Yes. I mind," Paul protested, too late. Reaching across him, Shepherd retrieved the folder and flipped it open. Inside were three sheets of lined, yellow tablet paper. Erratic scrawlings were written on all three pages. None of them were decipherable.

"What is this? Some sort of shorthand?"

"Let me see."

Delgado took the pages, scanned them curiously, then grimaced.

"I have no idea what they mean."

"Code, perhaps?" Shepherd retrieved the folder, catching a glimpse of the writing from the corner of his eye. Viewed in that manner, unencumbered by forced effort, the gibberish seemed to make sense. The words were not English, but a corruption of Latin.

But not that, either. His throat constricted at the revelation.

Pre-Latin. Or more accurately, the roots of Latin.

In a fleeting moment of hysteria, he wondered whether Delgado had too much time on his hands and had taken up with the Gypsy next door. He clung to the irrational rationality, twitching as the reporter broke into his speculations.

"Why would I write in code?"

Shepherd conjured his own demon to drag the information from the reluctant informant. "I don't know. Why would you?"

"It's not like I'm working for the FBI. Ms. Elvina is only a...."

"Only a – what?"

"A very beautiful woman." Peculiarly, the verbalization seemed to come a full second after his lips moved, simulating the effect a TV viewer saw when an actor did a poor job dubbing his lines.

"Yes. She's very beautiful. Did you sleep with her?"

Delgado's expression turned reflective.

"Who wouldn't?"

"But did you?"

"Did I – what?"

"Screw around."

"I was invited up to her apartment.... Yes! I did interview her!"

Shepherd pressed closer, eyes aflame.

"What did you ask? Where are your notes?"

"Right there... in your hand."

Backing away from himself, he demanded, "But this is only scribbles and weird symbols. Look. You've drawn the pentagram. Why?"

"I have no idea," came the weak protestation. "Silly of me, wasn't it?"

"Yes. Did you feel the need of protection?"

"Don't be silly." The sentence trailed off as he became cognizant of using the same expression twice in the same breath. Yet he added a lame, "Maybe," and crossed himself.

Shepherd would have bet him for an atheist.

"I can't read this. You'll have to tell me what she said."

"Tell you what who said?"

"Ericka Elvina. What questions did you ask?"

"I don't remember."

"What about her employer – the emperor, or king, or whoever he is?"

"She said he was... an old man." And then more vividly, "A very old man."

"What's his name?"

"I don't believe she mentioned it."

"Here," Shepherd prompted, shoving the notes forward. "Check and see if you wrote it down." Delgado cringed, whipping his hands behind his back.

"Some of that... isn't my handwriting."

"Try to remember. What country does he rule?"

"Whatever."

"He rules a country called 'Whatever'?" The tension between them grew palpable.

"No, no.... He rules a country named.... You name it."

"I can't. That's what I'm asking you."

Averting his head, Paul Delgado put a hand to his temples. The harder he tried to remember, the worse they throbbed.

"I can't tell you anymore. Go, now."

His denial sounded oddly reminiscent of Maleva's admonition to Larry Talbot. Shepherd did not appreciate playing the werewolf-in-waiting.

"You've got to. Surely she mentioned something about her native land. It's important."

Delgado jerked away, crossed back to the window and pressed against it, giving Shepherd the uneasy feeling he contemplated jumping. When he spoke, his voice sounded tortured, as though the words were confessed on the rack.

"A very ancient land; somewhere in Europe. One of those... countries without boundaries. Like Doctors Without Borders." He laughed. The joke, if indeed it were, fell flat. "Not listed on any maps."

"Listen: I've subscribed to *National Geographic* since I was in the 7th grade. Everything is listed on a map. Or do you mean the *name* isn't listed?"

"She said it wasn't listed," Paul firmly reiterated. "I wasn't about to contradict her."

"You're a reporter. You're supposed to get at the truth."

"One *never* contradicts her," came the sharp rejoinder. "Or, rather, I should say, it never occurs to you to doubt what she says. She... always tells the truth."

"Everyone lies."

"Just as you lied to get in to see me," Paul remarked with eerie clairvoyance. His lips did not move. Ventriloquism. Another gift from the erstwhile Gypsy.

"I didn't tell a falsehood. Daniel Poole did refer me."

"You asked about a job. That's it," Delgado grasped, reaching for straws. That fact seemed to relieve him.

"I never mentioned a job. I have a job."

The older man shied away from the window with repugnance. "I'm sorry. I have no free-lance work to give out just now. Leave your card. I'll call if something comes up."

Puzzled at the insistence and change of mood, Shepherd clandestinely hid the manila file behind his back.

"Thanks. I appreciate it."

"That's all right. I owe Danny a favor."

"So you said." Walking to the door, Shepherd let himself out. Before leaving, he shouted one final question.

"It's all right, isn't it, if I use your name as a reference? For a job, I mean. With other journalists?"

"Sure. That would be O.K."

"Like Joe Warren. You know him, don't you?"

"Joe Warren? He worked for *People* didn't he?"

"Yeah. That's the guy."

"I thought he was dead. Died in a plane crash, or something."

"No. He's alive."

"I... don't know him."

"You just said you did. The guy who works for *People*. Remember? Good old Joe?"

"Joe Warren. Yeah. He's dead... or something. Thanks for stopping by."

"You're welcome. Any time."

Without bothering to leave his "card," Shepherd headed for the elevator. Sensing a subtle change in the dingy corridor, he stretched back, taking in the open floor plan. It took a moment before he identified the alteration. A different placard hung from the Tarot-reader's door. It read "CLOSED" in large block lettering.

"What happened to 'Always Open'?" he asked of no one, feeling strangely uneasy. On impulse, he removed a pen from his pocket and drew a five-pointed star over the seer's sign.

Superstition, he assured himself. *Just leaving graffiti. For fun.*

He had no way of knowing who would have the last laugh.

"Good old Joe," he spoke aloud, rolling up the purloined file and stashing it in his jacket.

If Joe were dead or "something," interviewing him would prove elucidative.

CHAPTER 8

Shepherd Kingston did not have a clue what Joe Warren looked like, but he had the uncanny feeling he would be a tall man with blue eyes and blond hair. All the men with even a remote association to Ericka Elvina seemed to fit that general description. Starting with Bill Ford, then working past Danny Poole to Paul Delgado, he had encountered three individuals, each younger, taller, handsomer and more fair-haired than the last.

Smoothing down his own golden locks, Shepherd waited in the lobby. It was nearly six o'clock when the person he identified as Joe Warren stepped out of the elevator.

"Mr. Warren," he tentatively hailed, waving an arm in a friendly gesture of camaraderie as he accosted him in the lobby. "May I have a moment of your time?"

Bracing for immediate rebuke, the reporter surprised him by cordially returning the salutation.

"Sure. What can I do you for, junior?"

Coming from a man hardly five years Shepherd's senior, the familiarity seemed odd.

"I'd like to talk to you. About a confidential matter."

"I don't buy or take blackmail," came the angry snarl. Shepherd held up his hands, earnestly shaking his head.

"It's nothing like that. I swear."

"Then what's the secrecy?"

"It has to do with Ericka Elvina."

"Ericka?" While recognition came immediately, the reaction was vague. "Ericka Elvina?"

"The Wall Street wizard. You're the only one who ever took her photograph and had it published." The prompt worked.

"Ericka.... That's right. But there was something wrong with that shot, wasn't there?" he whined, in the same tone he might have adopted had his French fries been delivered cold.

"Yes. There was." Shepherd debated whether or not to fabricate the facts, then uncharacteristically opted for the truth. "She wasn't in it."

Joe Warren laughed at the memory before his face clouded over.

"That's right. Sweet Jesus, I caught flack for that. But it wasn't my fault...."

"Whose fault was it?"

"I don't remember. I'm not certain. I think the editor picked the wrong negative... or something. Wasn't that it?"

"I'm asking you."

"It was a photo I took at the Drake last year. Or was it the year before? I take so many shots, I forget," he apologized. "It was supposed to be of Ericka, but it turned out it wasn't. Some other woman, maybe?"

"There were no women in the photograph at all. Just three men. But her name ran in the caption."

"Funny how that happened."

Shepherd leaned closer, imploring the man to help.

"No one's ever managed to get a decent photograph of her."

The effort went for naught.

"What's your point, junior?"

"Can I talk to you about her?"

Warren's face went from affirmative to doubt at warp speed.

"Sure. I mean, I guess so. Why don't you make an appointment? I'm pretty busy just now. Next week, maybe?"

"I'm in a big hurry. I have a deadline. Next week I'm shooting a layout for Campbell's soup. Can't put it off," Shepherd pressed, feeling his window of opportunity close.

"Oh. What agency did you say you worked for?"

"Could we go up to your office? Just for a few minutes?"

"To talk about... the soup layout?"

"No. Ericka Elvina."

"To my office?" He sounded horrified. "No. Not up there."

"Here, then – in the lobby. It's a public place. No clandestine meeting, O.K.? What about over there – on the couch? Just for a minute. Please? I really appreciate your time, Mr. Warren. You're rather a hero to me."

Joe flashed a smile, warming to the compliment. "All right. But I don't know what I can tell you. That photo was a mistake, or –"

"Or something. I know."

Restraining his impulse to lead Warren by the arm, Shepherd walked in baby steps, never letting the man stray more than a foot from his side. He did not speak again until they were seated.

"Some say," he began, "you not only photographed Ms. Elvina, you interviewed her."

"Not exactly an interview," Joe confessed, running a hand through his yellow hair. "It was more like a tit-for-tat."

"What does that mean?"

"I'd ask a question, then she'd ask one of me. That... seemed to be the way she wanted it."

"She was curious about you?" Warren shrugged. "Why?"

"She said she never had the chance to talk to a 'regular joe.'" He brightened at the innocent part of their conversation. "It was a sort of play on my name. 'Joe.' You know?"

Shepherd had the sinking feeling he knew more than "Joe." And it did not put him at his ease. While he contemplated his next question, Joe unexpectedly continued.

"She said she was looking for someone, and I might be he. We discussed going away together."

"Your place or hers?" The tease never got off the ground.

"To her native land."

"Did she give it a name?"

Warren chewed his lower lip, fleetingly aware how sketchy his memory had become.

"Not precisely. Or maybe she did and it had too many vowels to remember."

Shepherd rolled his eyes. "But you didn't go?"

"No. Shortly after I visited with her, I received a big commission. Totally out of the blue. I was gone from the country for a month."

"But you wrote the story when you came back?"

"No. I... couldn't get into it."

"Didn't you take notes?"

"Sure. But...." Warren looked off, frowning. "It was the most peculiar thing."

"What was?"

"My notes. I couldn't read them."

Ignoring the cold chill settling over his bones, Shepherd withdrew the pilfered file and shoved it under Joe's nose.

"Did they look something like this?"

Fighting his first instinct to the take the paper, Joe followed his second, far stronger one, and recoiled.

"Where did you get them?" he hissed.

"These are not yours."

Considerably relieved, Joe wiped his brow. "Good. You're right. They can't be mine. I... destroyed them."

"Why did you do that?"

"I don't know. Because I couldn't read them, I suppose. I have terrible handwriting," he added. "Happens to me all the time."

"That you can't read your own penmanship, or that you destroy notes?"

"Look: what is it you want of me?"

"I want you to tell me all you remember about Ericka Elvina."

"She's beautiful. Mysterious."

Joe faked a smile, forcing Shepherd to regroup.

"Did she say why she wanted to take you on a trip?"

"Yeah, she did. But I've forgotten. It was a long time ago."

"You're not senile, Mr. Warren! Come on! A woman like that offers you vacation of a lifetime and you cancel out?"

"I told you. A job came up."

"What could have been more important than going away with her?"

"An assignment that paid a lot of money."

"More than you could have gotten from an exclusive on her? What was it?"

"Something only I could handle. A revolt in... Central America." Warren shifted uncomfortably. "Not my area of expertise, really. I was surprised to get it. Thought maybe it'd propel me into network news."

"It didn't, though. You're still here."

"Nothing ever came of the revolt. The warring parties brokered a peace treaty. Or something. Anyway, it turned out to be a dud. Things like that happen."

"What did she say when you told her you were bowing out? Was she angry?"

"It was like she already knew. Wasn't surprised, at all. Anyway, by that time, our relationship had cooled. It was a relief to both of us."

"Relationship?" Sweat trickled down Shepherd's arm pits. "Did you go to bed with her?" On Joe's blank look, Shepherd prodded, "Sleep with her? Have sex?"

"Did I?.... I suppose we did."

"You just suppose?"

"Look, sonny boy, I've slept with a lot of women. It wasn't anything... out of the ordinary."

Shepherd knew a palpable lie when he heard one. His next question was prompted by knowing what Trent would ask, were he in his place.

"Did you tell her that – that you'd slept around a lot? Is that what cooled your relationship?"

Warren hung his head, finally placing both hands over his ears. When he spoke again, his voice had a far-away quality which it previously lacked.

"No. She didn't mind that, so much as... That's it!" he cried, relieved to clarify his vision. "I told her I had just gotten engaged."

"That made her angry?"

"Really mad. Furious. I remember, now. No, I didn't tell her I fooled around a lot. I just said I was engaged and she asked if I had consummated the relationship."

"And you told her –?"

"Yes. Celia and I had been a couple for two years. In fact, we were living together at the time."

"At the time? Where is she now?"

A look of sadness came over the journalist's face. "Dead. She died in a car accident. Horrible."

"When was this?"

"While I was away in Central America. We never did get married. It broke me up."

"Can you tell me how I can reach her?"

"Celia?" His tone expressed dread.

"Ericka Elvina."

"No."

Sensing Warren's restiveness, Shepherd hurried to press his advantage.

"How did you get to meet her? Did you call for an appointment?"

"Yes, I did. But no one ever got back to me. She never calls anyone back."

"Then how did you get into her penthouse?"

"It was after I'd taken the photograph. The one she wasn't in." His foot shook. *"She* called *me* the same night; after the party. Said she had heard a lot of good things about my work. She knew I had taken her picture; wanted to see it. And I was to bring my camera." He smiled fondly. "I think she's vain. You know women. They always worry they won't look their best. I thought she was going to permit a photo shoot; so I could get a better one."

"Did she?"

"No. Frankly, the subject never came up."

"She didn't switch cameras, did she? I mean, when you turned in your film, she wasn't there. Is that how it happened?"

"It was in my briefcase. Secured with a combination lock. I never took it out. She couldn't have gotten it. I would have known. I'm sorry, kid. I have to go." Standing abruptly, Joe Warren shot Shepherd a quizzical look. "Good luck with your soup commercial."

"Thanks. I'll send you the proofs."

Gritting his teeth in frustration, Shepherd made the first move. While Warren had undoubtedly told the truth, he had not learned enough to fill a thimble. Waiting for the older man to rise, he noted Joe had frozen in position. The youth had a suggestion.

Take a long walk off a short pier.

Before the idea fully formed, Warren woke from his sudden trance. Getting to his feet, he waved a fond farewell, evoking a peculiar feeling of guilt in the ill-wisher. Almost a premonition of latent, evil forces at work.

Hurriedly crossing the lobby, Shepherd drove his palm outward, attempting to blow the door open by unnecessary force. Before making contact, however, the steel and glass egress flew outward, causing him to stumble through the opening.

"Damn electric eyes," he grumbled, regaining his balance, but not his dignity. Once outside, he played back his original entrance, distinctly recalling the heavy door had required a pull of inordinate strength.

Chiding himself for lack of short term memory, he nearly dismissed the incident but a nagging doubt reared its ugly head. Retracing his steps, Shepherd placed his body at a point where the automatic sensor should detect his presence. Nothing happened.

"Open, sesame," he commanded. No movement.

A woman passed on his right. Gripping the handle, she attempted to enter. The door did not budge. Shepherd gallantly came to her rescue.

"Thanks," she mumbled, slipping past. "It's the wind. Blows so hard, it makes it impossible to get in or out. You'd think architects would take that into consideration when they designed buildings."

Like Joe Warren, Shepherd put his hands over his ears to block out what he knew was coming.

"Think someone would install an electric eye, so you didn't have to break your fingernails tugging on it."

She did not wait for an answer from the erstwhile doorman, which was just as well, for Shepherd's lips had gone numb.

Shivering from the horror of the revelation, he scurried away, chin neatly tucked between his collar bones.

It had happened again, when least expected. Denial was impossible, yet Shepherd did his best.

"Damn wind. Blew the door open. Just like that. You'd think someone in this damned city would take atmospheric conditions into consideration."

Three "damns" in under sixty seconds. While hardly a world's record, he had the uncomfortable sensation that "damn" ruled the day.

But he'd be damned if he'd worry about it.

Shepherd did not want to return to Trent's apartment, yet there were questions only he could answer. After calling ahead to reserve a place at supper, if not forgiveness in the old man's heart, he presented himself at precisely seven o'clock.

"Right on time," Trent greeted. "Only an hour later than I expected."

"I got held up in traffic."

"How? Rush hour ends at –"

"O.K. Quit the lecturing, Professor. I was driving around in circles."

"I couldn't have put it better myself," Trent grinned. "What are you drinking these days?"

"Whatever you've got," came the truthful response. "Should I have brought flowers to make amends?"

"The day you walk through that door with common sense, I'll never ask another thing of you."

"How 'bout a beer?"

"Help yourself, then come into the living room. I want to show you something."

Shepherd chose a Samuel Adams, bought exclusively for him, then wandered back, nerves on edge from the lecture he expected. Trent hated to be kept waiting, never failing to chastise his friend on the virtues of punctuality. But considering what had happened today, he almost missed it when the chastisement did not come. Somehow, he felt the need of a verbal thrashing to absolve him of sin. Which did not prevent him from groaning, "Oh, no, not those again," as he saw the photographs of Ericka Elvina in the older man's hands. "Now what have you found? The devil lurking in the background?"

He could ask that now, for he always found teasing Trent easier than confronting other, more frightening issues.

Rather than answer, Trent held the photos at arm's length, further raising Shepherd's ire.

"I've taken some measurements of the glow around the figure's head and body."

"Me, too. Thirty-six, twenty-four –"

"Pay attention!"

"I am. You said I photographed her aura. Her life force."

"Yes.... That's what I thought at first. But the measurements didn't bear that out. If it were her aura, then the ghostly shape would hold exactly to the contours of her body. They don't. Close, certainly. Close enough to fool the casual observer, but not exact enough to fool my calipers."

"Go on."

Trent put the glosses down and picked up a separate stack he had placed on the arm of the couch. "Look at these. They are exactly the same photographs, but on them I've outlined the glow. Study the outline."

Shepherd stared at the carefully depicted dots, finally shaking his head in frustration.

"Am I supposed to see something?"

"Try using your imagination, rather than your eyes."

"You're asking me to use my imagination?" he snorted. "You? I thought you were Mr. Stick-to-the-Facts."

"Ordinarily I am. But I think I have discovered what you would call *facts.*" Instead of belaboring the point, Trent indicated his handiwork. "Note the area around the head and face, where the glow is most defined. You can just make out a second image. One which is taller, with more sharply etched features."

Shepherd peered closer, suppressing a gasp of understanding.

"I think I see what you mean."

"What conclusion do you draw?"

The boy recoiled slightly, trying an easy grin.

"You missed your calling. You should have gone into stippling."

"It's the image of a man. The nose and chin don't have that softness normally associated with a female. There's no question in my mind that the apparition superimposed over Miss Elvina is that of a male."

"Some big bruiser standing behind her?"

"He's not a big bruiser. He is, what you might say, her male half; male counterpart."

Shepherd rolled his eyes in melodramatic denial.

"What *you* might say. I never said it."

"Shepherd, I think she's possessed."

"Oh, shit! I should have seen that's where you were leading. I go from a mundane, double exposure, to an aura, and now you say she's possessed. What next: she vomits green puke?"

"Possession is not unheard of in the annals of parapsychology."

"Now I get it," Shepherd cried. "You're just looking for material for your next book! You don't believe it any more than I do, but your publisher will eat it up like candy at a day-care center. Another best seller from world-renowned expert Abraham Trent. No, sir. You're not going to steal this from me. It's my exclusive."

"I'm not trying to steal anything," Trent explained. Normally his patience would have been at an end, but the seriousness of the situation stayed his temper, although he betrayed his inner turmoil by a quivering of jaw muscles. Ashamed of his weakness, he crisscrossed his legs, then abruptly rose and went into the bathroom.

He was two Samuel Adams long in returning.

Reentering the den, Trent thought he had calmed himself. He might have maintained his delusion if not for Athena.

The expression on the framed figure had altered. There could be no mistake. He knew her features as well as his own. Demoniac curiosity had replaced beneficent haughtiness. Stopping dead in his tracks, Trent found he could not physically tear his eyes away from the goddess in the woodcut.

Responding to the magnetic pull, he baby-stepped across the room until coming face-to-face with her. Any hope that a closer inspection would revert her features back to normal quashed instantly.

Willing himself not to panic, he worked his mind as other men worked their muscles when struggling with a weighty issue. Penetrating through the goddess' black and white orbs, he glimpsed a shadowy world, almost palpable enough to enter. The realization was horrific, for nothing in Jehovah's universe would have compelled him to commit such a suicidal act.

What are you staring at? he demanded, posing the order through the mental link which assuredly existed. He received no reply, but had no doubt he had been understood. Not by Athena, for he never once considered her real, in any sense of the word. He addressed the entity which peered through her two-dimensional image.

Go away. You have no place here. This is a dwelling of God's creatures.

He heard her laugh. Taunting, cold. Superior.

I command you, in the name of Jesus Christ, be gone!

A wavering, a flicker of doubt from the watcher. Trent pressed harder, wedging the knife of his will power deeper into the soulless shade. He prayed the Old Prayers.

My God – prevent this evil, seven or one – give to him what he has given to others. Keep the pure in safety – punish the evil one now!

One second, two. The grandfather clock kept track of time, which had always been meaningless in the world of gods and demons.

The flicker of an eyebrow, a questioning in the eyes, a twitching of the mouth, then it disappeared, departed as surely as it had come. Restored to her normal self, Athena smiled. Yet the old haughtiness did not bring relief. She knew, just as he knew, he would never look upon her in the same light.

Released from the spiritual hold, Trent stumbled forward, instinctively holding out an arm to break his fall. He did not mean to touch the artist's rendition. His fingers brushed it by accident. As if he purposely torn the frame off the wall, it flew outward, seemed to hoover in the air, then dropped like a stone onto the floor.

The commotion brought Shepherd over. Before Trent could stop him, he retrieved the woodcut, started at it lustfully, then replaced it. It hung crooked, but he did not notice. Trent made no move to straighten it.

"Subterranean tremors," Shepherd quoted from *The Haunting.* "Sunspots."

His timing and choice of subject matter were poor.

Grabbing him by the arm, the professor led the neophyte away from *It* who had gone and would return.

Reincarnated into a fiend of flesh and blood.

Jamming his hands into his pockets, Trent stared at the rug.

"Shepherd, I'm scared. Scared shitless."

His use of a crude phrase finally got through to the youth, even if he miss-guessed the reason. If Trent were reduced to Shepherd's own level of communication, then he meant what he said.

"What are you frightened of? Not of a picture falling off the wall." No answer. "Of being possessed, yourself? Of having someone take over your body?" Stoical silence. "Come on. Level with me. Who possesses people these days?"

Tempered by the exorcism, Trent understood on an intuitive level that he had driven away wickedness with an invocation to Christ and a summons of the Seven. That Truth he held close for it had sustained him all his life and would, onto death.

Or so he believed.

"The same 'people' who have always held the power of possession. The Old Race. The Evil Ones."

"Trent," Shepherd tried, eyes wide with sincerity. "No one believes that anymore. You may have made a career out of writing 'science fantasy' for the fringe set, but even *you* aren't allowed to teach that stuff at the University. Every time you propose a class on the occult, they show you the door."

"That doesn't mean it isn't true."

"The Old Race. You might as well believe in Dracula."

"Vlad Tsepes was a real human being."

"All right; wrong example. But you know what I mean. There aren't two races, Trent – good human beings and bad ones."

He flung his arms in the air, trying to lighten the suddenly dark scene.

"I never said they were human. Being human implies a common ancestor; evolution, along anthropologic lines. Those comprising the Old Race are not our blood kin."

"They spawned from a different ocean."

The wrinkles in Trent's face deepened as the room lighting fluctuated. Being such an old building, such brown-outs were a normal occurrence. If one did not believe in the supernatural.

The wiser of the two took it for a sign. Yet he had no option but to ignore it.

At his peril.

"I don't know that they 'spawned' at all. They were created *integritas,* not evolved from any ocean. Certainly not one on earth."

"What are they, then? Space aliens?"

"I can't answer that."

"Little green men from Mars? Vulcans? Guys dressed in rubber suits, stepping off the set of *Space: 1999?"*

Trent settled himself in his rocker, gyrating back and forth the way elderly people in nursing homes performed the feat. It offered a means of wiling away time before the Grim Reaper finally came to claim them. He might have been senile, speaking for his own benefit.

And for those spirits known to hover around the soon-to-be departed.

"No. They appear just as human beings. But they are not. It may be that their physical form is mere convenience; perhaps they can shape-shift. I don't know. But I do know references to an 'Old Race' predate the oldest Judeo-Christian teachings."

"So what? That doesn't make it true. It only proves cavemen had an imagination. Ghost stories; tall tales, whispered around a campfire."

"The stories persist, in one form or another, throughout the races of Eastern and Central Europe. With very little deviation."

"So have Grimm's *Fairy Tales,* and no one believes them, much less fears or worships them."

"The same could be said for the tenets of Judaism, Christianity and Islamic religions."

"I don't believe them, any more than I believe the Grimm brothers."

"But I do. And I am not alone."

As proof, he might have sited Athena, but did not.

"So, you tithe ten percent to the Church and feel saved. I can purchase an indulgence for a tenth of that and achieve the same result."

"You believe. Deep in your heart I know you believe."

"Now you're adding mind reading to your repertoire. What next? Balancing pie plates on your head? There's no way I'm going to buy this theory of possession, Trent. No more than I do your little dots. Sorry. I could put dots around her head and come up with an elephant, if I tried hard enough. And I don't even need calipers."

"All right," Trent agreed, melting into his chair. "I won't force you to accept anything you can't. And I don't want you to agree, just to pacify me. That would be worse than outright denial. I'm just asking you to consider what I say."

"Why?"

"Because when the time comes, my ideas may just preserve your – life."

"Soul, you mean."

"Both, in fact."

"I have no intention of dying. Not at the hands of the Evil Ones, and certainly not at the feet of Ericka Elvina. She's a mystery, Trent, but a normal, every-day mystery. She's a recluse, like Howard Hughes. People attributed him with all sorts of mysterious powers, but he was just a man, like everyone else. Just a man with money."

"No one ever photographed him with a glow around his head."

Turning away, Shepherd went back into the kitchen for another beer. Pausing to swallow a mouthful, he returned to the living room with a smile.

"Put those things down and let's have supper. Then maybe we can play Monopoly or something."

"So you can build up your paper kingdom?"

"Can't hurt. Maybe if I tell her I own Boardwalk and Park Place she'll grant me an interview."

"Then I better win," Trent promised. "If that's all it takes to keep her away from you."

"I haven't got close."

"No. Not yet. But she let you take her photograph."

"Let me? She didn't even see me."

"Yes, she did. She was looking right at the camera when you took those last shots. Or should I say, right through the camera. She saw you as clearly as you saw her. If she hadn't divined something which appealed to her, your film would have come out blank."

"Back to Dracula, again."

"I wish it were that simple."

The two ate the meal Trent prepared, Shepherd forgetting to ask his pressing question, then retired to his study to play Monopoly. Trent used a pair of loaded dice and won the game, being certain he purchased all the high-rent properties.

He only wished life was that simple.

CHAPTER 9

At seven o'clock next morning Shepherd presented himself outside the Stone Gate. He brought with him a bagel with cream cheese and a cup of coffee. Camera loaded with film and three new rolls in his pocket, he had everything required for a siege.

"All right," he declared, issuing a pep talk to the world. "Ready when you are, Miss Elvina."

He had no idea when, or even if, the celebrated recluse left the confines of her closely guarded dwelling, but he had exhausted every other avenue of pursuit. Storming the twenty-second floor could not be considered. It would undoubtedly result in his taking a short leap out of a high window sill.

The same activity Shepherd had ungraciously suggested for Joe Warren.

That left stealth.

By eight-thirty, he had consumed breakfast and been forced to abandon his post once to make the euphemistic "short trip" to the men's room. Upon returning, he had the uncanny feeling his quarry anticipated his human weakness and taken advantage, escaping in his absence.

He waited until nine-thirty, then cursed his luck and left. By 2:00 that afternoon, he had returned. Pigeons, recognizing a kindred soul, flocked about.

"Go away," he shooed. The last thing in the world he wanted was to be called the "Flying Rat Man." Were the mysterious Wall Street wizard to see him surrounded by the socially unacceptable birds, she would never take him seriously.

"Here," he whispered, removing a packet of saltiness from his pocket. Crumpling the crackers he had gotten at lunch, but saved for a moment of need, he tossed them on the ground. In less time that it took to discretely dispose of the cellophane behind his back, the food had disappeared.

"That's all," he announced, fully expecting the rock doves to comprehend the situation. Two dozen more joined their companions, cooing and fluttering around and over his feet.

"Go away!"

The admonition brought every pigeon in New York City to his homesteaded.

Shepherd abandoned his quest.

"I'll be back tomorrow," he promised. He meant it as a warning.

The following A.M. he returned with breakfast in hand. The pigeons were waiting, apparently with as great a taste for bagels as he. Berating himself for his ignorance of avian behavior, Shepherd stuffed the food down his own gullet before retreating behind a parked car. He did not see Miss Elvina emerge, but had the satisfaction of watching the meter maid write a ticket and stick it under the windshield wipers of his erstwhile camouflage.

Wednesday he struck gold. At eight twenty-two, a black limousine pulled up outside the covered entrance. Two minutes later, the object of his desire emerged from the building. She wore two body guards as decoration. Hands trembling, Shepherd snapped off a dozen marginal shots, then ducked behind a lamp post. Miss Elvina seemed not to notice his intrusion, for which he thanked his lucky stars.

Knowing for certain that what goes out must come in, Shepherd waited the entire day, amusing himself by counting the parking tickets issued by the metermaid. At twenty-five dollars a pop, he supposed the state of New York would not need to raise taxes ever again.

The chauffeur-driven car drew up to the front of the Stone Gate shortly after 4 P.M. The henchmen emerged first, one from either rear door. Seemingly without intent, their massive bodies shielded their mistress from the photographer's camera.

"God damn it!"

While his bitter invective did not startle the convention of pigeons, Ericka Elvina paused just as the footman opened the door. Stepping aside with a fluidity of movement and grace which took his breath away, she stared vaguely in his direction, smiled, then disappeared inside.

Had he been holding the camera, Shepherd would have had the perfect opportunity for a close-up. He did not and thus missed the opportunity of a lifetime.

"Shit a brick!"

This time, the pigeons scattered.

Assuming she would make no further appearances that day, Shepherd drove his old, dented car home. Twenty-four shots remained on the roll but curiosity could not be ignored. Wasting the remaining film on sundry items inside his efficiency apartment, he scurried into the darkroom.

Developing the film by rote, Shepherd purposely avoided looking at the forming images, determined to wait until they were printed on glossy paper before assessing his achievement.

Working backwards, he merely deduced that his unmade bed, dresser and card table which served as both desk and dining area, were sharp and in focus. Only then did he examine the remaining dozen.

They were adequate but fell far short of his wild expectations. While Miss Elvina appeared in all twelve, none clearly revealed her face. In each, her features were either hidden by a body guard, or she faced away from the camera. The glow around her body represented the sole outstanding feature of the photographs.

Shaken but not discouraged, Shepherd produced a new set of images, first under- then over-developing the images. The second set gave him a better view of her "aura."

What he would never have divulged under torture, Shepherd admitted to himself. Trent had been right. The halo, or life force, did not configure to that of a female.

"She is not possessed," he spoke aloud, fully expecting Trent to hear. Then, for good measure, he added, "And neither am I."

With a coldness settling over him, unusual in the warm temperature of the "dark room," so called because he had created it by hanging blankets from the ceiling, Shepherd snapped off the red light and retired to his living quarters. Ironically, the wider space of the kitchen-living room evoked a feeling of claustrophobia.

Peculiarly, it also felt hotter, yet the higher temperature did not comfort him. Shivering, then running both hands up and down his arms to ward off the flu he supposed he had contracted, Shepherd flopped into his second-hand folding chair.

"This is ridiculous. People in the 20th Century simply do not get possessed. They may have life forces, but they don't have their souls taken over by the devil."

Trent was being unreasonable. He had spent too many years pouring over musty old books. His brain had been affected by his monk-like existence. A man isolated in a cave could see anything.

"It might as well be the image of a saint, rather than the devil," Shepherd mused. "Perhaps she's God's instrument." While that idea had more appeal to his sensibilities, it seemed an odd thought for a man who professed disbelieve in any deity.

"Or better yet," he suddenly decided, "this *is* the 20th Century. She doesn't want to be photographed, so she wears some sort of jamming device. Right out of *Mission: Impossible.* Maybe she really is a spy. She's like Cinnamon Carter. She keeps a day job to hide her identity as a member of the I.M.F."

Striking himself on the forehead, he laughed aloud. Why hadn't he thought of that earlier? Why hadn't Trent? So intent on believing in the power of evil, the old man had overlooked the obvious.

Which raised the question that if Ericka really were a spy, what country employed her? The United States, or some half-pint European nation no one had ever heard of? Had she arrived in Manhattan to keep Wall Street solvent, or the opposite?

And what about her success? Was she really a genius with the stock market, or did the unnamed Secretary who gave Dan Briggs his assignments, feed her tips? If Shepherd exposed her, managed to get a decent photograph, would he ruin her cover?

Did he care?

He thought that he might, but if that were actually the case, she would have to tell him; confess her secrets. Only then could he make an informed decision.

Feeling better than he had all week, Shepherd fell asleep in the chair. The telephone, ringing from the far wall in the kitchen, failed to rouse him.

Replacing the handset in the receiver, Trent returned to his library. His shoulders sagged. Shepherd seldom failed to appear for dinner and his absence cast a pall over the apartment.

His study was cold. Or, rather, Trent felt cold, for the thermostat registered eighty degrees. The manifestation disturbed him. Cold indicated a visitation of the supernatural. When he had, on rare occurrences, experienced psychic phenomenon, the effort left him weak and badly chilled.

Yet there could be no question of psychic phenomenon here. He had not been involved with summoning spirits; nor had he been concentrating on the occult. Therefore, the unnatural sensation did not make sense. Particularly in light of the fact he had removed the woodcut of Athena from the wall, replacing it with one of a male god doing penance to an even higher power. That, he prayed, would blind whatever essence had stared out through her eyes.

Sighing heavily, he chose a title and settled in at his desk. Carefully pulling back the hard-bound cover, the pages opened by their own accord to an oft-consulted illustration. The ancient wood carving revealed a high priest, wearing nothing but a string of beads and a feathered headdress. In one hand the *presbyteros* held a perforator. In the other, a small clay pot for the collection of blood. Around his body hovered a second image, depicted by an intricately placed series of dots.

The antediluvian carver had taken care, but in the transference from wood to paper, some of the pinpricks had been lost, leaving the ghostly image more amorphous than intended. Without undo concentration, Trent could almost feel a life force escaping from the holes.

He could not be certain what the artist wished to convey or what possessed him to set the image in wood. The open-ended question made Trent shudder nearly as much as his unintended use of the word *possessed.* One thing he would have staked his reputation on, however: the depiction had not been created to convey a spiritual possession.

The caption, written by one Johan Tames, described the ritual as a sacrifice to the gods, making no mention of the aura around the priest. Perhaps Tames attributed it to no more than a careless transformation from impress; or the absorption of the unseen sacrificial victim's soul into that of the holy man. Yet it remained a peculiar omission.

Trent would have liked to ask the scribe, but the researcher shared something in common with holy man of whom he wrote: death. Trent had dated the published manuscript to the mid-1600's. Best case scenario, Johan Tames had been dead over three-hundred years.

Nor had Tames dated the woodcut or offered any explanation where he had obtained it. Most likely, he lifted it from earlier works, for the style bore a striking similarity to rituals practiced by the Olmecs 2,500 years ago. That indicated even the original wood carver could not have been contemporary to his time. Yet even through numerous reproductions, the vividness of the translation shone with stark reality.

Throughout the ages, mysticism had always been a topic of fascination. Books on witchcraft and the black arts were some of the oldest extent works, many of the earliest collected by the librarians at Alexandria in 290 BC. Most were written in cipher; many more had been burned in the hope whatever they contained would perish as easily as the papyrus, or the stone upon which they had been chiseled.

Fear of the preternatural predated even Man's desire to profit from its power, though in Trent's experience, they often went hand in hand.

In his research, Trent had discovered many ancient works describing, in infinite detail, the chants, incantations and magic potions used to break a possession. Few delved into the actual art of possessing a soul. Those which did were either encrypted to keep such knowledge from the unworthy, or were so vague as to be worthless.

Putting the book aside, Trent sought another. This one he seldom removed from his temperature/humidity controlled safe. He once explained to Shepherd the necessity of the lock was to prevent theft, but that had been a half truth. In actuality, he kept it hidden from himself.

Laboriously detailed illustrations filled margins, spaces between page breaks, even sandwiched between letters. Many of the graphics and wedge-shaped characters had faded; whole sections were worn away, or been purposely destroyed. After the passage of centuries, making an accurate determination of age proved nearly impossible, though Trent had his suspicions.

The author or, more accurately, authors, for the penmanship clearly indicated several, were unknown. No names had been affixed to the text. Not surprising in itself, the omission left more questions than answers. Who dared commit the very secrets of life after death – the gateway to another dimension – to posterity?

Perhaps more pertinently: how had "authors unknown" come by their knowledge and why did they risk certain torture to preserve it?

Who did they expect to benefit by their secrets? And why?

Written in no known language, the manuscript had laid undiscovered since time immemorial. In all the world, Trent knew of only two similar compilations describing in such detail these taboo subjects. Like his, all were kept behind locked doors, unavailable to scholars. Only the most erudite knew of their existence.

His text differed from like manuscripts by place of origin. The other two had been found amid the ancient ruins of Babylon and La Venta. The one he – possessed – came from an excavation in Eastern Europe.

Possibly, his copy had originally been written in another land and smuggled across continents, but he doubted it. From what little he gathered of other extant manuscripts, his contained far different incantations and referenced beings on other planes of existence. Nor had his been written on papyrus or inscribed on tablets. In fact, he had never been able to identify the specific medium on which his work had been preserved.

Trent had spent a king's ransom to obtain the forbidden. Had the previous owner been able to translate the script, he would have delivered it, free of charge, in order to be rid of it. The Old Ones were notoriously jealous of their power and had, according to legend, consumed other possessors and manuscripts in the purifying fires of hell.

Trent believed in legends, just as he did in the jinx placed on the Hope Diamond and the curse put on those opening King Tut's tomb.

Reconciling that with Christian faith proved an onerous and ongoing task.

In his early days, Abraham Trent spent countless hours poring over the mysterious symbols in his text. Complicating his task, the authors frequently altered the codes in which they wrote. Without a Rosetta Stone, or any link to previously identified cipher, his labor had been agonizingly slow and arduous.

Forty years later, he had no more than one third of the work translated. Though he prided himself on being a scholar, and thus immune from fear of the unknown, he had finally abandoned the effort, acknowledging with unamused obedience the oft used expressions of early horror films:

There are some things Man is not meant to know.

Some knowledge is better left to God.

Five hundred times Trent had considered burning the heretical text. Five hundred times he had stayed his hand, without knowing why.

He knew why now.

God meant him to have it. Meant him to finish the translation. Meant him to use it against the Powers of Evil.

Time was against him.

If he were to save Shepherd Kingston's life, he would have to work with alacrity.

Opening the bound pages, his eyes fell on the last translated sentence.

And behold, I live forever and ever; and I have the keys of death and beyond.

The words chilled the marrow in his bones. Without doubt he understood the prophesy to indicate his own demise. No one trespassed on forbidden ground without paying the ultimate penalty.

For knowing too much, the gods would exact their retribution.

On earth as it is in heaven.

CHAPTER 10

Morning did not bring the reassurance Shepherd anticipated. Gone his euphoria of the night past. Dissipated, too, his belief Ericka Elvina served as a clandestine member of the Impossible Missions Force.

It had been an errant wish. Childish, even. Satisfying the moment, nothing more.

But if she were not a spy, what then?

The story of a lifetime.

Promising to keep his imagination in check, Shepherd showered, shaved and resumed his post outside the Stone Gate Building. This time when the limousine appeared, he did not bother taking pictures. He had learned his lesson: never give yourself away. Seeking no more than eyeball proof of her departure, he planned a reception of a different sort for her return.

At 4 P.M. Shepherd reappeared at the scene, but did not assume his usual hiding spot. Ascertaining a clear coast, he positioned himself in the doorway immediately adjacent to the Stone Gate. This angle provided a clear view of his target as she emerged from the limo.

An hour later his feet ached and he had endured the annoyed command from the owner of the building to "Move along, or I'll call the cops," more times than he could count. After each warning he stepped aside, only to return when the irate proprietor disappeared.

By six o'clock, his chances of success hovered below the Dardanelles. Presumably, Miss Elvina had returned earlier than anticipated and he missed her. Only youthful arrogance held him in place. Arrogance and a sixth sense, warning the game was afoot. His prey had made herself available, purposely allowing him to determine her comings and goings. Once established, she failed to follow routine, dashing his hopes.

Were he to leave this night, Shepherd understood with an awareness stemming, not from logic, but second sight, he would never see her again.

The fact Shepherd had spent most of his childhood and all his adult life denying the possibility of psychic power disturbed him. To counter that effect, he opted to put a different slant on the situation. He stayed out of stubbornness, stubbornness being a common, everyday emotion.

A man with determination caught the goose which laid the golden egg.

His obstinacy reached an end by 7 P.M. With a vile, "Hell's bells," he abandoned his hiding place at the very moment the black limousine rounded the corner. Daring to smile, congratulations seemed in order. Perseverance had paid off.

Gambling that his presence would not immediately be noticed, he strode into the street as Ericka Elvina disembarked. No more than ten feet away, Shepherd snapped her picture with wild abandon. This preoccupation obliterated his vision of the outside world and thus he did not see the bodyguard approach. Not until a pair of incredibly powerful hands went around his arm did he cry in surprise.

"Leave me alone! Freedom of the press."

Unmoved by his protestation, the thug looked toward his mistress for guidance. Shepherd did not have to see his face to guess the silent communication.

Shall I squash him like a bug or stuff him down the sewer?

Fearfully following his gaze, Shepherd beheld Miss Elvina's features in sharp detail. They appeared even more stunning through the naked eye than via the camera lens.

A look of perturbation augmented the impression, for it implied a humanness Shepherd so urgently needed.

Making a curt gesture with her left hand, the bodyguard released his hold. The world resumed spinning on its axis.

A second, more radiant smile graced the youth's unlined countenance. In all the universe he knew no greater power than that of the press, before which even Wall Street wizards must bow.

Ericka Elvina disappeared inside the building, followed by her henchmen. Alone with his multi-million dollar prize, Shepherd swelled with importance.

"The world is my oyster."

An oyster's value is in the pearl it may or may not contain, he heard Trent preach. *Until you develop your film and sell the photographs , all you hold is –*

"Mr. Kingston?"

Startled to hear his name so softly spoken, Shepherd jerked in the direction of the voice. Seeing the mouth from which the question came, his astonishment grew in proportion. Before him stood another man, coming in at twenty-two stone if he weighed an ounce. He had not emerged from the car, nor could he have crossed the street in so short a time.

"Yes?" he replied, forgetting to ask how his identity had come to be known, or how the guard transported to his side. His first and only consideration lay in maintaining possession of the camera.

"My mistress would like to speak to you."

A swallow, and then, "She would?"

"In her penthouse."

Fear of losing his oyster battled smug superiority at having won the attention of Miss Elvina. Not surprisingly, fear lost.

Slipping the camera into his pocket, least the employee attempt a lateral movement and strip him of it, Shepherd followed the other's lead, proudly marching through the entrance of the Stone Gate.

What he expected of the interior with its recent "renovations," proved highly inaccurate, for the design had not been updated to modern standards. Instead of shiny chrome, he saw polished brass. Artwork on the walls depicted landscapes of darkly wooded forests and torrential streams, rather than amorphous, geometrically perfect squares, triangles and circles of present-day painters.

Overhead lighting played second fiddle to antique floor lamps, shaded so that the artificial illumination directed downward. On first glance the effect created a sense of gloom, but as he walked further into the lobby, his eyes adjusted rapidly, so that anything brighter would have blinded him.

The floor appeared to be layered with thin tile, not unlike meticulously placed slabs of shale. Rich, plush, throw-rugs were its only adornment, and they, in sharp contrast to the grey stone, were deeply imbued in purple and brown.

To the left, a reception desk of dark mahogany ran the entire breadth of the wall. Lining the counter were several over-sized ledgers, giving the impression the last entry had been made a century before with a quill-tipped pen. Behind the desk were old fashioned pigeon holes, most of which were empty.

No one attended the service area. Except for Shepherd and his guide, the lobby was totally deserted.

"This looks like a movie set," he observed in a hushed whisper. "Something out of the '30's. Where is George Raft when you need him?"

The man gave no indication of hearing.

"You know," Shepherd continued, stumbling over a contradiction, "standing outside, I'd have sworn this place would be a hive of activity. Where'd everybody go?"

"The mistress likes her privacy."

The statement did not answer the conundrum, but as Shepherd neared the ancient elevator, his attention turned toward that relic.

"A gated lift! I haven't seen one like this since I was a kid."

The lift might well have been drawn from his childhood, for it was exactly as he remembered the old "up-and-down" at the Montgomery Ward store his parents frequented on Saturday afternoons. Drawing air through his nostrils, Shepherd heaved a sigh of contentment. It even smelled of lubricating grease, underscored by the sharp, pungent odor of brass.

The operator, wearing a tight monkey jacket with gold trim, completed the memory. Seeing them approach, the elderly man permitted the passengers to enter, then squeezed himself in front. Closing the restraining gate, he manually drew the heavy inside doors together. Shepherd whistled.

"I didn't think there was anything like this left in Manhattan. I have a friend who would totally freak over this."

Receiving a silent cue, the conductor hauled back on a lever. The car ascended at a deliberate, uneven pace, as though the wheels might jam or the cables snap, should he attempt a faster acceleration.

"Nice effect," Shepherd marveled. "I bet the building inspectors had a field day with this. Where's the certificate, by the way? I thought the law required it be posted."

His companions effected deafness, conveying the distinct impression no one from the state of New York had ever stepped foot in the ancient conveyance. That gave rise to concerns about fire exits and the safety of electrical wiring.

Trent would "freak," all right, but not over nostalgia.

After what seemed an eternity and must have consumed an entire five minutes, the lift came to a quivering halt. The elevator monkey observed, "Penthouse," and worked the doors. Neither passenger moved before the gate rolled back on its track.

Accepting the mute invitation to disembark, Shepherd expressed a polite "Thank you," wondering if it were still considered good manners to tip. Before he could quite make up his mind, the gate closed. The bodyguard had not joined him.

"Just a minute!"

His fright at being abandoned came too late. The car labored down, abandoning him to whatever fate awaited.

"Wouldn't it be something if I wasn't expected," he muttered, stifling a sinking feeling that it would be a long wait before the car returned.

"That would make me a poor host," came a low, yet perfectly audible voice. Nearly jumping out of his skin, for he had neither seen nor heard anyone approach, Shepherd spun around, finding himself face-to-face with Ericka Elvina.

His host, or rather the more socially acceptable hostess, had exchanged her business attire for a floor-length gown of shimmering aqua. The form-fitting outfit would have conveyed sensuality in another, but on Miss Elvina the impression more closely expressed dominance, as though she had shuffled off her mortal coil for one of supernatural prowess.

"Hello," he grinned, feeling foolish at being caught off guard. The lady gave no indication of noticing.

"Mr. Shepherd Kingston, is it not?" The deferential, feminine tone belied the impression of power and sent a shiver down his spine.

"Yes," he agreed, respectfully bowing. "And you are Miss Elvina?"

"I am she. Welcome."

"Thank you. I apologize for –"

"If you will follow me?"

While spoken as an interrogative, she undoubtedly meant it as command. Totally unoffended, he obliged, trailing through a meandering corridor which led into a spacious living apartment.

Similar to the interior design of the downstairs lobby, this room reflected the quaint charm of yesteryear. Any association ended there, however, for the suite had been decorated with breathtaking magnificence. Velvet curtains of blood red and royal gold covered the side windows, setting off the jet blackness of the wall-to-wall carpet. Lining the back walls were tapestries of great age, offset by oil paintings done by anonymous masters.

A huge picture window, the only glass left unencumbered, dominated the west wall. Through its panes shone the city of Manhattan, motor vehicles and pedestrians reduced to the size of Lilliputians. Illuminated in the late sun, the artificial headlights and street lamps appeared starkly out of place in this chamber, stolen from another era.

A couch of white leather, flanked by two intricately carved side-tables of dark mahogany, faced the vista. Smaller stands and a matching sideboard displayed a vast array of art from the pages of antiquity. Exposed to statues and Medieval crafts from Trent's personal collection, Shepherd identified several of the items, including those once employed as crude but highly stylistic weapons. The room smelled faintly of wood and incense.

A quiet, almost subliminal sound of music caressed the interior space. Shepherd could place neither the orchestration nor the composition, though he knew enough to date it as pre-Christian.

"Some red wine, Mr. Kingston? I am afraid I find your hard liquor so distasteful."

"Yes. Please," he agreed, experiencing the rush of alcohol course through his veins before ever sipping.

Ericka glided effortlessly to a side-table, poured two glasses of deep red wine from a beautiful crystal decanter, then handed a matching goblet to him.

"It is a tradition in your country, is it not, to offer a toast the first time two... friends imbibe together?" Flushing at the unexpected familiarity, he enthusiastically nodded. "To what shall we dedicate our sharing of wine?"

With Trent screaming *"No!"* in the recesses of his subconscious, the youth smiled engagingly. "The blood is the life," he articulated in his best Hungarian accent.

"The blood is the life, *Mr. Kingston,"* Ericka repeated, amending the sentence, then touching her glass to his. Assuming she used his name as a substitute for "Mr. Renfield," thus completing the quotation from *Dracula,* he delicately placed his lips around the rim and drew in the liquid.

"It's excellent," he finished. The subsequent lines of dialogue from the 1931 classic, "Aren't you having any?" and the reply, "I never drink... wine," were unnecessary, for Miss Elvina readily joined him.

"Now," she declared after receiving his nod of appreciation, "shall we be seated?"

"This is really very nice of you," Shepherd replied, following her to the couch. "I had hardly expected so warm a welcome." While undoubtedly true, the tone of voice indicated a confidence that his charms were equal to the occasion.

"Why is that?"

Pausing for her to sit, he graciously placed himself at the other end.

"Others who have attempted to photograph you have not been so well received."

"Who says that?" Ericka hurtfully demanded. Noting the small blush of color reddening her cheeks, he immediately regretted his harsh words and brushed them aside.

"Oh, nobody. Just people I've been talking to."

"Give me their names." Again the hurt tone, but this time with the latent promise of retribution. Shepherd demurred to his baser instincts.

"No one important."

"But you must tell me. I insist. I am a foreigner in your country, as you undoubtedly know and I have offended without knowing."

Further attempts at obfuscation were not only impossible, but reeked of poor breeding. At any rate, Shepherd reasoned, his information could bring no ill, and might, perhaps, do good.

Had he his wits about him, or had an impartial observer witnessed the scene, the interpretation more aptly would have been that Shepherd could refuse her nothing.

"I was trying to get an introduction; I spoke to all the people I could find who might have known you." Like a good spy, he gave up the least of his sources. "Sammy Greeley and Bill Ford."

And like a good interrogator, she probed for more.

"Who else?"

He swallowed hard and offered up "Danny Poole and Paul Delgado" without quite comprehending his reticence.

"And yet another?"

Shaking off the peculiar sensation Miss Elvina already knew, he completed the litany.

"Joe Warren."

Bracing himself for her reaction, for surely her memory of Mr. Warren would be greater than the reporter's recollection of her, Ericka's expression did not change.

"Five men. To have offended so many. I am so sorry."

"Perhaps I overstated the situation," Shepherd hastened to correct. "None of them actually used the word 'offended.' It was more like... their memories were affected. Notes written in gibberish. Conversations forgotten."

Reacting sharply, she held her hand to her breasts in a quaint, European gesture, more suited to the court of the French Sun King.

"Now, *they* have offended *me.*"

"It is pretty hard to believe." Shepherd drank more wine. "But then, you must admit, an aura of mystery *does* surround you."

"The same can be said of any woman," came the teasing admonition.

"You're not just any woman."

"I shall take that as a very nice compliment, Mr. Kingston."

"Shepherd, please."

Ericka reached an arm over the back of the couch in a seductive posture.

"You are most kind... Shepherd. An interesting name, I might add. One I am unfamiliar with as a first name. Is it a –? What is the term? A nickname? Or were you... baptized with it?"

"That's what my parents put on my birth certificate. You may use 'Shep,' if you prefer."

"No. I do not think I do. Shepherd," she repeated, rolling the word over her tongue the way a foreigner, unfamiliar with the language, might do when encountering a strange sound. "I like 'Shepherd.' It has a meaning, does it not?"

"A tender of sheep," he observed with less than pleasure.

"It is not a Christian name, then?"

"No."

"Your parents were shepherds?"

"My father was an archeologist; my mother studied anthropology."

"Indeed? Where is the connection with sheep?"

Above them, the low, underlying music faded out. The loss, however subtle, caused Shepherd a stab of pain.

"I don't know."

"I am prying?"

"Not at all."

"It is curious. When I find a conundrum, I wish I know the answer."

"I don't know why they named me what they did."

"Not a family name? No shepherds lurking in your background?"

"They never said. When I asked, they had no answer. They just liked it, I guess."

Running her finger along the rim of the glass, she astutely regarded him.

"They made a good choice. The name fits you. Shepherd. Shepherd Kingston. You are of English descent?"

"Yes."

"What was your mother's maiden name?"

"Mason."

"Mason. Stone mason. An artesian who works with stone." Noting his face twitch, she smiled. "That was common, I believe – to take one's surname from a trade or occupation. And *King*ston...?"

"I suppose the significance has been lost to posterity. My father was hardly a king."

"A servant to a king, perhaps. In the long-distant past."

"A lot of good it does me now."

"You might perhaps ask your father."

"Both my parents are dead."

"How sad. They never made a family tree?"

"I was never interested," he finished with a pout.

"But you should be. The bloodline is all important."

"Not to me. I've always felt actions speak louder than inheritance."

"You are wise beyond your years, Mister – Shepherd," she corrected, although it hardly sounded like a mistake.

"I will accept that as a compliment, although in America one does not generally like to be reminded of one's youth."

"Now you puzzle me again." She laughed and the sound of her pleasure brought a flush to his cheeks. "It is my impression yours is a culture of youth. Growing old is not considered desirable. Am I not right?"

"No one likes to look old. But then, neither does one like to be proofed. Especially men. I suppose that's because we fancy ourselves... mature beyond our years."

"But surely you have obtained your majority?"

"I am twenty-four – almost twenty-five," he amended, then felt foolish for the vanity.

"An excellent age."

"One you admire from close proximity."

Ericka laughed at his flattery while refilling his glass from the decanter he did not remember her bringing with them to the couch.

"I am more – worldly in experience than you."

"I am experienced enough," he pouted, proving, to her silent delight, the contrary.

"Drink your wine and we will discuss this interview you have come to obtain."

Gulping too fast, Shepherd nearly choked. To hide his embarrassment, he turned away, holding a hand up to his face in order to stifle a cough. It required a full minute to sufficiently recover.

In that matter of sixty seconds, however, much transpired. The evening sun, dipping just below the upper level of the picture window, cast a phenomenal spectrum of red and orange light into the room. The couch, once white, blazed red, while the curtains, already a crimson color, stood out in stark relief, the shimmering gold piping giving the appearance of super attenuated life.

A draft of cool air, coming, he presumed from the air conditioning, stirred unseen wind chimes, igniting the entire room with its faint music. Half human, half bestial in tone, the otherworldly sound seemed more a wail of immortal agony, than any created by finely coordinated strands of metal.

Shadows danced upon the rug, leapt from the tapestries, darted behind, then out from the heavy gilt picture frames. The scent of incense, barely perceivable until now, rose up in twisted glory, filling his nostrils with memories of great conflagrations, burning flesh, funeral pyres and sacrificial lambs.

Frightened by the subliminal images, Shepherd drew back, then forced his disobedient eyes to locate his hostess. Like the room, she, too, had metamorphosed, though in the opposite direction. While the penthouse had come alive, Ericka had turned to stone. Her naturally pale skin glistened in imitation of marble, while her fiery orbs, bright and sparkling only a moment before, were fixated on the spectacle unfolding through the window.

Every muscle in her body had gone rigid, making the veins in her neck and hands appear more prominent than generally observed in the female form. Even the muscles in her arms pulsated with sublime strength, conveying the impression of commanding physical power far beyond the human ken.

Though he understood, on a rational plane, that she yet breathed, Shepherd could detect no movement of her lungs or abdominal muscles. The light, although intense, did not make her blink.

Drawn as a slave to an all-powerful master, the sunset wrapped itself around head, shoulders, legs, covering her in a sheen of shared glory. Unlike the vague glow he had witnessed in photographs of Ericka, this starkly etched outline made it appear as though her life force had captured the sun, framing her in its red and golden radiance.

The longer she stared, the deeper her trance. Mind rushing madly to explain the phenomenon, Shepherd could get no closer than a priest imbibed in religious communication with his god. Had stigmata appeared in the palms of her outstretched hands, he would have fallen to his knees in supplication, not to the unknown deity she worshipped, but to the creature herself.

Had she suddenly transformed into the lupine figure of an ancient werewolf, his reaction would have been the same. Time altered. His consciousness, cast into a swirl of past and future, witnessed the wilted body of Jesus on the cross, heard the pitiful moans, strove to make out the cry, torn from a bleeding heart.

"Father, forgive me, for I have failed."

His own heart accelerating to fantastic rates, Shepherd worked on the puzzle, frightened to the marrow of his bones.

No! he cried, though he made no noise. *No. That is not what He said. Those are not the words.* Struggling violently to beat back a lethargy of will, he dragged that which was not a memory, but a shared belief, to the front of his mind.

Say it right, he demanded in righteous indignation to the human on the cross, so soon to perish. *Say the words, 'Forgive them; for they know not what they do.'*

This Christ was beyond hearing, however, and as Shepherd absorbed the image through his pores, the hanging figure expired, a look of supreme agony on His wasted, sunken, tortured countenance.

Before the soul of the departed fled its mortal shell, the sun dipped below the window, stripping the room of color. Nearly thrown to the floor from the finality of the release, Shepherd caught himself, shuddered in abject terror, then fell back against the cushions. In a state of confusion, he covered his face, pressing fingertips into his eyeballs to erase the vision.

Frightened beyond comprehension, he would have crawled into a ball and lay on the rug, had he the power. He did not, and in this weakness, his hands dropped. All he had left was the power to open his eyes.

Preparing himself for Satan's triumph over the defeated God, he witnessed quite a different scene. He was not at Calgary, but in the penthouse, now muted into near obscurity by the rapidly darkening room. It did not appear as he had left it, however. Gone were the walls with their tapestries and paintings; disappeared were the end tables, covered with objects d'art and ancient weapons. What remained of this world was the window, now shrouded in black, the Hades-colored rug, and the woman by his side.

With the wonder of a child waking from a nightmare only vaguely understood, Shepherd gaped as Ericka reanimated. Her breathing restarted with a minute gasp, the veins and arteries retreated beneath pink skin and finally, in imitation of the Golem, she moved her torso.

In a moment, no more, her flexibility of movement returned, so that he could not believe she had once been carved from marble. All returned to what it had been before, save one exception. Her eyes. As though belying human origins, the orbs were catlike, with pupils vertical, rather than round.

Blinking away the image, the saline fluid beneath his lids transformed her from feline to feminine. Noting his twisted features, Ericka's mouth crinkled at the corners.

"The wine, I am afraid, has gone to your head." Though spoken in a normal voice, he strained to hear her words, half expecting her to communicate in tongues. "It is a danger, I am afraid, for those unaccustomed to partaking of such a potent beverage. Come," she offered, rising to her feet with no more effort than wind emerging from a storm cloud. "Take my hand."

Brain screaming to disobey for fear her flesh would be as cold as stone, Shepherd offered up his hand. Her fingers felt warm, firm and female. Without dedicated effort, Shepherd found himself on his feet, whisked up by magic.

"What has happened?" he implored, adoring her as an acolyte would his carved idol.

"The wine," she repeated softly. "It has many strange properties. It affects Otherworlders in peculiar ways."

"Otherworlders?"

"Those not from our country."

"Yes," Shepherd tried, vainly attempting to focus. "I wanted to ask you about your country. No one knows anything about it." Safety lay in the tangible.

"That," Ericka laughed, though he did not see the humor, "is surely an exaggeration. Many people know about it. Those who live there," she added, noting his pout.

"But *I* want to know. I want to know everything."

"That," she admonished, coyly pulling away, "is a dangerous petition. To be all-knowledgeable is to be –"

"God?"

"You are speaking of matters upon which I will not comment further." Though her jaw line set, Shepherd detected a note of fear. His masculine sensibilities instantly rose to defend her.

"Tell me," he pleaded. "I want to know more about you."

"You wish to know...everything?" The impishness returned. Running her gaze seductively over his tall, youthful frame, Ericka succeeded in raising his color.

Because he could not back down from such a challenge, Shepherd bravely stared at her own lithe form, working his way up from the long, slender legs, lingering at the ample curve of breasts, then resting his hungry stare on her face.

"You are beautiful."

This time, her laughter sounded girlish.

"So that is why you wished to take my picture. Because I am beautiful?"

"Yes," he avowed before realizing the patent falsehood in his answer. Hanging his head, his lips pursed while debating whether to speak the full truth.

"Come," she encouraged. "I will have it. Like you, Shepherd Kingston, I want it all."

He believed her implicitly.

"And you shall have it. Anything and everything I possess."

"Now you are acting like a love-struck boy." Ericka stepped back and he followed her movements with reverence. "Explain why it was so important you take my photograph."

As ideas formed, she reached for one of the objects on the table. He did not know its identity, but recognized it as a primitive stone idol. The thought, *Central American* flashed through his overwrought mind and he nearly spoke the words aloud, asking where she obtained it, for the god bore a striking similarity to the one in Trent's flat. The idea muddled, however, as his blood pressure rose watching her fondle it.

Although she could not know his thought, Ericka flexed her fingers, summoning him to continue. He regressed to her previous interrogative.

"No one has ever been able to photography you; no one knows anything about you. I thought if I could get your picture... and maybe an interview," he dared add, "I could share your story with the world."

"And in this quest you were acting altruistically?"

Shame overcame, then surpassed his mounting desire. "No. I hoped to sell it. I am a photographer, you see. That's how I make my living."

"You are a famous photographer, that you dare stalk such big game?"

Reacting to her taunt, he responded rapidly.

"You know that I am not."

Gliding away, stone object still cradled in her hands, Ericka shook her head.

"Like me, an aura of mystery surrounds you. We might, perhaps, nurture our uniqueness, to our mutual benefit. But for now –" Without completing the sentence, Ericka tossed the tiny god in his direction. Responding by instinct, Shepherd attempted to catch it. He was not quick enough, however, for it struck him on the left side, then bounced to the floor.

"A photographer, but not an athlete," she good-naturedly observed as he retrieved the carved stone.

"I hope it's not broken."

"I think that very unlikely. It has withstood much in its lifetime."

"Lifetime. That's a peculiar expression." Handing it back, he added with more bravado, "Toss it to me again."

"No. It is not a toy to play with. But I grow weary." Placing a hand to her forehead, Ericka affected tiredness.

"You are not ill, I hope?"

"Fatigued. Making money for someone else's profit is an arduous business."

"I'd like to know more about it."

"Your request is a bold one."

"I can be bolder."

"We shall see, Mr. Kingston. But not this evening. You will come back?"

"With bells on my toes."

She frowned at his expression, then, as comprehension came, she flashed white teeth.

"I shall require nothing so drastic. Although it is a... quaint idea. She we say tomorrow night? Eight o'clock? Presuming you have no prior engagements?"

"None," he swore. "I am accountable to no one but myself. And now, to you," came the gallant addendum.

"You are most kind." A man appeared from the side entrance. Shepherd could not see him clearly, but did not think him one of her bodyguards. "A moment, if you will, Shepherd."

"Certainly."

With a nod of familiarity, Ericka floated from the room, the servant retiring with her. He watched them go, rubbing his hands in anticipation. The act symbolically eradicated the so-recent memory of death from his soul. Trent had been wrong. There was nothing supernatural or evil about her. She was flesh and bone like any other woman. Her beauty, he decided, had set his mentor off, sparking jealousy over Shepherd's affection.

As well you might be, he silently warned any listening spirits. Before him lay not only the story of a lifetime, but the prospect of delights beyond any mortal man's fantasy.

As Ericka's "moment" drifted effortlessly into minutes, Shepherd amused himself by wandering around the room. Lingering over the side-table where she had taken the little god, he noted she had replaced it in a different spot. Smiling at her forgetfulness, he picked up another object d'art, this one seemingly out of keeping with the collection.

Unlike the others, this was not of stone, but comprised of a golden material. Neither a human figure, nor that of any animal, it represented a pyramid. Holding it to the light, Shepherd detected rows of intricate writings inlaid, rather than etched, on all three sides. How ancient artists achieved the effect, he had no guess.

Worried that he might be caught trespassing among the treasures, he started to replace the object when a very definite idea popped in his head. Pyramids were thought to bring luck to the possessor. Grasping the implication, he slipped the small prize into his pocket. In case Miss Elvina forgot her invitation, he would have an excuse to return.

Hearing the swirl of her floor-length gown, he stepped away from the table to dissociate himself from guilt. Unaware of the theft, she offered an apologetic smile.

"Do forgive my absence."

"I forgive you anything."

"You Americans; so forthright. That is what I like about men from your country. You are afraid of nothing."

Bowing in acknowledgement, Shepherd accepted her proffered hand.

"Until tomorrow?"

"Eight o'clock."

"I look forward to it."

"As do I. Now, good evening, Mr. Kingston. My servant will escort you out."

Sweeping her hand in the direction of the door, Shepherd saw the servant waiting. He had not heard him return with his mistress and did a double-take.

"Your carpet covers a multitude of sins."

"Not only the carpet," Ericka agreed, gaze resting knowingly on the table where a small gold pyramid once sat.

Waving her a good-bye, Shepherd followed the bodyguard outside, the weight of his purloined gift resting lightly on his conscience.

CHAPTER 11

The lateness of the hour accounted for the lull in evening traffic, but as luck would have it, the sidewalks were congested with pedestrians. Ruing the fact he had opted for caution over convenience and left his Chevy blocks away from the Stone Gate, Shepherd managed to take several elbows to the rubs and narrowly avoided tripping over a low-hanging purse in his haste to make the corner. Missing yet another "Walk" signal, he jammed on his feet brakes a moment before a BMW jump-started the changing red light.

Casting a one-fingered salute at the driver, he shouted after, "Hey! Watch it, buddy!" The driver, as might be expected, ignored him.

In retrospect, the idea of parking his car a light year away from the building appeared ill-conceived and unnecessary. Originally concerned that Ericka Elvina's henchmen would discover his transportation and steal it as a means of teaching him a lesson, he cursed his prudence.

"I might as well have parked on the moon." He might also *have taken a cab,* as Trent often lectured. But a taxi cost money, and until he had real spending cash in his pocket, he could ill afford the luxury.

Waiting for the light to change, Shepherd slipped the purloined pyramid from his pocket and examined it more closely. Deftly upending it, he observed that the base bore no marks whatsoever; not even scratches, which the ravages of time might fairly have dug into the metal.

Returning to the sides, he focused on the inscriptions. The characters ran one into another in a peculiar cursive style, giving the appearance of having been scripted from right to left. Unable to adequately separate more than two words, those were enough to stop him cold.

XILKA.

BESA.

He did not know their meaning, but the latent power they seemed to convey as he repeated the syllables aloud served as a warning not to probe further by himself.

"Trent will help me," he decided, although that act held the potential of being a double-edged sword. The professor would translate, but the effort would evoke a lecture and a torrent of warnings.

"If you don't want to hear what I have to say, then why do you ask?" he imitated. "You could look them up for yourself; you don't need me."

"But I do need you," Shepherd cajoled in his one-sided argument.

"Yes: you need me for a free meal and a roof over your head after you've been locked out of your apartment for non-payment of rent," he concluded on his mentor's behalf.

Replacing the pyramid, mind still dwelling on the pending confrontation, his head shot up as a terrified shriek rent the air. Turning to the left, he witnessed a young woman caught in the cross-hairs of an oncoming truck. Moving forward, more from instinct than self-preservation, he plunged into the street.

Fright had the opposite effect on the potential victim, for she froze, feet rooted to the pavement.

Apparently the driver did not see the young lady, for he made no attempt to slow his forward progression, or veer away. In fact, as Shepherd sprinted to her aid, scattering the fainthearted and the curious, the truck actually increased its acceleration.

Too far away to reach her in time to avert disaster, Shepherd nevertheless threw out his hands, willing her body to move. Without making physical contact, the woman was lifted off her feet and catapulted to safety. Landing awkwardly, she stumbled into Shepherd's arms as he caught her lunging body.

Throwing himself around her, he spun them away as the truck hurtled past, wind created by its close proximity nearly blowing them over. Both struggled for balance before slowly separating, huffing hard from exertion.

"Thank you!" she gasped, badly shaken. "I never saw that truck until it was nearly too late. And I looked before crossing. Where did you come from?"

Shepherd shook his head, unwilling to answer.

"Damn fool! The driver must have been drunk, or something. I'm sure he saw you, but he never slowed down," he replied instead, shaking from a fright not so easily explained away.

"You saved my life." Her profuse thanks might have gone on, but as realization struck harder than physical impact, she withdrew, frowning. "How... how did you do it? You were too far away... weren't you?"

Shrugging his shoulders in denial, Shepherd rubbed his arms, feigning hurt from his herculean effort.

"I – I don't know."

"Well, no matter. If the impossible was made possible, who am I to complain? Bless you. It was a miracle."

"I – I didn't mean to," he stuttered, then abruptly reversed himself. "I mean, I suppose I was closer than either one of us thought."

"I would have been killed." Taking stock of her still intact body, she grinned. "I guess it wasn't my time. You must be my guardian angel, or something."

Eyes wide with horror, he demurred. "Anyone could have done it. There was nothing miraculous about it. Are you all right?"

"I think so." Holding out her hand, her face beamed with gratitude. "My name is Shelley Larson. I'm very pleased to meet you."

"Shepherd Kingston," he introduced. "You sure you're O.K.? Do you need to go to a hospital, or anything?"

"What I need is a stiff drink – and a proper opportunity to thank you. Will you see me home? It's not far." He hesitated, then responded more to the offer of a drink than her gratitude.

"Sure. No problem."

Taking her arm, Shepherd guided Shelley across the street, down the sidewalk, then up the steep flight of steps of a modern apartment building. Opening the outside door, Shelley indicated a lower-level apartment.

"That's mine."

Slipping a key into the lock, she turned it, then stepped aside so he could enter first. Close behind, she shut the door and tossed her purse on a table. After running a shaky hand through her windblown hair, she indicated the living room.

"Please; have a seat. I'll just straighten my face and be right with you. The booze is over there, in the corner."

By the time she returned, he had fixed drinks. Grabbing hers with two hands, Shelley gulped it down, then handed the glass back for a refill.

"What a day," she admitted, taking her drink to the couch. Plopping down, she indicated he join her. "When you have a close call like that, it makes you appreciate life a whole lot more."

"I'll say."

"You must be some sort of Olympic runner to have reached me in time." Drawing back to stare at him, Shelley ran her eyes appreciatively over his slim body.

"Just luck," he demurred.

Fortune being more agreeable to him than any reflection on his prowess.

"Call it what you will; I say a godsend. There must be some way I can repay you."

The fear of death, the wearing off of numbing shock, the alcohol and the close proximity of two healthy bodies made her tacit offer immediately attractive. Bending forward, their lips met.

One exploratory kiss lent itself to a protracted one of passion. Without further discussion, hands probed one another's bodies, tentatively at first, then with excitement. As emotions rose, Shelley slipped down onto the couch, Shepherd beside her.

Unbuttoning her blouse, he kissed her warm flesh, then went to unzip his fly. Before he completing the task, however, he cried in pain, arms wildly flailing.

Pulling out from under him, Shelley demanded, "What's wrong?"

"Hot!" he hissed, fumbling in panic at the folds of his jacket. Wrapping his fingers around the triangular shape of the pyramid, he cried again and hurtled the object onto the rug.

"What is that?"

"Nothing. A knickknack."

"It's burning my carpet!"

Almost too scared to look, Shepherd did not need eyes to confirm her statement, for his nose immediately filled with the stench of burning fibers.

"Put it out!"

Embarrassed and confused, he struck out his foot, kicking away the golden treasure. His action seemed to turn it "off," but the spot where it landed revealed a distinct burn mark.

"I'm really sorry."

More curious than angry, Shelley bent down and held her hand over the pyramid. Deeming it cool enough to touch, she cradled it in her palm. "It's all right now. What is it? It looks like gold."

"It is. I guess we were just too passionate for it."

"But gold doesn't conduct heat," she reasoned, turning it over. "What made it get hot? Is it some sort of a trick?"

"I don't know."

"But you must know," Shelley insisted. "You brought it with you."

"I... borrowed it... from someone. I had no idea it exhibited... properties."

"You better be careful what you borrow from now on. Maybe it's some sort of alien device."

"Maybe," he unhappily admitted, suspecting Ms. Larson had come closer to the truth than she realized.

Losing interest, Shelley tossed the pyramid back onto the carpet, then repositioned herself by Shepherd. "Where were we?"

Grinning sheepishly, they kissed again, this time more curiously than before. The pyramid immediately began to radiate heat. When they broke off, it appeared to cool.

"If you're not controlling it, then it certainly has a mind of its own," she dryly observed. "Maybe it doesn't like me. Did you get it from another woman?"

"Yes. I did."

"I think it's jealous."

"It's inanimate," he protested, but this time he could not put her off. Shelley removed her blouse and stared at the small object on the floor.

"Shepherd and I are going to make love," she announced. The carpet beneath the gold object d'art burst into flame. "All right! Stop! I won't touch him." The fire extinguished. "Shit. What is that thing? I mean, really, what is it?"

"I don't know. I swear I don't."

Retrieving her blouse, Shelley distanced herself from Shepherd. "I think you better leave. And take that thing with you. I appreciate what you did, but now you're scaring me more than that truck."

"I'm sorry."

Retrieving the stolen pyramid, Shepherd hesitated, then shoved it into his pocket.

"I'm glad you're O.K."

Showing himself to the door, he slipped out and ran from the building, mortified and more frightened than he had ever been in his life.

"That's a very good question," Trent declared, turning the pyramid over. "How did it 'turn itself on and off' like that?"

"If I knew the answer, I wouldn't have asked," Shepherd pouted, his sulking attitude used to disguise fear. As a tactic, it failed miserably.

"Want to tell me about it?"

"I already did," Shepherd protested, attempting to retrieve the object from his friend. Anticipating his action, Trent held back.

"I'm not done with it, yet." Sitting behind his desk, the professor turned on a high-voltage lamp. Holding the pyramid under the rays, he studied the ancient text on the sides. Determining Shepherd had retreated from his object of reclaiming the prize, Trent copied down the letters, speaking as he worked.

"You haven't done anything of the sort. I get half a story about how you saved a young woman's life –"

"Half a story!" the youth protested, inadvertently moving too close and casting a shadow over the old man. Trent moved sideways.

"That's right. If you think you can satisfy me by telling only part of the truth, don't start in the first place."

"Well..."

"Never mind 'well.'" Pulling back, Trent started keenly at his companion. "It happened again, didn't it?"

Feeling his face redden, Shepherd nodded. "Yes."

"The young woman didn't realize?"

"I'm not sure. She convinced herself I was closer than she thought."

"And you didn't tell her?"

"Tell her! I'm not even certain myself. I mean... how could I have – willed her away from danger? Normal people don't have that ability."

"You do."

"But I don't want that power. I deny it!"

"Some would call it a gift from God."

"And others would say it's the work of the devil."

"What do you say?"

Rather than reply, Shepherd held out his hands in a supplicating manner.

"Trent, why do these things happen to me?"

"You were caught off guard; reacted before you had time to counter the effects of your gift."

"It's not a gift, damn it!" Seeing Trent's frown, he immediately rescinded his statement. "It's not a gift. It's a curse; it's... abnormal."

"Granted," came the easy reply. "But 'abnormal' does not necessarily mean 'bad.'"

"It does to me. Why do I have to have this *gift,* as you call it? Why can't I cede it to you?"

"Psycho-kinetic power cannot be transferred. It is a wonderful possession when used for good. You saved Miss Larson's life with it."

"My parents didn't have the ability."

"I dare say it is not something genetically transmitted."

"Then where did it come from? And I don't like that word you used."

"It's no more than a scientific term. I employed it, hoping to alleviate your horror."

"There's a scientific word for *werewolf,* too, and knowing it wouldn't save anyone during the three days of the full moon."

"Lycanthropy."

"Can't you take this 'psycho' power away from me?"

"No."

"Then can't I be taught how not to use it? Like seeing auras, or receiving premonitions of death? You told me there are ways to break people of those bad habits."

"What I said was that most children born with the power of seeing auras lose their ability as they grow older, whether from being overwhelmed by the constant input they receive, or because adults denied what they witnessed. The same holds true for a psychic ability to predict death: it's not only depressing, such certain knowledge can drive you mad."

"Well, I'm going mad. I can't stand being different, Trent. It's... queer." Realizing his poor choice of words, Shepherd pouted, then stubbornly refused to correct himself.

"It is a sacred talent. Bequeathed to you for good."

"You still didn't answer my question: bequeathed by whom? And don't tell me God," the troubled boy angrily protested.

"All right. I won't. I don't have to."

"I don't believe that religious crap. I don't believe people can use their minds to move solid objects."

"Then how do you explain your own ability?"

"I'm the devil's spawn."

"Hush, boy!" Trent hissed, shocked by the assertion. "Never say that again. You are a child of God. As are we all," he added with reverence.

"I don't believe in God."

"Then you had better not believe in the devil, or you shall make for yourself a very one-sided universe."

"To hell with that. All I want to know is how that stupid, dime-store pyramid burned a hole in the rug. And what those letters mean."

"You translated the characters yourself," Trent guessed. "You know the Theban alphabet. I taught it to you."

"A lot of good it did me. There wasn't one damn... one question on the SAT's about ancient languages."

"A pity."

Shepherd stomped his foot. "What-do-they-mean?"

"In this context I cannot be certain. An incantation of some sort, surely. Possibly, the placement of text around the pyramid has something to do with its power. A more apt question would be: why did Ericka Elvina let you have it?"

"She didn't let me; I stole it."

"Yes: that's what she wanted you to believe. You're not going to put anything over on that woman so easily, you know."

"I took her photograph," Shepherd bragged, eager to redeem himself. "I was brought in for an interview."

"In which you learned exactly nothing."

"I'm invited back."

"Yes. And she won't give you an interview then, either."

"Then, what does she want?"

The answer took long in coming. "I wish I knew."

"All right. Maybe she won't say anything. But I still have the photographs. When I sell them, I'll be famous."

Pushing the pyramid away, Trent switched off the lamp. As he did so, a chill descended over the room, as if it had been heated solely by the wattage of the bulb.

"Have you developed the film?"

"No."

"There won't be anything on it. No pictures at all."

"Again? I can't believe that."

Trent stretched his arms, trying to ease a sudden tightening of the muscles.

"She tossed a stone idol at you, you said?" Shepherd nodded. "And it bumped against your side?"

"Yes."

"What did you make of it?"

"I'm not an expert on ancient gods," Shepherd protested. Trent rolled his eyes.

"Her action. Why did she do it?"

"She was being playful."

"In that you may be right," Trent sarcastically grimaced, "but I doubt it was playful in the sense you mean. I wager one-thousand-to-one that idol had strong magnetic properties. She was erasing your film, my lad."

"I don't believe you."

"Check your watch. If I'm right, the force would have affected that, too."

Shepherd quickly examined his wrist watch, then shifted his gaze to the old time piece on Trent's mantle. His expression revealed more than he wanted to admit.

"O.K. So my watch needs a battery."

"Take the film home and develop it. Then call and tell me I'm right."

"It couldn't be that easy."

"It's just that easy. She's not going to let you have what she's withheld from so many others."

"That's what you think."

Startled by the obvious bravado, Trent rose from his chair, eyes clouded with concern.

"Stay away from her, Shepherd. I don't know who or what she is, but she's dangerous."

"I can handle her."

"You can say that after witnessing the power of that pyramid? Think again after you discover your film is blank."

"So, she has a magnetic stone idol and a gadget from Woolworth's which turns hot at odd moments. Ericka Elvina is still a woman, Trent; flesh and blood, like any other."

Paling at Shepherd's obvious blind spot, Trent drummed his fingers on the desk. "If that were all, I'd wish you well. But you know it isn't."

"I know nothing of the sort! Everything that's happened has a perfectly rational explanation. Including the fact she finds me attractive – as a man," he imperiously added.

"Oh, dear God. Is that what you think?"

"Yes. It is."

"Then let us pray the Lord protects fools from their folly."

"Just because she's your rival –"

"Shut up, you god-forsaken fool!" Trent screamed in uncharacteristic blasphemy. "She is not my rival. I have no claim on you. You're free to come and go as you please. I've never interfered with your love life. You know that. I've never been jealous. Your friendship is all I've ever asked, and if that's too much to give, you can take your hot pants and get out of here."

Face torn by emotion, Trent indicated the door. "And take this pyramid with you. You shouldn't leave it here."

"Why not?"

"Because Miss Elvina meant for you to have it. I have a sneaking suspicion she can trace you through it; see what you're seeing; divine what you're thinking. I don't want her to find me through your eyes."

"You're afraid," Shepherd accused, barely concealing his own nervousness.

"Yes I am. Deathly afraid. She's been looking for someone a long time. You said so yourself; all the men she permitted to get close were pale imitations of you."

"Why... me?"

"I have no idea. Maybe because of your psycho-kinetic power. Maybe there's more to it than that. She wants you for some great purpose and it sure as Hades isn't your sexual ability."

"I don't believe you."

"Your belief or denial is already a moot point. She's got you under her spell. You'll go back there, despite anything I say. All I can do is warn you. And perform some spells of my own to protect you. And *pray* they work."

As though to mock Trent's hope, the temperature in the room plummeted. Both men shivered.

"You're right. I will go back. She's beautiful, Trent. She's mysterious, she's rich and she wants me. You can save your prayers for yourself; I don't want them. I don't need them. God abandoned me a long time ago."

"God never abandons anyone. Remember that."

"Not even Ericka?"

"No, Shepherd." Shepherd smiled, but relief was short-lived. "I'm very much afraid God never had Miss Elvina."

The room grew colder still.

CHAPTER 12

Not until dinner had been consumed and Trent returned to his research did either speak. Bored at having to amuse himself, Shepherd finally wandered into the study.

"What did you find?"

"Are you asking in the hope I found nothing, or that I found something?"

"I translated some of it."

"Then come over here and get the rest." Pushing his book across the arc of light cast by the reading lamp, Trent indicated the ancient text he had been consulting. Shepherd read the title and grimaced.

"Grimoire of Honorius."

"A first edition. 1670."

"What is it?"

"A handbook of magic. Look: this is what is written on the pyramid. Xilka, Xilka, Besa, Besa."

"What else?"

"Only those two words."

"It looks like more," Shepherd protested. "The sides are covered."

"Different languages – symbols – are used to represent the same thing."

"What do they mean? I said them myself in the street and felt... weird."

"As well you might. In conjunction, they create a chant to conjure a demon."

Reacting sharply, the boy arched his neck.

"Are you saying it wasn't my power which saved Shelley, but – demons?"

Trent peered over his reading glasses. "Which way would you have it?"

"I'm... not sure."

"It is well you said that or I would question your sanity." Pushing the spectacles back up the bridge of his nose, Trent grew reflective.

"Saving Miss Larson's life was an act of goodness. Demons do not serve God, nor are they evoked to work what you or I – or Miss Larson – would consider a miracle. No doubt, it was your own unique talent which preserved her." Stroking his chin, he hesitated, then finally speculated, "Possibly running counter to the spell you wrought."

Uneasy with the explanation, Shepherd swatted the air.

"Whatever. I'm not saying I buy any of it. But your explanation doesn't explain why it turned hot, does it?"

"Not in any logical sense."

"And it doesn't mean Ericka meant for me to take it, much less see through it. Isn't that what you said? It enables her to read my thoughts; look through my eyes?"

"It's possible she uses the demon of the pyramid as a 'familiar;' a tool to do her bidding."

"We aren't even certain she understands what the incantation means. Maybe she collects pyramids; people do, you know. Aren't they supposed to have some kind of healing powers?"

"Not ones with the Theban alphabet written on them," Trent snapped.

"That still doesn't prove Ericka knows how to use it."

"You met her; spoke with her. Does she strike you as the type who would have such an object in her possession and *not* know what it represents?"

"The apartment was cluttered with stuff. They couldn't all have evil connotations."

"Why not?"

A question for which no simple answer existed.

Shepherd left Trent's flat in a foul mood. Hands stuffed inside his pockets, he prepared to face the outside chill and was surprised to find the night air unpleasantly humid. The temperature, in sharp contrast to the cold inside the building, did nothing to appease his temper.

"Stupid old man!" he muttered. "Always running his air conditioning on high." Old people, he perversely reasoned, were always hot.

Too early to go home, the idea of developing his film only to fulfill Trent's prophesy held scant appeal. Protestations to the contrary, he anticipated nothing but blank or unusable photographs.

"So, what if they are?" he argued, ignoring the puzzled glances of passersby. "I hope the stone idol was magnetized. That, at least, is a rational, down-to-earth explanation." His own exclamation hit pay dirt. "No wonder Danny Poole's camera was 'corrupted.'" As she had done to him, Ericka managed to destroy the photographer's film by maneuvering him too close to the idol.

A sense of camaraderie, almost kinship, washed over his body. Good ol' Danny Poole. Shepherd wondered how the soup layout had gone.

"Say cheese," he laughed. A man walking his poodle, repeated the word. Shepherd shot him an annoyed glance. "Go to hell," he urged. The man tugged at the lead and hurried away, mumbling under his breath.

An overwhelming desire to pay his respects to "good ol' Danny" took possession of the youth. Although after business hours, the odds were good he would find the photographer at his studio. They could review his dailies, ogling the long-legged models.

It was long past time Shepherd developed personal acquaintanceships with his fellow photographers. They could go out and have a drink. He just bet Dan would appreciate hearing of Ms. Elvina's tricks.

Such a revelation would strip the lady of her mystique. Give them both a shot in the arm.

He found the studio open, but Mr. Poole was not alone. Not in the sense of being without companionship, although he could hardly be said to appreciate the company.

The place crawled with cops. Standard yellow tape had been stretched across the entranceway, denoting a crime scene investigation.

Shepherd did not want to ask what happened. He did not want to, but he did.

"What's going on here?"

A uniformed policeman eyed him with professional nonchalance.

"What's it to you?"

"I know the guy who owns the studio. I work for him. Part time," he added, least he be called to account for the little white lie.

"Yeah? What's his name?"

"Danny Poole."

"Well, I hope Mr. Poole didn't owe you any money."

"Why not?"

"He's no longer in a position to repay it." Taking a closer look at Shepherd, the officer narrowed his eyes. "What's your name and where were you two hours ago?"

"Shepherd Kingston. I was having a meal with Professor Abraham Trent. Of SUNY. He can vouch for me."

"May I see some identification, please?"

After the pertinent details were inscribed in the officer's book, he waved Shepherd away. Walking around the corner, he counted to ten, then turned back, merging into the flow of interested spectators.

One turned out to be a tenant of the building. He pointed out his window.

"It was me called the fuzz. I heard the screams."

"Screams?"

"Horrible," he testified. "Made my blood run cold."

Shepherd did not appreciate being reminded of the chill so recently experienced.

"What happened?"

"I don't know. At first, I heard voices. Well, Mr. Poole's voice. It was raised high and frightened. I thought one of his models was giving him trouble." He winked and the men in the crowd overhearing the conversation grinned vicariously. "He was a photographer, you know. All sorts of women worked for him. High priced, too."

"You said voices," Shepherd intervened. "Who was in there with him?"

"Sounded like a woman. Didn't catch what she said. Had a sweet voice – kind of foreign. Like you hear on those PBS series."

"British?" Shepherd guessed. While he had not detected a British accent when Ericka spoke, he remembered the conversation from the hotel where the financiers described her as speaking with an English dialect.

The tenant shrugged. "Maybe. Then this man started talking. Foreign, too, but with an edge to it. Nasty." Shepherd remembered Ericka's henchmen. "Nasty" described them as well as anything. "Then Mr. Poole screamed. Begging. Sure startled me. Men don't beg."

They do when their life is in danger, Shepherd thought, but kept the sentiment to himself.

"There was a loud crash. It was then I smelled fire. Acrid. Like chemicals burning."

Or sulphur.

"He must have tripped and spilled some of his developing fluid," Shepherd suggested, more for his own sake than that of his listeners.

"Could be. One spark and the whole place went up. I was lucky to get out alive. The insurance investigators are going to have a field day."

To say nothing about the mortician. Shepherd doubted anything remained of good ol' Danny's face to make presentable.

Closed casket.

With the lid up or down, he knew he would have a vision of Danny Poole's charred remains the rest of his life.

Which brought an even more unpleasant remembrance. Words spoken in anger.

If someone took a torch to the place, no one would ever miss the occupants or the work produced there.

"Terrible accident. I'm sure they didn't mean to kill him. That only happens in the movies," the witness sniffed. "Not in real life. He should have been more careful who he stiffed, though. Some of those models can be pretty tough. Bet it was her boyfriend who came calling."

That was one bet Shepherd decided he would take. For sanity's sake.

Left without the option of renewing *olde lang sine* with Danny Poole, Shepherd wandered the streets, head buried between his collarbones.

"Terrible accident," the ear-witness had said. Terrible? Certainly. But an accident? He knew how Trent would explain it.

Tying up loose ends.

But for what purpose? That rationale didn't make sense. Poole had already told him all he knew or surmised about Ericka. At that, it hadn't been much. No betrayed secrets, no details divulged – or withheld. Of that Shepherd felt certain. He had gotten all the photographer had to give.

"No!" he argued, kicking a wadded McDonald's bag like a soccer ball. The Trent of his mind overreacted, trying to make something mysterious out of coincidence.

After all, Trent had never seen her, never had the opportunity of staring into her lustrous eyes. If only Shepherd could bring them together, he felt sure the old man would.... Would what? Fall under her spell? Bad expression. Would find her as lovely – as innocent – as he did?

Shepherd finally grinned, resuming his one-man game with the street child's ball. Trent, the perennial bachelor, would not be sexually attracted to Ericka, but he was a man, after all. Even he could appreciate the beauty of the female form.

Scoring a "goal" by depositing the crumpled bag between two parked cars, Shepherd did a quick-step soft shoe dance before hurrying his pace. Lacking a destination, the need to arrive on time proved paramount.

Jaywalking with the righteousness of a native New Yorker who realized all the idiots in the world came from "out of town," he dashed into a crosswalk. A bus nearly ran him down. Shaking his fist at the public transport, he inadvertently caught sight of a large, handwritten notice someone had plastered against the rear window.

"The end of the world is nigh!!"

"Nigh?" he questioned, holding his head back in perfect imitation of a man wearing a neck brace. "No one uses that word anymore. No one even knows what it means."

Still chewing the prophet's archaic word choice, he reached the opposite sidewalk. Only then did the admonition strike home. The blow hit with less force than the bus but with equal life-altering potential.

He must return to Paul Delgado's building and see whether the Tarot card reader had reopened for business. If "Mystic Joe" were in, he would have his fortune told.

Just for kicks.

Avoiding cracks in the sidewalk the way baseball players skipped over foul lines, Shepherd reached the building and scampered inside. Eschewing the elevator, he clamored up the steps, two at a time. The effort took a toll and by the time he reached the third floor, his lungs heaved for air. Forced to slow, reason overcame curiosity.

What in the world had he really come for? If Delgado spied him lurking around, there would be an unpleasant scene. He might even remember Shepherd had purloined his notes and demand them back. Call the cops. Or turn him over to his other neighbor, the private dick, for a good, old fashioned thrashing.

He should have left, he wanted to go, yet his feet stayed the course.

"There's no fool like an old fool," he joked, reminding himself that at his age he did not qualify as old.

The CLOSED sign had been exchanged for the "Always Open" one. Relief as tangible as scratching off a lottery ticket and winning ten bucks in the "Instant Winner" game washed over him. Feeling foolish, despite his tender years, he knocked on the door. A voice from beyond called out, "Enter."

The interior looked as tacky as he had envisioned it. Over-large posters, depicting '40's style artwork lined the walls. Men with faces of wolves; women wearing low-cut dresses withering under the rays of a full moon Multi-pointed suns with esoteric expressions; clusters of stars looking vaguely like the Big Dipper.

A round table dominated the room. Beside the obligatory crystal ball, a deck of Tarot had been spread out in what appeared to be a game of solitaire. Standing by the rear wall hovered a genderless person wearing a black robe. Unfortunately for the completion of the scene, the pointed witch's hat had been omitted.

The seer invited him to be seated. Shepherd inched forward but declined the chair.

"I was looking for Mr. Delgado," he lied, suddenly afraid to have his fortune told.

The person raised its head, scrutinizing him with beady eyes, which from a distance appeared dull and lusterless.

"He is gone."

Suspicion tempered relief.

"Gone for the night?"

"Gone."

"What do you mean – gone?"

Having encountered one man "gone" this evening, the word held particular distaste.

"He will not return."

"Get thrown out for back rent?"

"He has been summoned."

"Come on, grand... dad," Shepherd guessed, taking the fifty-fifty chance. "It" might just as easily have been "grandma." "Speak plainly. Where's he gone? Who 'summoned' him?"

The wizened old hag made a low, croaking noise, akin to choking. Running his/her hands over the crystal ball, it's lips parted, revealing blackened teeth.

"The spirits."

"You mean booze got him?"

"He vanished."

Perspiration, which had nothing to do with his recent exercise, ran down Shepherd's arm pits.

"Don't play games with me." Looking around to be sure they were not being overheard, he lowered his voice conspiratorially. "I owe him money. I came to pay him back. My name is –"

This brought a reaction faster than the mention of cash, something he supposed which did not happen very often. If ever.

"I do not want to know your name!"

"All right," he placated, extending his hands, palms outward. "If you'll just tell me where I can find him, I can make good my debt and get out of here. Look," he added, removing his wallet as proof of his assertion. "Moolah. I owe the guy, and –"

"I do not want anything you have touched," the medium responded.

Who had verbalized that exact expression just recently?

Danny Poole.

An odd coincidence.

Queer. In the sense of being peculiar.

Danny no longer needed money. Or anything else, for that matter. Except, perhaps, his prayers.

Shepherd decided he would put the ten in the poor box, next time he passed a church.

Just so *Trent* would be on the side of the angels.

The safe side. Or so believers alleged.

"Come on. Don't fool with me."

"I never fool."

"Then tell me where he's gone. Or when he'll return."

"He will never return."

"Sure. I know," Shepherd began, pointing to one of the posters. "It's midnight and his coach turned into a pumpkin and the rats ate him." He stomped closer in a threatening movement. "What-happened-to-him?"

The ball-gazer withdrew, eyes sinking into its skull.

"Life is precious, even to the aged. I treasure mine. Go away, shepherd."

He gasped, failing to realize the word had been used in its lower case meaning, rather than as a first name.

"He couldn't have simply vanished. This is Manhattan. It's the 20th Century." Receiving no further confirmation, Shepherd backed away, feeling the walls close in. "Never mind. Forget I bothered you. I'll ask the detective next door."

"He cannot help you."

"He will if I pay him –"

"He cannot locate Mr. Delgado. No one can. He is not to be found in this world."

"O.K. Fine. I guess that wipes out my debt."

Cramming the wallet back in his pocket, Shepherd retreated, backtracking out of the office. He did not turn his back on the seer until the door shut.

"They shouldn't let people like that run loose. Someone sprinkle me with faerie dust so I'll wake up from this nightmare."

He had a feeling if someone did, he would wake to find himself in a place no one in their right mind would wish to be.

As of yet undefined.

Which completed the circle, bringing him back to Ericka Elvina. She worked for an unnamed king in an unnamed country.

A place Paul Delgado never got to visit.

One of them counted his lucky stars as Shepherd descended the stairs, one at a time.

Ericka. It was she he really wanted to see. The hell with Danny Poole and Paul Delgado. They were after-runs, second place finishers. The race belonged to him.

He hot-footed it all the way to her office building.

Oddly, the doors at the main entrance to the Stone Gate Building were locked. Nor did there appear to be a doorman in attendance. Peeking through the plate glass window, Shepherd noted the lights had been turned down. Only two small lamps illuminated the interior. Rather than appear inviting, the harsh glow served to repulse the casual inquirer.

He knocked, then sought a bell. Finding none, he stood back and stared upward, much the same as he had done at the SoHo Grand. As he had that fateful night, he hoped to catch a glimpse of someone looking out a window. Although a yellow-orange glow, strangely reminiscent of fire, bathed the penthouse, no one lingered near the curtains.

"This is an odd way to operate an apartment complex," Shepherd mumbled. "How do the tenants get in and out?"

He had never before questioned the simple fact Ericka Elvina might be the only occupant. Rich she might be, but the sole renter? That seemed improbably and extremely wasteful.

Jiggling a pocketful of change, he decided to call and announce his intentions before remembering he did not have her phone number.

"Stupid," he chastised. Instead of stealing the pyramid, he should have copied the number from her telephone.

Riffling the pages of a directory chained to a nearby phone booth, he finally abandoned the idea in disgust. Not surprisingly, her number was unlisted, and he did not know the name of the company under which she transacted business. Nor were there any listings under "Stone Gate," either as an enterprise or a dwelling.

"Damn!"

No sooner had he expounded the curse than the name Joe Warren popped into his mind. He would have her phone number. While it might be problematic he would part with it, it seemed a chance worth taking.

Besides, Shepherd acutely felt the need of company. Figuratively, he had already struck out: Danny Poole had caught the last train for the coast, Paul Delgado turned up "missing" and Ericka Elvina was not receiving. His luck, he decided, could only go up.

Like Miss Elvina, Mr. Warren's home had an unlisted phone number. That meant seeking information at his office. Unlike the Stone Gate, Warren's place of employment would be open 24/7.

Feeling giddy, almost light-headed, Shepherd stepped out of from booth. He drew in a deep breath to rid his nostrils of the stench of urine from the "public toilet," then hailed a cab. The sight of a familiar face, no matter how unfriendly, presented a better option than the biting loneliness destroying his stomach faster than a bleeding peptic ulcer.

Glancing down from the twenty-second story of the Stone Gate Building, a tiny, almost tender smile graced the alluring features of Ericka Elvina. Shepherd guessed correctly: he needed to reach Joe Warren. That he would come closer than anticipated she had no doubt.

Afterwards, but not immediately, Shepherd would go crawling back to his mentor.

It was unfortunate, she decided, that she would never have the opportunity of meeting Abraham Trent in the flesh. Undoubtedly they would have much to discuss.

From opposite sides of the Known Universe.

Leaping from the taxi and passing the driver a bill, Shepherd raced up the broad cement walk fronting the mega-complex where Joe Warren worked. Brushing away the wrinkles of his shirt to make himself presentable, he prepared to enter the establishment when he felt a friendly tap on his shoulder. The grin on his face froze when he saw no one behind him.

"What the –?"

Certain he could not have been mistaken, Shepherd's eyes were drawn upward just in time to witness a body hurtling down through the damp night air. It took no more than a fraction of a second for his mind to go from puzzled query to hard truth. He arrived in time to witness a suicide.

The afternoon's image of the photographer, standing alone and frozen in the office lobby prompted Shepherd to jump backwards. Ironically, his feet were off the ground at the exact instant the body struck *terra firma.*

The force of impact shattered bones. Although twenty yards away, even a layman could interpret the twisted angle in which the body fell as indicative of a broken neck.

Deader than a door nail, flashed through Shepherd's overwrought imagination. And then, just as quickly, *You can't get deader than dead.*

For the first time in his life, he doubted that old truism.

He did not know for certain the smashed face bleeding over the pavement had once belonged to Joe Warren. It might as easily have been any one of the two thousand employees working there. For all of that, it could have been a total stranger who had walked into the building for no better reason than the doors were open.

Suicides from the top of the Empire State Building were passé. The poor unfortunate might simply have wanted someplace more novel to terminate his earthly existence.

Errant thoughts. Without the slightest doubt, the mangled corpse had once housed the soul of Joe Warren. He had gone to join his fiancee.

Whom God has jointed, let no man tear asunder.

Or something like that.

Shepherd no longer wished he were in Joe Warren's shoes.

CHAPTER 13

Shepherd read about Bill Ford's death in the newspaper the following morning. The writer described the incident as "unfortunate." Apparently, Mr. Ford had been a regular patron at the Bottoms Up, a club in the seedier side of town. He had gone in last evening, as usual, to share a drink with an employee named Daisy Petal. A strobe light had broken loose from its mooring on the ceiling and struck him on the head.

Death had been instantaneous.

The rest of the blurb dealt with building code violations and ended with a quote from Hemingway about, "for whom the bell tolls."

Wrong time, wrong place.

Which did not make the death any less of a shattering coincidence. All four of the men who had given him information on Ericka Elvina were now dead. By itself, the facts were startling, but inconclusive. People died.

Fire.

Summoned.

Suicide.

Accident.

Nothing actually could be attributed to Ericka – or the Black Arts.

Trent, he supposed, would put a different slant on it. But Trent was steeped in the occult. To his discredit, such beliefs had never made him wealthy.

Not like someone who dabbled in the stock market. Money had become the only reality his ward understood. Money made the world go 'round.

Having all day to kill before his 8 P.M. appointment with the great lady, Shepherd decided to stay in and rest. That seemed a better alternative than looking up Sammy Greeley.

Sammy lived a dangerous life, after all. He made his livelihood as a petty stooge. On any given day, he might just wake up to find himself being rowed across the River Styx.

Far more disturbing from a personal perspective were Shepherd's own peripheral involvements with the collective demises of his informants.

In his own, inimitable way, he had wished each of them ill.

Sammy Greeley's face he had likened to a dead high-schooler.

Bill Ford had been summarily dismissed from the land of the living by a wave of his hand.

He had written off Danny Poole by mentally burning down his studio with the photographer inside.

Shortly after drawing the pentagram on the office next to Paul Delgado's, evil spirits whisked him away.

Joe Warren had been the recipient of his bitter deprecation to take a long walk off a short pier.

All his wishes had come true.

In spades.

The black cards. Harbingers of death.

But how could any of those expirations be traced back to him? He had not really meant his errant desires to be taken seriously. They were no more than wistful thinking.

Or had they been? He had surely meant the threats at the time. But to have them all come true? At his behest?

Impossible.

It simply could not be. He was – how would Trent describe him? A child of God.

A God he denied.

"I'm innocent!" he cried, wiping his hands on a paper napkin to wash away his sins. "I don't have that power! No one does."

No one who was not linked, in one way or the other, to the supernatural.

The dim room grew darker by the minute. The only illumination came from a small globe, set on a distant side-table. The occupants of the suite appeared oblivious to the deepening gloom.

A young and comely maid finished pouring wine into a decanter, then turned to her superior.

"Mistress, will he bring the pyramid back?"

"He does not have it. He left it with another. A very foolish man." Ericka left unsaid whether she referred to Trent or Shepherd.

"Will he use it to summon forth the spirit within and use it against you?"

"He does not have the power." The presentment rang with smugness. "Though he may say the words, perform the rituals, the... deviling... belongs to me, alone. Only I may summon it." Vainly adjusting her long locks of jet black hair, Ericka flexed long, slender fingers in a beckoning gesture. "That I have never done so is indicative of my own, inherent strengths."

Gliding effortlessly toward the couch, Ericka set herself to receive the visitor. She radiated an aura of vitality, not un-similar to the glow of the pyramid in Shelley Larson's apartment. "Others of my kind have required – devices – to augment their position. They were weaklings. Inferiors. I have no equal. I need no familiars."

A cruel smile twisted her otherwise stunning countenance. "Go to the door."

Silently obeying, the servant did as bidden. Opening it without further summons, she beheld the elevator doors part. Shepherd, clad by two close-fitting bodyguards, stood in the car. The perfect timing of the action temporarily disconcerted the youth. Before he could quite recover himself, the hostess spoke from afar.

"Come in, Mr. Kingston. You are expected."

Crossing the threshold, he found himself alone. Neither bodyguard followed him inside. The maid vanished into the shadows.

"Good evening," he greeted, making a small Continental bow. Ericka returned his gracious gesture with a slight inclination of her head.

"You are right on time. The wine has just been set out to breathe. Will you take some refreshment?"

Utterly transfixed by her presence and more than casually affected by her revealing attire, he eagerly nodded.

"Yes. Thank you."

Dressed in a form-fitting gown of fiery black, decorated with streaks of jagged red lightning bolts, the effect seemed to crackle with electricity. A gem, the color and intensity of fresh blood, hung from a gold chain around her neck. If it were indeed a ruby, then its carat weight and value far surpassed those ancient India treasures displayed in museums behind walls of protection.

Pouring the wine herself, Ericka first tasted it, gave her approval, then handed him the glass.

"It is very old. The last of its kind."

"Excellent," he judged, delicately sipping. "I appreciate you sharing it with me."

"I could do no less."

She indicated he be seated and Shepherd placed himself on the couch. Waiting for Ericka to join him, his eyes wandered toward the picture window. Unlike the previous evening, the curtains were drawn, shutting out the world below. For the first time in his life, Shepherd missed the dazzling Manhattan lights.

Carelessly joining him, Ericka inquired, "You were pleased with the photographs you took of me?"

He had no thought of lying. "The film was blank; there were no images on it."

"I am sorry."

"I know how you did it," he boldly pursued, assuming a control over the situation he did not feel.

"You do?" Ericka laughed, the sound of her pleasure tinkling like silver bells.

"Magnetism. That stone idol you tossed at me."

Amusement drifted into her reply. "Who put that idea into your head?"

"No one," he parried. "I did some research."

"You are suspicious. Come: let me put you at your ease. The room is warm, is it not? Please remove your jacket. You appear uncomfortable. I had not imagined you would come so formally attired."

Fighting the instinct to refuse, the closeness of her body overcame his reticence. With her help, Shepherd removed his coat, then fumbled awkwardly to loosen the knot of his tie.

"That is better," she decided, taking in the full form of his body. "I see so many men in the course of a business day, and they are all trussed up like – Thanksgiving turkeys. That is the expression, is it not? When I am at home, I prefer a more casual atmosphere."

"And yet, you are dressed for entertaining, yourself," he protested, eying the gem suspended delicately above ample breasts. Pleased at his compliment, she fingered the jewelry, making certain the facets reflected the lamp light.

"You like it?"

"It's magnificent!"

"A royal treasure; from deep within the earth of my country."

"I would not have imagined your people had the technology to mine so deeply."

"Oh, we have our ways," she admitted, as though delighted to share a secret. "It is all in knowing where to look. And how to obtain that which one truly desires."

"What do you desire?" he whispered in a husky voice.

"I think, perhaps, it is more pertinent to discuss what you desire."

With the room closing in, Shepherd withdrew from her nearness, sipping his wine as an excuse to move.

"I want... success."

"But you do not know how to obtain it." Ericka gracefully removing one evening slipper with her other foot.

"I do."

"Taking my photograph. Interviewing me. I understand," she sighed, the suggestion clearly too petty to bother with. "Is there not some – better way?"

"Better?"

"More direct. More commanding. I would think a man like you would be able to achieve far greater heights if he... put his mind to it."

"How?"

The innocent question deepened her already broad and voluptuous smile.

"I think you know that already."

"No," he protested, weighed down by the sudden remembrance of his complicity in the deaths of four, possibly five men. "I know of no other way."

"It may possibly take someone like me – an innocent bystander – to open your eyes."

Innocent. Their common denominator. Shepherd swallowed more wine, feeling a surge of power ignite his soul.

"I would do much for you."

"Much?" she teased, gracefully smoothing an errant strand of his long, silken blond hair. "Or anything?"

The avowal lay on the tip of his tongue, yet he could not say it. Ericka moved closer, brushing her lips close to his.

"Do you like this dress? It is silk." She took his hand and placed it on her thigh. "Created exclusively for me by my countrymen."

"You have silk worms in your kingdom? I thought they were the exclusive providence of China."

"Do I not look Chinese to you?" she coaxed, drawing closer.

"No."

"What nationality do I appear?"

"I don't know. I'm not very good at that sort of thing. Eastern European?"

"Come: your informants told you that much."

"Then tell me more."

"Let us say I come from a very old line." Her vagueness and the effects of the wine emboldened him.

"Where does it originate?"

Rising from the couch, Ericka paraded past, the soft swish of her dress making a lovely accompaniment to the music of her voice.

"In all your investigations, you have been unable to find out?"

"No one knows."

"You did not hear it from the financiers at the party the other night? Nor from Sammy Greeley, Bill Ford, Danny Poole, Paul Delgado, or Joe Warren?"

Hearing the litany of the dead sent a chill through his heart.

"Not from them. They... knew nothing."

Although too late to protect his sources, some undefined, twisted logic caused Shepherd to hold his tongue. Neither surprised nor offended, Ericka moved to the window, stroking the curtain the way a master might fondle an expensive, unloved pet.

"And your friend, Trent? He made no guess?"

Flushed from her startling revelation, Shepherd frowned. "Not specifically. But... how do you know of him?"

"You mentioned him when you took the pyramid. You said you were going to consult Abraham Trent. Of SUNY. He is your... mentor. Is that not how you expressed it?"

"Did I?" His mind a whirl of conflicting emotions, Shepherd could not exactly recall mentioning the professor, or of having been given permission to take the object d'art.

Radiating with the glow of animal spirits, Ericka returned, standing over him with the majesty of one born to command.

"What was it he told you about the cryptogram?"

"He – he translated it," Shepherd stuttered, struggling for control.

"How very clever. What did he say it meant?"

"A summons for a demon," he got out in a gush of excitement. Stimulated less by the memory than the woman's presence, he put a hand to his throat in a vain attempt to increase air flow to his brain. Her hands beat him to it.

"Let me help you." Further undoing the fastenings of his shirt, her cool fingers slipped across his bare chest. "Did you summon this demon and bring it with you?"

"I don't believe in such things."

"But you should. Trent does."

"He believes in Santa Claus, too," Shepherd mocked, kissing the flesh that lingered too long by his mouth.

"But surely he gave you something – to ward away evil?" Ericka insisted. "That would have been like him. He loves you so."

Foot spasmodically jerking, Shepherd crinkled his nose.

"No. He gave me nothing. He merely indicated he would say some... prayers. But it was not from love," he pouted, fearful least Trent's affection be a slur on his own rising manhood.

"One must never spurn affection...or concern, where it is well meant. Tell me," she breathed into his ear. "What prayers?"

"I don't know." Shepherd drew his lips away for her hand and redirected them toward her face. They met hers in passion, held, then only reluctantly parted. Watching him pant, Ericka continued the interrogation.

"He said them over you?"

"I wouldn't let him."

"Why not?"

"I was embarrassed." Then, only slightly more seriously, "I should have, but only because they mean so much to him. He... thinks they hold sway over evil."

Ericka's laugh tinkled merrily.

"Then why not to you? He has taught you everything he knows?"

"I never listen to him. I didn't want to be taught. That was an agreement we had... from the beginning. He has his ways and I have mine. Trent is an old mother hen," he added with a pout.

"Then you did not believe him about the summons? Or the power of prayer?"

"I have no faith in his superstitious nonsense. But there *was* something peculiar about that pyramid."

"I know all about that," Ericka dismissed. "Come with me."

"Where?"

"Must a woman reveal all her secrets?"

He responded to the invitation by saying, "Yes."

"To my bedroom."

"I would follow you anywhere," he vowed, standing on wobbly legs.

"I may ask you to do just that. But come; our journey this evening is a short one."

Taking him by both hands, Ericka led the willing boy across the living room, down a dark hall and into a private chamber. This, too, was dark, but of a deeper, more penetrating void than he had yet beheld.

"A moment, *shepherd,*" she warned, leaving him just inside the entranceway. Breath coming in ragged gasps, he waited as she lit a small corner lamp. Rather than cast a circular glow, the sphere directed a beam toward the left-hand wall, where a massive oil painting, seemingly suspended on air, hung over the bed.

In the absence of wider light, Shepherd's eyes were drawn to the art. Before reason overcame instinct, he cringed, one arm shielding his face from the fearful images.

Had his eyes been melted out of their sockets by searing hot pokers, Shepherd Kingston would have lived the remainder of his days with the palpable, surrealistic figures of Ericka Elvina's painting burned in his memory.

A sense of timelessness, muted by age, yet no less vibrant, assaulted Shepherd's senses. Mouth hung loosely by slack muscles, he beheld the amorphous figure of a blond youth, helplessly cringing under the dominance of a hovering winged creature, vaguely female in form. Attired in nothing but rags, heavy links of chain mercilessly weighted the male against the mountainside.

In vivid contrast to the lines used to wretch the boy's body from the canvas, the spirit's face appeared vague, obscured by an aura around head and shoulders.

Adhering an unspoken command, Shepherd ripped his orbs from the disturbing scene to view a second painting, hung in the middle of the triumvirate. On this broad panorama he beheld a wild, windswept hillside covered in dead grass. A looming tree with gnarled black branches held left foreground, while a figure, enshrouded in robes consumed the center.

Against his will, Shepherd deciphered the identity of the faceless shape beneath the cowl: the Angel of Death. Never having lived in a corporeal sense, this harbinger of eventuality clutched an ancient wooden scythe between fleshless hands.

Deathly frightened by the prophesy, Shepherd directed his gaze toward the last of the paintings, the specter of horror made visible by the magical readjustment of interior lighting. The three stark crosses of Calvary, Golgotha's instruments of agony, were silhouetted against a grey, threatening sky. A skull of tarnished white lay by the foot of the middle cross. A raven, beak parted in a soundless cry of rage, perched on the cross-arm above.

Three paintings: three seconds, three minutes, three hours, three lifetimes. An unholy Trinity. Moaning in immortal pain, Shepherd staggered forward, lost his balance, then lunged forward, seeking solace from the one human being who could protect him. That hope died an ugly death, for beholding a pair of burning eyes, he drew back, suddenly doubtful of her origins.

Once, twice he tried to speak. Not until the third attempt could he give birth to the word.

"Ericka."

Three syllables matched his solitary enunciation.

"I am here."

Unable to penetrate the darkness beyond the arc of illumination, he cringed, terrified least her voice reveal what his heart would not admit. Yet they were soft and comforting, spoken not by a winged creature, nor a dark angel; not from the skull or the black bird, but by a warm, living body. Sobbing in relief, he groped again, this time grasping the familiar body he longed to possess.

"Ericka!"

Her smile, transformed from the malignancy of shadow to one of seduction, invited intimacy.

"I will light a candle."

Without appearing to move, Ericka reappeared across the room, her form highlighted by the sudden flash of fire. Holding match to wick, a candle sputtered, caught, waxed and waned, then grew bold.

Released from an inner sanctum of conflicting images, Shepherd stared in abject fascination as she lit two other candles, finally encasing the chamber in a soft, flickering glow.

"My bed," she pronounced through barely parted lips. "I trust it is to your taste."

Tearing his eyes away from her sharply contoured form, Shepherd radiated with anticipation at the sight of the huge canopied bed. Blood-red drapes covered sides and top, the fabric matching a red satin coverlet shot through with swirling black, the opposite of her dress.

"You will come to me?"

"I will come to you."

Lacking any sensation in his feet, Shepherd floated forward, allowing Ericka to engulf him in her arms. Guiding him to bed, the mysterious woman of Wall Street undressed the willing body, then snuggled close, flesh against flesh. Passion mounting, they intertwined, and where two had been, one became. Sinking within the feather mattress, they coupled violently beneath the living world.

She on top, he beneath, the comforter above and around them, bodies merged into an otherworldly entity of thrashing, driving need. Never separating, never satisfied, alive with ageless passion, they mated, struggled, evoked the bonds of stamina, challenging the gods of love, until time, that unknown, incomprehensible entity, closed in, and Shepherd became Ericka's as surely as if she had claimed his soul at Hell's auction.

CHAPTER 14

The telephone rang and he ignored it. When it rang fifteen minutes later, Shepherd muffled the sound by tossing a pillow in its general direction. When it rang a third time, he cut the cord.

He was not as dexterous with the door. Despite his less than hospitable warning to "Go to hell!" the annoying visitor on the other side kept banging. The thought of sleep finally banished from his mind, Shepherd rolled to the edge of the bed, gingerly swung his legs over the side, then attempted a vertical movement.

Once on his feet, navigating his way to the entrance became child's play. Swaying like an adventurous toddler, he finally reached the wall, steadied himself, then turned the knob.

"Shepherd!" a familiar voice cried. "My God, I was about to go to the police."

Staring at his friend through blood-shot eyes, the youth made a vain attempt to clear his vision by rubbing away the encrustations of deep slumber.

"Good morning to you, too," he muttered without the least hospitality.

Pushing past, the older man entered the apartment, made a cursory inspection of the room to be certain they were alone, then shut the door with resolve. It did not ease his feeling of being watched.

"It isn't morning, it's afternoon. I've been trying to reach you since last night."

"I didn't get in until after 3 A.M."

"Where were you?"

Offended by the accusatory tone, Shepherd shrugged, debated whether or not to explain, then managed a grin.

"With her; with Ericka. And you said it couldn't be done."

"What couldn't be done?"

"Her acceptance of me. As a lover," he added with an undisguised brag. "She's awesome, Trent. Incredible. I don't know what hit me."

"That last I believe."

"I mean it. She's all woman, Trent. All human female. Well, maybe she *is* part animal," he grinned, rubbing his sore muscles. "What a workout. We must have been at it for hours."

"You had sex with her?"

Surprised by Trent's uncouth interrogative, Shepherd bristled.

"What's so surprising about that? I'm not unattractive, you know."

"Yes; I do know. But I don't see the fascination."

"Really?" Shepherd dug, squinting his eyes. "Then that's one thing you don't share."

Ordinarily, Trent would have been hurt by his ward's implication, but the situation had progressed beyond personal considerations. Nervously pacing the room, he shut the blinds, then scanned the ceiling. He identified nothing out of the ordinary, nor could he locate a trinket or talisman which might serve as a communicator to the beyond. Yet the nagging doubts would not be dispelled. As if in response to that fear, he hit harder than intended.

"A fascination with you? Don't deceive yourself, boy. It's not your body she's after."

"Could have fooled me," he yawned. "Make some coffee."

"Make it yourself," Trent angrily snarled. "I'm not your servant. And I suspect you can use the practice."

"What does that mean?"

"That if anyone plays servant, it'll be you."

Under Trent's watchful eye, Shepherd padded barefoot into the kitchenette, ran water, filled a pot, then rapidly made coffee.

"That's where you're wrong, old boy. She has plenty of servants to do her bidding. And a whole country of them at home."

"How would you know?" Receiving no reply, Trent shoved his face close to Shepherd's. "Did she tell you that?"

"Yes," he snapped. Withdrawing from the close proximity of the old man's body, he tried to continue their conversation, then abandoned the attempt. This reticence spoke louder than words.

"Exactly what did she explain?" No answer. "About her country full of servants. Come on. You were glib a moment ago. Tell me the rest."

"I... don't exactly remember," the youth groggily admitted. "We had a long talk. She's very knowledgeable. She told me... a lot. All about her country."

"Did she? Then you tell me, so we'll both know. Where is it? What's it called?"

"Oh.... something or other. Some long name with a lot of vowels."

"That'll make a great story for the Sunday supplement. I thought you were a reporter. Where's your journalistic recall?"

"I'm a photographer," he protested, pouring black coffee from the half-filled pot into an unwashed mug.

"So you like to flatter yourself," came the droll reply. "What about your great snapshots? How did they turn out? I'd like to see them."

"I... didn't develop the film."

"I know better than that. You developed it, all right. And it was blank, just as I said it would be. Wasn't it?"

"O.K. So you were right. Pat yourself on the back, pass 'Go,' and collect two hundred dollars."

Drawing up one of the rickety kitchen chairs, Trent planted himself at the table.

"And that doesn't concern you?"

"Why should it?" Shepherd asked, perching on the other. "I'll have plenty of other opportunities. Besides, there's nothing mysterious about blank film. You explained the phenomenon. The stone idol; magnetized, you said."

But he had passed beyond that. "How, 'plenty of opportunities'?"

"I'm going away with her." The color came back into his cheeks.

"Going away? Where? To her country – the one with no name?"

"It has a name. I just don't remember it."

"Where is it? What part of the world?"

"She did tell me," he began, staring into his mug. The face peering back held no reassurance. "I forgot, all right? I was drunk," he added. "We drank a lot of wine."

"That's not like you."

"Maybe it isn't, but that's what happened. I was feeling good. I was floating, you know? After we made love, we slept for a while, then got up and talked. We killed a bottle of wine."

"That's when she asked you to go away with her? Think, Shepherd. It's important."

"No...not right away. Ericka told me about herself, about how homesick she felt. She's been in this country a long time. Made a lot of money. Millions. Billions, for all I know. Now, she's being recalled."

"By whom?"

"Her employer."

"What did she call him? Does he have a name?"

"She didn't call him anything; just 'my employer.' The king, or something."

Trent slapped his hand against the table.

"What in God's name does she want with you? Why do you have to go?"

"Maybe she likes me, Trent," he snapped. "Have you ever considered that? I told you. She said she was lonely."

"If she's being recalled, then one might suppose she won't be lonely anymore," the visitor, or perhaps at this point, the interloper reasoned. "She must have family, friends in this mysterious 'realm.' The king, perhaps? She isn't married to him, is she?"

"No," Shepherd scoffed. "He's an old man. I don't think she likes him very much." He paused to scratch his unshaven chin, then smiled. "I think he's dying. That's why she's being recalled."

"So she can make a last accounting? Think, boy. You've remembered this much. He's an old man and she doesn't like him. What else? What's her position? Who succeeds him?"

The face in the coffee mug scowled. "She wasn't clear about that. I did ask her; shit, Trent, I don't want to get caught up in some third-world power struggle."

"No. You don't."

"She said not to worry; that the line of succession was all worked out. I almost got the impression *she* expected to succeed him."

"She? She! Is she his daughter, then?"

"I tell you, I don't remember."

"Just like all the others."

"What do you mean?"

"All those photographers who got close to her. They didn't remember anything, either."

"Yeah, but they were just..."

"Pale imitations of you."

"Yeah, well now she has the original."

A hesitation, a twinge in Shepherd's voice alerted Trent much had been left unsaid. Leaning back in his chair, he studied the face before him. Shepherd's foray of the night before had done nothing to alter the intrinsic innocence of his demeanor. Yet lurking in the shadows of experience he detected fear. He deduced correctly, but for the wrong reason.

"She knows you've had experience – sexual intercourse, before last night?"

"Oh, for Christ's sake, Trent, she's not looking for a virgin sacrifice!"

"But she does know? The pyramid stopped you from coupling with Shelley Larson."

"Yes, she knows. I told her all about myself."

"And about me?"

"She... already knew about you," he whispered, suddenly shamed.

"But not from you." Trent sank back, hands suddenly going limp. "Through the pyramid."

"I... may have told her more than I should," Shepherd weakly protested. Waving his hand derisively, he got up and made himself a bowl of cold cereal. "I simply cannot accept the fact she, or anyone else, has the power to see through the eyes of a gold object."

"Not through the 'eyes' of the pyramid; through whatever demon lurks inside."

Shepherd kicked the table. A splash of milk cascaded over the lip of the bowl. Annoyed, he brushed it over the edge, then wiped his fingers on his undershirt.

"Trent, I tell you, she's no different than you or I. She has a mystique around her, like an actor, but that's all. A persona. She doesn't summon monsters from hell and she doesn't murder people."

The enormity of the statement was so startling, Trent nearly tipped over backward.

"Murder people?" The fear appeared again in his boy's eyes. This time, he did not mistake it. "Who has died?" he demanded, shaking the youth by the arms until his teeth rattled.

"Accidents –" Shepherd tried, vainly attempting to pull away. The fact he could not, surprised him, for he had never considered Trent a threat.

"Who-has-died, you son-of-a-bastard-stupid shithead?"

The force of Trent's fingers around his biceps caused him to cry in pain, but the foul language more than the grip nearly brought tears to his eyes.

"Trent, please – don't curse like that. I know you're upset, but for Christ's sake, calm down." Only his invocation to the Lord took the edge off the professor's rage. Taking several deep breaths, he released his stranglehold, then, for lack of something better to do, clasped his hands behind his back.

"I'm listening," he tried. His voice shook.

"Someone I interviewed about her." He dared offer more but it did not satisfy. Trent's eyebrows furrowed, almost running to the bridge of his nose.

"Someone? Or someones?"

"Four," Shepherd confessed, then rapidly added, "but their deaths were all accidents... suicide. Carelessness." He meant for the statement to be taken at face value and was thus disappointed when a disentangled finger shoved its way under his nose.

"Four," Trent gasped, staggered by the enormity. "When did these deaths occur? Why didn't you tell me?"

"Yesterday.... The day before. I don't remember. I didn't have time."

The furrowed eyebrows knotted into a Chinese puzzle.

"You didn't want me to put two and two together. But surely even a love-sick calf knows the difference between coincidence and the willful destruction of life."

"She wouldn't kill. She can't. She isn't evil, Trent. I lay beside her, for God's sake. Don't you think I'd be able to sense something wrong with her, being that close?"

"Yes," he sadly declared. "I think you would. And I think you did."

Flushing with shame and indignation, Shepherd shoved a mouthful of cereal in his mouth, then swallowed without chewing. He choked and spewed forth bits of soggy, un-masticated breakfast.

Trent's face reflected nothing, though Shepherd knew him well enough to divine his thought.

I wish the devil were cast out as easily.

It did not comfort him. Nor did the fact of his seeing the old man slump in his chair add reassurance. Reaching out, Shepherd gently touched Trent's face.

"I know you care, and I appreciate it. More than I've ever said. Let's not quarrel, please, old friend. I need your support."

His words strengthened Trent, but the heart had gone out of his argument. He spoke now for the future, rather than the present.

"You said you told her all about yourself."

"She asked if I were married," he agreed, hoping to ease over the distance forming between them.

"And you said no. What else?"

"The usual stuff: who'd miss me? What family I had."

"You told her your parents were dead. But she *was* curious about them, wasn't she?"

"What makes you say that?"

"You didn't answer my question."

"I told her a little. You know I don't like to talk about them."

"Did you tell her their professions?"

"Yes."

"And how they died?"

"More or less," he admitted, absently picking bits of damp cereal off the table.

"And about your power?"

"No!" Shepherd cried, raising his head and turning savagely on Trent. "I never mentioned that." Pushing away from the table, Shepherd stood, looked around the cheap, depressing apartment, then shook his head.

"How could she ask about a 'gift' she doesn't know anything about? When two people who are attracted to one another have a heart-to-heart, the subject of telekinetic power doesn't just pop up, you know."

"No," Trent softly acknowledged. "I suppose it doesn't. Especially when she already knows."

"How – could she know?"

"You're forgetting the pyramid, son. When you saved that young woman's life. A very carefully staged 'accident,' by the way. A test. One which you passed with flying colors. Did she ask about it, by the way – about her little gold pyramid?" Shepherd shook his head. "But it did come up in conversation, didn't it?"

"Funny," he mumbled, running a hand over his face. "She knew I took it. She even acted as though she gave it to me. That's it!" he yelled, stamping his foot in childlike remembrance. "She knew *you* had it!"

"I?"

"Yes. Trent. She called you by name."

"But surely you never mentioned me?"

"Of course not. How could I? When I took it, I didn't even know I was going to give it to you. I just wanted a keepsake... something to use as an excuse, if she didn't want to see me again."

"Then how did she know my name? What did she call me?" he pressed, snatching Shepherd's hand to prevent him from picking at the tablecloth.

"Trent. My mentor." Red rose up his neck. "She should have said 'ward,' shouldn't she?" It was a humble admission. One Trent could not afford to sentimentalize. Applying pressure to the hand he still held, he urged the youth on. "I told her you had translated the words on the pyramid; that it was a curse for summoning a demon."

The weight of predestination bore down on the professor. Despite the foregone conclusion he had physically lost Shepherd, the call to battle once again stirred his soul.

"This is very grim. She witnessed your power, then she prevented you from making love to that girl. Now you tell me she knows I translated the cuneiform. Did she ask for it back?"

"No."

"She will."

"Then I'll give it to her. It's hers, after all. It's probably valuable."

For the first time, Trent smiled. It was neither tender nor humorous.

"It is. But not in the way you mean."

Shepherd rolled his eyes.

"It's gold."

"It is, in her eyes. And pray that is all it is."

Trent reluctantly released Shepherd's hand, allowing him to move away. The separation hurt, for it symbolized a far greater one to come.

"Tell me one thing," he requested. He sounded kind. Shepherd would always remember him that way.

"If I can."

"Think carefully before you answer. *Why* are you going with her?"

The question baffled.

"Why? Why? How can you ask that? Because she's a beautiful woman, that's why."

Again, the feeling of being watched. Trent squirmed in his chair, shaking his shoulders to ward away the impression. It only grew stronger. Carrying on the conversation with his mouth, he used his mind to delve into the un-seeable.

"Are you in love with her?"

"No."

"I won't dignify the question by asking if she's in love with you."

"You think it's impossible that someone love me?"

The tug at his heart strings brought Trent to his feet. Like a puppet with only one side of his wooden body properly functioning, he wandered into the living room. Shepherd watched, wondering if he were growing senile. "Arthritic" would have been a more sympathetic description, but his feelings were wounded. Fortunately, his guardian could not read his mind. His senses were elsewhere, although his consciousness focused on dialogue.

"I think it's impossible that *she* love you. No matter what you may think, love is not part of her makeup. So I ask again, why are you going with her?"

He posed a valid question. One in which Shepherd had given much consideration. The oppressiveness of his living quarters, the dim, nearly nonexistent chance he had for making a name for himself poured from his lips.

"To get her story. Maybe a lifetime of stories. Just imagine, Trent: an exclusive about an unknown kingdom. *Ancient dynasty meets Wall Street.*

Old Meets New. It's a natural. It's the kind of thing I've been seeking all my life."

Pausing for breath, Shepherd hurried to the old man, eyes glistening. "This penny-ante stuff I've been doing – hoofing around parties, hoping for a break. Trailing after celebrities; making pocket-money for a photograph. It's not what I want out of life. I'm destined for bigger things than that."

"I always thought so," came the thoughtful response.

"Well, here it is: not just a break, Trent, but an adventure. A chance to see the world. To be a part of it. Ericka is. Think of it: she rose from the obscurity of a rinky-dink kingdom, to become a major player in the stock market. Now she's going home, for who-knows-what-purpose. Maybe to become queen. Or maybe as adviser to a new king. What a story."

The irony did not go unnoticed. A twisted perversion of a smile worked its way horizontally across the old man's warped features.

"So, you're going to play Anna to the king of Siam?"

"Why shouldn't I? Don't you think I'm worthy? Or do you think I'm no better than all the rest – that I have no more talent than the guy taking mug shots at the motor vehicles department?"

Noting the hurt in Shepherd's voice, Trent softened.

"I've always believed you have talent. I've supported you in everything. I would have put you through college –"

"I know I disappointed you, Trent. For that, I'm sorry. You've been good to me. But this is my chance, and I'm going to take it." Stuffing his hands in his pockets, Shepherd faced his mentor. "You've taught me a lot. Now it's my turn to walk on my own two legs."

To prove his point, he stomped his feet, which only served to underscore his lack of age. Trent shook his head slowly, meeting Shepherd's gaze with unhappy, wet eyes.

"If only it were that, boy, I would send you with my blessings."

"It is just that simple, Trent."

"For God's sake, if not mine, don't close your mind. You must swear to me you'll be careful."

Holding up his hand, he started to make the sign of the cross. Shepherd let out a yell, pushing him away. The half man-half puppet staggered before regaining control. His glare expressed tremendous displeasure at being stopped from such a pious act.

"She's not an ogre, Trent! She's a woman. She likes me – a lot. She said so, and I believe her. Maybe I'm not your idea of the perfect male, but you're not a woman."

"Get it out of your mind, you fool! She is not infatuated with you. She doesn't want you for stud service and she will never permit you to write one single word about her, the country of her origin, or this ancient monarchy, of which you know nothing."

"Then what does she want?" Shepherd demanded, regretting his rash action, but not knowing how to make it right.

The reply took long in coming.

"I wish I knew."

"Well, I know. And your jealousy won't stop me."

Tearing himself away from the pleading in his friend's eyes, Shepherd stormed into the bedroom. Trent followed, but kept his distance.

"When are you going?"

The reply was curt and unemotional. "Today."

A coldness washed over Trent's body. Clenching his fist, he looked up, then through the ceiling of the cheap apartment. For a moment, no more than a split second, he saw *it*. Eyes, peering down at him. Not at them, not at both he and Shepherd, but directly, solely upon him.

Black eyes. Large, luminous, intent. Malignant. Powerful. More powerful than... but he dared not finish the thought. It bordered on blasphemy. His foundations shook. He would not let them become unglued.

"How?" he whispered, lowering his shoulders, and thus his head, toward the floor. Any excuse not to look up. "You don't even have a passport."

He had not meant for Shepherd to answer, but one came. "Ericka's making all the arrangements."

Shifting his eyesight to the threadbare carpet, Trent addressed it, rather than the boy.

"And nothing I can say will stop you?"

"Nothing."

"Then promise me one thing." Before Shepherd could protest, he hurried on. "One thing, only. And that for what we have been to one another."

"I'm listening."

"Before you go, let me give you something. I want you to take it and put it in your luggage without inspecting it."

"What?"

"A gift; no more. A... farewell present. You must not to look in it, nor mention it to Ms. Elvina. Just pack it away and forget about it."

"What kind of a gift is that?"

"One I pray will save your life." He forced himself not to choke. "Remember it only in time of dire need. I don't know if I have the power... or that you will have the opportunity to use it. Or even if it will help. But knowing you have it will ease my mind. Is that too much to ask?"

"Not money?"

"No. Money I give you freely." Reaching into his wallet, Trent withdrew all he had. "Take this. It isn't much. If I had time, I would cash in a savings bond, but she has arranged otherwise."

"I can't take your last dollar. Besides, Ericka is rich. She'll give me money if I need it."

"It's only a token, son. It won't buy your freedom. It won't even buy you a plane ticket home. But it might be enough to bribe a servant or two."

"I told you. I don't need it."

"Take it, anyway. You've never refused money from me before." As Shepherd reluctantly nodded, Trent handed him the currency. "I must go now. To prepare your gift. How soon are you leaving for the airport?"

"Not until this evening. You can meet me at the terminal."

Trent grimaced at the word. "No. That will not do. I will come back here. In an hour. Please: no matter what, wait for me. Swear you will."

"I swear. But you're upset for nothing. I'll call you when I arrive in the Kingdom."

"Yes." Trent agreed, knowing no such thing would happen. "You do that."

"I swear."

But enough swearing had already taken place. What remained lay beyond the power of oaths.

CHAPTER 15

The man stood alone in the airport terminal, hiding behind a cart stacked to the rafters with luggage. He remained so still, he might have been mistaken for a porter.

Had he been twenty pounds heavier, three inches shorter and in possession of a British passport, someone might have mistaken him for George Smiley.

Like the famous spy, his was a mission of stealth. To fail held the possibility of death. To succeed offered an outcome only slightly more optimistic.

The baggage terminal where he hid was nearly deserted. There were no suitcases on conveyer belts, long lines of impatient passengers waiting to be scanned for dangerous substances. There were no X-Ray machines, no federal employees milling about looking important.

While such unpleasantness were the reality of commercial travel, those flying by private jet slipped by in a world of their own.

It had taken Trent the better part of an hour to locate the gate where a private plane was scheduled to depart for Europe. It had cost him nearly a month's salary to discover the plane would refuel in London, then immediately continue its journey eastward. Not even the addition of a fifty dollar bill bought him the knowledge of its final destination.

"Ask at Heathrow," had been his informant's best suggestion.

Had he the wherewithal, Trent just might have taken him up on the suggestion. In fact, he considered the idea, then abandoned it nearly as rapidly. It stood to reason no one at Heathrow would tell him and he had doubts Ericka Elvina's plane would actually stop there.

Had the clerk said, "The plane is refueling in Wales before going on," he might have believed him. Wales was a small, quiet, unobtrusive country. A private plane could land there, refuel and depart without raising an eyebrow. But not London. London was too open, too cosmopolitan. Too susceptible to smugglers and terrorists. Passengers on private aircraft would be scrutinized, if not physically inspected. Something Trent very much doubted Ms. Elvina would approve.

Where was she taking Shepherd? To Hungary? The Czech Republic? A castle in the Carpathian Mountains? The plane had enough maneuverability to land almost anywhere.

Even in a kingdom in which *National Geographic* had never run a cover story.

Hard to believe, but possible.

It had to be possible, or Shepherd might just find himself on a longer journey that he anticipated.

The kind where passports were extraneous.

Trent saw the limousine long before the driver slowed down, prefatory to stopping at the terminal. There were no other motor vehicles in the disembarking lane. No doubt of the occupants.

Leaving the engine running, the chauffeur got out. With stiff, clipped motions, he opened the rear passenger door. Ericka emerged, carried nothing with her, not even a purse or handbag. Trent had never known a woman to travel without one. The omission did not steady his already jangled nerves.

Obviously, she did not carry what she did not need.

Shepherd popped his head out the opposite door before the driver had time to scoot around the automobile and open it for him. Even from a distance Trent saw the youth's wide, shining, innocent eyes. They frightened him more than anything.

Words were exchanged, which he did not hear. Shepherd nodded agreeably, then wandered away as the servant removed luggage from the trunk. As Ericka busied herself with details, Trent made his move.

Without leaving the protection of his hiding spot, he made a quick motion with his hand. Fortunately, Shepherd saw him. Moving with the loping purpose of a tourist set upon seeing all the sights, however mundane to the seasoned traveler, he joined his friend. Grabbing his arm, Trent drew him behind the cart.

"I waited for you at your apartment," he chastised. "You didn't come back."

"I meant to, but –"

"Never mind. Here. Put this in your pocket. Quickly."

Reaching out a hand, Trent thrust a small package into Shepherd's.

"Are you going to tell me what's in it, now?"

"No. And you are not to look."

"I wish you'd forget all this secrecy."

"And I wish you'd take this more seriously. Promise me, whatever happens, you won't say anything about my present. If you have to empty your pockets before you board, don't worry. There's nothing... dangerous in it. Just get it back as soon as you can and hide it."

"All right."

"If she sees it by accident, say it's a gift from a friend. But whatever you do, don't tell her who it's from."

"She doesn't even know you," Shepherd good-naturedly argued.

"You told her all about me. Remember?" Trent snapped, then wished he had not. Regaining control of his emotions, he smiled. He was a poor actor, but Shepherd failed to detect his dissembling. "Did she ask for the pyramid back?"

"No. I think she's forgotten about it in the excitement."

"Good."

"What are you going to do with it?"

"I'm going to... try and use it. The same way she did – to follow you. It's my only chance."

"I wish you'd stop worrying."

"And I wish you'd start. You've got to believe me. You're not going on a vacation."

"I know. I'm going on a job. I'm going to write a series of articles – help her bring the 20th Century to her land."

"Is that what she told you?" Trent choked, struck dumb that Shepherd could actually be that naive.

"Yes. I'm the first otherworlder to ever set foot on her native soil."

The professor quivered, mentally capitalizing "Otherworlder." Fearful least he say too much, he felt equally torn by the fear of explaining too little.

"What I've given you may help. I've written instructions. Read and obey them implicitly, for God's sake."

"When?"

"You'll know. And wear this."

With an unsteady hand, Trent withdrew a small golden chain. A plain cross hung from the links.

"For your mother's sake," Shepherd quoted. For once, his knowledge of old films did not bring a smile to Trent's face.

"For your own," he corrected.

"I am not Renfield."

"No. And Ericka Elvina is not Dracula. I wish she were."

"You didn't put any wolfbane in that package, did you?" Shepherd protested, rolling his eyes. Trent shook his head.

"More effective than wolfbane, I pray."

"Will you stop with the melodramatics?"

"Shepherd?" Ericka called. Trent squeezed Shepherd's arm, then drew his face toward him. He debated whether or not to kiss the boy's forehead, then decided against so overt an action. Instead, he rapidly made the sign of the cross over his head and torso. This time, Shepherd permitted the action, but not without a weak protest.

"You know I don't believe –"

"But I do. And so will you, before this is all over. God will protect," he added with less than total conviction.

"Shepherd?" More commanding, now. Gone the familiarity, replaced by what could have been interpreted as ownership.

"Bless you, Shepherd," Trent whispered.

"I'll call," Shepherd promised, a smile on his face. "I'll buy you some artifacts for your collection."

Before Trent could warn him off such a course, Shepherd disappeared. Ericka greeted his return with a smile. One devoid of warmth.

"There you are."

"This is exciting, isn't it?" Had he been acting, he could not have sounded more convincing. For that, at least, Trent silently expressed gratitude.

"Yes," she agreed. "Very exciting. Come. Our plane waits. I am eager to be off."

Taking him by the arm, she examined him briefly, then made a curt motion over him with her left hand, as if to brush away a stray hair. Witnessed by a casual observer, her action bespoke no more than a friend's concern over his appearance. Trent knew better.

She had wiped away his blessing.

His heart sank.

He did not move again until the youth and the woman were out of sight. No point trying to follow them further. He would be stopped at the gate. Worse, she would be alerted to his presence and grow suspicious. If nothing else, Trent did not want her to question Shepherd about any other parting "gifts" he might have received.

He had given Shepherd all he could, but he had bestowed upon the youth no more than a blessing, a gold cross and a mojo bag filled with holy items to ward off evil. Three gifts. A sacred number. The first had already been mitigated, if not actually destroyed. That left two.

Between the Father, the Son and the Holy Ghost, Shepherd had only two remaining.

The Father and the Son.

Suddenly, Trent felt old.

Powerless.

With nothing left but life, itself.

Old. Powerless. Life. Two were no good without the other.

Shepherd looked around himself in amazement. Not until the plane began taxying down the runway did he actually believe they had the aircraft to themselves. Noting his expression, Ericka smiled.

"I told you."

"Yes, you did. But – I mean, how could anyone imagine being on a private jet? This isn't first class, this is something out of a dream."

She nodded, appreciating his choice of words.

"A dream. I could not have put it better."

"But surely not for you. You must fly like this all the time."

"I was not referring to the accommodations."

Rather than elaborate, she turned her attention out the window. Landscape moved rapidly across their horizon, then diminished quickly as the craft became airborne. Before New York City vanished, the seat belt sign dimmed and died.

With isolation, Ericka seemed reborn.

"Let us celebrate our adventure," she decided. "Champagne."

Anticipating her need, an attractive young stewardess appeared from the forward compartment, carrying a tray. Crossing to the pair, she set it on the seat opposite, then looked at Ericka.

"Open the bottle."

The stewardess did so, hands trembling. She managed to pour two glasses, but spilled a drop as she handed it to Shepherd.

"I am terribly sorry," she apologized, her fear out of proportion to the misdemeanor. As Shepherd took the glass, she immediately attempted to wipe the spill. The action went unappreciated by her mistress.

"Leave us," Ericka demanded. Handing the second glass to the speaker, the stewardess made a low bow, then backtracked several steps before finally turning and scurrying away.

"I think you intimidated her," Shepherd observed.

"Did I?" came the uninterested response. Then, with a shake of her long black hair, Ericka raised her glass. "To us," she toasted. "To our new partnership."

Shepherd touched his glass to hers, then sipped his sparkling wine.

"Excellent," he sighed. "Is this what you drink in your country?"

"It is what *I* drink," she acknowledged. "Much of my country is very backward; French imports are for royalty, not serfs."

"Are you going to tell me more about it – your country, I mean? I'm eager to learn. If I'm going to write about it, I'll have to know a great deal."

"I will tell you much; more you will discern when we land. I hope you will not be shocked. You will witness that which is strange and unusual."

"Good. I want to. I hope I've brought enough film to do a thorough pictorial. There are places I can get it developed?"

"No."

"Then how –?"

"All things in the proper time. The... king is anxious to meet you."

"And I he." Squirming in his seat, Shepherd faced her, face flushed. "I don't know much about proper manners. I've never met a king before. Will you help me?"

"Certainly. I will guide you in everything. Have no fear on that count."

"I brought a suit jacket, but –"

"That will be sufficient. We do not stand on ceremony. Not with those to which you refer," she amended. "Drink your wine."

He willingly obliged, though she drank no more. When he finished, the stewardess returned. This time, however, a marked change had come over her. Her smile seemed friendlier, her demeanor more relaxed.

"Is there anything else I can get you, sir?" she asked after refilling his glass.

"This is fine."

"Whatever you desire, please ask. I am here to serve."

She did not look at Ericka, nor did she repeat the offer. Bowing a second time, she retreated, immediately turning her back to the pair.

"I guess she's new," Shepherd decided. "Trying to impress."

"In that, she has failed," came the tart rejoinder. "But think no more of her. Relax. We will arrive at our destination before you know it."

"I've spoken to people who've traveled to Europe. They say the flight is long. And boring. I was hoping we could take the time to get better acquainted. I don't want to appear ignorant. If you'll just tell me what I need to know..."

"Of course. But finish your drink. Then we will talk."

"I want to take notes...."

Before Shepherd thought to reach for his pen and pad, however, he stifled a yawn. As his eyelids fluttered shut, Ericka took the glass from his hand.

When he awoke, the glare of the seat belt sign flashed.

"Are we in London?" he sleepily inquired.

"No. We have arrived in the Kingdom."

"So soon? Did I sleep through it all? How could I have? I wanted to see England."

"Another time. Perhaps."

Fastening his belt, Shepherd stared out the window. Nothing he had prepared himself for met expectations. Below them appeared a wild, windswept airstrip, seemingly no more than a crooked cow path. From his vantage point, he saw no buildings, no signs of civilization.

Craning his neck for a wider vista proved equally unrewarding. Beyond the landing strip were high, rough mountains, covered in pines. What attempts at agriculture he saw were crude and unproductive. A lone figure, standing by an oxen-drawn plow, gave no indication he witnessed their arrival.

"You implied your country was set back in time," Shepherd observed, fighting a gnawing suspicion. "But this is – primitive."

"Yes. It is."

He glanced Ericka, expecting to see her smile. She did not. Instead, her face reflected grimness.

"How could you have made so much money in the stock market, and still your people live like this?"

The answer should have been self-evident. "I did not earn it for them."

"But surely the king uses some of that vast wealth to help his subjects."

"Surely, he does not."

"Is he a despot, then?"

"That is your word. His is an ancient blood line; he rules by right of inheritance. His word is law. No one acts against him. No one questions him."

"Not even you?"

"There is an aristocracy, of sorts, but none his equal. I must warn you: do not displease him."

"But surely you," he pursued, noting her reticence. "You are not afraid of him?"

"I have my fears," she thoughtfully conceded.

"Where is the nearest city?"

"There are no cities."

"I see no power lines, no telephone poles."

"We have no use of such 'conveniences' here."

"Then how do you live?"

"As our ancestors did."

With a growing sense of isolation and a gnawing fear gripping his insides, Shepherd rested his head against the seat in front.

"It looks more like the 12th Century than the 20th."

This time, her lips curled into what might have passed for a smile.

"Nothing so advanced as that. But look: you can see the castle from here."

Staring beyond the Land that Time Forget, Shepherd beheld a huge, ancient structure rising out of lowland mist. Set in the mountains, trees and high outcropping of rock partially obscured the stone edifice.

"I promised my – a friend – I would call when we arrived. He'll be worried if he doesn't hear from me."

"I am afraid that is impossible."

Before Shepherd could comment further, the plane's wheels touched ground. With solid earth beneath them, Ericka suddenly turned to him, eyes flashing. Her expression did not prepare him for the revelation.

"There is something I must confess. It is nothing which would have altered your plans to accompany me," she hastened to add. "In fact, you will find it to your benefit. The old king for whom I worked has died. His son now rules this land. It has taken him this long to... acclimate himself to the throne. He has now recalled me; with you. An invitation," she menacingly included, "the old king would never have extended."

Startled, Shepherd nearly choked on the saliva suddenly pooling in his mouth.

"Wait a minute; why didn't you tell me this before?"

"I saw no need."

"But this new king – how well do you know him? What's he like? Is he better or worse than his father?"

Her face assumed a preeminence, born of breeding and arrogance.

"Much superior."

"That which we discussed – does it pertain to the old king, or the new?"

An aura of un-emotion descended over her countenance.

"Customs have been handed down for hundreds of generations. Can you ride?"

"Ride?"

She pointed outside. The airplane taxied to a stop before a duo of saddled horses. He swallowed nervously.

"Only the kind of horse which runs when you put a quarter in the machine to make it go."

As a joke, it fell flat. Almost as flat as his heart.

CHAPTER 16

"I don't think they like me," Shepherd announced, staring dubiously at the mounts. The fact they were magnificent, broad-chested beasts with wide-spaced eyes and long, yet muscular legs proved little compensation for the city slicker. Sensing his clear trepidation, the beast destined for the interloper flattened its ears at his approach. Ericka made no response, forcing him to ask in a more deferential tone, "What breed of horse are they?"

"They are peculiar to this country." Shepherd shot her a look, frightened to receive yet another evasive reply. The orbs which met his stare, however, were innocent of complicity. "And totally unknown outside it. We guard our secrets well, Shepherd Kingston."

"So I'm beginning to realize." The weak smile he fashioned held no trace of levity, implying that he fully comprehended her warning.

We guard our secrets well, Shepherd Kingston.

Very well, he thought. *So well, in fact, one has to wonder why you brought a photo-journalist with you.*

Did this maybe-queen desire to introduce her Kingdom to the world? To indoctrinate the actual king in the ways of the late 20th Century? Had Trent been correct when accusing him of playing Anna to the king of Siam? Did his worth lay in the procurement of napkins and proper place settings?

Four-thousand odd miles away, Shepherd had scoffed at the idea. It now seemed preferable to his other choices.

Ericka had continued speaking while his mind wandered. Jerking back to reality, he scuffed his foot.

"I'm sorry. What were you saying?"

"You will find our riding accouterments quite unlike your Western saddle. I hope you will not have difficulty keeping up."

He worked on widening his grin. "Keeping up with you shouldn't be hard."

The mistress frowned, sending a chill through him. He had meant the statement to be taken on its wider sexual connotations. Instead, his jest had been taken for an insult. Had he not witnessed her subtle change of personality on the plane, Shepherd would have tried again. Instinct warned, however, her accommodating manners had faded with the miles.

Gone, the charming, mysterious, yet willing woman he had known in the penthouse apartment. The person before him had re-formed into a stranger.

All pretenses at equality were gone. In her element, as he was out of his, their relationship, or, rather, his fancied camaraderie, had disappeared.

While maintaining the surface decorum of her late persona, Ericka Elvina had transformed. Wherever they went from here, it would be on a new basis, with entirely different rules.

"I meant," he apologized, finding his efforts more desperate than anticipated, "riding. I'll do my best."

"Yes. Your best," she repeated, eliciting a sinking feeling she did not refer to four-legged transportation. Before he could comment, Ericka directed a steely gaze at the liveryman. The servant cowered in much the same way as the stewardess, before a similar silent command altered her attitude into one more acceptable to Shepherd.

"Eldrich will help you mount. Use the block," she ordered, vaulting unassisted into the saddle, if such it might be called, for in reality, it resembled little more than a flat leather blanket. The steed reared, snorted, then settled uneasily into a waiting mode, ears rotating wildly, like the head of a trapped owl. No affection existed between rider and mount. Like the servants, it obeyed from fear.

Remaining mute, Eldrich indicated the mounting block. Stepping up, Shepherd wavered, then swung a leg over the horse's back. Without waiting for him to establish any control, Ericka dug her heels into the black stallion's flanks. It plunged forward, leaving the erstwhile guest in the dust.

Shepherd hissed, then attempted to catch the eyes of the servant. "Thank you," he tried, but the man appeared oblivious to his statement, as though his powers of animation were solely controlled by his mistress. Out of her presence, he seemed to lack the energy to move.

"Thank you," Shepherd restated, raising his voice. The man hesitated, then waved his arm. Without uttered a word, he made his intent clear: *Hurry*. Taking the offering as a peace gesture, the Otherworlder nodded, then gingerly kicked his mount. Out of all proportion to his urging, the horse broke from a standing position to one of instant motion.

Thrown back by the force, Shepherd grasped for the saddle horn, forgetting, in fear, that none existed. Crying in dismay, he clung to the flying mane for dear life. Bouncing in an awkward up-down, side-to-side motion, the novice attempted to slow the horse, but it ignored his feeble effort, heeding a more powerful inducement. Teeth chattering, limbs flailing, the rider managed to hold on long enough to near his companion who waited for him atop a rise.

The nearness of Ericka's presence, more than any direction from Shepherd, prompted his horse to slow. Out of breath and badly shaken, he finally drew alongside, expecting, at least, a compliment for the unorthodox ride. Expectation died hard.

"Up there."

Shepherd followed her direction, much the same as the horse slowed at her silent command. Literally carved from the side of a mountain, the vast, foreboding fortress elicited more horror than the fleeting magnificence Shepherd had originally attributed to it from the air.

Constructed entirely of grey-black stone, sealed together by intricate placement rather than any fixative, the imposing walls towered above the landscape, dwarfing the ancient pine and deciduous forest surrounding the structure. Turrets held sentry positions at either end, while jagged edges of broken stone ran across the highest parapets, meant to repel boarders.

In contrast to the dry road and the long wood ahead of them, a clammy, clinging mist shrouded the base of the castle, obscuring more salient details of its construction. Had Shepherd not known better, he might have assumed the fog manmade for just such an effect.

Although hidden from sight, Shepherd could easily picture ten thousand skeletons strewn across the ground. Accumulated over centuries of armed conflict, the unburied bones of defeated warriors served as proof of impenetrability.

"Is it not grand?" Ericka demanded, attention directed toward the battlements.

Unable to vouch more than a trembling, "Yes," Shepherd did not dare add his impression of unearthly terror.

"There is nothing like it in all the world." Oblivious to, or perhaps more correctly, drawing strength from his fear, Ericka continued, "It is its own beginning, its own end." Her peculiar emphasis on the word "end" caused him to flinch, unable to determine whether she meant there would be no end, or that its end was nigh.

Ericka gave him no time for reflection. Reaching out a hand, she drew his face toward hers.

"I must leave you now."

"Leave?" Dread overcame pride and Shepherd attempted to grab the reins of her horse. The animal sidestepped before he completed the act, leaving him utterly defenseless. "Where are you going? Back to New York? Without me?"

Contempt enveloped her expression.

"I am through with New York." Implicit in the statement came the unarticulated, *And so are you.* "I go on ahead. My... employer is expecting a report."

Roused to jealousy born of fright, Shepherd bristled. "Is that all he is expecting?" She made no reply. "When will I see you again? Soon? Tonight?"

"Not tonight. But the king will serve as your host, as he has been to no other. No one, Shepherd Kingston, has ever crossed that threshold as guest. You are the first. For that, be grateful."

The blatant insinuation, *You are the last,* rang too clear for appeasement. Unsuccessfully attempting to control the pounding in his chest, the invited guest probed further as a means of delaying the inevitable.

"This king... the son who has become ruler. He is your employer?"

"The *King* is everything." The reverence in her words underscored the significance. Reluctant to give up, he tried harder.

"The luggage?"

"It comes on a horse-drawn cart."

Twisting in his saddle, Shepherd peered into the distance. "I saw no cart." She stopped him from further foolishness.

"Look again. One must use more than one's eyes in this country if he wishes to survive."

Blinking, then shaking his head, Shepherd stared back the way they had traveled. Out of nowhere he heard the creaking of wheels, then saw the dog-cart slowly emerge from a bend in the road.

"How did you know?" he softly inquired.

"Black magic." Waiting for him to react, Ericka finally smiled. "The luggage is always brought that way. A thousand times, it never changes. Wait for the cart."

Before he could protest, she rode ahead, controlling the spirited mount as though born to the saddle. Afraid to disobey and follow, Shepherd resigned himself to wait. Half an hour later the cart arrived, bringing with it the dawn of night. Glad to see a familiar face, no matter that of a servant, Shepherd familiarly hailed him.

"It's good to see you," he began, then suddenly bit his tongue, for the man gave no hint of recognition. Passing by without so much as a glance, the driver continued up the path. Fearing to fall behind, Shepherd debated whether to spur his horse forward when the animal broke into a walk, falling in behind the cart like a well-trained dog. In that manner, Shepherd made his way to the gates of the castle.

The heavy wooden doors of the outer barricade stood open. Passing through, he loitered just long enough to be assured they would not seal automatically, then returned his attention to the courtyard. In debunking one myth, he inadvertently created another for in the short time he looked away, the two-wheeled wagon and its silent occupant had disappeared.

"Hello?" The word echoed off the cold stone, returning just as frightened and solitary as first issued. For a moment he did not recognize his own voice and in the repetition, attempted to rectify the weakness. "Hello?"

He might have been summoning the ghosts of pre-Christian warriors, for the wide, deserted space gave rise to impressions of a battlefield, haunted by the spirits of defeated aggressors.

Craning his neck for a better view, Shepherd absorbed the weathered stone, the feel of desolation, the utter dearth of life. Within the confines, no trees, shrubs or desultory weeds grew, augmenting the total lack of color. As though some unseen hand had thrown a switch, the world had turned to black and white.

Slipping, rather than dismounting from the horse, he rubbed his hands together, deriving no warmth. A penetrating cold seemed to slip through the cracks, or more likely, settle over the yard, for he detected no wind. It brought with it no refreshing scent of pine or grass, however, though the forest grew to the gate. Mouth slightly open to augment his sense of smell, Shepherd tried to identify what odors prevailed. The closest he came were the stolid, damp, musty ones present in a mausoleum. They brought no comfort, nor were they intended to.

Freed from its charge, his horse picked its way across the court, moving cautiously, as though fearful of stepping in a depression or catching its hide on unseen brambles. Having no better destination, Shepherd followed.

The animal came to a stop outside the stable, double doors bolted to stone by heavy, rusted hinges. Although it made no sound, a groom responded, stepping out from the darkened interior. Behind him no light fell, granting the outsider slim chance of seeing beyond. Taking the reins, the servant soothed the horse in an unexpected display of affection before shifting dull, glassy eyes on the stranger.

Without one syllable of greeting, he pointed toward a series of steep, twisting steps leading to the castle entrance. Accepting that as an invitation, Shepherd nodded and backed away. While not his custom to depart without speaking, words seemed out of place, almost forbidden. Not trusting his powers to break the omnipotent silence, he dropped his head and redirected his feet.

Finding what might be construed as a walkway, he crossed the courtyard, coming slowly upon the stairs. Though the upward exertion was not arduous, thin air loitering in the high elevation hardly sustained his need and he fought off the effects of vertigo while debating whether or not to knock.

This inward debate turned moot by the appearance of yet another unheralded servant. Drawing back the portal with considerable difficulty, he stood beside the six-inch thick door as sole welcoming committee. Like the barn, nothing could be seen of the interior but enveloping blackness.

A man of short stature, dressed in a drab leather tunic draped over an open shirt of crude manufacture, the man presented an odd picture to Western eyes. Instead of buttons, the fastenings of his wardrobe were laces, slipped through small-bore holes devoid of metal eyelets. He wore threadbare trousers, over which were calf-length boots, constructed of poorly tanned leather. These, too, were laced with latigo and lacked heels.

Tangled locks of dirty blond hair, reaching past his shoulders, swayed gently as he bowed to the guest. Shepherd guessed his age to be thirty-five, though he might have erred ten years on either side, for though the individual's face had been carved with deep lines, he exhibited a youthfulness belying the accumulation of time.

Beyond the peasant costume, the most startling aspect of his demeanor were his eyes. Of an unusual, almost washed out blue, both pupils were fixed and dilated. On impulse, Shepherd passed his hand in front of the man's face, eliciting no response.

Perhaps feeling the breeze, the servant withdrew a step, then bowed, creating a sweeping arc with his hand as he indicated the interior.

"My master bides you welcome. Enter as friend."

"Thank you," Shepherd crossed the threshold in the same manner he hoped to leave: as friend. "My name is –"

"Shepherd Kingston. You are expected. A room has been prepared for you. My name is Dongal. I have been assigned to see to your comfort, *as long as it pleases my master.*"

Doing a double-take, Shepherd returned the salutation. "You are very kind." He would reserve judgment on the "master."

Dongal frowned, feigning ignorance of the expression, though he spoke perfect English, albeit heavily laced with a foreign accent. The observation brought Ericka to mind. Notwithstanding others' assumption of a British dialect, he would have assumed her for an American. Clearly, she had worked long and hard to eradicate any trace of dialect.

"Your command of language is impressive," he flattered, taking advantage of the man's sightlessness to scan the interior.

Tiptoeing inside, he found himself in a huge, high-ceilinged antechamber, lit by torches placed in sconces. A half dozen tapestries of gigantic proportion decorated the walls Unlike those in Ericka's apartment, however, these bore no recognizable symbols. Bold and dominating, they could have served in the vestibule of a house of worship, but seemed out of place in the foyer of a castle.

Stepping closer, Shepherd determined them to be great antiquity, yet the colors were luminous, despite close proximity to the open flame. He guessed they had been recently cleaned and treated with a preservative. One, no doubt, purchased with the funds garnered from Miss Elvina's Wall Street successes. That, at least, seemed a link between epochs, serving to convince him his past life had truly existed.

Several corridors led off in either direction. Though they did not appear to be sealed off by partitions, his vision failed to penetrate a single foot.

"It's all done with mirrors," Shepherd decided, trying to find a reason to grin. Left to his own devices while Dongal busied himself refastening the outer door, he ambled away, trying to absorb the strangeness, drink the ambiance of tangible legend.

"What a story this is going to make. If only you could talk," he marveled in a low, almost inaudible voice, addressing the structure as he might a living entity. "Who has walked these hallowed halls before me? What fate of nations did they decide? What battle plans were drawn? Who did these mysterious people conquer; who tried to dominate them?"

Only then did he note a total void of portraits. No illustrious forbearers wearing ruffled collars and bejeweled necklaces stared through oil-painted orbs, watching the comings and goings of their heirs. That struck him as odd. Listening to Trent speak of ancient British castles toured as a youth, he always dwelt on the paintings. A source of pride to their progeny, he said; ancestors revered as the architects of the nation.

Perhaps, Shepherd mused, *those who reigned "the Kingdom" were superstitious of having their likenesses committed to canvas, fearing the loss of their soul the way American Indians in the 1800's refused to have their photographs taken.*

He would have to ask. It would make a fascinating side-bar for one of his articles.

No warmer inside than out, the temperature felt uncomfortably chill. Rubbing his hands over his arms to warm them by friction, he paused, caught in a sudden draft from a distant section of castle. Nose twitching with the commingling scents of earth, burning reeds, wood fires and something sweeter, he identified dried herbs, probably used as potpourri to offset more unpleasant smells. Their effect, he illogically decided, only augmented the prevailing cold.

A stone staircase of astonishing dimension beckoned from the right. Seemingly growing out of the floor like a petrified tree, it rose in a circular fashion before disappearing in the dimness. Nothing about the unseen chambers, the artwork, or the allure of upstairs bedrooms appeared cheerful or inviting.

A series of locks clicking into place alerted Shepherd that Dongal had completed his work. All access to the outside world had been sealed off, subtly altering the perception of a royal dwelling into that of a dungeon.

Feeling the loss of freedom like a stab in the side, Shepherd returned his attention to Dongal. If he were to survive in this strange new world, he desperately needed an ally.

"I suppose there are many servants here," he began, before abruptly halting when an echo, similar to that experienced in the courtyard, repeated itself.

"The master keeps few servants." Imparted unemotionally, the tone seemed staged but reluctantly imparted. "The groom is called Hest. The man who brought your luggage is Eldrich. He is the most highly-placed."

"But surely you are a favorite?"

Dongal grimaced. "I am – different from the rest."

"I see." Shamed at the ill-chosen expression, he attempted to make amends to the blind man. "What I mean is –"

"If you will follow me?"

"With pleasure." Dongal tilted his head, conveying the impression that like French cuisine, "pleasure" remained the sole province of the master.

With unerring accuracy, Dongal led the guest through the hall and up the stairs. Though they rose high, no hand-railing protected those ascending or descending the heights, nor had any carpet been placed on bare stone to aid traction. One careless footfall could plunge the walker to certain death.

Eyes trained on his feet, Shepherd noted that long usage had worn the center, while rock on either end remained rough. Although well-swept, he could not dismiss the idea that centuries-old accumulations of dust lingered in the cracks.

Losing count at thirty-four, he reached the upper landing with aching calves. Unaffected by the steep climb, Shepherd surmised the servant went up and down many times a day.

"An elevator would make a nice addition to the decor." The half-hearted jest met with stolid silence.

Down the corridor, then around a bend in the stone walls, the pair came to a dark-stained oaken door. Shut, but unlocked, Dongal turned the metal latch, then flattened himself against the side, allowing Shepherd to proceed ahead.

Foreboding stone walls rose upward toward a twenty-foot ceiling. Situated with at least one side facing outward, the chamber had but one window, and that, no larger than a man's fist, situated well out of reach. Bordering it lay a huge chimney, the hearth two feet off the floor. Blue-orange flames leapt from a newly-lit fire, spitting and hissing as sap boiled and burst within the logs. It offered no means of escape, for even a desperate man would fain attempt to shimmy up the narrow, red-hot opening.

Opposite the fireplace, an oversized, four-poster bed, more suited to giants than mere mortals had been situated. A richly woven comforter of silk, streaked with black and gold lay atop it, covering two amply stuffed pillows. Without touching, Shepherd presumed them filled with goose down. The mattress, he decided along the same lines, must be filled with feathers.

The idea might have aroused erotic expectations of spending time with Ericka, but did not. Although she could be no more than a landing away, her physical presence felt as removed as Trent's. Unable to reach either by phone, mail or simple shouting, he was as isolated as the Man on the Moon.

A bedside stand, a narrow table with one chair, and a wardrobe completed the furnishings. The floor revealed an unworn nakedness, proving Ericka's assertion that no invited guest had ever come to this place.

Not until completing a circuit of the room did Shepherd observe the painting. Affixed high on the wall, it dominated the chamber with its life-like oils. Sucking air through his teeth in horror, he stepped closer, though he need not have, for the image was as starkly etched in his mind as though he himself had painted it – or more accurately, posed for it.

Without doubt, this depiction had been created by the same master who painted the first of the three works in Ericka's Manhattan bedroom. It was, in fact, so strikingly similar, it conferred upon Shepherd the impression the one in New York represented a rough draft of this finished masterpiece. Like Poe's unintentional trilogy, "Bernice", "Morella" and "Ligea," the author plagiarized himself, reworking his creation until he got it right.

With sure, firm brush strokes leaping from a suddenly inspired mind's eye, the artist had transformed the female figure into that of a male creature, more demonic and authoritative than the preliminary. Talons glistened at the end of over-long, claw-like feet, while the mythological beast's open mouth revealed sharp, pointed, wolf teeth.

The devilish fiend hovered malevolently over a pale young man, chained helplessly to a rocky mountain peak, as was Prometheus. Both legs, devoid of clothing, were shackled to the ground; arms stretched piteously outward. Upper torso clad only in rags, the figure with wildly dilated pupils stared upward, eyes riveted in horror upon the incarnation of evil above him.

Beyond the depiction of lingering, torturous loss of mortal existence lay a tearing asunder of spirit. No heaven awaited this mortal's arrival. Rather, the sure and certain condemnation to Hades drew the observer in, forcing him to identify with the victim.

With a cry of anguish, Shepherd stumbled back, heart hammering. Horrific to contemplate without added symbolism, the victim's face represented the true import of the painting.

Down to the last detail, Shepherd stared at his own countenance.

"Dear God!" he choked, sweat dampening his hairline and causing his shirt to stick against his flesh in ineffectual protection. No doubt, no escape from reality. He comprehended what he had been brought four thousand miles to see.

His own image, sacrificed to Lucifer.

Turning toward the cry, Dongal addressed the guest.

"Something wrong, sir?"

"That painting – the one over the bed. The figure chained to the ground. It has my face."

As if gifted with sight, the servant turned toward the wall. While his features remained expressionless, his voice held a tone of calmness.

"Mr. Kingston, that painting has hung in this room since the old master's days. In fact, it has *always* been here. How can it be *you,* sir?" Shepherd made no reply. "I shall bring you wine. Refreshment might, perhaps, restore you."

"Thank you."

Whatever secrets the painting held, he would not get them from Dongal. Nor would he do his cause any good by protesting. Yet, it was all he could do to prevent his eyes from returning to his face on the wall.

Not until alone did he dare take a second look.

A closer examination did nothing to dispel his fright. The face *was* his, if, in all fairness, he could be said to recognize himself, contorted in hellish agony.

Nothing in Shepherd's life had prepared him for this situation. While his parents were ardent believers in the "great beyond," their son had rejected their views, choosing to believe in the "here and now." Not even Trent's patient, loving explanation of grace and holiness had swayed him.

That he had never altered his opinion was a testimony to the lack of any significant challenge in his life, coupled with a near total avoidance of serious introspection. Trent had warned him such was the case, but Shepherd had not believed him. Now, a former conversation returned with haunting clarity.

"Why should I need religion?" he demanded one day after waiting impatiently for Trent to return from church and prepare their Sunday repast. "God is only for those who need to beg favors."

"Or, to be thankful they don't need to beg favors," Trent dryly pointed out.

"Which are you?"

With a sigh, the professor stared deep into Shepherd's eyes. "I am both, although I choose rather to substitute the word 'ask' for 'beg.' I ask God to protect you, and I thank Him that you have – so far – kept yourself out of serious trouble."

"Don't you pray for yourself?"

"Of course."

"What do you pray for?"

"I pray, with thanks in my heart, for my trials, great and small."

"You're kidding."

"I am not."

"Why would anyone be thankful for trials? Unless he's an out-of-work barrister," Shepherd punned, using the British word to further irritate.

"Because each is a learning experience. Without the ability to grow, one becomes stagnant. I wish to advance in all aspects of knowledge, so that I may use it when I move on."

To which the boy groaned. "By 'move on,' I assume you're referring to ascension into heaven?"

"Absolutely."

"And if there is no heaven?"

"There is."

"Say, for sake of argument, there isn't. What, then? Both your vast accumulation of knowledge and your supplications will have been for naught."

"Obtaining knowledge is never useless. And as for my prayers, if there is no being universally thought to be 'god,' then there is a cosmic intelligence."

"Didn't I see that on an episode of *Space: 1999?*"

"You are being impudent."

"I don't mean to be. I'm serious. If there is no God, won't you feel like a fool?"

"If death is an end, then I suppose I shall never know it, for I shall have ceased to function as a thinking human being. However, I know in my soul that God does exist."

"Then I guess I'll go to hell, because I don't have a soul."

Despite his controlled demeanor, the statement distressed the professor. "Do not say that. Deny God, if you must, but never deny your soul."

"What's the difference?"

"I pray you never find out."

That had ended the discussion. Shepherd wished now he had paid more attention, for he suspected Trent's final prayer would go unheeded by something so godless as a Cosmic Brain.

He was incorrect in only one aspect of his new-founded fear: Trent's *final prayer* would come years after that innocent conversation.

CHAPTER 17

Trent was working at his desk in the study when the pyramid began to glow. He did not notice it until heat radiated onto his hand. Remembering Shepherd's experience and how it had singed the carpet in Shelley Larson's apartment, he shied away.

Not daring to touch it with his finger, he prodded it with the end of his pencil. The eraser spat as the edges melted.

Nodding wisely, for he had anticipated such an eventuality, Trent grabbed the corner of a glass ashtray. Employing the unsharpened end of the pencil as a lance, he shoved the pyramid into the ashtray. A small, square burn mark remained in the wood.

"I've guessed right, haven't I?" he demanded of the object. "You are her instrument. Can you see me, Ericka Elvina?"

He did not expect a verbal reply and was not disappointed. However, his words did elicit a response, for the gold glowed more fiercely.

"You have Shepherd, despite all I could do to prevent it. Where have you taken him?"

The pyramid continued to glow, making the glass ashtray warm to the touch.

"He is not such a fool as you think, Ericka," Trent continued, addressing the pyramid as though it were a conduit to another world. "I have taught him well. Protestations to the contrary, he *does* believe. And that belief will save him from your evil intentions."

A flame flicked at the tip of the pyramid before dying out. The glass grew too hot to touch. Looking around, Trent spied a metal tray. He pushed the ashtray onto it.

"He was baptized as an infant. Did you know that? He belongs to God, not to you or your Master. God will not forsake him."

Although near no electronic equipment, Trent's ears began to ring. Putting his hands over his head did nothing to lessen the intensity of the high-pitched noise. He raised his voice.

"At the age of twelve, he was confirmed into the Christian faith. He knows his prayers."

Over the squeal came a type of inhuman, robotic speech.

Prayers... will ...not ...help him. Your... protection... is impotent.

The thought came through his brain, not his ears, which were nearly deafened by the ringing.

Individual syllables were pronounced carefully, with long separations between words, making it appear the controlling entity had difficulty with its own system of communication. Or that the speaker was unaccustomed to using the English language. A fact Trent knew to be untrue, for Shepherd had assured him Ericka demonstrated proficiency in her speech. This, then, demonstrated a manifestation of weakness, proving the malevolence in his den was not all controlling.

"Yet God is all powerful," Trent coolly pursued. "In a contest between good and evil, the dark powers can never win."

That... is what... you have based... your faith on, Abraham Trent. I know... all about you.... I have... read your mind... through the... instrument... of your destruction.

Trent's eyes went involuntarily to the pyramid. The glow around it had grown so intense, it had lost its shape, appearing almost spherical. The heat had turned red-hot.

"I suspected," Trent agreed, refusing to give in to fear. "That's why you let him steal it, knowing he would bring it to me."

Such an... instrument... was put in place... long ago. In its... long history... it has served well... as a gift... acknowledging one master... while rendering... obedience to... another.

The enigmatical statement made no sense. "The demon," he began, biting his tongue to concentrate on pain and thus enable him to rework the swirling contradictions. "Xilka, Xilka, Besa, Besa. A summons...?"

Smug, haughty laughter filled his brain. *So it has... been supposed... old man. By others... more versed... in the black arts... than you. Did you... try and... conjure it?*

"You know I did not."

The pyramid... is a... fickle present. In its... illustrious history... that supposition has stood... as fact uncontested. No recipient... has ever succeeded... in making it respond.

Backing away, Trent fixed his stare on the object, vainly attempting to combat the overriding presentment of doom. With introspection came an overwhelming sense of being watched and the correction of his error.

"You are not Ericka Elvina."

More tinny laughter, convoluted with traces of insanity. Annoyed that he could determine nothing about the voice, including gender, if, in fact, it possessed one, Trent jutted his chin. The angle served not only to give him an aspect of defiance, it allowed him to see, via peripheral vision, the increasing intensity of the glowing pyramid.

Am I... not?

"No." Less certain than a moment ago.

Whom am I... then? Again, the leering superiority, evoking rage. Trent had seen Ericka Elvina only once, but that glance had been enough to convince him of her unmitigated ego.

"You are the devil incarnate!" Trent shrieked, thrusting a finger at the pyramid. For a moment, the glow subsided, causing him more consternation than if it had exploded into two billion shards of magnetic energy.

You are... both more... and less correct... than you suppose, the voice whined, playing up and down the scale in varying octaves. *But what... you know... or think you know... will not help you... Abraham... Trent.*

"You may kill me, but you cannot destroy the boy."

Destroy him? The gyrating, dizzying laughter in Trent's head increased. *Is that... what you... think? That I... wish to... destroy... him?*

Dumbfounded, Trent pulled back, frantically attempting to regroup. If the Evil did not wish Shepherd's death, when then did it want?

"Nor can you take his soul. That belongs to the God of Light."

If you are... going to play... Daniel Webster with me... Abraham... you had better... have your legal... brief well prepared. Remember... when I made... you doubt? That day... not so... long ago... when I watched you... through Athena's portrait?

"That was you?"

It was I.

"I... held you back. I said the prayers – performed the *legal brief,"* he reiterated, throwing back the reference meant to humiliate.

You wanted to believe in your success, the voice sneered, speaking more normally now, *but I tricked you.* The voice, speaking now in vivid clarity, almost evoked remembrance. Where had he first heard it – at the airport? Out of Ericka Elvina's mouth? No. Ironically, that would have been a relief. It had come to him on a more subliminal level, when he sat alone, hunched over his forbidden manuscripts. The voice had come then, instilling his mind with the intangible presence of Another beside him.

Negligently, Trent had supposed the whisperer to be the ghost of the long-dead author, helping him discover secrets so carefully and foolhardily committed to paper. Aiding him for good. He realized now the grievous mistake. Some one or some thing had allowed him to proceed, but not on God's behalf. Unknowingly, he had assisted Satan.

"No! I will not allow you to pervert me!" This influence, this devil's advocate, attempted to instill doubt. "I will not be swayed from the path of righteousness. I do believe. There is a God. 'God is great; God is good.'"

And I thank him for this food. Amen, the insanity mocked, merging with the incessant ringing in his ears. *You resort to a simple child's prayer for succor, Abraham? How amusing.* Waves of intolerable pressure forced him to scream.

"I did stop you! I did hold you at bay! The woodcut flying from the wall was a farce! I have the power!"

He did not say and hardly dared think that he had secretly passed on this gift to Shepherd. Out of charity, one human being to another.

You discovered much in your immoral manuscripts, Abraham. I read over your shoulder. To whom did the prophesies refer?

"Shepherd is not the one," Trent cried, desperate to place a doubt in the ancient consciousness. "You have made a mistake."

No mistake. Behold.

Ripples of space crossed Trent's line of vision. When the scene cleared, the revelation sent chest pains tearing through his heart.

Shepherd stood alone in a medieval chamber, eyes distended, lips twisted in horror. Before him, ready to escape its canvas prison hovered a beast, so lifelike Trent could almost hear the flutter of wings. Beak parted in silent rage, talons extended, black pupils flashing an unearthly hatred, it posed over a chained boy.

Look at the face in the painting, came the order, though hardly necessary. The old man's eyes were pinned to it the way the chest cavity of living laboratory specimens were held back so elementary students could view the beating auricle. Even a father's protection could not dispel the similarity. The figure represented Shepherd, or more accurately, a painter's rendition of a countenance he had never seen in life, but knew well from unholy premonition.

"Good God! What can this mean?"

The fulfillment of divine inspiration.

"You will sacrifice him to that?"

I will not sacrifice him. He will submit himself.

"What use can he possibly be to you?" Trent begged for a moment's sane consideration. His child, his beloved ward, was a human being, not a devil. What part could he play in Lucifer's Kingdom?

The explanation was forthcoming, but Trent did not understand it. The piercing, lance-sharp whining in his head overwhelmed his cognitive senses. He managed to decipher no more than *False hope.*

False hope.

The malignant enemy had stripped away his purpose for existence.

To his left, the ashtray began to melt. Pooling in nearly perfect circles, the molten glass flamed, streaks of fire escaping the metal tray and dripping to the floor. As each glob struck, it ignited a small area of carpet. The acrid odor of burning fibers quickly filled the room.

Now you know.

"Shepherd! Shepherd!" Trent screamed, praying his words would travel across the psychic link. "Shepherd! Come back to me! For God's sake!"

Either Shepherd could not hear, or he was rooted to the spot, held powerless by the symbolic chains restraining the victim in the canvas.

You waste your breath, the malevolent voice warned Trent. *And you have precious little left. He has made his choice.*

He might have listened, had not a flicker in Shepherd's terrified orbs alerted him otherwise.

"Shepherd, save yourself; remember your prayers," he unselfishly begged. "God is great; God is good." Repeating the words made them seem the mere babbling of a condemned man. He tried harder, with greater faith.

"God is the greatest power in the universe. All others must be subservient to Him. Remember that. Call upon God to save –" He stumbled as flames licked up around his ankles. Doubt came on the spearhead of burning flesh. "– you from temptation. Believe in... mercy."

He had been right all along: faith came easily to those far removed from evil.

Trent shrieked from pain and righteous indignation. "I have sinned, yet I will not succumb!"

So brave a martyr. But martyrs have no right to recruit innocence to their Cause. See to your own tainted soul, Abraham Trent, before it escapes.

"Shepherd, remember! I have given you the key. Use it. Good shall triumph over wickedness."

A wall of shimmering liquid fire engulfed Trent. Just as Shepherd stared at his own face, stricken and immobile, Trent watched as the flesh melted from his hands. Exquisite agony shattered the conventional wisdom that once burned, nerve endings ceased to transmit pain.

"Fight for God's Kingdom!"

As his clothing burst into flame, adhering to his body like an outer layer of skin, Trent lost the power of rational thought. Unable to cry, he writhed, twisted, spun in a semi-circle before crashing to the floor. In a second – the same time required to engender life – his spirit fled his body.

To his mortal essence, that second lasted longer than eternity.

Long after the fire had consumed the earthly remains of Abraham Trent, a pair of eyes continued to observe the proceedings. They were black orbs, watching with calm, evil intent. Behind them, however, simmered a satisfaction older than the Human race.

False hope, they seemed to say. *False hope.* Over and over again in endless repetition.

Neither the quick nor the dead were there to listen.

"It appears the fire started in an ashtray," the firefighter observed, kicking absently at a still-smoldering piece of wood. "The old man was probably smoking. He put his cigar into the ashtray without realizing it was full of paper scraps. I've seen it before. Gum wrappers; sticky notes; a half dozen candy bar papers. The end of the stogie caught the trash and ignited it. In five minutes the desk was engulfed in flames."

The fire chief nodded, turning away from the charred remains of what once had been a human being.

"The medical examiner won't have much to do with that one. Who was he?"

"A professor at SUNY. The building superintendent said there were a lot of rare books up here."

"Too bad. They're ashes, now. Hope they were insured. Where's the family?"

"He lived alone. The 'super told me a young man used to live here with him. Still came in and out a lot. Thought he might have been one of Mr. Trent's former pupils, or something. We're checking with the university, now. Maybe he was his son," he graciously added.

"Yeah, well, don't release the name until we get hold of the kid, just in case. What kind of professor was he?"

"Taught occult sciences. Something like that."

The fire chief grimaced. "When I went to college, we studied math and English. None of this off-the-wall stuff." He turned to survey the damage. "Guess his charms and incantations didn't save him."

While the interior of the flat had been entirely destroyed, one small section of wall had miraculously escaped the inferno. Both firefighters had witnessed such phenomenon before. In their line of work, the unusual was commonplace. Such experience did not prevent the supervisor from throwing back his head in surprise, however, as he observed precisely what had been spared.

"Will you look at that!"

The bright orange of his companion's helmet bobbed and dipped.

"Didn't notice that before," he confessed, picking his way across the debris of burned wood and broken glass. As his heavily booted foot stomped carelessly on a puffball of bloated ash, particles resembling spores ascended around him. "A painting."

"A sketch of some sort," the former student of math and English imperfectly identified. Scrutinizing the perfectly preserved wooden frame, the immaculate glass and the woodcut beneath, he sought an identifying caption. Great his irritation to find none available to elucidate them as to the subject's identity.

Seeing consternation on his chief's face, the subordinate grinned. "Maybe she was the old boy's mother."

"Well, she wasn't his wife," came the derisive snort. "If our professor studied mysticism, she's most likely a witch, or something."

"Must have been a pretty good one, to save herself like this."

Despite his easy banter, the NYFD member felt uncomfortable. He thought he saw the eyes move. Shifting his gaze suspiciously toward his friend, he ascribed the chief's change of mood to the same observation.

"Maybe they burned her at Salem," he pursued, compelled to make small talk. "This was her way of getting back at the establishment."

Neither man moved. The otherworldly allure of the nameless figure held them in her power.

"Think we ought to take it down? It seems a shame to leave her all alone when we go."

"Don't tough her."

They referred to the figure as though she were real, as opposed to being merely ink and paper.

"Maybe the M.E. can I.D. her for us."

"Yeah.... I'd like to know." His avowal was a lie. The chief hoped he would never find out. He had a dreaded superstition that were they to discover her name, the beautiful woman with the large grey irises would haunt them to the grave.

"Creepy sort of place."

When Athena smiled at the observation, both men simultaneously jumped away. Freed from her grip, they inadvertently rubbed shoulders in their hurry to turn their backs on her.

The firefighter resumed his patter. Hearing himself talk was better than taking the chance their lady friend would fill in the void.

"Funny thing, sir. The fire was completely contained before we got here. Didn't burn through the floor to the apartments below; didn't get through the walls to the neighboring apartments."

The chief took up the conversation, asking questions to which he already knew the answer.

"Somebody come in with an extinguisher?"

"No one's admitted to it. The guy next door did say he heard the professor talking to someone just before the fire broke out."

The answer had to be simple. Nothing consequential.

"Oh? Find another body?"

"No. Just the one."

"Then maybe he was on the phone. Or listening to the TV. Sounds get distorted through walls."

"That's probably it."

A glint of metal attracted his attention. With a feeling of doom, the chief pointed to a small golden pyramid perched on the floor. "What's that?" and then, "Careful," he admonished as his lieutenant went to pick it up. "Might be hot."

"Gold doesn't conduct heat," the subordinate reminded his superior, stooping down to pick up the object. "It's heavy, too. Wonder if it's solid gold?"

"Whatever it is, it looks valuable. Better hold onto it."

The fireman started to place the object into a collection bag, then changed his mind. He had no particular reason to hesitate; the bag contained what few items remained intact from the intensity of heat and flames. They had been gathered as evidence and to keep them out of the hands of the curious and the insurance investigators.

"What's wrong?"

"I don't know," the man admitted. Though not a practicing Catholic, he felt compelled to cross himself. An old habit. One he had not resorted to since childhood. "Somehow," he confessed, "it doesn't seem to fit with the rest."

"Don't put it in your pocket, or someone might accuse you of stealing it." Had it been the Hope Diamond, the firefighter would not have been tempted. "Put it with the rest."

The man did as instructed, then stepped away, being careful not to trample any more "mushrooms." He crossed himself a second time.

It was as close as he could get to asking forgiveness from the dead man for transgressions, past and present. Why he thought one Abraham Trent, former SUNY professor, could absolve him of his sins remained unanswered.

The pyramid did not appear on the list of valuables removed from the apartment. No one remembered to question the omission.

Neither the Fire Department nor the police ever identified the former student of Professor Trent's, who may or may not have been his son. The insurance policy on the old man's life went uncollected.

CHAPTER 18

The low, snake-like corridor absorbed all noise, so that his footfalls echoed soundlessly against the enclosing walls. Hand-carved from solid rock by the hammers of one thousand long-dead laborers, the tunnel angled steeply down, toward the bowels of Perdition.

The only light came from regularly placed wall sconces, themselves dug deep into the stone. As the tall, slender form passed one, it flickered. The slight diminution originated not from the stirred air of his passing, but rather from the intensity of his being, radiating with latent energy so intense it might have been the source which originally lit the burning reeds.

Striding between pools of light, the man appeared more shadow than substance, but as he approached another torch, his features sang out in stark prominence. He was a startlingly handsome man with sharply chiseled features, denoting a first born.

While his origins were difficult to place, the slim shapeliness of form, the smooth grace of mannerisms, the aura of absolute superiority would mark him in a crowd.

He was the kind of man to whom a new acquaintance would bow the head, if not the knee, and receive for his unconscious supplication a royal wave of the hand, acknowledging his exulted place in the universe.

Barely above a score of years, there existed about him an impression of timelessness, as though he had been reincarnated in the same form since the beginning of Mankind's existence. Or, possibly, like Dorian Gray, he kept a hidden portrait of himself locked away, using the oils to absorb whatever transgressions he might have committed.

The obsidian irises of what could have been an Eastern European face were alive with passion. Not the type men reserved for women, but of that unique variety bestowed on those who knew the world as their plaything. A casual nod, a twitch of the eyelids and ten thousand men would be put to their deaths without a moment's hesitation.

It might be surmised the man knew no fear: that in his lifetime he had never come face-to-face with his equal. That supposition would be incorrect, but would have pleased the walker, for that was his intent.

Jet black hair hung loosely about his shoulders, melding into the collar of the cape he wore. His style of clothing was old-fashioned, but not out of place in the underground passageway. Here, time had ceased to exist. What had been, what would be, were narrowly confined in the present, although exactly what "present" meant remained elusive.

Pausing a moment in his unholy travel, the walker cocked his head, as if listening to a conversation. His long locks swayed with the movement, revealing slightly elongated ears. No one would ever mistake him for an elf or a faerie, however, for his sharp canines, revealed when he smiled, marked him for a far different breed of supernatural being.

Whatever voices he heard were not transmitted audibly. They originated from far across space, so distant it could not be calculated in miles.

The information he received seemed to please. At his acknowledgment of pleasure, the walls breathed easier. When the young master evinced satisfied, life, in all its myriad shapes and forms, received permission to continue.

The journey recommenced. The angle of the tunnel slanted ever downward, so that one unaccustomed to the steep descent would lose his balance, falling upon the cold, unyielding stone for support. Receiving none, such an unfortunate guest would cry out, refusing to go deeper, for the final destination surely had to be the bowels of hell.

The prince, suffering no such trepidation, recommenced his journey with long, swift strides. Eventually reaching the farthest length of the passageway, this lone man stopped before a door of black stone, so dark and impenetrable it appeared to have been made of onyx. He smiled again, this time at his own reflection which jumped out at him through the distant firelight.

Attired entirely in black like a monk, which he was not, his face shone as the only discernible image. Suspended six feet from the foot of the stone floor, he seemed the bodiless man from a second-rate peep show.

The analogy would not have pleased him. It was as well he did not make the connection.

Flashing his left hand out in a stiff-armed salute, he waved it over an invisible sensor. The door slid back. He entered. It closed behind him. All transpired without a sound.

Ara entered a chamber the exact opposite of the sloping, twisting, torch-lit corridor. As the egress sealed, an entirely new world sprang into being, as had Athena from Zeus' head.

A new world, in the sense of change, for the rough-hewn, cavernous apartment was as old as the hills. Those same hills which had witnessed the briny oceans spewing forth multi-celled creatures; the same rock upon which tree-dwelling apes first walked upright. The exact burning fire which beheld cavemen scratching images of their hunts on soot-blackened walls.

"New," in this ungodly seat of worship, dated back to the birth of God.

Genuflecting at the knee, the young man shed his mantle of impenetrability, leaving it behind the way a snake gyrated out of dead skin. Unlike the reptile, that ancient representative of evil, Ara would redress himself in the same arrogance he checked at the door. But not here: not in the presence of the Father.

Immediate obligation completed, Ara, prince of Satan's Kingdom, removed his cloak, baring his chest to the rage of the magnificent flames burning in a hearth so great, it easily accommodated the logs of twenty full-grown trees. Not close enough to be singed from the heat, he nevertheless steeled himself against the searing temperatures.

Ara's master was a fickle God, one moment basking in his supplication, the next destroying what He had created. Just as ancient scribes of that other Deity had admonished their followers to fear the wrath of He who ruled the heavens, so too did Ara fear his liege.

The difference between the two behemoths in this regard, being slight.

Stripping himself naked, the youth bowed again, this time at the waist. When assured his worship would be accepted, he crossed, barefoot, to a round stone table immediately to his left. Amid the hiss and crackle of the conflagration, his footfalls on the hardened earth were absorbed into the greater whole.

Humbly retrieving a soul-black robe lined with blood-red silk, he slipped his arms through the flowing sleeves. Flexing his rippling muscles, Ara allowed himself a moment to absorb the raging energy generated by the costume before clasping a wide, unadorned length of supple gold, around his middle. The interwoven tentacles of the belt, of the type which might have been spun by a gigantic spider, caught the reflected glow, casting a billion sparkles outward, toward the Master's portal.

Also on the table lay a ring of gold. Wrapping his fingers about it the way a child clutched a precious toy, Ara warmed it with his body heat before threading the loop through the wedding ring finger of his left hand. Like bonding ceremonies throughout time, this ritual, too, represented a union of like spirits.

Not to profess undying love, but rather to pledge one's will to another.

A ruby set in the jewelry, the size and intensity of a man's iris, stared back at its earthly possessor, both impatient and implacable.

Never having lived, the precious jewel seemed in no hurry to die.

Silently communicating with the troth, Ara's lips moved reverently, praying words incapable of translation. Only when reaffirming his intentions had been fully comprehended did he make a thirty degree turn to face another table, which had been, until that moment, obscured by a preternatural space, devoid of light.

Like the first, this three-legged table consisted of rock, but carved entirely from one boulder, the way Michelangelo's *Pieta* had been sculptured from marble. Upon it lay a ceremonial dagger, the ornate hilt heavily encrusted with diamonds after the fashion of a civilization which prized appearances and the status of earthly wealth.

Beside it, standing guard duty like a lone sentinel, sat a chalice, so plain in its simplicity it might have appeared out of place, but for the inner shine radiating from metal lips.

I am hungry, it communicated to the petitioner. *Feed me.*

Acknowledging the tacit command with a brief down-casting of his lids, Ara's hand trembled slightly as he grasped the vessel in his right hand. Only then did he assume control of the knife.

In contrast to the temperature of the chamber, which waxed and waned according to penchant, this instrument felt corpse cold. No amount of heat, whether from the fire or the man's flesh, would ever warm it. To a soul who begged for mercy and received none, it could be likened to God's heart.

Clasping both objects to his breast, Ara glided toward the fireplace. He did not dare glance into the lapping, orange-red-blue flames, but kept his eyes averted. An observer, had there been one, might have remarked that Ara hesitated staring into the intensity, for fear of what he might see emerging from the furnace.

One second, two passed without further activity. Then, slowly, with the motions of an old man, Ara bowed his head. His lips moved. The muscles in his jaw quivered. Whatever words he prayed were lost in the angry snapping of the inferno.

Without the addition of one single log, the flames leapt in anticipation. This was Ara's cue. Lifting his head, he transferred the chalice to his left hand and the dagger to his right. Pulling back the flowing sleeve of the robe, he kissed the blade, then made a deep, vertical incision in his forearm. The effort was not without cost, though the black eyes betrayed little of the pain he endured.

This was not a place to display weakness.

As the blood merrily gurgled from the potentially fatal wound, Ara collected it in the chalice, taking extreme care not a drop should be spilled, or worse, splashed onto the fabric of his robe. That would target him for the ultimate sacrifice, something he would avoid *at any price.*

Despite his overt rendition of worship, Ara had no intention of offering his mortal body. Blood was precious enough, without adding the final ingredient. One mistake, no matter how trivial, would mean his life.

Although the agony of the bloodletting elicited excruciating pain, causing his skin to drench itself in a sheen of greasy perspiration, his hand never wavered, his tensed muscles holding the collection cup firm. Not until the bleeding staunched of its own accord, filling the receptacle two-thirds full, did he dare move.

Allowing a minute outpouring of relief that the operation had terminated successfully, Ara licked his lips, pink tongue running carefully over bone-white teeth. No other cut, no injury of any sort must tear his flesh, for that, too, would invite the Recipient to take other gifts, not as freely offered.

Setting the chalice on the floor, then backing away, least he inadvertently knock it, Ara pressed the flat side of the dagger to the gaping incision on his forearm. Eyelids fluttering shut, he employed what powers of concentration were left him, healing the wound.

As it had countless times before, two chasms of severed flesh reached out to one another, at first hesitantly touching, like strangers performing a mating dance, then consummating their foreplay by painstakingly knitting together, two separate entities becoming one.

When satisfied not the faintest semblance of a scar remained, Ara sank gratefully to his knees, a limp bag of bones, tendons, sinews and pious gratitude.

Another prayer followed, longer this time, more intricate. Written with the cadence of poetry, his invocation brought into open adornment the worship he held for the unseen deity.

Supplications finally at an end, Ara rose awkwardly to his feet, swayed a moment, then steadied himself with internal fortitude. Weakened from self-inflicted anemia, the intensity of inner conflict kept his spirit at a fever pitch.

With the acceptance of one who has performed his duty, he shoved the blade beneath the golden sash, then placed both hands around the chalice, cupping it for protection from the heat.

Perhaps sensing his actions were less humble than resentful, the fire rose in indignation, flames leaping for him with mind-numbing purpose. He reacted quickly, but not fast enough to prevent his eyebrows from being singed.

Interpreting the action in the only way possible, Ara raised the goblet, for the first time looking directly into the spitting flames. Making eye contact with an ill-defined shape lurking behind the red-hot embers, he flung his life's fluid into the fire. When the intensity of the blaze overgrew its bounds, spilling across the floor like raging flood waters over a dam, he knew his offering had been accepted.

This time the fire did not burn the supplicant, but merely licked his form before retreating back from whence it came.

Not without gratitude Ara retreated, never turning his back on the demon hovering in the flames until reaching the safety of the table.

Breathing heavily, he removed the belt and then the robe, always cognizant of the fact no errant drop of blood should stain the silk. Before donning his own clothes, the naked youth gripped his fists tightly, until the knuckles appeared as uncovered bone. Confidence restored, he threw back his head in defiant contemplation of the sated spirit within the fire.

"Soon," he vowed. "Soon I shall have a shepherd, Father, to tend *my* kingdom whilst I rule without the threat of usurpers. It is time, Father, for the old to give way to the young. Time," he added in a whisper, lost to all but unearthly ears, "for the prophesy to be fulfilled."

With a smugness of one who believed destiny favored him, Ara removed the ring, placing it on the table. The robe and belt followed, folded and positioned exactly as before. The dagger he held longer, staring at it with introspection before returning it and the chalice to the smaller table.

Time and prophesy. He had waited all his life for the coming struggle. The pieces had fallen into place. Let the games begin.

From her temple called Parthenon where she had returned, Athena knowingly smiled. Being the goddess of wisdom was a great asset. It allowed her to see more than other, lesser gods. It augmented her sense of superiority.

Gently stroking the owl, her favored pet, and receiving for her trouble a blink from its magnificently round eyes, she pressed her hands together, palms touching. She did not bestow a blessing, but rather congratulated herself.

Let the games begin.

Indeed. Ara was not the only one impatient for the final contest.

Time and prophesy played a role in all the destinies of the principle athletes. That none knew precisely the prowess of the players against whom they would pit themselves fell under the slightly reworded colloquialism, *Whom God destroys He first makes impervious.*

The moon hung in transition, half black, half white. Its rays penetrated the small, narrow rectangular window of Shepherd's bedroom, falling upon the sleeper. Weak and impotent against the backdrop of the fire raging far below, they nevertheless disturbed the tranquility of repose.

Moaning in a dream-trance, Shepherd raised an arm, grasping for something too elusive to touch. He was back in New York, in Ericka's apartment, following her down a long, twisting, snake-like corridor. She taunted, daring him to follow. Titillated and frightened, eager and cautious, Ericka seemed to understand his conflict, for her features, made more beautiful in the torchlight, smiled tenderly.

"Come," she commanded though lips which did not move.

"I will follow you anywhere," he avowed, passion rising.

"Anywhere?"

"Anywhere."

She laughed, a coy, delicate sound of satisfaction. She beckoning and that emboldened him.

Without moving, Ericka dissolved into thin air. Shepherd cried, hurried forward, stumbling against her bedroom door, no longer wood, but stone as thick as a man's skull. Too solid for his mortal frame to pass, he bounced back. Fists pounding against the unyielding barrier, he cried, "Let me in!".

"One must be careful what one asks." Not a warning, but a challenge.

"Let me in. I want you," he begged.

"Not nearly as much as I want you," Ericka retorted in a voice assuming the lust he craved to hear. "Use your mind, Shepherd. Your mind is the key; your mind has the power. Cross the threshold."

"I cannot," he protested, attempting to turn the doorknob with frantic energy.

"Use your mind. That is the only way you may enter."

"No," he sobbed. "I am not like you. I am human."

"You have the Gift."

"No, no, no," yet he did know. Struggling against the three-dimensional world, Shepherd concentrated, visualizing himself on the other side of the door. To encourage him, Ericka's spirit wrapped her arms around his body, pressing wet, red, voluptuous lips to his.

"Come to me. I want you. I need you. We have been separated too long, my shepherd."

And then he found himself on the other side, drawing her flesh to his flesh, tearing at her clothes in a frenzy of need Before he had begun his consummation, however, an unholy shriek froze his blood. He worried, innocently, he had inflicted hurt, but reality proved far more heinous.

Tearing away, Shepherd staggered back, only to be struck from above by the vulture, freed from its oil and canvas cage. Shielding his face, he stumbled, lost direction and pitched forward. Reeling, almost too late, his trajectory carried him toward the living image of Calvary. Reversing in terror, he hurtled to the right, where he supposed Ericka to be.

Not finding her, he fell, face down onto the carpet, the mad beating of wings pummeling his body. Out of all proportion to size, the vulture dominated the youth, ripping his skin, tearing away exposed flesh with unnatural talons.

"Save me!" he wept, curling into a protective ball. "Save me."

Save me! a voice repeated, but it did not originate with Ericka. Shivering at the plea, coming from so unexpected a source, Shepherd rolled away, exposed eyes riveting on the painting. There, come to life as surely as the bird, writhed the chained victim. Arms outstretched, the boy with a face so like his own, begged for salvation.

"Save yourself!" Shepherd ordered, then immediately regretted the heartless command as the painted figure began to sob. Responding with an empathy outshining his own dire predicament, Shepherd crawled toward the wall. "I *will* save you," he promised.

An empty vow.

With a mad screech of unrequited desire, the raven landed on Shepherd's head, weighing it down. Darkness encompassed him. With fading consciousness, he smelled fire. Burned rug; singed carpet. The unmistakable scent of charred paper.

A familiar odor. Too familiar, though he had never before smelled so overwhelming a combination. Blackness swelled, leaving only the red of the avian's eyes to color his world.

"Trent," he sobbed. "Trent, where are you?"

It was past the power of his friend to answer.

He had gone beyond, to a time and a space Shepherd denied.

Slipping away into swirling mists, the beginnings of faith touched the heretic's heart.

Too little, too late, he heard, succumbing to the pseudo-death of sleep.

Had it not been Trent's voice, he might have disbelieved.

CHAPTER 19

Shepherd did not want to wake, but the oppressive heat deprived him of escape. Ripping at the collar of his shirt, then screaming in the dull, ineffective sounds of tortured sleep, he shot bolt upright, red-rimmed eyes fixated with horror.

Vision clearing, Shepherd beheld a man standing by the fireplace. He did not recognize him. He had not been not part of the nightmare. Neither mentor nor avian, the stranger had no place in the recently departed netherworld, where actions, situations and emotions were dictated by the caprices of an over-active imagination.

If the dreamer were fortunate.

Hand to his head, more to fend off blows from the nightmare rather than any threat this new individual posed, he mumbled, "Trent," as the last vestiges of sleep fell away.

"Beg pardon, sir?" Softly spoken, the low, sibilant interrogative sounded concerned, eliciting both gratitude and embarrassment.

"You're Dongal, aren't you?"

"Yes, sir."

"I didn't mean to startle you. I was caught in the grip of a nightmare. I haven't had bad dreams like that since I was a child."

"It is, perhaps, the fact that you find yourself in a strange place," the servant offered with more doubt than conviction. Shepherd would have had it otherwise, but brushed his suspicions aside.

"You're probably right." Glancing at his wrist, he frowned in irritation. "What time is it? My watch has stopped."

"Nearly suppertime. I have brought a basin of water and a towel. The master thought you might like to refresh yourself before making an appearance at his table."

Until that moment Shepherd had taken for granted there would be running water and toilet facilities. Finding himself without the most basic trappings of civilization disconcerted him.

"Your master is a thoughtful host."

"It is the least he can do, sir. For so honored a guest."

If this were the "least," Shepherd wondered what the "most" would be. For the first time, he suspected the distance between the two were closer than he dared surmise.

But it would not do to display fear to a servant. He forced a smile.

"There's a great deal I have to learn about your country. I hope to have the opportunity of seeing much. I'm a photographer. A photojournalist, if you will."

Dongal bowed slightly, then resumed his business of tidying the apartment.

"I am afraid I do not know to what you refer, sir."

"I take pictures, and occasionally write descriptions to explain the subject matter."

"You – are a painter?" Dongal posed the question from kindness rather than any desire to solicitation information.

"No. I work with a camera." The blank stare did not encourage. "Let me show you."

Disregarding the servant's blindness, Shepherd swung out of bed, forgetting his dream-weakened condition. His legs buckled and he would have fallen, had not Dongal anticipated the event and stepped in to grab him.

"I'm sorry," Shepherd muttered, wrapping his arms around the man's powerful shoulders. Dongal immediately retreated.

"You must never apologize to me."

"Why not?"

"I am only a servant, here to see to your comfort. It would be out of place to seek kindness for that which is my duty."

"I was being polite," Shepherd disagreed. "Where I come from, politeness is considered a virtue."

"You will discover few such virtues here, sir." The threat, if such it were, caused the visitor to shudder. "I trust you are strong enough now to wash. The master is waiting."

This time, Shepherd could not mistake the warning.

"You... are afraid of the king?"

No reply confirmed the statement. Thanking his lucky stars at his status as guest and not serf, Shepherd tested his legs, found them steady and crossed to the low wardrobe.

"Kindly thank Eldrich for me," he continued, unzipping the suitcase. "I appreciate him bringing my luggage from the plane."

"It is not my place to speak to Eldrich, sir."

Shepherd shrugged. "Then I shall thank him, myself." When he did not find that which he sought, Shepherd searched through his other case. He found his clothing in order, but no camera or film containers.

Irritated and alarmed, he emptied the items, discovering his toiletries and a small mirror he had packed as a jest. For a moment, the sight offered relief.

"Well, Trent, the master cannot be a vampire, or he would have taken the looking glass."

The thought of his old friend stirred longings and with them a disturbing premonition that things were not as they should be. The idea of fire recurred: fire contained in a monstrous hearth and fire unrestrained in a familiar room. Perspiring under the influence of tremendous heat, he drew back from his suitcase before realizing the discomfort came not from the hearth but a subliminal impression.

An overwhelming sense of loss struck, and he nearly doubled over.

"Trent? Trent?" This time, the servant did not mistake the query and made no reply. Impressions of an inferno assaulted Shepherd, and above, or rather through them, the words, *Shepherd, remember. I have given you the key. Fight for God's Kingdom!*

In panic, the youth to whom the last cries of a tormented soul had been directed, searched the pocket of his overcoat. Relief equivalent to salvation filled his mind as he discovered the parting gift. A victory. But it did not explain the missing items.

"Where is the rest of my property?" he demanded, removing Trent's packet and hiding it more securely in the toe of a shoe. Wild fear flashed behind Dongal's eyes.

"That is all I was directed to bring. Is something missing?"

"Yes. My camera and film."

"I know nothing of it."

Biting his lip, Shepherd dismissed the problem. He did not suspect Dongal.

"Never mind. It is a matter of no consequence."

Again, a bow from the servant. "You will wash now, sir?"

The master does not like to be kept waiting.

"Of course."

Shepherd had never washed in a basin of cold water, much less attempted to shave and refresh himself with such amenities. He completed the task quickly, ran a comb through his hair, then debated whether to change clothes. His traveling suit was wrinkled and his shirt stained with perspiration. Yet Ericka told him the customs of the country were casual. Using that as his excuse, he declared himself ready.

In truth, Shepherd did not wish to undress. While not unduly modest, the thought of stripping down to undergarments frightened him. As little protection as the suit offered, depriving himself of comfort seemed unnecessary and dangerous. Any state of nakedness also brought him closer to the chained victim in the painting. Placing a separation between them seemed wise.

"I will show you the way."

Following Dongal, Shepherd had the eerie feeling of abandoning sanctuary. Only the thought of meeting Ericka emboldened him to proceed.

The sight of the dining room staggered. Dominated by a huge, dark-wood banquet table which extended wall-to-wall, fifty men could have fit at opposing sides without crowding. Six mammoth candelabras sat atop a richly brocaded cream-colored tablecloth, each holding twelve candles. Recently lit, little wax had spilled down the sides. As testimony to the stillness of the air, none of the small flames wavered.

Highly decorative china, sparkling with gold accents rested on matching chargers. In contrast, plain silverware, consisting only of forks and knives, were placed one to a side, forks to the left. There were no napkins, making Shepherd speculate that, like Anna, he would be required to remark on their absence.

Tapestries lined the stark stone walls, but unlike those in the entranceway, these depicted graphic hunting scenes with the spilling of blood the one outstanding theme. As a stimulant to appetite, the guest found it held the opposite effect.

Late to arrive, Shepherd found the young king already seated at the head of the table. Contrary to expectations, the youth rose to greet his guest.

"I am Ara. I bid you welcome." After formally bowing, an act Shepherd copied, the monarch extended a hand. "This, I believe, is the customary greeting in your country." While he toyed with innocence, Shepherd suspected Ericka had versed him well in Western manners.

"Yes, sir."

Although only two syllables, Shepherd had trouble articulating, for the king's countenance struck his so forcefully, he nearly lost the power of speech. Had he not known better, he would have sworn some prior friendship. Unable to dismiss the impression, he stumbled on. "Forgive my boldness, Your Grace, but –"

A wave of the hand prevented further comment. "I am Ara; master, here. All you see – and much you do not see – belong to me. I believe Miss

Elvina has told you that I do not stand on ceremony. Ah, I see that she has," he added, staring critically at Shepherd's attire.

"I meant no disrespect," Shepherd flushed, regretting his *faux pas*.

"None taken. You see? You may hold Miss Elvina to her word. She is my *most trusted* servant." Shepherd's blush deepened. "I chose an incorrect word? Or is it that you resent the fact she is my *servant?*"

The guest backed down from the challenge, but not far enough.

"In New York she controlled an empire of her own."

"A 'Wall Street wizard,' was she not?" Shepherd nodded, noting with trepidation the use of past tense. "So I understand. Not from her own lips, but from others. With me, she is... more than modest." He laughed alone at the private joke.

"Everyone admired her – envied her. She *is* as successful as enigmatical."

"Secretive," Ara corrected, noting the verb change. "But certainly successful. How *is* it you came to catch her fancy?" Standing back, he critically eyed the newcomer. "Yes. I see you are a pretty boy. Not so tall as me," he bragged, "and not as handsome. But you have... appeal. What do you say, Dongal?" he suddenly demanded, spinning on the servant who had, until that moment, blended into a shadowed corner of the room.

Shepherd thought that an odd question to put to a blind man, but said nothing as Dongal stepped out of the darkness. Bowing to his master, he answered with perfect sincerity.

"You are the most handsome man I have ever beheld, master."

"It is well you agreed." Ara returned his piercing gaze to Shepherd, lightening it with boyish anticipation. "He was not always sightless. His... affliction is of a rather recent nature. Is it not, Dongal?"

"Yes, master."

"I am sorry to hear it," Shepherd interrupted the private conversation. "Perhaps something can be done for him. There are many medical advances in the United States which might restore his vision. If he may accompany Ericka when she returns –"

"Miss Elvina will not be returning. Her work there is done."

Although warned by Ericka, hearing such finality from the king sent shock waves through Shepherd. Holding down a panic attack, he looked from servant to master, then threw caution to the wind, believing that whatever Ericka's position with the "master," she would save him.

"I was invited here to make a photographic study of your country, sir. Yet when I unpacked my bags, I discovered my camera and film missing."

Ara's face assumed a pose of rage. "What is this?" he demanded of his servant. "There are items missing from Mr. Kingston's luggage? How can this be? You had personal charge of them."

An expression of pure horror took hold of Dongal, diminishing him as he quavered before his lord. Shepherd quickly came to his rescue.

"There was another man – Eldrich, I believe is his name. He brought my luggage from the plane. Perhaps he –"

Shepherd immediately regretted his well-intentioned interference.

"Eldrich is my favored servant. It is impossible he should have stolen your camera. And film," Ara slyly added, imparting the distinct impression the news had not come as a surprise.

Striding across the room, Ara raised his left hand and struck the hapless servant. Dongal reeled backward, crashing into the wall with a dull thud.

"Have you now added theft to your many accomplishments?" Holding a finger to his bleeding mouth, Dongal made no attempt to deny the charge. Ara brusquely nodded before addressing his guest. "You see how it is here."

"Yes. I see how it is."

"This is most unfortunate. *Ericka* will be displeased that your items have been stolen. You can hardly be expected to complete your assignment without the proper tools."

"I could send for another camera," Shepherd tried, hoping against the obvious. "If you will allow me to communicate with my friend in New York, he will gladly send me another."

"As to that, I am afraid it is impossible. We have no telephone service, as I am sure you were informed. Neither do we have a postal service."

"How... how do you communicate with the world?"

"We find we have no need for... communication. It has long been the policy of our kings that we allow no outside corruption to taint our culture. My step-father followed those rules. I shall continue the tradition."

"But Ericka lived and functioned in Manhattan –"

"Ah. Yes. Ericka." Ara repeated the name with particular emphasis, raising Shepherd's ire in that he implied more than casual familiarity. "She was the exception. My step-father wished that she go to New York. But he is dead, now. The ring has been passed to me. I do not wish Ericka to leave my side."

"But she *is* so successful," Shepherd pleaded despite the futility. "She made a great deal of money for – you."

"So she did." The smile slowly returned to Ara's finely chiseled features, peculiarly deepening the cleft in his chin. "But, what use have I for money? Without contact with your so-called civilization, I find it rather superfluous."

"With money, you could build schools, hospitals. Bring your subjects out of the Dark Ages."

Ara did not appreciate the observation. He scowled, eyebrows melding into a "V" over the bridge of his nose. "Ours is a very ancient and well-revered culture. It has stood for thousands of years. No one here complains of living in the 'Dark Ages.' Do they, Dongal?"

"No, master."

"We find our way of life perfectly suited to our needs. But I am forgetting myself. You are, no doubt, hungry after your long journey. Pray, be seated."

A shiver ran down Shepherd's spine. It occurred to him that while much "praying" went on in this strange country, little found itself directed further upward than Ara's imposing frame.

Unless, of course, he meant "prey." *Prey, be seated.* In that case, the guest had little doubt who the "prey" would be. And what Trent would call it.

The Most Dangerous Game.

Seeing that his guest would hold his tongue, Ara reseated himself. Uncertain of his place, Shepherd hesitated. Dongal supplied the answer by drawing back a chair on Ara's right.

In obstinacy, the guest repeated a previous mistake with a bold, "Thank you." Dongal cringed as Ara stiffened an arm in his direction.

"Bring us food."

"Yes, master."

In his haste to leave, Dongal stumbled into the table, righted himself, mumbled an apology, then scurried out.

"I trust the meal will be to your liking. I ordered it especially for you."

"That was most kind."

"Lamb's tongue and heart of stag. Plus a blood pudding, dark and rich. I favor that, myself. The blood is the life."

Shepherd's eyes narrowed, suspecting the king mocked. Determining he did not, the revelation frightened him, for he would have preferred the contrary.

In due time, two manservants delivered the steaming food. After serving Ara, generous portions were heaped on Shepherd's plate. Assignment completed, both disappeared, leaving the pair alone.

"Eat," Are ordered, a fork full of meat suspended before his mouth. "I wish you to keep your strength."

Believing he would need it, Shepherd forced himself to comply, hoping his stomach would not rebel against the foreign sustenance. Chewing without breathing, he managed to swallow with only minimal offense to his uninitiated taste buds.

Supping in silence, Shepherd survived the ordeal, only daring speak once the plates had been removed.

"Will Miss Elvina be joining us this evening?"

"Alas, she is busy," Ara lightly dismissed, pretending not to see the disappointment. "But do not fear. You will see her again."

"In the morning?"

"We shall see."

As a promise, it hung like a broken vow.

CHAPTER 20

After supper, the king directed his guest into a chamber across from the dining hall. Like the bedroom, a large fireplace dominated the room. Oversized armchairs, draped with spun cloth of red and gold were set in a semicircle around the hearth. Similar in appearance to other castle furnishings, the chairs appeared to have been designed for men of gigantic proportions. No one Shepherd had yet seen came close to fitting them. Mentioning that fact, however, seemed a breach of etiquette.

Ventilation came from huge windows reaching to within a foot of the ceiling. All were covered by thick draperies, tightly drawn. Shepherd did not recall seeing them on his approach, so he presumed the room faced west. Lacking particular cause, he would have laid a bet iron bars fortified the casements, giving rise to the unpleasant speculation that guests may be invited in, but departing presented an entirely different scenario.

A fire, recently set, hungrily devoured logs the size of limbs. Placed directly on the stone flooring which lacked a grate, adequate ventilation prevented smoke from escaping. Although summer outside, thick walls kept it at bay, giving the interior the cool dampness of a cave. Without the warmth and broad, flickering light, the interior would have been utterly cheerless.

Unlike other rooms to which Shepherd had been exposed, the den featured heavy panels of unstained wood, so seamlessly placed he could not detect where one board ended and another began. Devoid of tapestries, paintings, bookcases or reading matter of any sort, a recumbent had no amusement other than the contemplation of his thoughts, or whatever conversation he could extract from a servant.

Shying away from the fire, for he had developed a fear of it since his startlingly realistic dream impressions, Shepherd chose a chair furthest away from the flames. Harboring no such inhibitions, Ara placed himself dead center, basking in the warmth.

"Come," he invited. "Sit closer. The nights are cold. You will suffer, sitting over there."

"Then why are chairs placed in such a manner?" Shepherd countered. While meant as a delaying tactic, for he knew now Ara would have his way in all matters, the question held relevance.

The master laughed, delighted at the opportunity to display his ascendancy.

"The answer should be apparent, even to one unaccustomed to the privileges of rank. Those who sit closest to the fire, and thus to me, are favored. Those placed at the end freeze to death while paying their homage. Now come: sit closer. I – request it."

Realizing that to lose Ara's sheen of politeness could easily equate to certain death, Shepherd complied. Copying the master's technique, he held out his hands to warm them. Only then did he appease the king.

"I should not want you to catch a chill. Such ailments have been known to be fatal. It is explained by our healers that once the chest is weakened, evil spirits creep into the body, destroying it from the inside out."

"You believe that?"

Ara gravely nodded. "Most certainly."

"Have you never heard of germs? Bacteria? It is not evil spirits, but a disease process which kills. Treatment with antibiotics cures that which beads and rattles cannot," he sourly added.

Ara frowned, failing to appreciate his guest's deprivation of manners.

"Be cautious," he warned with intent. "You will find your science does not work in this kingdom. Cling to the past – *your* past – and you will perish. Most unpleasantly. You have come to a new reality, Mr. Kingston. The 'old' rules do not apply."

"But surely they must," Shepherd protested, averting his face from the intense heat. "We are all human beings, descended from a common ancestor."

Ara contemplated the statement, closing his eyes to draw from memory an appropriate response.

"Darwin," he finally articulated, taking care to enunciate the word, as though the syllables were difficult to pronounce. "Darwin was a fool. He saw no more than the nose before his face. Which is an interesting expression, is it not, inasmuch as one cannot see one's nose." He smiled at his cleverness, prompting Shepherd to ask, "Did Ericka teach you that?"

A momentary confusion crossed the master's face before he grasped the implication.

"Yes," he slowly replied. "She is a multi-linguist. The only one in this country. Having no desire to leave, the rest of us have no use of such knowledge."

"Yet you speak English; as does Dongal," Shepherd protested. "You have seen fit to learn the language of international commerce. Surely," he pursued, "you would not have studied it for my benefit alone."

"For you I would do much," came the enigmatically reply. "Your coming has long been anticipated."

"But how? I met Ericka less than a month ago."

"You saw the painting in her apartment? Not a perfect likeness. Call it a likeness in progress. I was not sure, you see. Not *completely* sure. I had some details, but not all."

"I don't understand," Shepherd protested, shifting his weight in the chair, then crossing his legs to cover his discomfiture.

"But you will. Be not impatient. Your time will come."

Meant as a warning, Shepherd took it as such. The huge chair augmented Ara's dire premonition, for it created the effect of making the newcomer feel like a helpless child.

"My time? For what?"

"To fulfill your destiny, Shepherd Kingston."

Whether Ara meant for him to pursue the ominous subject or not, Shepherd could not hold his tongue. He spoke, despite the sudden correlation between that sentiment and of having eaten tongue for supper.

"The painting in my chamber – the similarity to me is much more accurate." Ara nodded, copying his guest's style by placing one leg over the other. "How could that be?"

Shepherd had not meant to be amusing, but his concern prompted a smile from the host.

"It... altered," he explained as if the phenomenon were of no consequence. The guest leaned to his right, a subtle desperation highlighted by the crackle of wood in the fireplace.

"You mean it was repainted?"

"No."

"Then how was it changed?"

"Do not bother me for details. It is enough I have told you what I have."

Squirming under a direct light which suddenly outlined his face, Shepherd attempted to blink away his mounting doubt.

"Dongal said it was very ancient."

Casually sweeping his left hand through the air, Ara's gesture had the effect of redirecting the light. Rather than move it away from his guest's face, he increased it, forming an amorphous spotlight on his subject.

"Did he? I am afraid Dongal speaks too much. It is a flaw; one I have tried hard to exorcise. He is usually more obedient to my wishes."

In a display of free will meant to impart the fact Ara dealt with a man and not a sheep, Shepherd repositioned his chair away from the beam. His effort went for naught, as the firelight followed him, further increasing Ara's mirth. Whether or not he could read Shepherd's mind, his expression conveyed the idea of his guest's *childlike disobedience.*

"What of his free will?" Shepherd continued, finally dispelling humor into ire.

"Free will," Ara snapped, "is the sole domain of royalty."

"Of which you are the only one?"

"Precisely."

"What of Ericka?"

"It is her pleasure to serve me in all ways," the king easily decided, relaxing back into his chair. "Her will is my will."

"I cannot accept that."

"You will accept that and much more before your purpose here is complete."

Placing both hands on the armrests, Shepherd again attempted to move. This time, however, he found the chair firmly rooted into place. The disconcerting revelation did not dispel his desire for argument.

"God gave all Men free will."

"God?" Ara's eyes opened with wonder. "You preach God's teachings to me?" And then, more directly, "I was lead to understand you did not believe in God."

"Who told you that?" Shepherd demanded, feeling sick at the pit of his stomach. He did not recall ever mentioning religion, or his beliefs, to anyone but Trent.

"I know many things."

Angered by his inability to extract one elucidative statement from his host, Shepherd rocked in the chair, speaking over his ineffectual actions.

"How? What else do you know?"

His action and the tone of demand finally succeeded in offending the ruler.

"Did not Ericka warn you about evoking my ire? You would do well to remember her admonition."

"I beg your pardon, master," Shepherd hastily replied, relinquishing his hold of the chair while falling naturally into the expression used by Dongal. He chose his words well, for Ara immediately relented.

"Apology accepted. But remember your place, Otherworlder. I am unaccustomed to reminding my souls more than once. Infractions are very severely punished."

Shivering at the use of the word "soul," though he knew it to be an old-fashioned term for a king's "subjects," Shepherd bowed his head.

"I do not wish to displease."

"I should think not. Enough said. We will take wine."

No time elapsed before the door opened and Dongal appeared, balancing a tray upon which he had placed a decanter and two glasses, both already filled with wine. The crystal looked precisely the same as that in Ericka's apartment, but before Shepherd had time to comment, a scene broke out.

"What do you mean, handing me a goblet I have not seen you pour?" Muscles in his neck taut with fury, Ara pushed away the offering. "You think to poison me!"

"No, master."

"Drink it yourself," Ara ordered, shoving the glass back. "Drink it all, to the last drop."

In utter terror, Dongal brought the goblet to his lips, then hesitated. Noting his anxiety, Ara shot a look of pure hatred toward Shepherd.

"This is how it is," he explained. "A dog wishes his freedom, and so thinks to kill his owner. But a dog cannot rise above his station. A dog is meant to be beaten into submission."

Shocked by the accusation, Shepherd attempted to defuse the situation.

"I do not believe the wine is poisoned, your excellency. I have spoken to Dongal. He is loyal to you."

"Is he? You know so much? Then drink the wine, yourself. Drink it," he menacingly added, "as proof of your fealty to me. Give him the glass," Ara directed, "and let us see the mettle of his conviction."

Trembling profusely, Dongal handed over the wine, making no attempt to establish eye contact and thus prove the drink untainted.

Having gone too far, Shepherd unhesitatingly put the glass to his lips and drank, not taking breath until the entire contents were consumed. Finishing with a look of triumph, he stared at Ara, expecting to see an expression of contrition. He beheld a far different expression.

Instead of displaying contriteness at his false accusation, the master appeared radiant, as though it were he who had protested Dongal's innocence, and Shepherd who had condemned him. He did not speak, but in his jubilee, Shepherd knew beyond doubt he had made two mistakes: first in interfering between master and servant, and second in displaying his courage with unnecessary bravado.

Where it would lead he could only guess, but he doubted it bode well for either himself or Dongal.

A full minute passed before Ara verbally acknowledged the feat.

"It appears you have found a champion, Dongal."

"Such was not my intention, master."

"Very well. Let it stand that it has served another purpose. Leave us."

The servant bowed and departed, never once turning his back. With his absence, the room grew chill. Determined not to be outdone, Ara took the untouched glass and drank from it. He did not finish the contents, however, but merely sipped before returning it to the tray, reminding Shepherd of Ericka's actions on the plane. In this instance, the similarity offered scant comfort.

Demurely wiping his lips with the back of his hand, Ara continued.

"I understood it was your intention to write about my Kingdom." He smiled cordially, without warmth.

"That *was* the idea. But without a camera, my words could hardly be substantiated."

"We will see what can be done about returning your equipment. I am sure Dongal did not hide it carefully. When it is found, it shall be returned."

Something in the tone reminded Shepherd again of Ericka. It held the same intonation she used when taunting him about the photographs he had taken of her. Passing off the impression as a reflection they both undoubtedly had the same English instructor, he smiled.

Ara did not know how to interpret his guest's silence.

"You smile?"

"I was merely wondering about something."

"Ask me and perhaps I can lay your wonder *to rest.*"

"Whether your photographic image would have a glow around it."

If he expected to catch Ara with guilty knowledge, his hopes were dashed.

"Explain, please."

"When I photographed Ericka, there was an orb – a glow, if you will – around her head. Her features were not sharply defined, making my pictures useless."

"Useless – ah, you mean unworthy of publication. Yes, I see. An interesting supposition, although why that same phenomenon should affect me, I do not know."

"Neither do I. That was why I wondered."

"I see." The explanation seemed to satisfy. "I cannot say, inasmuch as I have never had my photograph taken."

"But, you have had your portrait painted?"

"No."

"I thought that was something all monarchs did. Surely you want your subjects to be familiar with your likeness. I understand in England, the Queen's portrait presides over all government buildings, as well as in schools and many private dwellings."

"An enlightened idea," Ara readily agreed. "I approve. But that is quite unnecessary here."

"Why is that?"

"My subjects all recognize me on sight."

"Really? How is that? Do you have so few that you have come in contact with them all?"

Too late, Shepherd realized he had inadvertently given Ara an easy way out.

"That is it, exactly! Like my 'sister,' Queen Elizabeth II, I often go out amongst my people. But unlike her, I am an absolute ruler. In the United Kingdom, unfortunately, much power has been stripped from the throne. A pity," he added. Shepherd did not doubt the sincerity of his conviction. "There are so few of us left – those of royal blood," Ara continued, warming to his subject. "And of those enlightened countries still maintaining a monarchy, their royal houses have been diluted by commoners."

"Some would argue that makes the line stronger."

"Some. But not all."

"Not you, for instance?"

"I trace my heritage back to the first ruler of the kingdom. To the first," he craftily added, "and greatest ruler of any country."

"I should like to study your heraldry."

"And so you shall. I will teach you, myself, for no one is better versed than I. But not tonight, Shepherd. I see your eyes grow heavy."

Shepherd had not been, until that moment, tired. But as Ara's statement settled over him, he suddenly felt an overwhelming desire to sleep.

"I believe you are right, your grace," he admitted, rising from his seat. "If you will excuse me, I think I will retire."

Ara rose with him, but not without one final, parting comment.

"Not 'your grace,'" he corrected. "I accept 'your majesty,' if you will, but that other was refuted for all time by my dear royal 'brother', Henry VIII of England. It was he who instituted the title of 'Your Majesty.' He felt the other too... plebeian."

"You admire Henry?"

Ara's eyes sparkled. "How could I not, when he established himself as supreme ruler of the English church, thus forever diminishing the power of the Bishop of Rome. Of that, I approve most heartily."

Shepherd swayed uneasily, attempting to clear his head before speaking.

"Are you head of the church here?"

"I am the absolute ruler of everything. The grass does not grow without my permission."

Tempted to argue, Shepherd thought better of it. Already reminded of Ericka's admonition not to incur the king's ire, he did not wish to go against her advice.

"Good night, then, sir. I wish you pleasant dreams."

"And I wish you the same," Ara replied with a beneficent smile. "Until tomorrow, then."

Seeing himself out, Shepherd opened one of the double doors and had begun to slip through when his eyes beheld a small item on a side table. Heart catching in his throat, he gagged, swallowed bitter bile, then fled.

Without doubt, the small gold object d'art was the same pyramid he had left with Trent.

All the way to his chamber, Shepherd tried to convince himself it was a duplicate, a copy, a twin of the one he had stolen from Ericka, but he could not believe it. Even if it were possible to have two exact pyramids, this one had Trent's feelings all over it. Were he to examine it for fingerprints, he knew without rational explanation, Trent's would be there.

Equally certain, the pyramid reeked of death.

Someone who had touched it within the last two days had perished.

That meant either Trent, or Ericka, who must surely have retrieved it from his friend.

In either case, he felt greatly diminished.

And very, very alone.

CHAPTER 21

Shepherd dreamed again and knew it in the same way those witnessing a tragedy wished they were asleep: horror, however encountered, could not be denied.

Fire, the type of spontaneous combustion which could not be combated because it had no source, crept up his legs. Try as he might to slap it down, the flames grew larger, more intense. Painful.

Shrieking in agony, he tried to run away. The added oxygen increased the inferno. Tripping over some unseen object on the floor, he cried and went to retrieve it. The action made no sense but he had no power to question his actions.

Recovering a small, triangular object, Shepherd cried in fright.

"No! It's cannot be the same pyramid! I left it with Trent."

Summoned by the repetition of his name, the SUNY professor with no known living kin appeared. Peculiarly, the fire did not touch him, or when it did, had no effect. The old man sadly shook his head.

"I tried to tell you, but you would not listen."

His words were out of keeping with the threat Shepherd faced. The boy beat back the flames. They retreated but more in mockery than fact.

"Trent, help me. Can't you see what's happening? I'm burning up."

Trent did not see, for he had closed his eyes.

"Xilka. Besa."

Shepherd cringed in horror.

"For God's sake, what are you doing?"

"Conversing with a demon."

Shepherd misunderstood. "It has already escaped. Set fire to the room. Send it back."

"Only you can do that."

Shepherd stared at the object in his hand. It burned his flesh. He tried to throw it away but found the sides adhered to the skin. He shrieked. The fire grew hotter, crept nearer.

"I haven't the power."

"Then, why ask me? You are the one with it in your possession. I no longer have it."

"But I left it with you."

"It was taken –"

"By Ericka! But when? When I left, you said...." He tried to recall Trent's exact words. "That you would use it. The same way she did – to follow me. How did she get it?" He trembled. "By magic?"

"I thought you did not believe in the supernatural."

The fire grew hotter. The room smelled of burnt flesh.

"All right. I was wrong. Tell me –"

"She summoned it. After it had done its work."

"For Ara," Shepherd accused. "This is his doing."

"Think what you will." Neither a confirmation nor a denial.

The convert reached out a hand. It went through the body-shape of his mentor. He sobbed.

"Trent, come and get me. I need help."

"You know I cannot do that." He smiled. It lacked amusement. "I do not know where you are."

"In the Kingdom –"

"– that Time Forgot," Trent finished. He sounded mocking.

"I am burning. Put out the fire."

"Those are the flames from Hell. A Christian has no authority over the devil's domain."

"A Christian must fight the powers of evil."

"Dare I tread where God does not?"

"God is everywhere."

Trent appeared sad. "I think I must reassess."

"No! You cannot. You are my rock; my foundation."

"You have another master, now."

"I am your ward."

"Ah. But you have forsaken me."

Through the crackling of the fire, Shepherd heard a cock crow. Three times.

"I repent."

"There is no going back. You have chosen. Find your own salvation."

Shepherd began a mad tap dance, high-stepping away from the flames.

"From Ericka? Will she will save me – from Ara?"

"Perhaps it shall be the other way around. Who can say?"

"The other way?" Shepherd heard himself screaming. He writhed in agony. "What other way? Ara shall save me from her?"

But Trent had stopped listening. His body began to disintegrate.

"I must leave you now.... I bid you a fond farewell."

"Don't leave me. I need you. Trent, I never had the chance to say, 'I love you.'"

A tongue clucked. "You had the chance. You just never took it."

"Then I say it now. Trent, I love you."

"Too late, son. I should have known your affection was always destined for another. But I played my role of foolish old man." He sighed. "Not well enough."

"What does that mean?"

"I opened my door to you and through it came evil. It destroyed me. And my faith."

"Our Father who art in heaven...." He could not finish the prayer. "Trent, the words!"

"I have given you the words."

The boy fell to his knees. Fire spread over the top of his head. "Kneel with me. We will repeat them together."

The professor had no knees. They had disappeared, along with the rest of his corporeal form. Only the voice remained, and that faint and growing more distant.

"... he makes me lay down in green pastures...."

Shepherd Kingston screamed.

He had detected the dissembling. An education, not gone for naught.

"... he makes me *lie* down in green pastures...."

A grammatical mistake one should not make in heaven.

Shepherd awoke, convulsed in fear. Beating away the still too-real fire from his limbs, he struck nothing but the soft cloth of his nightclothes. Finally staying his hand with the numb realization that the flames had come through a crack in time, he sobbed for that which he had lost.

"Trent. Oh, my God, Trent." Unable to finish the sentence, *You are dead,* for that would firmly nail the black wreath to the kindly old man's coffin, he shivered in abject misery. His first nightmare in this brave, ugly world had been a premonition. This last one, stark reality, perverted by the castle's aura of evil.

That Trent had perished he could no longer deny. That his death lay at Shepherd's door the youth he found easier to lock outside the realm of culpability.

"No. Not I. That other."

The temperature in the room dropped. He did not want to get up. It would have been easier to crawl deeper under the covers, telling himself the psychic images were no more than wine-induced fantasy. That would have been a lie, but at three o'clock in the morning, the explanation might have satisfied his overwrought brain. But not his conscience.

The pyramid had been the last piece of the puzzle. Not a duplicate, a copy, a clever twin, but the actual object he had stolen from Ericka's apartment. It no longer mattered how it had been retrieved. The true significance lay in the irrefutable fact it had returned to its true owner: Ara, Master of the Kingdom. He had purposely left it where he knew his guest's eyes would fall.

There are more things in heaven and in hell than are dreamt of in your philosophy, Shepherd Kingston.

More mockery. He must regain control; divine how the king expected him to act, and perform the opposite. In that direction led life.

And probably madness.

Wrapping a blanket around his shoulders to ward off the bone-numbing chill, Shepherd slipped out of bed, feeling naked and unprotected. Creeping across the floor on tiptoe, he tentatively tried the knob, finding it unlocked. This occasioned no surprise. While any number of excuses could be made why Ara desired him kept inside, the invited guest knew he was meant to wander this night.

The characters in his dream had said so, without once mentioning the fact.

Furtively glancing up and down the narrow stone corridor revealed no lurking shapes. Nor had he expected to find any. The master wished him to feel safe, secure in his stealth.

Assuming that as his cue, Shepherd scurried rapidly down the hall, descending the staircase one step at a time. His feet froze under the stone. He wondered how long it had been since that rock felt the sun's warmth. Five hundred years? One thousand? Two thousand? As long as the unbroken blood line which terminated, at the moment, with Ara?

He did not know where instinct would take him, only that his inner ear, as a substitute for his third eye, would direct his passage. Not to any place on ground level. He must go below.

Deep down below.

To the subterranean chamber and the subliminal voices which had awoken him from repose. Not to find Trent or Ericka or even himself, but others. Ara, around whom the world revolved. And secondary characters, about whom Shepherd would need to know much more before the drama played itself out.

Unfamiliar with the layout of the first floor, having seen no more of it than the dining and den, he hesitated. Numerous choices beckoned.

"The lady or the tiger?" he asked, attempting, by grim humor, to bolster his waning courage. For his effort he received no answer.

Pausing in the middle of the expansive foyer, the youth made a slow circle, head cocked to one side.

Look again. One must use more than one's eyes in this country if he wishes to survive.

Ericka's admonition. He paid heed.

Turn to the left. Walk down the corridor; at the end, open the door to the right.

Those were not his words, not thoughts which originated within his brain. They came from elsewhere. A guide had come. He pinched himself, the classic gesture all sleepwalkers made to convince themselves they were awake. He need not have bothered. This time, there could be no debate.

Turn back. Turn back.

Other thoughts, equally strong. A second mind at work. One evoking him to follow, the other to run.

He had no choice. The die had been cast.

Turning left, he walked down the corridor to its end, then opened the door on the right. A stale, putrid draft struck his face. He identified the odor as must, which constituted a lie. He had covered enough accidents in his short career as a photographer to recognize the stench of fresh blood.

Shepherd descended, placing one hand to the stone wall for support. He expected it to be slimy, but although rough-hewn, the wall felt dry. That indicated a low water table. He congratulated himself on a command of the trivial.

Twenty steps, twenty-five, before he stopped counting. It served no point other than taking his mind off what he would ultimately discover.

Perhaps two dozen more steps, before the staircase ended at a solid wooden door. It came so unexpectedly he almost ran into it before drawing back in time to save himself a smashed nose. Groping for the handle, he found none. Pushing inward, the barricade swung open. Well oiled, the hinges made no sound.

Behind the door he found neither lady nor tiger, just another long corridor. Unlike the pitch of the stairwell, sporadically placed torches lit the way. Above them were dark, erratic stains, deeply etched into the surface, testimony to soot and ash. Thousands of incendiaries had burned here; as many had died.

Passing the first, a rat scurried out of the shadows, paused to look back, appraising him for an easy meal, then abandoned the idea and ran ahead.

At least I'll be announced, he thought. An errant idea, like the fluttering in his heart.

He continued to walk, taking more care, least he come upon another rodent, this one less eager to abandon a bare-footed dinner, but encountered no more.

After what seemed an interminable time, Shepherd observed light pouring out from beneath a closed door. He hesitated, steadied his shaking hands by clasping them together, then inched ahead. The stench of blood grew stronger. Although it seemed unlikely voices could travel through solid rock, he heard the conversation clearly.

"Where have you hidden it?"

Ara's voice, heightened to a pitch of fury. "If not Dongal, then you."

"No, master, I swear," came a voice Shepherd did not recognize, but attributed to Eldrich. "I would not." The sharp whistle of a whip lashed out, followed by a man's scream. "Why would I?" the voice continued, now laced with pain. "I do not even know its purpose. Why would I steal such an object?"

A pause, then the whizzing of a whip being swung over the wielder's head. When the sinewy leather finally struck flesh, a shriek of unendurable magnitude filled the cave. Holding hands to his ears, Shepherd turned and fled.

He could do nothing to save Eldrich. No protestation for mercy, no rational explanation that the value of the camera did not merit the punishment meted out, would suffice. Ara meant to assert his authority, and do it, he would.

Running headlong the way he came, Shepherd emerged from the stairwell out of breath and covered in sweat. While the upstairs rooms were no brighter, prolonged exposure to the netherworld gloom had sharpened his eyesight. Using that edge to guide him, he hurried through the corridors with one thought only: to return to his bedchamber before he was missed. If the master would punish so favored a servant, what might he do to a guest who strayed?

Reaching the stairs, he pivoted too quickly, turning his ankle. Flung forward, Shepherd waved his limbs in imitation of a windmill before righting himself. The accident and subsequent regaining of balance turned him around, so that by the time he righted himself, he faced the den. Nostrils flared, he crept forward, more cautious than before. Entering the room, he saw that the fire had been allowed to die down. What light remained proved sufficient to illuminate the small table by the door. Scanning the surface, he sought the pyramid.

It was gone.

"What are you looking for?"

The question so startled him, Shepherd's knees buckled. Spinning around, he beheld Dongal.

"My God, you scared me!" An expression of unease crossed the servant's face, but he did not explain, prompting Shepherd to add, "I didn't hear you come up behind me."

"One learns to walk on cat's feet," the servant whispered.

"I... couldn't sleep."

"You should not wander about."

The warning, although well meant, served only to rouse Shepherd's interest.

"What happened to the pyramid I saw this evening?" Dongal's eyes shifted from Shepherd's face to the table.

"There was nothing there."

"Yes, there was. A small gold pyramid. I saw it distinctly as I left the room."

"There was nothing there," he repeated in exactly the same tone of voice. So precisely enunciated, Shepherd could have believed it a recording.

"About this big," he demonstrated. "And made of pure gold."

"You are mistaken, sir. The firelight –"

"Why are you lying? I took you for a friend."

The simplicity of the avowal warped Dongal's expression.

"Go upstairs quickly. Before the master returns."

"Do you know where he is?" No reply. "What he is doing?" Stony silence. "I heard him below. He was punishing Eldrich for stealing my camera."

The servant's eyes opened in dull astonishment.

"Punishing Eldrich? That cannot be."

"I heard him, I tell you. In the dungeon, or whatever you call it. He whipped him." Dongal raised a hand to shield his eyes. "Ara said that if you did not take the camera, then it had to be Eldrich."

"You heard him? In the dungeon?"

"Yes."

"That is impossible."

"Why?"

"Because... Eldrich is his favorite."

A lame excuse, fraught with half-truth.

"That is not true," Shepherd gambled. "You are his favorite."

Dongal's arm shot out, pointing upward.

"Go. Quickly. Do not speak of such things. It is dangerous."

"I will," Shepherd promised to Dongal's obvious relief. "Only if you tell me what happened to the pyramid."

"It... was never there."

Reacting in unanticipated anger, Shepherd grabbed the man by his loose-fitting clothing.

"Tell me!"

"I do not know where it has gone!"

"Who put it on the table? Ericka?"

"Ericka?" Dongal gasped, barely able to enunciate the name.

"That's right. It must have been she. Where is she? I must speak to her."

If Shepherd thought Dongal frightened by Ara's earlier accusation of theft, it paled in comparison to the expression which shrouded his face at this new demand. Pulling away, the servant made an obscure gesture then backed away, nearly running into the doorframe in his haste.

Shepherd watched him go, deeply troubled. Why had the mention of Ericka's name so terrified the man? Surely she could not be the source of his horror. It must, then, be Ara's protection of her.

Jealousy rose in Shepherd's breast. Despite denial, it seemed the new king must either be her lover, or her husband.

Choked on emotion, Shepherd almost missed a more obvious connection. One Ara might have given away by his coy statement, "The blood is the life."

Working his mind around the solution, he smiled in grim satisfaction. If Ericka were not paramour or wife, then she must be Ara's sister. He could not decide if she were older or younger but it made scant difference. In a backward kingdom where tradition dictated every facet of life, it seemed unlikely women would wield power. Therefore, while Ara, the heir, remained behind to "acclimate" himself to eventual ascension, she had been dispatched overseas.

Once the king died, her brother assumed his rightful place. Presuming it took him several months to entrench his power, the call had finally come.

Return to me, dear sister. Come home, where you belong.

If not to rule beside him, then certainly to bolster his claims. Any monarch required vast amounts of wealth to maintain a firm grip on his subjects. That explained where her fortune had gone: to bolster her brother. Bribing the nobility. Fortifying the army.

It also went a long way toward justifying her inclusion of an "Otherworlder." Old men might not be interested in what lay beyond their borders but a youth, better educated and more aware of technology, had seen fit to offer the invitation.

One the old king would not have extended.

To Shepherd's eager mind, the rationale went so far as to justify his selection. Indeed, this country had backward traditions. New ways were not easily introduced. In order to do so, Ara required a link with the past. That explained the necessity of finding someone who resembled the man in the painting.

Likely, the oil held some religious significance; belonged to a prophesy, passed down from generation to generation. As there had been in Ericka's apartment, he supposed there were a number of connected works. Innocence dominated by evil. Innocence fighting back. Innocence triumphing.

While he did not appreciate playing the role of "Innocence," Shepherd felt he could use it to advantage. Just as Ara needed him to be the conduit to the 20th Century, he could maneuver that position into becoming spokesman. When the camera was returned to him, or with another, purchased from a neighboring country, he really could introduce the world to the Kingdom that Time Forgot.

Pictorials. Interviews. An entire series of articles on Ara, Ericka, the peasants, their ways of life without electricity, phones or televisions. He might even become ambassador. Open trade, negotiate pacts, bring in select heads of state.

Howard Carter had become famous by discovering King Tut's tomb. If memory served, that had been in 1922. Nineteen *twenty-two.* A number Trent regarded as... mystical and equally fearful. Shepherd closed his eyes. Now was not the time to dwell on that. He would be famous. How many more accolades for the man who brought an entire country out of the Dinosaur Age?

His name would be on everyone's lips. Instead of being the interviewer, he would be the one interviewed. International travel. Private sessions with presidents and popes. He had been right all along and Trent –

Trent. What of Trent?

But he was being foolish. Trent had not died. It had all been a nightmare. When he got to civilization, he would call his beloved mentor and explain the entire situation.

Yes, Trent. There are things we do not understand; things you might even say which are beyond our Western comprehension. The pyramid. The startling realization that in our modern existence of satellites and moon walks, an entire country had managed to remain hidden. But there you have it. The Ninth Wonder of the World.

Cheery thoughts.

If Shepherd Kingston believed them.

And more to the point, if he had actually guessed right.

If he had not, then he had willingly and with innocence aforethought, walked open-eyed into the devil's dominion.

CHAPTER 22

Little exterior light filtered in through the lone window in the bed chamber, but it served as an alarm clock and Shepherd sat on the edge of the bed awaiting the summons. When it finally came, he sprang up and answered the door, finding Dongal, as expected, with a towel and basin of water.

Accepting the primitive offering with a newly reworked humor, he carted it over to the stand where he had set out his toilet articles. Washing his face and hands, he dried them before turning to the servant, ruefully extending the wire from his electric shaver.

"I trust it is accurate that Ara does not stand on ceremony because I am unable to shave. How is it you remove the hair from your cheeks?"

"With a straight razor, sir."

Shepherd mistook the servant's intonation as dread of wielding so awkward an instrument, when he should have realized it stemmed from the informality of using the king's name.

"I do not think I care to brave such an instrument of torture." This time, he more accurately guessed the cause of pain and quickly apologized. "I do meant torture as in –"

Dongal had no interest in pursuing the subject.

"If you have completed your ablution, I shall escort you to table. The master is already up and impatient."

"There is really no need for you to see me downstairs. I know the way."

The servant flinched, making a crosswise motion with his hands.

"I will escort you," he replied. In repetition, it sounded well practiced.

"As you say. I do not wish to step on toes." Frowning at the expression, Dongal stared at his feet, then gave a slight indication Shepherd follow. Curious, not about idiomatic phrases but freedom, he casually pursued, "Does this mean I am not to wander around alone – even in the daytime?"

"That, sir, is a question best directed to the master."

"Do you actually mean, best not broached at all?" The man debated whether to answer, started to reply in the affirmative, then simply hung his head, causing the guest to take pity. "A moment, and I will be ready."

Running a comb through his hair, then splashing a palm-full of cologne over his face, Shepherd took pains to straighten the wrinkles from his shirt. Not completely satisfied, he sought an ascot to wear in lieu of a tie. The search took him to the wardrobe, where his hands instinctively went toward his shoes. Finding Trent's parting gift still safely hidden, his lips moved in quiet prayer.

"Thank you, Trent. I don't know if I'll ever need what you gave me, but I do appreciate the foresight." With this sentiment came guilt, for he had scant belief in the efficacy of beads and rattles. *If your potions were so powerful,* he reasoned in the cool light of day, *whoever stole my camera would have taken them, as well.*

The thought depressed his spirits, for he knew the gift had been well intentioned. Positioning himself for privacy, he withdrew the small bundle and unwrapped the outer covering, intending to inspect the contents. His eyes froze on a small silver cross affixed to a chain wrapped around the packet, holding the edges neatly together.

"So, you anticipated my doubt," he chuckled in false bravado. While conceivable Trent had placed the cross around the packet to assuage Shepherd's skepticism, he felt it far more likely the actual intent had been to prevent unholy hands from removing it.

Shoving the gift back inside his shoe, the ostensive ward of Abraham Trent clasped his hands in supplication. If his suppositions of the night before were accurate, he would never have to find out if the cross and related items had the power to hold evil at bay. If he were wrong, then his life would depend on them.

Finding the neckwear he originally sought, Shepherd made himself presentable, then followed Dongal into the corridor. Descending one after the other, the follower tried hard to dispel the illusion of being a pull toy.

All things considered, there were worse ways to emulate a game piece.

Ara greeted his guest by offering a cheery wave from his seated position.

"Good morning. Ericka warned me 'New Yorkers' slept late, but she did not say they snored the day away. I have been up since dawn."

"That is because you have a kingdom to rule, while I am on a working vacation." He hoped that sounded pleasant enough, considering Ericka's absence. "Will Miss Elvina be joining us?"

"Not for the break of fast. But later. She is most eager to see you."

"And I, her."

Accepting the invitation to sit, he observed the grandeur of the preceding meal had been dispensed. Pewter replaced fine tableware, heavily scored by innumerable knives slicing through tough fare. Matching them for wear, the wooden chargers were so scarred they appeared dog-eared. In place of multi-armed candelabras were plain silver candlesticks, placed at the head of the table. All chairs but two had been removed. The remainder were set against the walls, backs to the diners, giving the impression that latecomers would eat in the corner like naughty children.

Without cue, Dongal served from three covered pots, adding thick slabs of very rare red meat, boiled potatoes and a heavily spiced stew before each diner.

Nose tingling from the smell of charred blood and the commingling of spices he could not identify, Shepherd quipped, "The breakfast of champions." Fortunately, the king did not take offense.

"Undoubtedly, not what you are used to. My people do not have a taste for sweets, as I am told is common in less civilized nations. But surely you eat *pork?*"

Comprehending the reference, the guest nodded.

"Bacon; crisp. Usually with hash browns and eggs; or cinnamon buns."

"Ah. You will find this repast infinitely more fortifying. Although, should such be your desire, I could send Dongal out into the brush to scare up half a dozen birds' eggs."

The idea of eating unborn robins presented an unappetizing picture and Shepherd hastily refused the offer. Picking, instead, at the oxblood-colored concoction, he inquired, "What is this side dish?"

"I think the closest word you might understand is 'goulash.' The spice is paprika."

"Of course. I should have recognized it, yet it is far more... pungent."

"That which you are familiar is a poor substitute for what you will find here. No one from my kingdom would willingly consume the pale, flavorless spice sold in New York as 'paprika.'"

"I understand," Shepherd pursued after swallowing a bite, then washing the pungent, wild flavor down with water, "that paprika is common in Eastern Europe – Hungary, Romania. Are we near those countries?"

Ara chose to ignore his guest's curiosity, while indulging his own.

"Ericka tells me you can ride, after a fashion. We will take exercise after you have eaten."

"Very well. But tell me, your grace, were you able to find my camera? I would hate to pass up a photo op."

If Ara did not comprehend the journalistic expression, he gave no indication.

"From what I have learned, you did not bring a camera with you."

Shepherd looked up sharply, meeting Ara's gaze with a steady one of his own. Making a point by calling the king a liar seemed ill advised.

"It is possible I forgot to pack it. I left in quite a hurry. If that is the case, I apologize most profoundly."

"Consider the matter forgotten."

Shepherd accepted the dismissal, though both men fully comprehended the issue had yet to be buried.

Completing the meal in silence, the pair then retired to the stables, where a stableman awaited with two saddled horses. The first, a tall bay Ara indicated for his guest, while the second, a majestic black stallion he assumed for himself. Acting nonchalance, Shepherd reached for the reins of his mount, but the animal immediately flattened its ears and lashed out with a hind foot. The groom made a valiant effort to control it, with little success.

"Our horses are spirited," Ara commented with obvious pride. "I fear they are not fond of strangers."

Assuming he meant to include the groom, Shepherd inquired, "You are a foreigner, then? Like me?"

Responding to the question, Hest failed to articulate a single word before his wind pipe constricted. Dropping the reins, both hands went to his throat as he fought off invisible fingers threatening to strangle him. Glancing obliquely at the king, Shepherd noted a dark, concentrated expression, reminiscent of Ericka when the situation did not please her. Holding that thought for the moment, he responded to the groom, thinking to alleviate his distress by loosening his collar.

"Do not touch him."

"But he is choking –"

"A reminder, only. Hest is being punished and not allowed to speak."

"But how –?" The intense, hungry look dissipated from Ara's countenance and the servant fell back, released from the implied but untouched stranglehold. Confused that he had brought about the situation, Shepherd attempted to express his concern. "Are you all right?"

Hest flinched, then merely stooped to retrieve the reins. The red in his complexion faded as Ara petted his horse, resuming the conversation.

"Diabolus was a royal gift, bred for me, alone. There is none like him in the world. But, you were saying?"

By "saying," he implied "thinking," and Shepherd blushed.

"Your facial expression, sir – so like that of Miss Elvina."

Ara danced lightly on the soles of his feet.

"Put your mind at ease. I am neither father, *brother,* uncle nor cousin to her. Nor am I her lover – or husband," he added with a faint, knowing smile. "Let us ride."

Vaulting with the ease of one born to his situation, the master motioned Shepherd follow his lead. Hardly "put at ease" by the king's assertion, he tried and failed, falling back to earth with an undignified thud.

"No saddle horn," Ara chuckled, this time with genuine good humor. "We have no 'cowboys' here. Our tack is of a very ancient design, in use long before Mankind ever dreamed of riding."

Having already heard that once before, Shepherd trudged toward the mounting block. Finding it more solid than the reasoning which had been knocked out from under him, he grabbed the bay's mane and used that to assist him into place. Before he had gained any semblance of balance, Ara motioned forward and dashed off, quickly leaving his guest in the dust.

Feeling the fool and driven by fool's pride, Shepherd attempted to regain some standing in his own eyes by touching heels to the horse's flank. He regretted the action instantly as the animal broke into a full gallop. Bouncing like a sack of grain, he would not have caught Ara, had the more experienced rider not slowed the pace he set. When Shepherd finally drew abreast, they proceeded at a walk, allowing for a more thorough contemplation of the countryside.

Viewing the land from an elevated perspective enabled Shepherd to realize how far up the mountain he had come. Trees were abundant, yet those closest the castle displayed thin foliage, sporting copious dead limbs, leaves wilting in impending death. Further down the slope, the pine, oak and maple grew healthier, giving rise to speculation of a miasma hovering over the sole habitable dwelling.

Further down, interspersed between sections of forest were cleared areas where tall grasses waved languidly in the breeze, adding, rather than detracting from the bleak, almost desolate picture of stagnation and hopelessness. Half an hour's journey took them into a deep, but not impenetrable valley, dominated by rolling hills. Little had been given over to agriculture. What plowed fields he could see were given over to scraggly crops.

Keeping to a slow trot, they bypassed several small villages comprised entirely of wooden dwellings with thatched roofs. None were in good repair. Windows were either left open to the elements, or patched with what appeared to be oiled paper, while paths, seemingly leading nowhere, were strewn with weeds. Had Shepherd viewed the scene as early 19th-

Century, set in a harsh, unforgiving American West, they might have been considered inspirational. Appraised from a 20th-Century perspective, however, they represented the model of a lost land.

Repulsion rising, Shepherd sought a starting point for conversation.

"How many people live here?"

"That is hard to say. No one, so far as I know, has ever undertaken a precise count. There are as many as there are."

"But surely," Shepherd tried, hoping to hit upon a point of agreement, "they must pay taxes – or homage, or whatever you call it."

"That is true."

"If you don't know how many families live here, how can you be certain they have all paid their –"

"Tithe?" Ara completed, a steely look completing the sentence before the answer emerged. "No one would dare omit such a display of – loyalty. It is beyond comprehension."

"But if they did?"

"That would be considered an act of unpardonable aggression: remedied by death."

"What if their crops are bad? Their business fail? What then?"

Ara dismissed the idea with a wave of his gloved hand.

"Then they pay in things other than money."

"Such as?"

"An arm or a leg."

"You jest."

Pausing to stroke Diabolus' neck, Ara stared at his guest with a calm, deadly expression. "No."

"But that is... barbaric."

"Did not Ericka warn you this was a harsh land?"

"She did. But I realize now I did not fully take her meaning."

"That is unfortunate."

They rode again in silence before the quiet grew ominous. Without bird or insect to break the monotony, Shepherd squirmed in his saddle.

"Why is it you have kept the modern world at bay? Surely radios, telephones, medicine would not threaten your rule, and might, in fact, strengthen it."

"There is no need of such here. Besides, I do not wish it. I prefer things the way they are. It is more comfortable for me this way."

"Then why the stock market?"

Ara paused, debating whether to answer. When he finally spoke, his words rang true.

"As I have explained, that was my step-father's wish."

"But he didn't seem to use the money for anything. Even the castle shuns technology."

"There are other things."

"Such as power?"

"Power is everything. Without it, there is only humiliation and everlasting subjugation. What do you say," he abruptly offered, "to a race back to the castle?"

"What's in it for me?" Shepherd demanded, reminding the king that he had heeded well his words. His offer was well taken, the reply immediate.

"If you win, I shall permit you to see Ericka tonight, much sooner than I might otherwise have permitted."

"And if I lose?"

Casting about for a suitable answer, Ara replied with charming innocence.

"You must agree to pay me tribute in the manner of my country."

"With money?"

Ara smirked. "You do not have sufficient remuneration. Shall we say tribute – taken to mean worship? Will you accept such a challenge on those terms?"

Inasmuch as Shepherd divined he had little choice, he accented. "Certainly."

The two men brought their mounts even.

"We shall return by a different route," Ara directed, sweeping his arm across the landscape. "Do not fear: there is little change of your becoming lost. Ride in that direction and follow the trail. But do not stray from it." Giving Shepherd no time to digest his warning, the cry of "Go!" set them off.

Determined to make a credible account of himself, Shepherd urged his bay into a gallop. The horse responded with amazing speed, falling naturally into a smooth, fluid gait. Leaning forward, the city boy exhilarated to the feel of wind and the spray of foamy white perspiration, blown from the horse's lathered neck.

"On! On!" he cried, becoming, in his mind, the epitome of the Lone Ranger and all the other cowboy heroes with whom he had grown to adulthood. Pretending to be a character from a well-scripted Western, he thrilled to the taste of victory, urging his horse to greater speed. In a struggle for ascendance, he pitted Good against Bad, white hat against black.

Ara fell behind, first by a nose, then a neck, until Shepherd gained a full length. On, on, he flew, faster than the speed of light, the distance between the two riders growing wider, more pronounced. Daring to glance over his shoulder, he caught the master's eye.

Perhaps trailing for the first time in his life, Ara transmitted dismay at his unanticipated predicament. Consternation shot from those black orbs, commingled with something equally identifiable: mortification. Inebriated with his own prowess, Shepherd's orbs danced. *Look at me! You took me for a fool and you were wrong! The old must give way to the new.*

Around a curve in the path, then plunging headlong into a long wood, the horses raced. Nostrils distended, necks outstretched, hooves barely touching earth, they ran, for it was the nature of a horse to run.

Faster, faster and Shepherd dared look back again, dared show his contempt for one who had never known defeat. This time, however, the appearance of loser had vanished from Ara's face, replaced by an expression of pure evil. Waiting for the very moment of Shepherd's triumph to make his move, Ara opened his mouth in a twisted grin, revealing a bottomless red cavity.

Without any obvious instruction, Diabolus increased speed tenfold. Within a heartbeat he drew upon the bay.

Losing complacency, Shepherd whipped the bay, kicked wildly with his heels, to no avail. Black passed off-white easily, moving ahead with little effort.

Not yet ready to admit defeat, Shepherd pressed closer, urging his horse forward. The animal responded, but clearly outmatched, continuing losing ground. When nearly out of sight, the front-runner turned, seeking contact one last time before disappearing into the forest.

The eyes which met Shepherd's were narrowed in vindictive triumph, clearly transmitting the truth to the "unwary fly." Never had the contest been in question, they mocked; it is all a game, a tease, a torment, for the sake of sport.

Heart hardening at the mockery to which he had been maneuvered, Shepherd bit his lower lip, drawing blood. "On!" he screamed. "On!" But too late. In a moment, Ara vanished, leaving him alone with only the stench of upturned turf and the sting of humiliation to keep him company.

Deprived of his expectations, Shepherd slowed the bay, finally reducing its pace to a walk. With time, now, to more fully observe his surroundings, he found this wood to be of a far different character than that previously traversed. Grass grew green and lush, the forest dense. More like the landscape of upstate New York, he used the familiarity to calm jangled nerves.

"I never expected to win," he spoke aloud. The shrubbery along the trail seemed to agree, for it bent in silent acknowledgment. This gave Shepherd the impetus to breathe through his nose and savor the fresh smells healthy of growing plants. Distanced from the poison air around the castle, the area exuded hope and the renewal of faith, verdant shades of brown and green and yellow rejuvenating the soul.

Here, Shepherd experienced a sense of normalcy. Around the bend and one hundred miles beyond lay Budapest, or Prague, or Warsaw; cities swarming with people. He had not been separated from civilization after all.

A two hour ride would bring him to the border of a known country. No matter how strange or peculiar Ara's kingdom, it represented a mere flyspeck in the vastness of the world. He had not been trapped in a netherworld far from Earth, but merely a visitor in a foreign land.

"The blood is the life," he quoted the immortal Bela Lugosi. "Transylvania never looked so good."

Mood improved, he allowed his mind to wander. Whether from that renewed attention, or some inner alertness, Shepherd's eyes fell on an area of brush, blackened and charred by fire. Not a random burning, of the type caused by an errant strike of lightning, but one forming a path, snaking back into the wood as far as he could see.

Interest piqued, he debated whether or not to follow the trail. The choice was an easy one, made more from spite than curiosity.

"Why not? I lost the race and must pay the consequences. But I will do it in my own time."

With a smug sense of satisfaction at having his revenge, Shepherd slipped off the saddle, landing lightly on his feet. Attaching the reins to an outcropping bush, he abandoned the horse.

There could be no doubt the line of charred vegetation resulted from careful deliberation, for it lead through heavy underbrush, straight and true, nearly two hundred yards. At that point, the burned path veered sharply right. Without hesitation, Shepherd turned with it, climbing a low hill into a stand of oak.

The first and most obvious attraction were the trees themselves, wider around than the width of two men standing hand-to-hand. Having learned something of ancient forests from Trent, who often spoke longingly of the one-thousand-year-old oak at Yorkshire, he put the age of these specimens into the same category. Unlike those living monuments in northern England, however, these had been burned from the bottom up, to a height of nearly fifty feet. What few dead branches remained were suspended at varying angles along the trunks, resembling those preserved on canvas within the castle walls.

Shaking off a feeling of *deja vu,* he continued his assent, finally arriving at the top of the incline. From that height he beheld a sharp decline as the land dropped off into a narrow, flat valley. All vegetation had been burned away and the area well trampled, leaving a startling view of center stage. Set within the clearing were thirteen huge boulders comprising an outer circle. Clearly hewn by hand and shaped into pillars roughly the shape of playing cards, Shepherd placed their age at somewhat older than 1,000 years.

It did not take a scientist to guess the date, for the entire rim of the valley lay covered in monstrous oak. Without a gaping opening through which to drag the stone, he deduced the pillars had stood in place since the time before the trees had sprouted.

Within the enclosure he counted nine black obelisks, twice the height of a very tall man.

Breathless at the discovery, Shepherd scrambled down the blackened slope into the vale. The moment his feet reached the perimeter of the outer circle, overhead light dramatically diminished. Glancing upward, he could no longer see the sky.

"A low-lying cloud," he decided against common sense. "Descending to the tips of the dead trees."

If the absence of the sun were a warning, he ignored it, compelled forward by an intense sensation of awe. Here he behold something ancient and modern, speaking of rituals and sacrifices still practiced, as they had been, since time immemorial.

Working his way forward, he passed the outer circle, getting a closer and thus a more complete view of the inner arrangement. Beyond the obelisks, at dead center, stood a nine foot stone, surrounded on three sides by immense chairs carved from rock. Six chairs were set on either side of the center stone, while a thirteenth, larger and more commanding than the others, faced ahead. Interspersed throughout the enclave were tripods, atop which were placed shallow, curved discs used as fire holders.

The nearer Shepherd got to center, the more intense the pall, until he feared his breathing would be affected. He need not have worried, for though the air felt thick, he had no trouble inhaling.

A thick layer of ash covered the valley floor, so deep in places it crept up the foot of the stones, creating soft peaks such as he had seen sand around the pyramids.

"I must have been a fool to come down here."

A fool, indeed, yet nothing could have kept him away. A power greater than his own had meant him to feel the allure, be drawn by the fateful attraction.

Stepping carefully to avoid disturbing the settled dust, he arrived at the center stone, finally observing that which had been obscured: four iron chains, complete with shackles, positioned to imprison the arms and legs of a human being.

Failing to comprehending his fascination, Shepherd reaching his hand into the ash. Discovering a small, hard object, he withdrew it, then blew off the clinging powder in order to identify what he held. As his brain correctly interpreted the item, his stomach violently contracted.

"Good God!" Flinging the human molar from him in utter disgust, the tooth struck one of the smaller chairs, bounced off and disappeared into a new pile of ash. "What kind of a place have I come to?"

No one answered, for which he gave thanks. Reminding himself not to tempt fate by speaking aloud again, he propelled forward, stumbling into a flat stone altar, clearly the focal point of the arrangement.

Breathing through his mouth for fear of smelling a not quite burned-away stench, he reacted with horror at two cut-away channels meant for the passage of blood. Almost as horrific were the bizarre characters etched into the apex of the altar.

Compelled by forces beyond his control, Shepherd eagerly examined the hieroglyphics, face lining in concentration. The deeper his thought, the more a sensation of vertigo descended, until he could no longer make out the characters. Working in concert with the dizziness, waves of intense heat wafted before his eyes, distorting his vision.

Flailing his arms in a somnambulistic trance, he crept upon the master's chair, mumbling incoherent supplications to the invisible presence. Unable to comprehend his motives or the words which poured from lips under another's control, Shepherd brushed against the arm rest. Instantly his limb soldered in place as though it had become magnetized. Crying with numb, ill-defined fright, he attempted to break away by planting his feet in the earth and tugging. Nothing he did broke the electrified spell.

Jeering at his struggles, an energy force pressed against his back, knocking him to his knees. From this position, Shepherd's gaze riveted to the base of the seat.

Characters similar to those chiseled on the altar leapt out from their stone encasement. Although he had not changed, the force controlling him transferred the power of interpretation, enabling him to read the cryptic symbols. Not fully cognizant of the strange, obscure meanings, his head drew back, forcing his attention upward, toward where the head of a man would be, were he sitting in the chair.

Speaking in tongues, Shepherd rattled off a series of incantations or supplications, oblivious to their import. Completing the last with the familiar yet dreaded, "Xilka. Besa," he plunged face down into the ash.

This act served to clear his vision and in an equally bizarre moment, the miasma encompassing the valley dissipated. Everything around him took on the stark unreality of a dream, larger and more intense than life. No longer day, but night, torches burned with ferocity, casting grotesque shadows in the form of beasts, throughout the enclave.

A naked youth was chained to the altar. Before him stood a man clad in a black, cowled robe, affixed with a golden belt. He wore an immense ring, set with a blood-red stone on one hand. In the other he grasped a sacrificial perforator. Though Shepherd could not make out the wielder's features, he received the impression of an old man, taller and broader than Ara.

Around him swarmed a buzzing, likened to that which might originate from a gigantic bee hive. Only through the most intense concentration did Shepherd distinguish it as the singsong hum of human chanting. Coordinated with the actions of the high priest, the sound rose and fell according to the position of his dagger. The culmination came when the point touched to the victim's heart, then reached an almost deafening crescendo as the priest drove it through that auricle.

Open-mouthed in synchronization with that of the victim, Shepherd screamed.

His cry of immortal terror dissolved the night sky, returning him to the present. In a panic known only to those who have experienced death and yet lived, Shepherd crawled away, nearly choking on the dust upturned in haste. Not until reaching the outer limits of the sacrificial arena did he find the power to rise.

Unsteady on his feet, he plunged forward, stumbled, scraped the palms of his hands on the hardened earth, then righted himself. Using a burst of strength summoned from the depths of his soul, he raced up the incline, then back down the other side without pause.

He did not slow until coming upon the horse, and only then for fear of spooking the animal.

"Easy, boy, easy," he cajoled. "It's all right." His words lacked conviction, yet miraculously, the steed steadied long enough for him to mount, which he did, with unanticipated ease.

Without his former conviction that beyond the hills lay Budapest, or Prague, or Warsaw, Shepherd rode, certain now that all paths led to hell.

CHAPTER 23

Everything at the castle appeared as he left it, giving the impression nothing had altered in his absence. Yet Shepherd sensed a latent awareness that whatever transpired in the valley had been carefully scripted – not only for his benefit, but for that of others. Feeling soiled and used, he left the bay horse with the silent Hest and slowly trudged his way up the steps to the fortress.

Dongal greeted him at the entrance the way he might have admitted a tenant of long standing. Or a wayward dog.

"The master is waiting, sir."

His tone suggested that the rent might be past due. Or that the pet had been caught committing some transgression and would be led to the den for a less than friendly blow to the nose with a rolled newspaper.

Angered and distracted, Shepherd nodded.

"I'm sure he is."

Before the servant could render further caution, Eldrich appeared from a side corridor. Dongal's reaction conveyed the impression this did not bode well for either of them.

"You are to come with me," the favored announced to the new arrival. "And you, Dongal, are also summoned."

Swallowing this command with ill-disguised terror, Dongal's head bobbed.

"Of course."

Impatient to have his assignment fulfilled, Eldrich scurried ahead to inform Ara that Shepherd had returned. This gave the two who tarried a chance to conduct a private conversation.

"Ara challenged me to a race. I never had a chance."

"Diabolus is unbeaten, sir," came the hesitant response.

"So I gather. A mysterious type of horse, bred in your mysterious country."

"Not *my* country, sir," came the immediate protestation, as Dongal's plodding feet ground to a halt. "I was not born here."

"Not born in the Kingdom?" Shepherd responded, taken off guard. "Then why the hell are you here?"

Dongal lowered his eyes, but not from shame.

"I was sold by my father."

"That was damned white of him," Shepherd bitterly muttered, pausing to take a closer look at the man's features. Learning that Dongal was a foreigner aroused immediate sympathy.

"He sold himself as well, sir," Dongal forgivingly whispered. "Times were hard, sir. It was life or death."

"But to sell himself... and his son. How barbaric."

"It is an ancient tradition one resorts to... when times are hard."

Ignoring the lame excuse, the photographer leaned forward with ill-disguised interest.

"I was led to believe no one had ever been brought in – that I was the first."

Dongal shrugged, begrudgingly offering his information.

"The first from... over there," he explained, pointing his finger in a vaguely eastern direction. "Occasionally, some of us – my people who live near the border – do enter the Kingdom."

"Willingly?"

The question brought an immediate reaction.

"Yes, sir. That is most important."

"You're not recruited – not dragged over against your will?"

Dongal appeared shocked. "Never. Yet... to *cross over* brings great change to one's status."

His listener cringed at the expression. In his experience, "crossing over" meant only one thing: bridging the gap between life and death. With hesitation born of extreme trepidation, Shepherd reached out and placed a hand on the man's shoulder. It encountered no more and no less than flesh and bone.

Steadying himself from the shock he did not receive, he forced himself to continue.

"What kind of change?"

It did not require a crystal ball to divine Dongal's thoughts. *One must sacrifice one's soul, sir.* The verbal reply he actually gave was only slightly better.

"One gives up one's freedom, sir."

Closing his eyes until a wave of vertigo passed, Shepherd motioned him on.

"How old were you when you... came over?"

"Fifteen years of age. The Old Master presented me to his stepson, Ara, who was but an infant at the time."

"Then you are Ara's personal... slave?" Noting the expression of dread, he immediately recanted. "I'm sorry. Forgive me. Pretend I never said it."

"It is too late," came the sorrowful answer. "The master already knows."

Uncertain whether that meant Ara could read minds, or had some other form of divination, Shepherd held his tongue and the two hurried after Eldrich.

They did not go to the den, but to another room Shepherd had not seen. Outside the chamber rested a small, round table upon which had been set a decanter and two glasses. Stepping back, Dongal permitted the guest to enter first. Unlike the former, this spacious room had no furniture of any kind. A large picture window dominated the west wall, running from one end to the other. Heavy drapes hung on either side, fastened by thick gold cord. Open or drawn made little difference, however, for the view presented scant cheer. As Shepherd witnessed earlier from the courtyard, no houses, villages or signs of cultivation were within view. If a fire had not somewhat lightened the mood, both interior and exterior landscape would have been overtly depressing.

Ara stood somewhat off-center, awaiting their arrival. Eldrich was not present, indicating he had delivered his message and departed.

The master's amicable voice bid them welcome. "Come in! You must be thirsty after your ride, Mr. Kingston. We will take refreshment."

Waving his hand with the expectation Dongal would act on his wish, he waited until the servant had procured the wine and poured a glass before continuing. Unlike previous ceremonies, Ara indicated the visitant be offered the first taste.

"Drink."

Shepherd complied, offering a flat "Congratulations on your victory," before swallowing.

"Come now," Ara beamed. "You must be a better loser than this."

"I must?"

"Take your cue from Dongal," he chided. "He loses often – and well. And *he* never fails to pay his debt to the gracious winner. Do you?"

"I try my best, master."

Dongal poured a second glass and offered it to Ara. His hand shook so badly, however, he spilled a drop, incurring instant wrath.

"How dare you!"

The servant ducked from a blow he expected, but was not forthcoming.

"I – I beg pardon, sir," he stammered, hastening to wipe the spill with a cloth retrieved from his tunic. "I will refill the glass."

Temper assuaged, Ara watched with bemused contempt as Dongal cleaned the goblet before offering it again.

"You see how I am served," he noted, taking the offering. "What a shame I have no better. And to think – this is a very special vintage. For a most auspicious occasion."

He meant for Shepherd to pursue his veiled reference.

"Special?"

"We have cause to celebrate. Tonight, you will learn more of our customs. How fortunate. That is why you came, is it not?" Shepherd nodded, aware that his true feelings had already been made known. "I am terribly sorry you shall be deprived of Ericka's most pleasant company, but the loser cannot expect to claim a prize he did not win."

Reacting to Shepherd's expression, Ara burst into raucous laughter.

"The look on your face," he teased. "Miss Elvina must have made a great impression on you. She makes a great impression wherever she goes. Remember the first time you saw her, Dongal?" he joked, taking in the scene with unmitigated amusement. "How enraptured you were!"

"Saw her?" Shepherd questioned, curious to add to his knowledge. "When was this?"

"Not so terribly long ago," Ara answered for him. "When Dongal still possessed his sight. Even now, he is not permanently blind. But his moments of 'enlightenment' are few and far between."

Failing to fully comprehend the well-played act, Shepherd innocently protested.

"If that is true, then Dongal's blindness may be caused by hysteria or shock, rather than some organic cause."

"Yes. I believe that is a sound diagnosis, Mr. Kingston. Shock. But as we have no physicians here, alas, it may be said his condition is incurable."

"I don't believe –"

Ara silenced him by slapping a hand against his thigh. "Your faith in 'modern medicine' is not at issue. I cannot permit him to leave for treatment. I would miss him so."

"He has been with you... all your life?"

Ara dismissed the question, his eyes burning brightly.

"Let us agree that between us there shall be no dissembling. Inasmuch as Dongal has already informed you of my 'gift' of second sight, it is safe to acknowledge I have owned him since childhood."

"A present from your father," Shepherd clarified.

"Yes. My dear departed stepfather," Ara amended, sarcasm dripping from his mouth the way wine had rolled down the side of his glass. "God rest his soul. How thoughtful he was."

Shepherd did not know how to take the reference to God and let it pass.

"You did not get on well with him?"

"I think not. He was fond of saying that although I was precocious, I often acted like a child."

"And you disagreed?"

"My stepfather's words were not always well chosen. Perhaps he bore a grudge."

"Why is that?" he began, but Ara waved the question away. On this subject, however, the foreign caller felt at liberty to delve further. "But, surely it was he who taught you how to rule –"

"Yes, indeed," the king agreed, sipping his beverage with hedonistic delight. "Though perhaps not in the manner you suppose. Or for the reasons one might conjecture."

"It appears you do him honor," Shepherd tried, feeling awkward at having to stand throughout the conversation.

"That is an interesting observation. That I do my *father* honor, you may well believe. Let us say I have learned much on my own."

"And I congratulate you for it."

"Thank you. Though it may not appear so to you, there is much which requires my personal attention."

"I do believe you." Inching forward, Shepherd pushed home the advantage he hoped he had gained by his flattery. "And Ericka? Does she help you? In ways other than making money?" Ara's face betrayed a momentarily hesitation, as if he did not have a ready answer. "You mentioned it was your father's wish she go to New York, not yours. You did not inherit her, then, as you did Dongal? She is a free woman?"

"You might say –"

Ara abruptly ceased speaking. His smile faded and his concentration, to that point directed on Shepherd, dramatically altered. Suddenly oblivious to his visitor, the youthful king crossed to the window, where the first rays of sunset danced along the glass. In contrast to the dull, cheerless visage of mountain and trees, a brilliant array of sparkling vermilion, pumpkin orange and royal gold assumed precedence, giving rise to the speculation that the portal had been designed for exactly that effect.

Puissant rays shot from the setting orb, eradicating all but its own majesty. Transfixed by the panorama in exactly the same way Ericka had been when watching the sunset from her New York apartment, Ara pressed against the window. Arms outstretched, he drew power from the energy until his entire body assimilated into the natural phenomenon.

His flesh changed hues, subtly altering from pale white to striking red; the black of his wardrobe, once the absence of color, assumed a radiant brilliance of scarlet and platinum, altering Ara's shape from humanoid to amorphously alien. Over his head, a fluctuating, luminescent halo developed, pulsating with energy derived from the heavenly star. The more intense the spectrum, the more encompassing the aura, until it stretched the length of his body, encapsulating the beams within.

More striking than this physical transformation, Ara's countenance displayed an expression of rapture, almost a transcendental exchange of intelligence with a higher medium of intelligence.

Beyond worship flickered wonder, victory, fear and defiance, making Ara appear he were in a battle with the sun for ascendancy. In this contest of man against nature, both sides waged war to the death, first drawing then repelling the other, until the entire room sparkled with the fierceness of the contest.

Unlike the horse race, no preordained winner declared victory. Back and forth, first one, then the other gained dominance, until it seemed neither could possibly triumph.

Curiosity gripping his soul, Shepherd leaned forward, all concentration on the combatants. Opening his consciousness, he allowed his mind to expand through the wavering dimensions. Waxing and waning from the intensity Ara drew in, then repulsed, Shepherd found himself inching closer to the window.

Swirling memories, half-formed images, remembrances of his own religious instruction battled with the beguiling pagan concepts which wormed their way into his brain through all open orifices.

Give yourself over to me, for I am the One. Through me is the path to salvation. I am the power; I am the will. I am the beginning, I am the end. Worship at my fire and be damned, for within me is evil greater than any good. I am the Protector and you are the Chosen.

Thrown back from the sheer horror of the unexpected revelation, Shepherd broke contact. In that instant, he caught sight of another scene unraveling before him.

Like him, Dongal inched forward, features contorted in concentration. Shepherd's initial impression that the servant meant to worship alongside his master dispelled instantly by the sight if a dagger tightly clutched between white fingers. He sought neither cleansing nor oneness, but assassination.

Nearly deranged by the awareness his intended victim did not have the strength to resist, Dongal crept through the former's shadow, praying his resolve to hold. An inch, two inches, then a foot nearer the captivated youth.

Detecting a new player in the contest, the Essence within the setting sun surged brighter, more daunting and thus more dominating. Ara's body leaned closer to the window, craving absolution by the destruction of a force more ancient than time. Insane desire pulsated from his very essence. The white aura surrounding him fluctuated, stretched, then appeared to solidify. His fingers curled inward, nails biting into flesh, then forming fists.

No strength on Earth could break the celestial contest. Although a daily struggle, Ara had no desire to refuse the challenge. To back down – to step away – acknowledged defeat, succumbing his corporeal existence to the elements of self-destruction.

In his limited fashion, Shepherd comprehended that Dongal possessed complete awareness of his master's inability to defend himself from any outside combatant. Figuratively chained to the sun, Ara's worldly powers were neutralized. Perhaps for the first time on his life, the slave saw his chance for revenge.

One he had cultivated since the age of fifteen.

Another foot closer. The dagger glistened with sparks of blue-white, reminiscent of metal pressed against a madly rotating sharpening stone.

Time dragged slowly toward its predestined end, giving Ara a slight ascendancy in his struggle. Unlike men, sunsets had but a short time to live. Though they would appear and reappear over the course of ten million centuries, their span of dominance lasted only minutes. Ara's eyelids fluttered. The skin around his nose twitched.

Awareness stirred. Acutely, frighteningly aware of impending danger, he could not – for the moment – disengage himself.

The beams metamorphed, blood red to anemic pink, Halloween orange to drab brown, newly-minted gold to tarnished pyrite. Seeing his master flinch, then begin to withdraw from the contest, Dongal panicked. Failing to consummate his act surely meant his own demise. Insanely furious, he raised the knife blade shoulder high. Features contorted in effort, he drove the point home. Ara cried, throwing his head back in an unconscious reaction to the pain he expected... but did not feel.

A deep, dark hissing noise emanated from between Dongal's clenched teeth. Though he had plunged the dagger downward, his arm had been stopped in mid-action. Not by Ara, still held by the semi-mesmeric trance of his combatant. By a totally unlooked for source of power.

Shepherd Kingston.

Gasping in horror, the servant turned quickly, first angry, then pleading. Trembling with impotent abandonment, he raised his empty hand, imploring Shepherd to free him.

"In the name of all you hold holy," he begged. "Release me."

Shaking his head in mute denial, for in truth, Shepherd did not have the ability to undo what he had begun, the dagger wrenched from Dongal's hand. It hung, suspended, for a fraction of a second, then dropped to the floor with a clang, drowned out by the low whimper of a condemned soul.

Dongal's chance had come and gone. With it went the hope of redemption.

Before his cries were absorbed by the undrawn window dressings, the sun dipped below the sill. The temperature dropped as the fading rays extinguished the warmth. A log crackled.

The knife rose from the floor. Dongal stared at it in dull fascination, then slowly lifted his eyes upward, toward Shepherd. He saw no explanation there. That actor's part had been written out.

Jerking in spasmodic fear, he turned to face Ara. The master's face, no longer bathed in red by the sunset, had returned to its customary pale sheen. In the growing shadows, his nose seemed sharper, his ears more pointed. Raising a hand for effect, his fingers looked longer, double-jointed, concluding at the ends with inwardly curled talons.

He smiled. Having escaped his own death, he desired to inflict that fate on another with merciless justice.

Holding his servant transfixed, Ara manipulated the knife through the dominance of his mind. The point rested at Dongal's Adams apple. With infinite patience, he worked it into the flesh, enjoying the spectacle.

"No!" Shepherd screamed into a void which did not acknowledge his presence. "I used my Gift, but only to spare your life. Do not turn it against the perpetrator."

"Dongal... my own Dongal," Ara crooned, his voice gentle, tender, contrasting sharply to the unmitigated sadism of his face. "We both have our destinies to fulfill. Yours is to suffer. Mine is to dominate."

"Master...." the servant begged, tears streaming down his cheeks.

"Yes. Master. Your lord and master. You would have me dead, Dongal, but that is not the Divine Plan. You were stopped." A quizzical expression briefly swept over Ara, as his eyes snaked toward Shepherd. "You. It was you who stopped him. You, who have left yourself open so that I may grow stronger. *I knew you were the one."*

"I could not help myself," Shepherd confessed, as he had done so many times before, both shamed and confused by his action.

"No. You could not. Your heart," he sneered, "is pure. You could not condone my murder. A pity for Dongal, Mr. Kingston. He forgot, you see. In his eagerness, he sought revenge by himself. My death was to be his triumph, and his alone."

"Forgot... what?" Shepherd whispered, afraid, yet compelled to ask.

"Why I have brought you here."

"Why... have you?"

"To complete a prophesy. Not," he menacingly continued, "to witness the taking of my life. How could you have been so forgetful, my little one?" he concluded, returning to his servant.

"Not him!" Dongal protested. "Surely not him. Do not use his power to kill!" but Ara laughed him off.

"Enough! It is time for you to expiate your sin."

Directed by the force of Ara's consciousness, the blade jumped again, pressing itself deeper into tender skin.

"Kill me, then!" Dongal screamed, startling Shepherd into a violent fit of trembling. "Destroy me, master, for I do not fear death. Kill me *dead,* and so I will finally have release."

Ara's eyes widened, an expression of amusement broadcasting his mirth.

"No, Dongal. Not *dead.* Again, you forget: the soul is immortal. It lives on, in eternity. For you, there is no release."

"Dead. Dead. Dead," Dongal chanted, employing his own concentration to propel the point inward.

Ara remained implacable. "That would be against my oath, old faithful servant. Remember my promise: never to allow you to take your own life? You belong to me: in this world and the next. To die forever would be too easy. I shall never forgive you, Dongal."

"Dead. Dead. Dead." But he had not the power to complete his desire. The knife spun away from his body, flipped over once, then settled on the floor.

"Pick it up," the master commanded.

"Ara," Shepherd appealed, struggling with his voice. "Please –"

"Silence! Do not presuppose your act of generosity has given you authority here. I am master. I am in control. As a guest, a small breech of etiquette may be overlooked. But in this land, one's status alters rapidly. Keep your place."

"What – is my place?"

"That is for me to know. And now Dongal knows it, too," he added with malevolence. "But your time is not now. Hold your tongue, or I will have it ripped from your throat."

Shepherd believed him. Hanging his head in shame, he said no more.

"Pick up the dagger, Dongal, and deliver it to Eldrich. He knows how to obey – and he would have your place." After observing the tear-stained face, he continued in a softer tone. "Let us agree that tonight we have come a long way on our journey, old friend." The unmistakable sound of affection tainted his otherwise reserved speech.

Dongal's shoulders quivered. Pausing to stare quizzically at Shepherd, the youth read resignation. Beyond that, the pages of Dongal's life were inscrutable.

"Leave us," Ara hurried on the slave. "I will speak to our 'guest' alone. Your person – for the moment – is spared."

Shrunken into submission, the servant retrieved the weapon, ran his fingers across the blade, contemplating what he had lost. Feeling the gaze of both Shepherd and Ara upon him, he slunk away, shutting the door quietly behind him.

The lock clicked into place. With it went a piece of Shepherd's soul.

CHAPTER 24

Without Dongal's presence, the life went out of the room. Shepherd almost dared remark on the phenomenon then abruptly held his tongue. Stealing a glance at the ruler, he was disturbed to see no such recognition in Ara.

As the king strode boldly over the floor, his booted feet soundlessly striking the carpet, Shepherd felt a tap on his shoulder. Responding precisely as he had done when experiencing the effect outside Joe Warren's office, he altered his position, expecting, without logic, to see someone behind him. As before, he merely confirmed his isolation.

For a moment his heart fluttered, anticipating the imminent arrival of Ericka. So sure, in fact, of her near presence, he crisscrossed Ara's invisible trail, going to the door. While the master drew the curtains, Shepherd peered out into the hall.

Empty.

Oblivious to the actions of his guest, Ara fussed with the low-hanging drapes, adjusting the cloth so that it hung smooth and unwrinkled. Taking advantage of this diversion, Shepherd locked them in, before turning his full attention to the room. While subconsciously denying his physic ability, he scanned the empty chamber, seeking that which his eyes could not register.

On a dare, he would have bet his soul they were being observed.

As foolish as it brave, he would have won.

Drawing back the hood from around his eyes, the tall, broad-shouldered spectre of a man malevolently smiled. Like Ara, his teeth were sharp and white, with irises black as pitch. There the similarity stopped, however, for although cast from the same mold, the observer differed from the young master in many ways.

Tarrington, for thus he was called, owned four score of years over the king. Greying hair spread over his head, combed back in a sweeping, almost careless style, although his attitude suggested anything but indifference. Dressed entirely in black, he wore a loose-fitting tunic under a flowing cape. Around his neck sparkled a gold chain, the links of which were interwoven without a seam to mar their symmetry. Although not a crown, the necklace radiated with the authority of mastery and command.

Watching the scene unfold as one who well comprehended his destiny, Tarrington radiated a glow of satisfaction. His thin lips crinkled at the edges, not accentuating laugh lines, but rather evil intent. *My work is not done,* his expression indicated, *but well begun.*

Rubbing his hands, then snaking his pomegranate-red tongue around prominent canines, he turned away, not in dismissal but satisfaction.

"Speak now, of prophesy, king-ling," he declared, with the aura of one who dictated other men's actions at whim. "Assure yourself he is the one. You have seen much. Believe more." With a smirk he added, "Trent did."

Tarrington possessed a deep but not unpleasant voice, and the words rolled from his mouth with anticipation. "Mark well the human's likeness to the painting."

As he spoke, his mind's eye transported itself to Ericka's Manhattan bed chamber and the picture on the wall. The ancient oils, dried for a thousand centuries, glistened anew as the youth on the mountain stared upward, the panic in his soul disintegrating into terror. With the photographic skill of a painter, whose ability to capture the very fundamental nature of his subject highlighted his talent, Tarrington reworked the art, fleshing in the final details of Shepherd Kingston's features.

"As it was foretold, so shall it *not* be."

Alive to his private jest, the demon-creature laughed, the sound of his mirth echoing off the walls of his private chamber like the cries of the damned reverberating off the gates of Hades. Reaching out to embrace both sound and flesh, a figure from another portrait came alive. Absorbing the noble's condemnation, Athena swelled in satisfaction and bade him continue. He was only too glad to comply.

"Your time is coming, Ara, stepson of Ruhvan. You know it. I know it. Prepare well for the sacrifice you must make, for He will receive it, *but not in the manner you anticipate.*"

Bowing his head, Tarrington turned his back on the images in the castle, displaying blatant insubordination to his earthly master. Maintaining an expression of smug superiority, he glided effortlessly toward a massive fire burning in a grate-less hearth. Flames leapt out toward him, licking impatiently against their bonds.

"Soon," he reverently whispered, neither to those alive or those supposed to be dead. "I have waited long."

In response to his promise, the pile of consumed logs collapsed, shooting balls of fire beyond the limits of their stone enclave. One such missile came to rest at Tarrington's feet. With a smile of unmitigated wickedness, he ground it out.

Athena, in her wisdom, winked.

A log cracked in the fireplace. Sparks flared upward, popping in the air like miniature firecrackers. This alone finally diverted Ara from his task of straightening the drapes. Staring at the flames a moment, he contemplated their significance before re-crossing the room to hurl additional fuel on the red-hot embers. He did not look up again until his offering had been greedily accepted.

Shepherd cowered away from Ara, still shaking from the sensation of being watched. Or, more accurately, trembling from the memory, for the acuteness had worn away, leaving only a dull suspicion.

More pertinent to the moment, he dwelt on Ara's vivid threat to Dongal. If this warlord could threaten the life of a man he had known all his life, what might he do to a guest whose status had "altered"?

Finally daring to meet the master's eyes, what Shepherd beheld did not match the picture of an enraged monarch. Instead, Ara's features had rounded into what Shepherd might have called "wonder" in a more sentient human being.

"You." One word, to begin a new relationship. "I *was* right. But I must know..... You will tell me, please," he gracefully amended. "*Why* you saved my life."

"I saw..." Shepherd mumbled, confused by the incident and of being called so suddenly to explain.

"It is true, then, you could not help yourself? This is a marvelous gift you possess, Mr. Kingston."

"I have never wanted it." Side-stepping away in dread of being put through a second test, he hastily continued. "In fact, I have spent most of my life denying its existence – looking for rational excuses to explain it away."

Ara's brows knit in concentration.

"But why? Such a *special* power raises you above the level of moral man."

Shepherd understood Ara meant his phraseology to sooth and ultimately flatter. It did neither.

"If it were up to me, I would abandon it all together." Noting Ara pout, he blurted in youthful protestation, "It has brought *me* no good!"

The king, his own age in years, broke into good humored mirth.

"As to that, I understand perfectly!" Clasping his hands in an unusual display of camaraderie, he quietly appraised the youth who had unwittingly exchanged his status as guest for one of servant. "We shall see what we can do about that."

"About exorcising my power?"

"You misunderstand. I refer to earthly rewards. Come," he sympathetically cajoled. "You pursued Miss Elvina because you sought fame and fortune. You wished to rise above anonymity; to have wealth, power through your photographic talents. Let us agree between ourselves that path is now closed to you."

"If it ever existed."

Ara waved the protest away.

"I offer you more. Cast your lot with me, Mr. Kingston, for I will not fail you."

Intrigued by the prospect, Shepherd made a noncommittal bow. He did not fully comprehend the offer, and suspected when it came to "rewards," he and Ara spoke of vastly divergent treasure.

"You and I are of different worlds."

"Not so far apart as you might presume."

"Are you asking me to... cross over?" he whispered, cringing from the vaguely comprehended idea of what such a notion entailed.

Like Shepherd, Ara chose his words carefully. He had much to lose and little to gain by saying too much.

"You ask a question but that is bad form, inasmuch as you have not answered mine. I asked why you saved my life."

Pressed on a subject he felt loath to pursue, Shepherd hunched his shoulders in awkward reflection.

"I never know when or how the... phenomenon comes about. I witness something happening and my mind responds... without conscious oversight."

"Have you never tried to *will* this power? To summon it on command?"

"Never!"

"Then we shall travel uncharted ground together."

"Please," Shepherd implored, torn by the consequences he surely faced. "Do not ask that of me."

A smile played on Ara's aristocratic lips. "Ask?" he toyed. "Or demand?"

"Either," he hedged, quickly surmising that his "gift" played an integral part in Ara's plans. "Before today, I have not used it in years."

"Ah. You think to put me off by falsehood. You have... employed it recently; by saving the life of a young woman." Putting a hand to his forehead in imitation of a carnival mind reader, Ara pretended to extract the scene from the atmosphere. "Shelley Larson, was her name, I believe."

"You had best believe it," came the foolishly bold retort, "for it was Ericka who told you."

Ara exploded with an amused guffaw. "You do not hesitate to speak your mind, Mr. Kingston. Indeed, you are correct. I learned it from Ericka."

"And she witnessed it through the pyramid. The same pyramid I saw in your den."

"How could that be, when you left it with Professor Abraham Trent?"

The image evoked sadness and anger and revealed more than he cared admit.

"Xilka. Besa," Shepherd quoted, damning the consequences. Ara drew away, whether in actual or feigned surprise he could not tell. "The demon in the pyramid brought it back to her and she returned it to you."

"So you believe in demons?"

He refused to answer the question, but failed to hide the color seeping into his cheeks.

"Did she report everything that happened?"

"Trust me when I say nothing which passed between you is unknown to me. Miss Elvina is... candidly honest. As well she should be, I being her master."

"But she is not your slave," Shepherd underscored, seeking to change direction.

"No. We do not have that relationship."

"And not your – lover?"

"No. As I have already assured, such is your distinction. For which I congratulate you. She holds her... affection dearly."

"When may I see her? I miss her. Without her presence I feel quite lost."

"You are not lost, sir: you are found. But do not fear. The time draws nigh. She is most anxious to see you. A lady must not be kept waiting, would you not agree? Even in this 'barbaric' land, one of high birth may not be denied forever. Have patience."

"I will try."

Turning his back on the ostensive guest, Ara stoked the fire with a long, savagely-pointed poker. Flames leapt up in wild abandon, the tips of their dragon-like claws nearly reaching his hand.

"What is it they say? Boys try; men do. 'Do' be patient, Shepherd. Do not 'try' my patience, for I am a temperamental ruler. An absolute monarch. My whim is law."

Had he been face-to-face with Ara, Shepherd might not have possessed the courage to speak. But protected, as it were, from his piercing eyes, he took a chance, failing to heed the warning just delivered.

"Be merciful with Dongal," he blurted. "I plead with you not to deal harshly with him."

The king straightened, holding the fire tool menacingly in his left hand, drawn across his body like a sword. Unlike Shepherd, his words were thoughtfully selected. Devoid of friendship, they yet contained a trace of awe, as well as challenge.

"You defended him once before – about the wine – and were correct. Tell me why you defend him now, when you have seen with your own eyes his murderous intent."

"While I do not understand his motives, I have witnessed – affection – for you in his face. I believe him to be good."

"He is a simple man."

"Those are not mutually exclusive, your grace."

"He is a slave. He is dung beneath my feet, although I admit he has – qualities." Without replacing the poker, Ara wandered the confines of the room, staring absently at the blank walls. The attention paid to the detail of the inlaid stone was of a kind Trent had once used to pursue Shepherd's photographs.

"Affection?" Ara continued finally abandoning his efforts to fathom some hidden message. "Possibly. But more likely, he considers me the lesser of two evils."

Hands akimbo, Shepherd confronted him. "Compared to whom?"

Ara formed the answer, but never uttered it. Instead, he chose a different track. "Do not lecture or question me, Mr. Kingston. And let me add fair warning: do not threaten, nor ever consider using your powers against me. I will extract terrible and immediate vengeance."

"You have powers yourself."

Replacing the poker between a pair of crudely fashioned iron tongs, Ara rolled his tongue before setting it against the side of his cheek

"What you saw... surely you understood?" Phrasing it as a question, he betrayed his own doubt.

"That you assumed temporary possession of my... Gift?"

"Yes."

"How was it done?" Receiving no answer, he tried a second time. "Trent told me I could not give it away."

Ara crept closer, until within touching distance. For a moment Shepherd believed he would put his arms out, completing some sort of a permanent transference. Surprising himself, for he had spent his life wishing to be rid of the power, Shepherd prepared a mental counter to the assault, but none came. Strangely, the boy-king backed off, muting the edge to his voice.

"He was correct. About many things."

Feeling the blood pound in his arteries, Shepherd choked back tears.

"Is that why you killed him?"

Only the most astute observer would have detected the subtle altercation which passed over Ara's face.

"I did not kill him."

"Have him killed, then."

This time, Ara frowned, shifting weight from one leg to the other, as though in preparation for flight.

"So far as I know, he yet lives."

"Liar!" Shepherd hissed, moving forward, fists clenched. Despite his posture, Ara neither fled nor put up resistance. "He is dead! Burned to death in a fire you started."

"I? Why do you suppose such a thing?"

The implied protestation of innocence did not put Shepherd off.

"I saw the conflagration. In my mind."

"When did this happen?"

"As if you don't know. Yesterday... the day before. As soon as I left New York," he concluded, uncertain himself of the precise timing. Ara worked the muscles in his jaw.

"I have no knowledge of such an event."

"Your pyramid started the fire."

Sensing danger, Ara retreated out of range.

"The pyramid has no power to kill."

"You called up the demon, then; whatever lurked within it!" Shepherd screamed. "Trent translated the writing. Xilka. Xilka. Besa. Besa."

"Shhh," Ara warned, bringing a finger to his lips. His complexion paled. "You are mistaken. I had nothing to fear from that old man. I did not wish him dead."

Pressing his advantage, Shepherd inched nearer, muscles tensed.

"But you killed Joe Warren – you, or one of your familiars pushed him from his office window!" On a roll, he threw caution to the wind. "You burned Danny Poole; you 'stole, 'or whatever you want to call it, Bill Ford away. You dropped a lighting fixture on Sammy Greeley."

"Ericka –"

"Not Ericka! I will never believe such evil of her. *You!*"

Gathering his wits, if not his composure, Ara finally worked a grim smile over his twisted countenance.

"Yes," he admitted almost graciously. "They were – what is the word? Tainted."

"From what?" Shepherd screamed.

"Too much exposure."

"To whom?"

"To Ericka. To you. Once she made up her mind you were the one, the others became superfluous; unnecessary. They set you on her trail. Their usefulness had... expired."

"And Trent? Had he become superfluous?"

Holding out his palms, Ara tried to placate the irate man.

"I had no hand in his death – if, in fact, he is dead. Which I doubt."

"Trust me," Shepherd warned. "I saw it." He pointed to his temple, voice choking from the vivid memory and the loss he could never make right. "Burned to a crisp."

"An accident, then. Surely not from the pyramid."

Reluctantly responding to the sincerity in the king's tone, he unclenched his fists.

"If not you, who, then? And don't try to make me believe it was Ericka." They had been down that path before and he could not face a repetition.

"No. Not she, either. She is as blameless as I."

Relief flooded the former ward's heart but it brought no relief.

"Who, then, perpetrated such a cruel and senseless deed?" Ara shrugged. "Someone here – someone with power to make the pyramid do his bidding."

A light glinted behind Ara's eyes.

"No one has that ability." *To act against me,* the unspoken conclusion.

"Then you deceive yourself. Trent has been murdered and we both have a very powerful enemy."

Straightening his shoulders, Ara assumed the mantle of a monarch. "I am absolute ruler here. No one would dare intervene in my plans."

"Are you so certain?"

Stung by the accusation, Ara's eyelid twitched.

"Yes."

Accepting his lack of complicity but not his flat denial, Shepherd sagged. His mind reverted to their former discussion.

"Is that why you brought me here? To steal my so-called 'gift' to fight your enemies?"

"That I cannot do," Ara softly confessed. "To use it, yes."

"For what purpose?"

"That is for me to know. But let it never come to a contest between us, Shepherd Kingston. That is not your place."

"What is my place?" the stranger pleaded, holding out his hands in desperation. "I understand so little of what has happened."

Moved by the sincerity of the plea, Ara's posture relaxed, and he offered his hand, so recently armed, in a gesture of tenderness Shepherd would not have believed possible.

"Your place is to work in conjunction with me. You and I – we are not natural enemies. Remember that. It is I who know your destiny. I, who will employ your talents in the manner decreed by He who created your soul."

"You say that to me? You evoke God's being?"

"Although this is a godless land, His name is not unknown here, my shepherd."

"You profess to comprehend His Divine Plan?"

Points of light flickered behind Ara's eyes. Shepherd needed to believe they were formed from reflected firelight, but the king was situated with his back to the hearth. Shifting awkwardly, he sought a mirror or pane of glass from which the effect could have come, and found none.

Confounded, he averted his gaze to avoid being blinded by the growing intensity as Ara spoke.

"Not *His* plan, certainly, although there are some who would avow that between God and Satan there are no secrets."

"Whom do you worship?"

"The question might better be put, my friend, whom do *you* worship?"

Images of his parents gently interlacing his child's fingers while repeating the Lord's Prayer assailed his memory. Scenes of Trent, reading passages aloud from the Bible, and of reverently placing the small cross around his neck, struck hidden recesses in his heart. To deny God meant to betray all he once loved, but he could not do otherwise.

"Neither," Shepherd intoned in a hushed voice, required to speak truth, yet afraid, for the first time in his life, of being overheard and believed.

Those who had called upon the Lord's name had not been spared. His mother and father, in their final moments, surely prayed for mortal salvation. Dear Trent, were he truly dead, must have cried for mercy and found none. God's power, then, was limited. Or worse, He turned a deaf ear to those children He endowed with existence.

Observing the myriad emotions tear through his visitor, Ara's form swayed as he ruminated on the transparent conflict. Curiosity aroused, he dwelt on the order Shepherd placed on God's supposed failing: the inability to supersede over a cavalier abandonment of His followers.

He thought Shepherd a fool. Or worse, an ignoramus.

"What is this all about? Does Ericka know?" Shepherd pursued, instinctively clasping his hands. "She was in Manhattan, looking for me. At your behest. What am I to you?"

"Perhaps she will answer that herself," Ara recanted, distancing himself from the petitioner.

"Let me see her, I implore you. Now! I must understand. How can I help you, or anyone else, if I'm kept in the dark?"

"Do not rush *blindly* ahead," Ara warned, his expression souring. "Everything in its place. This kingdom has stood since time immemorial; it will go on that much longer. As long as there is an Earth and longer still. What is meant to be, will be."

"I don't believe in this destiny you speak of," Shepherd cried. "I am a man. I forge my own way in life. My actions are not dictated by –"

Before he could finish, Ara raised his hand, stopping him. The grimness of his expression spoke louder than his admonition.

"Enough. It is as well to hold your tongue. I grow weary. We will speak again of Miss Elvina at supper."

"Very well, your grace," Shepherd magnanimously replied, forgetting, for the moment, the admonition not to use that expression, banished forever by King Henry VIII. He bent at the waist without questioning his unanticipated action. "Until supper. I shall look forward to your confidence."

Straightening with effort, he walked stiffly to the door, surprised to find that he, too, had been utterly drained of energy. It would do them both well, he reasoned, to rest before further confrontations.

"Shepherd." Ara's gentle salutation halted him in his tracks and he turned in a semicircular direction. "You were late returning to the castle after the race. I waited for you some time. What kept you from joining me?"

Meeting Ara's eyes, Shepherd benignly smiled. He did not choose the expression: a higher power selected it for him.

"I got lost."

"You strayed off the trail?"

"No. I... fell off the horse."

Had Shepherd realized his boots and trouser cuffs were soiled with ash and soot, he might have reconsidered his lie. Ara nodded in satisfaction, understanding that as Shepherd had asked for his confession, he was unwilling to make his own.

"Supper is at eight. Be prompt."

Unable to analyze his foreboding, Shepherd nodded and departed.

Unlike the previous evening, Dongal was not present to serve the repast. Noting his absence immediately upon arrival, Shepherd's face fell.

"Why so glum?" Ara challenged. "Surely you must be hungry after your exercise this afternoon."

Deprived of Ericka's company, and now even Dongal's steadying presence, the guest gave a noncommittal shrug.

"I'm still suffering from jet lag." Then, with unanticipated cunning, he added, "I don't usually suffer from such maladies. I've flown from New York to California, and that's three thousand miles; approximately the distance from Kennedy to Heathrow. How much further did we fly?"

"I think you will like the food I have ordered," Ara replied, taking the question as rhetorical. "Guess what it is."

"Chitlins and gravy."

"Guess again."

"Stewed rabbit guts."

"Shepherd's pie," the king informed with a toothy grin.

"I thought that was Engl –" Shepherd began, before getting the joke. He grimaced. "Am I the main ingredient?"

"No," Ara scoffed, snapping his fingers. A hitherto unknown servant emerged into the dining chamber, carrying an ornate silver platter in both hands. Atop it sat an immense meat pie, so hot, bubbles of grease still formed through cracks in the crust.

Pausing only long enough to obtain the king's assent, the waiter set the platter down before Shepherd. With steam rising to his nostrils, he accepted the mammoth knife and fork, cutting himself a generous slice. Suspecting some trick, yet espying nothing obvious, he then brought a forkful to his mouth.

Not until he began to chew did Ara complete his sentence. *"Dongal* is the main ingredient."

His delivery achieved the desired effect. Shepherd's throat constricted as his puckered lips expelled the offending delicacy.

"I'm sorry," he apologized, reddening from embarrassment. Wiping away the remnants from the linen tablecloth, he choked into his cupped hand, then hesitantly swallowed what small bits remained in his mouth.

"I see you are beginning to take me seriously," the king approved. "It is well."

Coughing again, Shepherd stared miserably at his plate.

"Yes, sir. But I trust... you were making a small jest?"

"Had I not been, I should have waited until *after* supper to inform you," Ara obliged.

"Thank you."

His meal spoiled, Shepherd picked at the food while his host accepted a robust helping.

"Come, my friend. Eat. You will need your strength for the trial to come."

"Trial?"

"The completion of your obligation." On Shepherd's frightened look, he supplied, "Payment of your debt. You lost the race: upon its outcome we placed a wager. Should I win – which I did – you agreed to pay me homage, after the fashion of my country."

"Was I foolish to do so?"

"On the contrary: it was a noble gesture. What would be foolish, would be to renege on your pledge."

"How is such tribute paid?"

"I shall explain. When we are in private."

Shepherd glanced quickly at the servant, hoping to catch, by his expression, a hint of the future. The man gave no indication of following the conversation, leaving Shepherd to surmise he did not speak English.

Poor consolation, at best.

Ara lingered over his food, consuming nearly half the pie, while Shepherd made the most of the wine, hoping to mute his senses before the coming ordeal. But as was common in such cases, the greater the desire to become inebriated, the less likely it were to happen.

Finally through, Ara clapped his hands. The servant cleared the table.

"I am glad to note we had one item on the menu which appealed to you," he concluded as the decanter was removed. Shepherd let it pass. "Come. We shall retire to the den. An interesting word, do you not agree?" Ara continued as a second servant drew back his chair. He stood, stretched pent-up muscles, then led the way from the room. "Den. Generally used as a place of refuge for beasts. I like your language; so picturesque."

"They say English is the hardest language to learn," Shepherd remarked, more from politeness than any desire for conversation. He felt nauseous and would have preferred to retire for the night. Knowing that impossible increased his discomfiture.

Turning the knob, then drawing back the heavy door himself, Ara stepped inside the "den." Once Shepherd joined him, he closed it. The lock clicked into place. While the room could not have been soundproofed by any modern methods, Shepherd understood that should he scream for help, no one would hear.

Distancing himself, the king rubbed his hands together in unmitigated glee. "Now," he began, savoring the mood which had begun with supper, "Homage is customarily performed while upon one's knees. You shall begin there."

Looking around for any measure of comfort, any sign of civilization from which to derive a belief he would survive the evening, Shepherd saw none. It would be all or nothing. In this land, "nothing," like the word "den," meant more than words described.

Seeing him hesitate, Ara's eyes narrowed.

"Shepherd, do not doubt my desire. I have told you how to begin. I am in earnest."

He believed him implicitly. Sniffing back a runny nose, Shepherd swallowed miserably, then sunk to his knees. It had not been his original intent to bow his head, but the position lent itself to that additional supplication and he did not fight it.

"Very good."

Crossing to within a foot of his recumbent petitioner, Ara held out his left hand upon which he had placed a gold ring. Needing no further instruction, Shepherd brought his face forward, prepared to kiss it. As his lips neared the symbol of royal dignity, however, he found he could not bring himself to complete the act.

Ara leaned forward, hot breath singing Shepherd's cheek. "Why do you resist me? I require no more than that which has been preordained before our births."

"Please," Shepherd cried, tears forming in the corners of his eyes as his courage failed. "I do not want to hear that again." In response, Ara gently caressed his bare head, tousling his hair until a stray lock slipped over his forehead.

"But it is a favorite story of mine, little one," he gently admonished. "Believe or not as you will, but recall to mind the painting."

Shepherd trembled under the sentence, for unlike Ara's physical action, this carried with it the weight of death.

"Then it *was* my portrait..."

"Hush. We will not debate that here," he whispered, touching his cheek to that of Shepherd's. "You have seen it; that is enough. Kiss my ring and avow your loyalty to me, as your one true master. Or you shall find yourself on the Field of Calgary."

"I am not God," he whimpered.

"Three crosses, Shepherd," Ara reminded him. "It is an agonizing way to die. Death comes slowly, by degrees. A man perishes by suffocation, his lungs unable to draw air from the weight of his own organs, yet he never loses consciousness. Hours, *days* pass before he expires. It is a horrible fate. One which tried the endurance of a god," he continued, wrapping his hand around Shepherd's hair, then inching his head back, until their eyes locked in mortal communion.

"You know enough to realize everything in this land belongs to me. What you do not understand are the Rules of the Kingdom. These will be explained in good time. But hark: once across the threshold separating God and Satan's territory, you forfeited your free will. Think of yourself," he debated, seeking the exact words, "as an angel. The harbinger who foreshadows what is coming. The good news," he chuckled with esoteric intent.

Immersed in the growing shadows of evil which settled over him like a blanket of doom, Shepherd struggled, attempting to extricate himself from Ara's hold.

"Please," he sobbed, hearing Trent's gentle admonition in his ears. "I am a child of God."

"In this kingdom, that is a sin, punishable by eternal damnation. Within the borders of this land, *I* am the way. Remember my words and heed them. In the travails to come, they may save you."

With a flood of utter terror, belief washed over Shepherd's gaunt countenance. Without cognizant thought; deprived of the power of reason, he kissed the ring, then withdrew, lips curled in a snarl, not of defiance, but of bewilderment.

It was enough. Savoring his triumph, Ara rocked back on his heels, stroking the penitent's head as he might a favored pet.

"Belief without faith is a wondrous thing, my shepherd. In all this land, you are an anomaly. Do not fear, for within you burns the fires of acceptance. You have come home."

"No," he gasped, shaking away the sensation of being drawn into a bottomless pit. "I do not belong here."

"And yet you came. Of your own free will. No one coerced you. You will acknowledge such?"

"I came for good, not evil."

To belie the innocent protestation, Ara laughed. The sound of his pleasure echoed off the walls, perverting the joy until repeated noises disintegrated into wails of torment.

"You accepted Ericka Elvina's invitation from greed... and lust. Hardly a resounding endorsement of purity."

"I wished no more than anyone else," he protested, made small and impotent and childlike by shame.

"Agreed. But others... those others you interrogated in your quest from light to darkness. They were not worthy. They would have failed, where you shall triumph."

"Over what?" he hissed, tasting sulphur on chapped lips. When Ara made no reply, he lifted a hand, though the effort cost much, for his appendage carried upon it the weight of lost innocence. "Those men. You admitted killed them."

"Say, instead, they were purged, eradicated for their defects. Even I must learn, Shepherd. They were stepping stones through the mire, both mine and yours. That which I discarded led you to me. Through Ericka."

"What do I have they did not?"

He dreaded the answer, "purity of soul," but what he heard resounded ten thousand times worse.

"Your gift, Shepherd Kingston. That which I have already noted; that which has lifted you head and shoulders over those minions of that Other's Kingdom. Marked you as one with the ability to... move beyond."

"The border of your land?"

"That is one passing."

"But I deny this power. I shall never use it again!"

"Listen to yourself," Ara mocked, teeth gleaming white until the absence of color dominated his face and his head appeared as a bleached skull. "In one breath you deny and in the second, you threaten. You cannot have it both ways." Exacerbating the impression of a skeleton, Ara turned perpendicular to the hearth, unnaturally elongating his slender body.

"When you were small, you used your 'gift' instinctively, helplessly. You were its pawn and it controlled you. How often did you unwittingly employ it to save the life of a rabbit from a predator, or a childhood companion from trauma, before others came to look at you askance? As... how shall I phrase it? *As different?"*

Shepherd rebelled against the accusation, holding up his hands, palms outward, to deflect the blows.

"You exaggerate. Two or three times, no more...."

"My dear friend, the truth is written in your eyes. Do not deny that which I, amongst all men, pay homage to."

Ara's sincerity took none of the sting from Shepherd's memory. Perhaps because of that, the king pressed him with greater urgency.

"How old were your parents when they fell victim to superstition and grew to fear you – shun you?"

Without waiting for a reply, Ara paced the room, savoring his majesty over the situation. Hands clasped behind his back, he fed off Shepherd's growing horror.

"That is the true reason they took a sabbatical, is it not? To distance themselves from their son. A pity, really. If they had brought you with them to Central America, you could have saved their lives."

"No," Shepherd protested, awash with guilt over facts so long denied.

"Yes," Ara corrected, pausing before the extraordinary man he had summoned from afar. "Had you accompanied them, you could have held back the landslide – or transferred them out of harm's way. Death comes to those of little faith," he concluded, running his tongue over his upper bicuspids.

Weakening under the barrage, Shepherd crawled to a chair, hoisting himself up by the strength of his arms. Ara tiptoed lightly to him, resting a friendly hand on his arm.

"Your parents were so-called good people; God-fearing Christians. Scientists. They should have welcomed you as a superior being, but they closed their minds, shunning you and your gift. That was wrong. Unchristian," he mocked, rolling the word over like fine wine. "Have you never wondered about that landslide – what caused it? But of course, you have. Why did it happen?"

"An accident –"

"Ah. The rational explanation for an unenlightened mind. Possibly Trent suggested something else. The act of angry gods?"

"No!"

"No? *He* believed in the existence of... alternate deities, did he not? He spent a lifetime studying ancient rituals; acts of revenge and retribution. When you told him about your parents, surely the idea must have occurred to him."

"He believed in one God – and in Christ, the Son."

"But he did not dismiss the Dark Powers, as you did. He feared them. And rightfully so. His mistake lay in underestimating their might."

Tears streamed down Shepherd's cheeks.

"But you said you didn't kill him."

"No, Shepherd." His heart gladdened before Ara continued. *"I did not kill him."*

"And not Ericka?" he choked. "You swear?"

"Nor she, either."

"Then who? I asked you that and you gave me no answer. Have you reasoned it out?"

Ara shook his head slowly, but his attitude on the subject had changed.

"Suffice it to say I am innocent of the deed."

Clearing his throat, Shepherd swallowed loving emotion.

"Then I say to you, whoever killed him has made a terrible mistake. He has sent Trent to heaven. There, his power, like God's, is unlimited. He will help me in my hour of need."

The denial came slowly, but the words were damning.

"He cannot help you here, for this is not God's Kingdom."

"Whose it is, then?"

"You know the answer to that."

"It is yours!" Shepherd retorted, quickly sniffing back the wetness in his nose. He reacted sharply as Ara broke out in raucous laughter.

"As good an answer as I could have given!" he cried, merrily tap-dancing around his invited guest. "Let us both agree, this is my kingdom."

"You rule it," Shepherd qualified, surprised by his own aggression.

"Indeed I do. But mark, Little One. I am only the king. Not the Master. As powerful as I am, even I serve another. As Christ served God," he darkly added.

"Who?"

"He, whom you will come to serve, as well. Through me."

"But how can I... change sides?"

Ara held out a finger, nodding wisely.

"A valid question. But have I not already explained it? In their fear, your parents accused you of being the devil's spawn. A quaint notion, but not without merit. From your inception, you have belonged to both worlds. To fulfill your destiny, you must choose one or the other."

"Then I choose God and His Kingdom."

"Unfortunately, another choice has already been made."

"By you?"

"You did it yourself. By coming here."

"I wanted no more than –"

"The photo journalistic story of a lifetime. So you told Trent. The chance at fame and fortune. And so you shall have it. Through the auspicious of ambition, you bargained away your godly soul, Mr. Kingston."

"But I didn't know what I was doing!"

"A trite denial from one who has, until this moment, denied the existence of his soul."

"I claim it now! For God!"

Ara waved his hand, dismissing the penitent.

"Do your damnedest to retrieve it. You have my blessing."

So saying, he prodded Shepherd with his foot. The boy rose from the chair, gagged, then vomited on the rug. Daring to turn his back on the prince, he staggered from the room.

Ara made no effort to stop him. He saw no need.

He and the Dark Powers had already won. They required nothing more than to claim their prize. Shepherd's latent enemy notwithstanding.

CHAPTER 25

When Dongal screamed, the cry was of such a pitch it might have wakened the dead. That was not his intention, however, and as Ara chided him to silence by holding a finger to his lips, he obeyed the command.

"I see, my faithful old servant, your eyesight has returned. Tell me: does that make the punishment more, or less painful?"

"Please, master," Dongal begged, sobbing hysterically.

"Please? Please, what? Please have mercy? You know better than to expect pity *here.*"

"Master, I swear. I will never raise a hand against you again."

"And I believe you. But that is for the future to judge. We are here to avenge the past. The recent past. Surely you could not have forgotten already. You raised a hand against your master. Had not Ericka's 'discovery' saved me, I would already be...." But what Ara saw was too horrible, even for him, to contemplate.

Fondling the whip to his breast, Ara strode around the dungeon, the heels of his boots making loud reverberations against the walls. There was much he needed to purge this night, not the least his own haunting fear. Inasmuch as he could not torture his enemy, he would take revenge where he could.

"There is no punishment prescribed for so heinous a crime as the murder of one's majesty," he continued, tucking the whip into his belt, then fondling a glistening knife. "Not by so lowly a creature as a slave. By your action – your malice aforethought – you have inscribed your name in the Book of Deeds. Are you not proud of yourself?"

"I beg forgiveness!" Dongal screamed, ignoring the question.

"Come: tell me." Peering into Dongal's eyes, Ara read only terror. Shrugging his shoulders with implied regret that he could extract no triumph from his servant, Ara placed the tip of the knife against the chained man's throat.

"Perhaps I should permanently record the guilt of your deed on your face. Though you shall never see it, it shall be there for the rest of the world to read."

Dongal struggled fantastically, sweat pouring from his brow the way precious bodily fluids seeped from dripping wounds.

"No," Ara argued with himself, prolonging the game of cat and mouse. "Not now. That would be so... messy. A useless sacrifice. If one is to give blood, it should be in a noble cause. Do you not agree?"

"I agree with anything you say."

"And you do heal so slowly. Were I to carve your face, that would deprive me of your service for days; perhaps a week. That would never do. You would miss attending me, would you not, old friend?"

"I would," came the miserable response.

Retrieving the whip, Ara cracked it over his head, then paused to listen to the echo.

"It is like music. Ancient poetry. The Old Ones knew how to stir the soul, did they not?" Dongal shook his head, afraid to answer. "Come now. In your twenty-three year service with me, you have seen much. Too much for your own good, but nevertheless, I have permitted you to witness the rituals. You will bear testimony to more, before your time is through."

"No more," Dongal pleaded. "Do not involve me."

"Do not involve you?" Ara mocked. "Pray, tell me why? Do you fear for your immortal soul?" He snorted. "How odd you should fear to lose that which you bartered away."

"I was a child –" came the brave response. Ara's eyebrows arched in mock surprise.

"So: there is fight left in you. I approve. However useless. Your father sold your body, Dongal, but you sold your soul. You signed your own name upon the pact. In blood. That same blood which yet courses through your veins."

"I had no choice...."

"As I have none. We are all born to fulfill our destinies, Dongal. My stepfather; you and I... All of us to exist upon this planet of earthly hell. Even Shepherd Kingston, of whom you have grown so fond."

"Let him go."

"Let him go?" Ara incredulously reiterated. "After I have sought him so long? After I have gone to considerable trouble to bring him here?"

"He is not the one."

This time, the master's laughter rang deep and satisfied.

"You cannot place doubt in my heart, old servant. And it would be well for you not to try. He *is* the one. Remember: your fate is linked to mine. Change loyalties in mid-stream and you will know what it is like to rot in hell's fire for all eternity, without hope of redemption."

"Kill me," Dongal pleaded suddenly. "Kill me. Dead. You have the power."

"But not the inclination. Death is too easy." Cracking the whip a second time, his parted teeth glinted with reflected firelight. "Look at me!" Dongal's pale orbs turned upward, seeing only that which the master permitted. "You have crossed my will for the last time. You would care to defend Shepherd? Then join his fate!"

"Not that!" Dongal cried, his words repeating themselves over and over in the enclosure. "Torture me, but do not condemn me. I swear to serve you faithfully – forever and ever. Burn me, cut me, whip me, only spare me that!"

"Enough. I will give you something to remember for the here and now." Snapping his fingers, he summoned forth two servants. The men unchained Dongal, then dragged his limp body to another set of manacles against the far wall. After restraining him in an upright position, they retreated back into the shadows.

The leather cracked against Dongal's exposed back. The man who wished to die for all eternity writhed under the force of the blow.

Nothing, his resignation implied, ever came easily.

Shepherd had no knowledge of what had transgressed deep down below. He did not have to. He understood, with a far better certainty than his belief in a merciful God, that work awaited.

Retrieving Trent's small, carefully wrapped package from its hiding place, he opened the packet, removing the articles one by one. Besides the unadorned cross, he found powders, talismans, a rosary, candles, holy water and a crucible. Folded at the bottom he found a hand-written note. He inspected that last of all.

"Shepherd," the missive began. "If you are reading this, then you are in trouble. I begged you to listen, but you would not. Enough said. Follow my instructions carefully. Within them contain the sum knowledge of my beliefs and my faith. I pray they are strong enough to protect you."

Shepherd's lips moved silently as he read. When he finished the note, he reverently kissed it, then tucked it back inside the suitcase. Should he ever get out of the country and the letter prove to be Trent's last words, he would preserve it. In life, he had not often shown his friend the affection he deserved. He would do so in death, if it were the last thing he ever achieved.

The first line of Trent's instructions advised him to take one of the three-inch white candles, place it in the small brass holder and light it. This he did, taking unexpected comfort in the arc of light it threw.

"I feel you beside me, Trent," he whispered. He *did* sense the old man's presence. If no more good came of his experiment with the occult, at least he had that.

Considering the odds against him, it constituted both a place to begin and one to end.

The second line of text advised him to clasp the bottle of holy water between his two hands, repeat a silent prayer, then sprinkle the contents around himself, thus making the beginnings of a magic circle.

No words, nor suggestions for a prayer were offered. Feeling uncomfortable, yet closer to his religious background than he had for many years, Shepherd found the text of the Lord's Prayer in the recesses of his mind. Repeating it without one single mistake, he rapidly scattered droplets of water over table and floor.

The second admonition for prayer, immediately following the unspecified one, had words. Without making any attempt at memorization, Shepherd stood, paper clutched in front of his face. From his right hand dangled a small charm, suspended on a black string, so thin it appeared invisible.

"Release me, evil power; please release me, the unfortunate victim of your malice." Turning one quarter circle, he continued. "Let me escape this evil thing and be happy again!" He made a second one-fourth turn. "If you do not release me, then I will abandon you at the next crossroads; and you will follow and possess another!"

Once again he made another turn. "Go, follow another; join the man who is my enemy. Strike him!"

Concluding the circle, he finished, "Talisman, boundary that cannot be taken away, boundary that the gods cannot pass; barrier immovable, which is opposed to malevolence!" Pausing for breath, Shepherd steadied himself against a lifetime of disbelief, then pursued the hope Trent had provided.

"Whether it be a wicked Gigim, a wicked god, a wicked Maskim, a phantom, a spectre, a vampire, an incubus, a succubus, a nightmare: let the barrier of the god Ea stop it!"

Breathing heavily, clothes damp, Shepherd lay the paper down, then crossed swiftly to the inner door of his chamber. From the knob he suspended the talisman. Pausing only briefly to inspect his work, he quickly slipped back into the circle.

On page two of Trent's notes, meticulously scrawled in the professor's neat, though hurried handwriting, were more guidelines. Scanning the entire page, Shepherd picked up a piece of chalk. Balancing it in his hand, he surveyed his territory – that which he claimed for his own – then knelt on the floor. Drawing a circle around himself, he recited.

"In the name of the Holy, Blessed and Glorious Trinity, proceed me to our work in these mysteries, to accomplish that which we desire."

In the den directly below Shepherd Kingston, Ara, master of the kingdom, sat, one leg carelessly thrown over the arm of a chair. His intense expression belied his casual posture. With head thrust forward, cat-eyes semi-closed, he directed his attention toward the roaring fire.

He held that position a moment, then slowly, meticulously repositioned his leg, so that both were flat on the floor. The flames grew in intensity, sparks leaping up the chimney in eager anticipation.

Shepherd's words filled the room, filtered so clearly there might not have been a floor between practitioner and listener.

"We, therefore, in the names mentioned, consecrate this piece of earth for our defense, so that no spirit whatsoever shall be able to break these boundaries, neither to cause injury, nor detriment to any here assembled."

Lowering his eyes, Ara scowled in intense fury. As his face blackened, his soul churned with the knowledge that it was he Shepherd defiled; he, whom the Powers of Righteousness were being summoned against.

Shepherd's voice droned on, assuming the singsong cadence of one falling victim to his own spell.

"But that they may be compelled to stand before the circle and answer truly our demands, so far as it pleaseth Him who liveth forever and ever, and who says, 'I am Alpha and Omega; the Beginning and the End; which is, which was, and which is to come, the Almighty. I am the First and the Last, who am living and was dead.'"

At the conclusion of Shepherd's words, Ara's lips parted, first into a sneer, then a smile of wicked triumph. Directing his gaze downward, his vision penetrated the carpeting and timbers and stone, to the room below. With sadistic pleasure, he waved his hand, extending the one-way line of communication.

In the dungeon, Dongal moaned, then pressed against his chains, sensing Ara's eyes upon him. He tensed, then relaxed, as no words came. His comfort was short-lived, however, for in a moment, he heard a voice. Not the one he expected, but that of another. Cocking an ear in the metaphysical direction of "upward," he listened, with no comprehension of how or why he heard beyond his own prison.

"And behold," Shepherd's voice rang true against the walls of stone, "I live forever and ever; and have the keys of death and hell."

At the mention of "hell," Dongal's head jerked back. A fit of trembling seized him. Whispering a word, which might have been "Shepherd," he placed his entire concentration on augmenting the prayer.

"Bless, O Lord! this creature of earth, wherein I stand; confirm, O God! thy strength in us, so that neither the adversary, nor the evil thing may cause us to fall."

Blinking away his life's moisture which threatened to obscure his vision, Dongal saw the image of Shepherd take shape before him. Half reality, half hope, Dongal pointed toward the image, willing it to persevere.

Two flights above, Shepherd crossed himself, then reverted to Trent's written word. Following the holy guidelines, he touched the cross his old friend had placed around his neck, then encircled a rosary about the burning candle. That complete, he surveyed his work, stifled a seizure, then continued.

Placing the candle holder within the crucible, he unscrewed a small jar of powder, dropping the nearly translucent flakes inside.

Without giving himself time to question, Shepherd retrieved a piece of paper and a pen, writing the word "Ara" on it in a bold hand. Underneath it he printed "ra," and finally under that, the letter "a." With Trent's words before him, he placed the paper inside the crucible.

"They are seven, they are seven," he repeated. "In the valley of the abyss, they are seven. In the numberless stars of heaven, they are seven. In the abyss, in the depths, they grow in power."

As time crept through its appointed course, Shepherd, Ara and Dongal, each in his own way, and for his own purpose, viewed the scene unfolding.

"They are not male, they are not female," the foray into the foreign wilderness continued. "They dry up the moistness of the waves. They do not love women, they have not begotten offspring. They scorn consideration and justice. They hearken to neither request nor prayer."

As Shepherd's concentration grew, Ara's face assumed an impish delight. Below them both, the manservant, staggered by the full import of the ritual, blended his prayers to the one above his earthly master.

"They who have revolted cause the gods to tremble. They are evil. They are seven, and again, they are twice seven. Spirit of the Sky, remember them! Conjure them! Conjure these evil spirits, spirit of Samas, King of Justice! Spirit of Annunas, mighty god, conjure them."

Looking up toward heaven, Shepherd concluded his text.

"And my God – prevent this evil, seven or one – give to him what he has given to others. Keep the pure in safety – punish the evil one now!"

Releasing the cross with which his hand had intertwined, Shepherd struck a match. Face flushed in expectation, straining with an otherworldly concentration, he dropped the flame into the crucible, watching the consummation of his prayer.

He dared to hope. And therein lay his vulnerability.

Shepherd was not alone with great expectations. Pressing against his chains, lips pursed in wordless prayer, Dongal waited. If Ara *were* right: if Shepherd was the one, then there existed just a chance his powers were greater than Ara's. That would be justice, indeed, to know that the master had hand-picked his own executioner.

Three participants in the scene; three varying degrees of anxiety.
Three hearts pounding.
Two possible outcomes.
One victor.
One common destiny.

With his back to the fireplace, Shepherd did not notice the flames growing in intensity. Only when he felt the heat did he dare divert his attention from the nearly charred paper in the crucible.

At first, he did not comprehend the true import, thinking, perhaps, that his prayers had stirred latent spirits: powers for good. Not until the circle of holy water began to bubble, then steam did he fully realize his misconception.

Not until the remaining water, left inside the bottle, burst the glass did he fully comprehend his failure.

Ducking away from the flying chards, his eye turned instinctively toward the door. The talisman suspended from the knob swayed wildly. Bang! Bang against the wood, then the cord broke, hurtling the sacred object across the room. Striking the floor, it died an ungainly death.

Next, the chalk comprising the magic circle sizzled, then burst into a blue-orange flame. Beginning at one end, the fire rapidly sped around the circumference, eating the white substance as though it were gunpowder, finally meeting itself at the beginning. Might clashed against equal might, extinguishing both combatants. They left behind no more than a blackened remnant.

Horrified, Shepherd cried aloud, throwing up his hands in despair. Two stories below, Dongal unintentionally imitated his action to the limits of his chains.

From a middle point between both, a laugh arose. It possessed a mocking, wicked sound, born of amorality.

Recognizing Ara's voice, Shepherd's eyes sought him within the confines of his own chamber. Alone, yet not alone, the laughter grew.

Furiously, Shepherd clutched the cross Trent had suspended around his neck, holding it out in pitiful defense. The metal grew red hot, burning his flesh. Ripping it away, he flung the offending, impotent symbol to the carpet. Like the pyramid, it began burning the fibers, the conflagration spreading to engulf the room.

Panicked to be trapped inside, Shepherd lunged backward, knocking over the table. Ash from his paper, the candle, holder and crucible plunged into the flames.

Ara's hysterical, triumphant laughter dominated his brain as physically as the acrid smoke burned his lungs.

Fire engulfed the door. Throwing his weight against it, Shepherd managed to break down the weakened structure. Tearing the remaining wood with his hands, he made an opening just large enough to pass through. Without a care of spreading the flames throughout the rest of the castle, he burst out. Breathing hard, eyes wildly distended, he dashed down the smoke-filled corridor.

And into the waiting arms of Ericka Elvina.

He did not recognize her at first. Only after recoiling in terror did his fervid brain identify she, who had become his savior.

"Ericka! My Ericka! Save me!"

Oddly unmoved by the danger they faced, she settled her voluptuous eyes upon him.

"Shepherd," she whispered. "My dear Shepherd. What have you done?"

"Nothing," he moaned, burying his face into the cool green, almost transparent negligee she wore. "I have failed."

"No, Shepherd," she consoled, wrapping protective arms around him. "You have done no such thing. Come with me, away from the fire. I will protect you."

"It will consume the entire castle –" he finally comprehended.

"Nonsense. Fire cannot burn through walls. They are of stone."

"But the door... I knocked through it."

"It is burning itself out," she observed, grabbing hold of his hands. Then, softly, "You have hurt yourself. Hurry. I must tend to your wounds *before it is too late.*"

Reacting to her emphasis, he stifled a sob and allowed himself to be guided away. With the tenderness with which one handles a child, Ericka led him down the corridor, then took him through the entranceway into her own bedroom.

The moment she shut the door, a feeling of utter peace nearly knocked Shepherd off his feet. Swaying unsteadily, he attempted a grateful smile. Returning it with radiant affection, Ericka pushed him gently into a chair.

"It is all right, Shepherd. Catch your breath. I understand what you have attempted."

"Ara will kill me for such audacity, Ericka!"

"No," she demurred softly, shaking her head. "I will not allow him to hurt you."

"But how can you –?"

A log in the fire cracked. Realizing how close he sat to the yawning mouth, Shepherd miserably whimpered.

"Please," he implored. "Too near the flames."

"I am sorry. Come." Holding out her hands, she accepted his, then directed him to her bed. "You will be safe here. See? The fire is contained. It cannot harm you now."

Her words had the power to control the elements, for the fire died down, leaving only the low flicker of flame over ash-covered charcoal. The room grew chill. Seeing him shiver, Ericka engulfed him with her bare arms. Though her flesh felt cold from exposure, her body heat instantly warmed him.

"I – I thought I would never see you again," he stuttered. "I thought Ara might have killed you."

"That is not within his power."

"Swear to me."

"I swear."

"On what you hold holy," he insisted, desperately needing conformation.

"On what I hold holy," Ericka repeated.

He believed her implicitly. Melting into a puddle of confused, frightened boyhood, Shepherd clung to Ericka for dear life.

"If it hadn't been for you," he began, but she stopped him by putting a finger to his lips.

"Shhh," she urged. "Save your breath."

Obeying her instructions, Shepherd dropped his head against her breasts.

Contained within lay the salvation he had failed to find with talismans, crosses and holy water.

Without knowing it, Shepherd Kingston had crossed another boundary.

CHAPTER 26

"Tell me what happened," Ericka requested, not with her lips, for those were busy kissing his feverish brow. She communicated through her mind. It seemed as natural as speech, and a thousand times more soothing.

"Ericka," he sobbed. "My God, I don't know where to begin. I don't know what I've done."

"Tell me."

"I've been so frightened. I never thought I'd see you again."

"Here I am. Tell me. Please. So I may take care of you."

"Can you?" She nodded, her eyes piercing through his vail of confusion and suspicion. Taking a deep breath, he steadied himself. "The painting in the castle bedroom – the one I slept in. You have seen it?"

"Of course."

"The face of the victim – it has my face."

Pulling away, her own expression troubled, Ericka's brows knit in concentration. When light dawned, her eyelids fluttered.

"Dear God! That's why you looked so familiar!" Recoiling from the intensity of her statement, Shepherd hesitated, then responded to the aura of kindness hovering around her body.

"Yes. Ara said it altered; the face changed. To more closely match mine."

"Is that what he told you?" Shepherd bobbed his head. She considered carefully before continuing. "That is interesting. It is very old. If it has changed, then the Old Ones identified you and manipulated the oils so you might be discovered by he who seeks your personage. Some say it depicts a revelation... or more accurately, I should say, it foretells the future. But I do not think that is true."

"You don't?"

"No. At least not literally."

"What truth does it... foreshadow?"

"I am only speculating, of course." Ericka spoke softly, the wonder of her voice wrapping itself around his tortured body, instilling the essence of warmth, such as he had never before experienced.

"The painting represents the domination of an innocent's soul. Your claim to immortality is far more complex than that."

"I don't know what you mean."

Ericka disengaged herself from his entwining arms, moving her body in a fluid, seamless motion.

"You are without stain," she praised, pushing back the hair from his eyes. "For an evil power to sacrifice you on the altar would be a mighty triumph. But to transport you to hell – that abyss of pain and suffering, with no greater purpose than having stolen one of God's children? No."

"What, then?"

"Yours will be a position of power – authority."

Shepherd abandoned her transcendental form as a means of escaping her prediction.

"But I don't want to go to hell! I serve no master, for good or evil. I am a free spirit!"

Taking his fisted hand, Ericka gently unfolded the digits, placing them to her breast.

"It is said that when one of God's minions dies, that soul transforms itself into an angel. But angels have no free will. What use do you see in that?"

Shepherd shook his head, confused and repulsed. "I don't want to die. I want to live," he articulated, the words nearly obscured by the quivering of his jaws. She tried to sooth his trembling, but he pulled away, protruding his lower lip like a surly rebel.

"He said I had come to fulfill my destiny – one elicit with evil. *You* brought me here," he concluded with an accusation. "And you work for him."

"I warned you," she regretfully parried.

"But not about..." Shepherd hesitated, feeling at once betrayed and desperate, yet the serenity of her face calmed him. Like a balm, it soothed and offered protection from the harshness of the new reality into which he had inadvertently plunged. Comprehending his misery, Ericka glowed with self-assurance.

"What were you doing in your bed chamber just now? What caused the fire?"

"He caused it."

"He?" And then, "Ara?"

"Yes. With his mind. I was –" He hesitated, debating whether to confess, then threw caution to the wind. If he could not trust Ericka, then he had lost, for she represented his final hope of redemption. "Casting a spell. Or more accurately," he amended, least she think him childish, "I was attempting to place myself beyond his reach."

"It did not work." Not a question but a statement.

"No."

"What you have done is put him on his guard. We must be careful."

"Tell me what to do. I will obey you implicitly."

"I will consider," she vowed. "Do not despair."

"I will try not to. Just tell me what must be done and together...."

"I will tell you," Ericka interrupted, but the tone of her voice had altered. "I will tell you many things. I will tell you..." But what she had to tell was lost as her lips found his. Responding immediately to the caress, Shepherd pressed back, allowing his passion to mount. After his near-death experience, Ericka's offer held the promise of salvation, rekindled by faith.

They intertwined, hungry bodies hugging one another. Eyes closed, they explored each other's outer regions by touch, falling back gracefully upon the sea of mattress and down-comforter. Slipping from his arms, Ericka positioned herself above, easily undoing the buttons of his shirt. With strong, knowing fingers, she massaged his naked skin, easing tense muscles, allowing relaxation to flow from her body to his.

Sighing in contentment, Shepherd gave way to her pressure, lusting with his eyes as she knelt over him, her own flesh tantalizingly charged and erotic. Working her way down his torso, she gently unfastened his belt, then slipped off pants and shorts.

As Shepherd removed his shirt, Ericka unlaced his shoes, dropping them over the side of the bed and out of the way. With the removal of his socks, he lay exposed before her, both man and child, clay in the hands of a master.

"Shepherd.... Shepherd," she whispered, turning easily from the articulation of his name into a low, melodic humming. The music stirred his blood, reaching inward to the recesses of memory, inspiring him to hum the long-forgotten, or perhaps never realized tune along with her.

Gently, skillfully rubbing his toes, Ericka made each a body onto itself, so that as she progressed upward, he grew into a being of gigantic proportion. Arriving at his shoulders, she beamed down at him, then reached upward, not to his head, but to her own. Gracefully, she cast back her long, silken black hair, so that it hung loose around her body.

With alien motions, combining both human and feline gestures, Ericka undid the tie at her neck, allowing the green silk of her negligee to fall back, exposing her own nakedness. With sensuous motions, she guided the fabric down, then rolled out of it, revealing her beautiful animal body to him.

Licking his lips with anticipation, Shepherd's arms reached behind her back, fingers interlocking. She allowed him this moment of glory before emitting a low, thrilling, tinkling sound. Slipping from his grasp, she took his hand and placed it against her abdomen.

Groaning in anticipated pleasure, Shepherd threw away his terror of death, forging ahead with his desire for life. His body stiffened with need to become one with she who had captured his soul.

In a primeval quest to forget all but passion, the two bodies on the bed mated in the ritual of renewal, twining together as one. Behind them, shadows cast from the firelight leapt upon the wall, dancing in hedonistic pleasure. The time had come to create a bond of flesh, transcending all higher emotions.

As suddenly as it began, their bodies separated. The action jarred, creating a sound of disgusting suction. Flames in the fire stretched outward, calling to one participant, repelling the other. Without full comprehension, Shepherd screamed. His partner responded, but it was not Ericka's voice which blended with his. It belonged to another, equally familiar, though totally foreign.

Looming over him, bare chest and powerful shoulders glistening with the sweat of sexual exertion, was the body of a male. In the split second between kiss and rending asunder, Ericka disappeared. The form leering over him belonged to Ara, Master of the Kingdom.

Shepherd's cry turned to insane denial, although reality afforded no escape into ignorance. It all became clear. When interpreting the photographs, Trent had been far more correct than even he dared concede. Shepherd had not captured an aura but a legitimate possession. Not in the sense of one being capturing another, but the act of one soul inhabiting two bodies. There never had been such a creature as Ericka Elvina. All along, it had been Ara, staging a diabolical farce.

"Good God! No!"

"Yes."

One word, so simple, yet so completely, utterly devastating.

"No! No! No!"

Too horrified to believe his own senses, Shepherd averted his face, but Ara would not permit so simple an escape. With all the strength of his male body, he grabbed Shepherd by the roots of his hair, viciously yanking his face so that their eyes met in mortal combat.

"Stop!" the master warned, all power and majesty. And then, in malignant triumph, "Who won this contest, Shepherd Kingston?" Repulsed and horrified, Shepherd's lips moved in soundless impotence. "Look, Otherworlder, into the face of Satan's son."

Willing his mind to rebuff the answer which must surely be revealed, he managed but a single syllable.

"How?"

"A simple trick," Ara admitted, the curve of a smile working its way across his smooth, handsome features. The attitude belied his true emotion, however, for an expression of deep hatred penetrated the depths of his eyes. "One forced upon me by my stepfather."

Shepherd questioningly mouthed the word "stepfather." Noting his confusion, the young master happily clarified.

"Stepfather: my earth father. The king, who has died." He held onto the last word, reveling in its finality. "My *real* father: a father in the true sense, Shepherd, is not only *my master,* but now yours, as well."

At the conclusion of this startling admonishment Shepherd tore himself away from Ara's grasp, leaping from the bed. Had it been his intention to run from Fate, the unexpected arrival of two guards foiled the attempt by entering the chamber. On Ara's signal, they accosted the guest whose status had changed, shoving him roughly backward. Off balance, Shepherd struck the bed, wavered, then toppled forward.

"There is nowhere to hide," Ara reproachfully chided. "You consigned your soul to Lucifer the moment your feet touched this sacred land."

"Sacred?" Shepherd shouted, premature wrinkles on his face accentuated like so many lines on a road map. "How can you use such a holy word to describe so –"

"Evil a concept?" Ara finished, raising, then lowering his eyebrows.

"Yes," Shepherd spat. Rather than offend, his defiance only served to placate the youth maintaining position on the bed, their symbolic field of battle.

"What is evil to you is holy to me."

"No," Shepherd demurred, shaking his head in stubborn defiance. "I don't believe that. Good and evil are universal constants. One cannot alter their significance to suit the situation."

"Believe?" Ara queried, tempering his interrogative with good natured surprise. "I was under the impression you did not *believe* in anything: good or evil."

Faltering in the face of his own doubt, Shepherd lowered his head. "That was true once." Shame burned in his heart for his own "stepfather," and the teachings he had rebuffed from that good man. "Trent tried to make me see; he told me and I would not listen. But I remember, now," he added, trembling violently. "I love him. He will protect me."

"Love? Protect? You thought that of Ericka, once, if I recall."

"I believed I wanted her more than I loved Trent. I was wrong."

"A pity. It seems you have lost them both." Ara clucked his tongue. "Abraham Trent, with his learned books and his talismans. He tried to shield you with holy water and ancient words. I found him... amusing."

Bristling at the mockery, Shepherd rallied his courage.

"He was a better man that you. A man who understood the real power in this world."

"And that is –?"

"Love."

"Love of another?" he repeated, as though the word held no meaning to him. "You disappoint me, Shepherd."

"Why? Because I have learned – too late – his lesson?"

"Love of self is the only true power; the sole gateway to eternity."

"No."

"Self-preservation; the prolongation of one's being. That is the one abiding force in nature. Professor Trent sought to keep his own life by saving yours. And how did he go about that, my young friend? Surely not by 'love' – either ethereal or carnal. He gave you potions; he bade you evoke the names of ancient gods. Those were not deities of love and compassion, Shepherd, but spirits of the Old Order. Evil spirits."

"He sought to save me by... fighting fire with fire," Shepherd protested.

Ara shrugged, dismissing the point as irrelevant. "Agreed. He sought to pit evil against evil for the greater good. Do you not see the contradiction? Do two wrongs make a right? I think not."

Swinging his legs over the side of the bed, the naked young master towered over his victim, savoring his victory, not only of the flesh, but of the will.

"When pressed to the limits of his fear, Trent choose evil to do his work. My evil, it appears, is greater than his. He failed."

"He fought you on your own level," Shepherd faltered, confused and frightened by Ara's explanations.

"But were he a man of good: were he a force of right, he would not have summoned the Seven. Or the Seven times Seven. He would not have armed you with chalk and magic circles. Think of that, Shepherd, when your own time comes. Mark it well. It was neither Jehovah nor Christ to whom he had you pray, but to my gods. Your 'holy man' did not send the sacred to defeat the profane."

Shaken to the roots of his own twisted self-identity, Shepherd writhed under the statement, more devastating to him than any whip.

"He sent both," he protested urgently, trying to recall Trent's invocations. "He placed a cross around my neck."

"A Christian symbol, to be sure," Ara commiserated. "And *I* burned it off you."

"But Satan cannot be more powerful than God. God is the beginning."

"Throughout all of time, and in that time before time existed," Ara reverently intoned, eyes as deep and black as the absence of light, "evil has existed. Who is to say which is more ancient – your God, or mine? Who among us may decree it was good which created evil? Is it not more likely evil begat good – as a perversion? A cosmic joke? Consider. What benign, loving Lord would institute that which was destined to destroy His own creations?"

Ara strode around the room. Passing the hearth, flames shot out, licking his flesh.

"What Force brought suffering into the universe, Shepherd? What entity devised the universal struggle of light against dark? Such a contest has existed long before your Earth formed. It shall persist long after its destruction by an imploding sun. Your friend comprehended that well, Shepherd. Despite his devoutness, he choose to summon the black powers. You asked if there were a heaven. If such a place exists, and I do not admit it with any certainty, then the soul of Abraham Trent has found hell by going through the back door."

He grinned at his cleverness but Shepherd no longer had the strength to grasp the subtlety.

"And now?"

"The Majesty of Evil seeks a Higher Order. In this, you were destined to play a role. It is no longer a contest between God and Satan, but one between the Dark Powers. I welcome you to the fold."

So saying, Ara bowed.

The end had become a beginning.

"Remove him," Ara ordered the servants. The men approached, hesitated, then exchanged glances. Ara, understanding their hesitation, waved them away. "He cannot hurt you. His power lies elsewhere. Take him to the dungeon."

He did not speak again until they dragged Shepherd's unresisting body to the door. Then, with almost an apologetic dismissal, Ara added, "Your status here has altered, Shepherd. You are no longer guest, but servant. You were warned."

Lifting his head which had hung between the men, the former photographer snarled bitterly at his host.

"Yes. I was warned. But not by *you.*"

Ara frowned until comprehension finally dawned. He attempted a tired smile.

"No. By Ericka. But she is gone. She is... no more."

"Then you have lied." Again, puzzlement from the master. "She told me you did not have the power of life and death over her. I made her swear it. On what she held holy. Now, you tell me she is no more." Desperation gave him courage. "She is dead. Ara killed her."

The boldness of his assertion froze the king, catching him in a tangled web of doubt. Not for the first time Shepherd saw fear in the shared orbs.

"I am alive."

"You are not Ericka."

"She was a part I played. No more than that. A character has –" He could not bring himself to say the word *died.* "Gone away."

"No," Shepherd demurred, remembering a conversation he had had with Trent years before. "Characters do not die. They live forever. No matter the outcome of a novel or a film, the characters remain as they were, immortal. Ahab yet fights the white whale; Quasimodo rings his bells; Dracula rises from his earth box."

"What are you saying? That I have not killed Ericka? So be it. Then I have not told a falsehood."

"I am saying that perhaps Ericka is the one with life everlasting; that if a life is wanting, it is *you* who shall perish."

Ara paled considerably, unable, for the moment, to deflect the unthinkable.

"No. That shall not be. I have already survived great trial."

"There will be others."

"How could you know?" Then, just as abruptly, the young monarch crossed to his new servant, fists clenched. "Yes. I forget: you have powers. I did not take you for a divinator, so I have underestimated your ability. But listen to me now, Shepherd Kingston. We speak of roles – the part I have played; the part you are to play. Both forced upon us by others. Yet enact them we must. Call us actors, then, in a great drama, penned by a hand far more powerful than either of us. I accept that. You must do the same."

"Must I?"

"You have no choice."

"Then tell me. Why it is I, and no one else you sought? My telekinetic power cannot be the only reason."

"No," Ara quietly confessed. "Of that I had no awareness. Not until witnessing it through the pyramid did I fully comprehend its usefulness. I sought you on the basis of the painting; and the prophesy associated with it. You identified yourself, just as I did."

"But what does it all mean? Tell me, Ara. Prepare me for what is to come."

"You are," he began slowly, forming the sentences as he went. "The shepherd of my kingdom. The watcher; the protector who abandons the ninety-nine to go in search of the one."

"You are that lost sheep?"

"I am."

"Then if I am the shepherd, your role-playing is not over, as you suppose."

"Explain."

His terse reply severed the heartstrings.

"You are the sacrificial lamb."

What Shepherd lost in combat, he regained by logic.

The master's tortured shriek followed him all the way to the dungeon.

CHAPTER 27

Pitch blackness encased the room. An odor of burned reeds stirred the lifeless air; an old scent, not of recent origin. Whatever light once penetrated the darkness came from some other era.

Chained to the wall, face pressed against cold stone, Shepherd dozed. He would not have thought it possible to sleep in such a position, yet the twisting and turning of his thoughts drugged his intellect, until he finally availed himself of the only means possible for release.

How long he slept he did not know. Lacking any way to gauge time, Shepherd saw no profit in belaboring the point. The fact hours passed he acknowledged as no more than the inevitability of nature progressing along a predetermined path.

The return of sensibility did bring with it the shocking realization of his predicament. Groaning aloud without fear of detection for he presumed himself isolated from all humanity, the sound of another responding to his plea, "Oh, God," caused him to jump.

"There is no God here," the voice replied. And then, more slowly, "There cannot be."

Shifting positions to transfer weight from one aching foot to another, Shepherd rattled the iron.

"Dongal? Is that you?"

"Yes, sir," came the low confession. "It is Dongal, and no other."

"What are you doing here?" But the question answered itself. "You are being punished, too." Stifling a sob, he listlessly kicked the floor. "I'm sorry."

The rattling of metal against stone advised Shepherd that like him, Dongal changed positions.

"Save your pity," came the surprising rebuke. "You will need it for yourself."

"I have enough pity for both of us."

So saying, they lapsed into silence, well aware that all the sympathy in the world meant nothing in Ara's hellish kingdom. This only served to deepen the gloom, making speech of any sort more preferable than the all-prevailing nothingness surrounding them.

"What do you mean?" Shepherd finally queried, startled by the sound of something human, after the dread of worse.

"Sir?"

"That God does not exist here. I refuse to accept that. It goes against all religious teaching. There can be nowhere, on earth or in heaven, outside the boundary of God's law."

A tortured clanking alerted Shepherd to the fact the servant moved, but this time, away from him. When he spoke, his words were muffled, for he had averted his face.

"There is much you do not perceive."

"Then tell me."

"It will do no good."

A wry smile fleetingly crossed the youth's face.

"I am a photographer. Not much of one, I grant you. But enough to stand by truth. Pictures do not lie. They stand as what they are: depictions of fact. I came here, not as Ara suggested, to 'sell my soul,' but to tell a story. I want to hear it – even if I am destined never to reveal it to another living soul."

He supposed Dongal would not understand. To his surprise, the servant responded, speaking over the last of his sentence as if he had been waiting this chance to share the story of his miserable existence.

"In a time before time, two identities existed, side by side. Neither dead nor alive as we understand it, they simply were. Which came first? I do not know. No one knows. Ara does not know." The simple and respectful avowal turned the saliva in Shepherd's mouth to gall.

"One spent His time in the creation of all things as we know them: the sun, the planets, the stars; the space between and beyond what our eyes behold. In these universes He made light and heat, water and dry land. Upon the mountains and valleys He set forth living things. The fish of the sea. The birds of the air. To amuse Himself and perhaps to keep him company, he bestowed the breadth of knowledge into certain select beings... not in his likeness, but in all manner of shapes and sizes.

"He took much joy and pleasure watching them grow. The tale is told that the other, His twin, if you will, was jealous of these creations. Having no desire to fashion life himself, it became his pleasure to cast adversity upon God's worlds. He introduced pain and suffering; he instilled doubt and finally death of the body, so that these creatures no longer praised their master, but shunned His love.

"All of this was permitted because the Bright and the Dark were equal entities, one no more or less great than the other. But a terrible falling came to pass over this trespass. Because they did not wish, or they could not wage war against each other, they made a pact.

"Inasmuch as Satan did not care to form his own universe, God created a black void. Anything which fell within its boundaries belonged to Lucifer. Not bound by the laws of nature, this hole drifted where it may. Over the course of eons, it has been many places. Wherever it tarries, evil – the perversion of good – reigns, with the Dark Twin as its master."

"Are you saying that black hole has settled over Earth?"

Although he could not see Dongal, Shepherd felt him nod in the affirmative.

"It claims a corner of this planet; a space where God has no influence."

The concept stretched credulity. "This kingdom Ara rules... is hell?"

"If hell may be considered a deprivation of God, then this is the physical manifestation of hell."

"There is another – level?"

"A metaphysical plane where souls exist in their true form; one without structure or substance."

"You mean heaven?"

"Heaven is for those who die under the Lord's eye."

"And those who die... here?"

"They belong to Satan. Their continuance is at his pleasure."

"With free will?" Dongal chose not to reply. "Are you saying those who enter this Kingdom are separated from God's mercy? Through no fault of their own?"

"You chose to pass over."

Again the dreaded expression, but this time, with an even more horrific implication.

"I did so without comprehending the import." The protest fell on deaf ears. "I do not acknowledge Satan's authority over me."

"Then you are greater than God, for even He has no direct influence here."

Spasms of terror contracted Shepherd's lungs, making it difficult to breathe. He struggled with his body as his mind worked ahead of physical effort.

"What is Ara? If it is true Satan did not create living beings, but merely played with those God made, is he a child of God?"

"He is a corruption."

"I do not understand."

Dongal groaned. Shepherd could not be certain whether it stemmed from the mortal pain suffered from the cruelty of the chains, or from some more penetrating agony.

"In your religion, you are taught to believe in Jesus Christ?"

"Yes," came the guilty admission from the penitent who has so long denied His teaching.

"And Jesus Christ is the human embodiment of God?"

"Yes, Dongal."

"As God is Christ, you cannot rightfully say He created Him. In the same manner, Satan issued forth devils to populate his kingdom. They are merely extensions of himself. Unlike Jesus, who had no companions, Satan chose to fragment himself. He made many from one."

"That one being himself?"

"Yes. Yet, *Satan's* living embodiments are not all equal. One, anointed monarch of this land, he made the most powerful; others less so. These do homage to the king."

"The devil made a world of himselves?"

Dongal choked, coughed, then cleared his throat.

"I am, perhaps, not explaining properly. Ara would know better, but he will not say."

"Why not? If Ara is Satan —"

"Ara is a corruption!"

Startled by the vehemence of the twice-stated assertion, Shepherd pressed against his shackles, attempting, in a feeble way, to protect the servant from the horrors of his own mind.

"Explain. Please."

The request took longer to fulfill and came with a sigh of resignation.

"Always before, Satan's favorite ruled here, and that ruler was the Dark Power. The other creatures dwelling herein worship him as god. Just as humans worship Jesus."

"The others? You mean, those who... look like people?"

"Yes."

"Eldrich? Hest? The peasant class?"

"Those, and more beside. There is also a hierarchy; a nobility. A cast of higher shapes. They are all evil, but some are better adapted to use it. These devils are jealous of the king, yet they fear him. There are those who would kill Ara if they could; usurp him and take his throne. That is the way Satan amuses himself."

"Others? Like you?"

Dongal gasped at the horror of the suggestion. "I wished only to free myself; not to take his place."

"If you had succeeded, where would you have gone?"

"I... I had not thought that far. Away."

"Home? To your own land?"

A low sob, followed by an admission. "Perhaps. If they would have me back."

Deprived of any ability to physically comfort, Shepherd stoked the naked air. "Who would take his place?"

"There is one; Tarrington. He... holds great power in the Kingdom. Many who dwell here believe him to be more evil than Ara, and thus the rightful ruler. But that is not for me to say," he unexpectedly added. "I pass no judgment."

Assuming that for an untruth, Shepherd pressed harder.

"Tell me the rest," he whispered. Time beat away reticence. His companion apparently felt the same, for he resumed the narrative.

"It has been as I described since God put Man on Earth. Only rarely have any of His creations been allowed to step foot within the confines of Satan's earthly dominion. Those poor souls," he continued, daring to include himself, "work as serfs for the demons, performing the lowest of manual labor. When they die, the fortunate ones are returned to the Land of Light. That is all I wish."

Something in his tone alerted Shepherd that such would not be the case with his friend. Eyes clenched to ward off unmitigated fury, he forced calmness into his voice.

"Is that why you asked Ara to kill you... dead?"

"Dead," Dongal repeated. "To release my soul. To let it fly heavenward. He has promised so many times, but now... I have lost my chance. Perhaps I never had it," he miserably added.

"What does he want your soul for?"

"So that he may dominate me for eternity. To prove... he is worthy of his Father."

"Is that what he wants from me? My soul? To assert his worthiness?"

"Be quiet!" Dongal warned, voice harsh and biting. "I will say it in my own way, or not at all."

"I'm sorry."

Metal rubbed against stone. The manmade against that of a divine hand.

"You are different. You are from the Far Beyond, sought for and discovered. Just as your kind believe in the coming of the Messiah, those here await the arrival of an all-powerful king. One who will rule for all time, wherever Satan's black hole settles. Ara thinks he is the one. There are certain signs favoring his interpretation. Yet he is a weak ruler. He was born a sickly child, but his stepfather, Ruhvan, the king, feared him because of the prophesy."

"You call Ruhvan stepfather.... I have heard Ara say the same. Who, then, is the true sire?"

A shuffle of weight, then, anger.

"Were you not listening? Satan is true father to all these devils. When he determines it is time to change the ruler of his Kingdom, he creates a successor."

"Why? The old one is not evil enough?"

"You ask me what I cannot answer," Dongal cried. "He does what he does. It amuses him to see his devils fight amongst themselves. In hell there must be no peace. Not even between the chosen. That is what I have heard. And I have heard too much," he added in an undertone, partly from shame and to a degree, from incomprehensible wonder.

Shepherd struggled, cutting his cheek against the roughness of rock.

"I am listening."

The disembodied voice continued but not without reluctance. Or perhaps, more accurately, with resignation.

"I was given to Ara as a companion in the hope that exposure to one of God's lesser creations would further weaken him. Because I could not fight back, Ara grew bold. I became the embodiment of his... sadism. With me, he was always superior. Unlike the true denizens of this land, I must bow before him without question.

"I am an example of *attenuation,*" Dongal carefully pronounced, giving Shepherd the uneasy feeling he had probed his mind for the correct word. "I was meant to be sacrificed long ago, but the pleasure Ara derives from tormenting me has made him selfish. The others know this. They look upon me as Ara's weakness, and so tolerate my continued existence."

"And yet, Ara became king."

"As it is decreed. As it has always been practiced. The stepfather raises the child who is bound to destroy him. Ruhvan taught his stepson the Rituals; Ara grew in strength. He worshipped and prayed, but his power never became absolute. You saw how the sunset affects him?"

Shepherd vividly recalled the scene in Ericka's penthouse, as well as the nightmarish struggle within the castle walls.

"The sunset is Satan's reminder to God of his own power. It reflects the fires of hell. In this place, the sunset is prayed to as the embodiment of evil. When locked within its grasp, Ara is vulnerable. He can do nothing to defend himself, for his power is subjugated to the Master. Were he to win...

ascendancy, that would fulfill prophesy and he would be worshipped as the Coming. There would be no question of right, and those who would challenge him must stand down. But he had never succeeded."

Shepherd heard, without the servant saying, *And never will.*

To his horror, he could not determine whether that boded good or ill.

The blackness surrounding him deepened, bringing with it the chill of a deep underground cave. Without light, his brain imagined forms and shapes where none could possibly exist. Mirage-like, people's faces appeared from nothingness, as clear and as sharp as though they were standing before the afflicted.

Unsolicited, Shepherd visualized a domineering mountain, so tall, its peak extended through the clouds and out of sight. Panning down the precipitous slope with the eyes of a camera, his attention briefly focused on an outcropping of rock clinging precariously to the side. He derived the distinct impression that the slightest disruption would cause the pile to break free and plummet downward, causing an immense and terrible landslide.

Far below, at the base, where the trunk of the mountain touched earth, a handful of natives had gathered. Dressed in bright, flowing garb, streaked with the colors of tropical fruit, from which they were undoubtedly dyed, their faces were streaked with concern. The men's attention was directed upward. One, whom the seer presumed to be a priest, waved a spear at the mountain. Another shook a stone idol, the eyes of which were made from semi-precious blue gems. It seemed to be very heavy, for the man had trouble holding it.

They conversed in a language Shepherd did not understand but his familiarity with various dialects allowed him to place the setting somewhere in Central America. Two other individuals, not of native caste, responded with a sharp rebuttal. Eyes drawn to the pair, Shepherd expressed a quick outpouring of breath as he recognized Dr. and Mrs. Kingston. His father extracted a small golden pyramid from their collection of recovered artifacts.

Holding out the priceless antiquity, the doctor of anthropology lifted it up toward the mountain. With gestures remarkably similar to that of the native priest, Dr. Kingston performed a prayer ritual, indicating that the powerful object held in his hand would hold back the impending landslide. Appeased, the laborers went back to work, digging in an excavated pit near the base.

Without direction, Shepherd's eyesight sharpened to the clarity of a microscope. On the golden *object d'art* were etched figures from the Theban alphabet. Without one shred of doubt he recognized it: the object he had stolen from Ericka Elvina's apartment.

He screamed, but the figures in the drama were unaffected by his warning. Perhaps they could not hear him. The revelation of his helplessness did not prohibit the onlooker from continuing his cries.

Watching the scene unfold, Shepherd was unaware of a surrealistic effect assuming dominance over the mountain until nearly too late, and only then because an unseen force directed his attention upward. Rays of crimson and vermilion from the setting sun dominated the sky, engulfing the towering structure of earth's exterior stalagmite.

"Get away!" he demanded in impotent rage. "Run!" but his vision did not permit him to intervene. Frantic with fear, a childhood rhyme ruminated in his memory, repeating itself over and over until it set him on the verge of madness.

> Wish I may,
> Wish I might,
> Have this wish
> I wish tonight.

As the prayer died in his heart, the rocks on the precipice tore loose from their moorings, tumbling downward in horrific anger. Clouds of dust spewed forth. As unlike the fluffy, blue-white sapphires inhabiting the heaven as ice was to fire, these clouds of pebbles and tiny boulders assumed a life of their own, tearing asunder other, more compact rock, until the entire mountainside pummeled downward on a journey of death and destruction.

Shepherd witnessed the avalanche, powerless to avert its tragic ending, but as suddenly as his mind had teetered on the edge of insanity, his emotions changed. Without will, his eyes, mind and soul wrapped around the glory of the sunset. Replacing nursery rhymes, hosannas rose in his throat, while tears of supplication developed, like dew at dawn. Eradicated from his consciousness was anything but the desire, the craving to offer homage.

His life, the life of his parents, the life of Trent, his friend and mentor. All these he offered and more. Entire cities, whole populations of countries he included in his tribute, until he set the world before the glory of the dominating hues.

Hearing the horrific crash as rock struck ground, Shepherd experienced no emotional turmoil. He saw, through the auspices of his third eye, the smashed, pulverized bodies of the natives; witnessed the last, agonized, unconscious writhing of arms and legs, once moving at the controlled behest of Robert and Marion Kingston.

And felt nothing.

Nothing, perhaps, but the stirrings of revenge and retribution. As they had abandoned him, so now he had sacrificed them. As it was in the beginning, is now and shall ever be. Wrong for wrong.

Two wrongs equaling one right.

The order of the universe had been restored.

Lying on the ground, unscathed by the unearthly destruction, sat the little stone idol, its bright blue eyes sparkling merrily at the death around it. *I shall live, where you have died,* it seemed to say. *What was created has been uncreated.*

That essence which was Shepherd, lost in time, prepared to conclude the prayer with an "Amen," when a voice intruded on his supplication. It was a cold voice, the voice of reason over emotion.

"Look away! Tear your mind from the scene."

Neither commanding nor angry, the words penetrated the blackness of Shepherd's hair, the thickness of his white skull, burrowing down into that metaphysical area of grey matter known as conscience.

"It is a trick; a fantasy. Your mind is being manipulated by the pitch darkness. Come back, Shepherd Kingston. Come back to the world where you belong. Do not tarry with the netherworld of another's making."

He did not wish to obey. The thrill of power exhilarated him. He wished to grab hold of the idol, steal again the pyramid and claim them as his own, but the voice unfroze his powers of concentration. The hues of sunset, the crimson of dripping blood, the luster of sparkling gold, the sentient blue of gem-orbs dissipated into the blackness of the absence of light.

Weakened and limp from his foray into a past he could not possibly have seen in a three-dimensional form, Shepherd gasped, then struck his head back against the stone of ancient Druid rock. The forceful blow sent sharp knife-points of pain through his brain. He repeated the action, discovering different thrills in the agony of suffering.

"Shepherd. Stop."

"Go to hell!" he cursed, reveling in the sensation of blood trickling down his back.

"Shepherd. Come back."

But to "come back" meant moving forward. It represented a contradiction, a conundrum.

"Shepherd."

"I am shepherd," he whispered, having no notion of the meaning.

Silence grew like mushrooms in the cave beneath Satan's castle. A congestion of wet mucus formed in Shepherd's lungs, finally compelling him to cough, filling his mouth with phlegm. He spat, grimacing as the congealed mass landed on his leg.

"Shepherd."

"I am Shepherd," he agreed, weary and bone tired from his struggles. His eyelids fluttered. In a moment, he slipped away into nothingness.

CHAPTER 28

"There is not much time. Are you listening?"

The words were foreign. Shepherd did not understand them.

"Go away."

"Listen." A command, from one *soul* to another.

"I am listening," he wearily sighed.

Dongal's voice sounded familiar, yet offered no comfort. He had been the one to draw Shepherd back from rewriting the past. He who had intervened. He, the Otherworlder, like himself.

The peasant-friend used his influence to solidify Shepherd's concentration.

"We were speaking of Ara – and his confrontation with Ruhvan."

"I remember." Remembrance seemed an age ago, yet his mind responded and he drew back within the present.

"The occasion of the demon son's twenty-first birthday has always been the date ordained for mortal combat between the present monarch and the prince who would be king. Never before had the son been vanquished by his stepfather, yet just this once Satan altered the rules, set hope in the breast of he who did not wish to freely abdicate."

"It was Ruhvan – Ara's stepfather – who made him assume a female form; the guise of Ericka?" Shepherd struggled with the words, concepts alien to his existence.

"Yes."

"But why?"

"As a humiliation. A punishment. No king ever goes willingly to his fate. During his time allotted, he does everything he can to balance the scale in his favor."

"And yet you said Satan altered the rules. Ruhvan did not have to lose."

Dongal sucked air between his teeth, as though hearing his own statement repeated back to him were blasphemy enough to condemn him. His voice thickened.

"Ruhvan was a dull, brutal man. He knew the prophesy as well as any."

"The one predicting this... Second Coming of Satan?" Shepherd whispered, a small cloud of condensation forming around his face as his breath froze in the deepening temperature of the subterranean chamber.

"Of the Second Coming, yes sir," the servant agreed. "Although not necessarily of Satan," he stressed. "Just as I was taught as a boy in the

Christian land of my birth, holy men prophesy of the Second Coming, yet in none of their works is it ever promised to be Jesus. So, too, is that encompassed within the tenets of this Kingdom's beliefs. Precisely who, or what they anticipate is unknown."

"An all-powerful demon?" Dongal rattled his chains, whether in rebuttal or agreement the questioner could not be certain. "Ruhvan thought he was the one?"

"The signs were inconsistent; some pointed to Ara, others to Ruhvan. There are even a handful of nobility who believe the supreme being will come from their class."

"Tarrington?"

"Without doubt he... and his followers consider that a possibility."

"And you?"

"I have seen that which would lead me to think so," came the reluctant answer.

"Where does that place Ara?"

Dongal's reply was on surer ground. "Ara, too, has cause to fear the most powerful nobleman in the Kingdom."

"Is Tarrington the one?"

Shepherd pushed too hard. Dongal cried, the torture of his predicament made obvious by the strain in his voice.

"Why do you ask me? I am no authority. I have no gifted insight. I am no more than a slave –"

"Who has seen too much," Shepherd interrupted. He meant to be kind, but his statement only inflicted pain. Attempting to sooth the wound, he hurried on. "You said you nurtured Ara from infancy. That your status only served to falsely increase Ara's sense of destiny."

"I have said more than I should."

"Think!" Shepherd commanded, straining against his shackles. "What you know may save us."

"It is too late for me. My life – and my soul – are already forfeit. I have signed away my birthright," he wept.

"Where the heart is pure," the youth quoted Abraham Trent, "redemption is always possible. You were a child when you gave away your freedom. Surely God will forgive –"

"God does not reign here!"

"All right," he hurriedly pacified. "Then some other means. I swear to you, if it is within my power, I will redeem your soul, if I cannot save your life."

His promise temporarily assuaged the humble man.

"I will do anything you say."

"Then tell me the rest. About the painting."

A sigh from the heart cast them both in a glow of white. The fog dissipated slowly as Dongal plowed ahead.

"The subject – the boy – with your face – is chained to a mountain."

"As a sacrifice?"

"To be used as a conduit – to augment the position of he who would be the everlasting ruler of Satan's Kingdom."

"Ara used my power," Shepherd miserably groaned. "In the room with the window. He levitated the knife and threatened to kill you with it."

"I overlooked that possibility," came the low admission. "I wanted to believe you... were not the one. But you are."

A pall settled over two human spirits, but Shepherd could not allow his depression to end the conversation.

"Why did Ara search for the... conduit outside the Kingdom? Logically, his ascension would hinge on another... devil."

"Use your eyes," Dongal snarled, tense and irritable. "The three crosses are a direct tie to Christ's death and resurrection."

"But He –"

" – attained eternal life," Dongal completed after his own intent. "While the two thieves are supposed to have gone to hell."

"Satan's 'Paradise' for sinners."

"Two warring combatants fighting over control of the Underworld."

"And the raven – is the devil?"

"It may be. I... try not to look at the painting. It frightens me."

"Tell me about the sacrificial human."

"The facial features." Dongal struggled with his words. "The innocence. Not one 'born' of Satan."

"All right. But why New York? Hardly the capital of virtue."

"Ara tried to explain once, when he was younger and more inclined to confess his reasoning to me. There are symbols hidden in the artwork." He rattled the metal as a means of expressing frustration. "I do not speak the language; I have not the training in the Old Religion. He thought he knew the secret." A pause turned into minutes. "And he did."

"If – I – am the one who can help him achieve final victory, why did Ruhvan allow Ara the liberty of traveling Outside?"

"He had no choice. But the king did everything he could to prevent Ara's success. He made him assume the body of a female against his will, hoping that would make his quest more difficult."

"And yet he used it to his advantage."

Dongal shrugged, slumping against the frigid wall, so that his weight hung entirely by the chains.

"I believe it was Tarrington's idea. He and Ruhvan conspired together. Tarrington said he would... watch Ara."

Shepherd's throat constricted. "How?"

"I do not know."

Shepherd believed him, but he did not need that answer. He already knew it.

Through a gold pyramid and a stone idol with blue eyes that Trent did not remember collecting.

"Tarrington."

The word tasted wicked on his lips as awareness soured his stomach. Tarrington had not only spied on the absent boy-king, he had played foul with Ruhvan. Tarrington had discovered the "missing link" long before Ara set out on a fool's errand. The aristocrat had manipulated Shepherd's life, overseeing the destruction of his parents, so that he would finally come under the protection of Trent. Trent, the kindly old professor of the occult, whose teachings would indoctrinate the boy in the Old Ways, making him that much more attractive to the dark prince.

Trent had not been killed as an example of divine power. He had not been the victim of sadism, nor even of tidying up loose ends. His death had been the ultimate test. By allowing Shepherd to witness the scene, Tarrington offered the final challenge.

Prove yourself by saving he you love; exert your will over mine and I will believe.

Shepherd had failed. In doing so, he ironically passed the trial.

Guilt washed over him, bringing with it bitter recrimination.

He *had* known; he had sensed the challenge, yet he had been too overwhelmed by his own fear of the painting to intervene. Trent *had* called and he ignored him.

Dear God. How could I have been so selfish?

But this time, Shepherd did not listen for an answer. He knew none would be forthcoming. Ara stood correct. He had abandoned God the moment he set foot in this accursed land. Worldly success meant more to him than anything.

Anything at all.

Satan had picked wisely. A damning condemnation.

Too late to save Trent, Shepherd had to believe it was not beyond his powers to influence the evil which had brought him low.

"You still live," he remarked with a casualness which startled him. "Why is that?"

"A weakness of Ara's. I am his... confessor. I know his heart," he caustically added. "But my time is near." He coughed but his listener did not respond. "Ara will offer me to his father. To prove his devotion. There can be no love here, Mr. Kingston – no matter how expressed."

To which Shepherd heatedly agreed, having discovered that fact to his cost.

"Why there are no female servants?" Shepherd asked, more for the sake of hearing himself speak, for he sensed their time drawing to an end.

"Ara cannot bear to be reminded of his role as Ericka. Though he has freedom to copulate with those he would *here,* the idea of intercourse is repugnant to him. In his true form, he has never known a woman... though he has been *known* as one," he added. "For which he will never forgive."

"By me....?" came the guilty interrogative.

"By Ruhvan, his stepfather, whom he loathes above all others."

Hanging his head in revulsion, conflicting emotions tore at Shepherd. Detecting the wavering loyalties, the slave hurried on, words tumbling from his lips.

"Controlling humans is easy, you see. Manipulating the..." He paused, working the unfamiliar concept over in his mind before continuing. "Stock market; toying with people. Destroying them in vicious, unyielding ways proved Ruhvan right."

"Why?"

"It made Ara careless. He thought himself all powerful. He failed to take proper precautions."

"But Ara did defeat his stepfather," Shepherd protested, clenching his fist, then making a futile attempt to pass it through the band of iron. Assaulted by creeping doubt, the blond-haired youth searched the blackness, seeking an answer. "He *is* king, isn't he?"

His own terror exacerbated by the noise, Dongal did not speak until hope extinguished and the reverberations died away.

"Ara is king," he faithfully repeated. "But his victory was... tainted. Incomplete." Both manacled victims shivered simultaneously. "I witnessed the confrontation when Ara and Ruhvan came face-to-face on a deserted road not far from here. I was hiding in the bushes."

"Tell me. Please." He did not want to know. Gone, like hope, was journalistic fervor, replaced by muted apathy.

Without the power to see, Shepherd sensed the negation.

"It is beyond the power of words. Close your eyes," Dongal continued, in a tone and manner remarkably similar to that of his master. "And I shall reveal to you what no Otherworlder has ever witnessed."

Shepherd did as bidden, letting stand Dongal's protestation than no Otherworlder had ever seen devils fight for the right to rule. If Dongal, human born and bred, did not consider himself an Otherworlder, now was not the time to challenge him.

In the absence of light, made greater behind the veil of fleshy, swirling tendrils of snakelike fog wrapping around their bodies, the unlikely friends were catapulted back to a time two years hence.

The sun burned hot in the sky, thought the temperature did not cause his perspiration. Squatting behind a heavy overgrowth of bush, Shepherd's eyes, which were not his eyes, but those of another, squinted through the brambles. Around him, nothing but preternatural silence. The wind, if there had been any, ceased to exist.

The only movement of which he had awareness was the throbbing of an artery in his neck. With nothing else to do, he found himself counting: thirty, sixty, ninety, one-hundred twenty-two.

His heart raced in anticipation of flight, though he knew he could not move. Moreover, fear paralyzed his limbs.

It was a peculiar sensation, anticipating that which Shepherd Kingston could have no knowledge. Yet he did, and more beside. Within him stirred an awareness that he shared a consciousness, yet he could not recall whose, or why.

Behind him came the sound of heavy footsteps; boots treading upon the earth with the authority of eminent domain. His eyes shifted to the right. Almost upon him emerged a figure he recognized, though he had never before seen. A broad, heavily-built man, powerful, with long hair bobbing from the aristocratic way in which he moved his head.

Attired in black, across his shoulders draped a cloak of deep, dark purple, the color of pressed grapes. A dull, evil-tinged aura clung to him like a second skin. The Dongal-thing knew him as Ruhvan, the stepfather, Satan's chosen, but his tenure was precarious.

Shepherd assumed an immediate hatred of him. It required no more than a glance to work up a loathing so intense it came near to splitting him at the seams. Were it within his power, he would have destroyed the creature on the spot, rendering him to ash with the glare of his own blue orbs.

A second set of footsteps, these lighter, though no less authoritative. The sound of twigs snapping, of dust stirring, then Ara, the stepson, appeared just below the tip of the horizon. He gave the appearance of having walked a far distance, though he showed no indication of being winded nor fatigued. Shepherd guessed traveling had refreshed, rather than tired him.

Oblivious of onlookers, the two spawns of Lucifer faced one another, fifty yards apart. A momentary appraising of the other's strengths – or weaknesses, Shepherd could not be certain – then Ara pointed down the road, indicating where the other should stand.

Ruhvan wickedly smiled, teeth glistening in the sunlight, a match to the gold clasp around his cape which flashed with earthly glory. Sure of himself and in his place as master, he paced off the required distance then set himself, legs parted, arms hanging loosely at his side. King Arthur, come to do battle with a knight of his own Round Table.

Silence reigned a moment longer, then Ara began to chant. A bird, startled by the sudden noise, fluttered upward from its perch. As its wings took flight, it inadvertently crossed over the contested area. Without a move from either man, it staggered, as though shot with an arrow, then dropped to earth, dead before it struck the ground.

Ara's recitations grew louder, more insistent, the cadence of a song as old as life. It swelled like the mighty ocean, forming an identity separate from its creator. Flexing his long, slender fingers, the youth held out his arms, stiffened his neck, then curled his fingers inward. The ground began to shake, then with a crack of thunderous proportions, burst apart. The stench of sulphur tainted the air.

Blue-tipped flames of peculiar configurations licked their way upward through the crevice. The ground around the opening blackened, clumps of dirt falling inward, never to touch bottom. A swirling mass of molten lava spun up from the rim, danced in midair until it formed a circular shape, then settled naturally into Ara's outstretched palm.

Shepherd's eyes wandered from prince to king. He, too, had performed the same feat, holding within his fist another ball of hell's outpouring. Simultaneously, the combatants raised their left arms, flinging their unearthly weapons at one another. The missiles struck, exploding into a cascade of intensity bright enough to blind a man. As the onlooker dropped his head in belated self-protection, bits of scalding embers rained to earth, igniting the intemperate underbrush which lacked the gift of locomotion.

Mightier than heaven's lightning, louder than a nuclear holocaust, the rockets from Hades' toy chest rattled the planet with the intensity of a falling meteorite. Long-dead dinosaurs and their present-day progeny quavered under the force powerful enough to extinguish their habitats.

Shepherd vainly attempted to make the sign of the cross over his sunken chest, but found his arms pinned to his sides. Not an act Dongal could have performed, his shared body refused to perform the ritual. Unprotected, and thus at the mercy of Another's whims, Shepherd riveted his full attention toward the dueling demons.

Another ball of fire appeared in Ara's hand. Tossing this one faster and with more purpose, it struck Ruhvan squarely in the chest. Sparks flew heavenward, igniting his cloak. Ignoring the inconvenience, the warrior staggered back, catching himself within a foot of his original position.

Ire roused at the unexpectedness of the hit, the king waved his hand, summoning a second projectile. Bouncing it lightly, and thus giving the impression it were no more than a featherweight, he leered at the challenger, then flung it outward with a casual, almost contemptuous air. His aim held true and would have found its mark, had not the younger prepared his defense. Jutting out his hand, palm extended, he deflected the blow, diverting it toward the ground. Cascades of flame scorched the road, charring the worn path into cinders.

Impiously daring to savor his victory, Ara did not sufficiently prepare for his opponent's quickness. Better directed, this fireball struck him in mid-chest, propelling him to his knees.

Howling in rage, his voice a combination of unrestrained imps and malicious demigods, Ara sprung to his feet and directed his attention to the ever-widening pit. Instantly, whatever powers existed in the inferno responded to his commanded, delivering two weapons, one to the right, one to the left hand. With ambidextrous ease, Ara pitched them toward Ruhvan, connecting with both. The older man cried, writhed in a sheet of all-consuming, red-hot flame, then danced away, weakened but not defeated.

Where his feet struck earth, pools of fire emerged, gained strength from the rejuvenated wind and spread across the road, creating uneven lines of demarcation. Pebbles, seared by the heat, exploded, shooting bits of rocks across the field. Shepherd/Dongal ducked, barely escaping one of the deadly chards. Seeing it about to ignite the dry tinder by his leg, he frantically dug the ground, using the dirt to extinguish the fire.

His act did no more than save his own humble hiding place, for the next moment saw the forest come alive with destructive patches of fire. Unable to contain, much less put out the flames, he cringed away from sight, finding more refuge in the fight than the fighter's inadvertent destruction.

Neither Ara nor Ruhvan paid heed to their surroundings. When their eyes shifted away, their gaze concentrated upon the never-ending supply of weapons. Growing more adept at their task, each tossed faster and more adeptly, until the arena hummed with the aftermath of missile striking missile.

As the shots deflected off their burning bodies, ancient trees along the roadway were reduced to ash, silently crumpling to earth in piles of grey-white mounds. In ten minutes, two hundred years of growth were wiped off the face of the earth.

With no awareness of time passing, Shepherd withdrew further, fearful least the encircling fires engulf him. Eyebrows singed, tips of his fingers raw from digging, lungs burned from blackened air, he drew into a circle, arms and legs protecting his quivering torso.

The contest continued, unabated, although not without cost. As each fresh projectile struck, the warriors weakened, staggered further, took more time garnering their waning strength. Sweat appearing on their brows immediately sizzled and evaporated, transforming the pink flesh of exertion to bubbling, boiling blisters.

Finally Ruhvan fell hard on his back. Ara laughed. Lips parted in a lupine leer, he gathered an armful of fire, heaving it atop the fallen master. The form, barely discernible, writhed, naked arms and legs protruding from the cone of flame.

Victory blazing in black orbs, shining through reddish sockets like marbles of obsidian, Ara gathered one last, tremendous ball of sputtering flame, so huge it required both hands to manage it.

"Damn you!" he hatefully cursed. "Damn you to Hell!"

Too weak to ward off the fiery projectile, it exploded in Ruhvan's face. A sheet of fire fifty feet high engulfed him, searing the tops of distant trees which withered and were rendered invisible, to reappear no more.

Obscured by the roaring inferno, Ruhvan shrieked in uncontrollable agony. The flames, twisted by ungodly fingers, wrapped themselves tightly around the figure, holding him secure as blood boiled and bones splintered.

Without losing consciousness, the melting mass writhed, floundered, crawled away.

One second, then another, timeless to the being enduring an endless death, before the shapeless mass emerged. No longer human in shape, it wavered, then seemed to roll off toward the left, destroying all which came in contact, as though it were actually lava from a volcano.

In the blink of an eye, he vanished.

The earth trembled, wailed, then slowly knit itself together, until the monstrous crevice appeared no more than a rent. From the far distance, an owl hooted. The howl of a wolf followed, lingering in the atmosphere like a funeral dirge.

Ara, strained to the point of breaking, tried a step but found strength had abandoned him. Sinking to his knees, sparks from live coals scattered in the wind. It took time before he could gather his tormented wits. Only then did he create a twisted smile over blackened lips. Using his right hand to steady his left, he held it up in triumph. Blood poured down charred wrists.

"The king is dead. Long live the king."

A pledge as old as time. And just as impotent, for the proof lay not in winning the contest, but in surviving it.

CHAPTER 29

The Dongal/Shepherd creature stirred. Before the interloper could influence the host, Dongal stood, casting about with prying eyes. With instincts borrowed from a rabbit, the servant let his nose and the hairs on the back of his neck alert him to danger. They worked better than Shepherd's ears. Before he identified any cause for alarm, the shared body dove to earth, flattening himself to the ground. All that remained visible were two eyes without the ability to blink, peeking into the distance.

A figure appeared from the west, standing with his back to the sun, inadvertently obscuring his features. Shepherd presumed him to be Ruhvan, returned from hell to renew the contest, but Dongal knew better. Whimpering into the flesh of his arm, he sunk lower, merging into the land to which he did not belong.

Ara's reaction came slower than Dongal's. Weakly raising his head, he staring upward in stark horror, identifying the newcomer in a harsh, raspy gasp.

"Tarrington."

The creature so addressed nodded carelessly, then stepped aside, affording Shepherd a better look. Towering over the supplicated king and the hidden watcher, he seemed a league high. Wide shouldered and heavily muscled, massive grey locks were drawn straight back, so they formed an arc over his head that drew light to it, creating a halo effect.

Attired in a form-fitting suit of black, over which hung a loose scarlet tunic decorated with amorphous shapes of gold, he wore calf-high boots fitted over the trousers. Surprisingly clean and highly polished, they reflected back the image of the would-be ruler. A massive link-chain necklace symbolizing authority completed the outfit.

"It is I," Tarrington gracefully acknowledged, condescending to bow, not from respect, but from breeding.

"Go away; absent yourself," Ara commanded. "I, your new king, do so command."

The nobleman's eyes glistened in mock denial.

"Your authority," he craftily articulated, "is questionable. Your triumph... incomplete."

Ara hissed, fingers digging into the charred earth.

"You – saw?"

"Everything."

"You had not the right."

"No one prevented me."

The booming voice, devoid of sympathy, evoked rage. Ara waved him away.

"I rule the Kingdom now. You are my vassal; sworn to serve the king."

Tarrington shook his head, a circle of mirth dancing from his proud, well-etched features. For all the world, he played master to Ara's servant.

"I serve no one but the Father. You are a poor representative."

"I won the right."

"You defeated Ruhvan; hardly the same thing."

"No!" Ara cried, struggling to his feet. Tarrington brutally arrested his upward movement by a heavy hand, placed squarely on his shoulder.

"You are not in a position to argue... Little One."

"Damn you!" Ara hurtled the invective as he had thrown the weapons of fire, but quickly realized words were far less effective, for he incurred no more than Tarrington's mirth.

"You may have condemned your stepfather, but you cannot damn me so easily."

Divining more than Tarrington said, but precisely what he meant, Ara quietly countered. "You cannot rule here. I am the next in line. I am Satan's chosen."

"As it has always been," his new adversary acknowledged, mockingly bending his knee. "For one full minute, you ruled, Sire. But your time is short."

"Impossible! Stand back. Obey."

"How will you implement the order, your grace? With thunder bolts from heaven?" He chuckled, stroking his chin to underscore Ara's weakness. "With fire from hell? The gateway has closed, the crevice sealed. It will not part again. Not for you."

"Nor for you," came the assertion as Ara cast his face toward the healed and charred earth.

"I do not need our Father's weapons. A knife will cut your throat and end your life just as easily." Removing a long, wicked, curved blade from its sheath, Tarrington ran it through his fingers, savoring the lethal feel. "While it was ordained you do battle with fire, this steel was forged in hell's furnace and presented to me at birth. Have you never wondered why?"

"Not to take my life."

"So you must now believe. But no explanation for the divine gift was ever given. Shall I run it across your neck, or plunge it into your vital organs and see?"

"No!" Ara cried, jerking his tormented body away from the would-be assassin.

"No," Tarrington repeated, savoring the fear. "You were always the weakling, Ara, the imperfect son. It is an abomination you should ever have thought yourself the Coming."

"Not you!"

"Perhaps not," the tormentor agreed, rubbing his hands together in blatant expectation of having his wish fulfilled. "But how shall we know, until we test the waters?"

Swishing the blade through the air, Tarrington inched closer to the being who would be king, eyes pinned to a position between carotid artery and jugular vein. Without looking where he trod, his right foot landed atop a live ember. The leather of his sole instantly disintegrated, exposing bare skin to the remnant of combat. Grimacing in unexpected torment, he jumped back, hopping on his left leg. Ara's laugh compelled him to put down the burned appendage.

"You have not prepared for this confrontation," the youth observed, eyes slanted against the rays of the piercing sun. "You have no spell to protect you. Whilst Satan may ward off fatal injury to his chosen, you were not included. Think well, Tarrington. Consider what you have to lose."

"Consider yourself," the elder hissed, extending the blade, so that light reflected off the polished steel. The moment had turned, however, and the son, prepared since infancy for leadership, assumed his rightful authority.

"You have no warrant – you are not the bloodline. The usurpation of power will come at terrible cost. Kill me if you dare," he challenged, baring his chest and exposing his flesh. "Rule in my stead. But be ever vigilant, for even your most trusted compatriots will turn. They desire power as much as you. One night, when the moon is full and you have drunk your draught of wine, they will attack, slaying you, tearing your body asunder. You know what they will do with it," he continued, straining forward from his lowly position. "They will drag it to the dungeon and cast it into the sacrificial pit.

"*I* may worship there, for such is my birthright, but no one else may trespass. To be offered to Satan at the mouth of hell is terrible to contemplate. That he will accept you is without question. That you will burn for all eternity, completely aware of your torment, is also a foregone conclusion."

"I will take precautions to protect my life."

Ara batted the protest away as he might shoo away a fly. "They will never be enough to save your earthly form. Death may come in any number of unexpected, unpleasant ways. Poison. Your fellow devils may steal into your bed chamber and smother you while you repose. A fall down a flight of stairs. Where you have dared, others will emulate. You know I speak truth, nobleman."

"You beg and squirm for your life," Tarrington defied.

"And you are a fool," Ara retorted. "You were aware Ruhvan and I would face one another, yet you have not said the proper prayers, made the sacrifices. You are as vulnerable as I. More so, for what you contemplate is treason, punishable by the most heinous torture."

Clearly moved by the vision of his own damnation, the would-be usurper wavered. But he had come too far, crossed too many barriers to be put off from the ultimate earthly treasure.

"I must have something," he began, choosing his thoughts for ears other than Ara's. "A position in your kingdom."

"You shall have it," came the response from he who had anticipated as much.

"I wish to be the most powerful... the most favored of your demons. To sit on your left side at table; to stand before you at the Rituals of the Plain of Stones."

"So shall it be."

"But I do not trust you, kingling," Tarrington wavered. "You promise much, but your pledge is fleeting. Once your strength has returned, I will find myself set upon and murdered."

"You have my sacred word."

"Your word," the noble scoffed, feeling the rise of hot blood. "I will kill you now and take my chances. It is better to rule for a week or a year than to be forever subservient."

"Remember the dungeon... and the fire," Ara reminded him, fighting a battle the equal of that which he had just passed. "Take my word as Satan's chosen. Assume your place as High Priest. That is within your grasp – and your right."

Tarrington's eyebrows knit in consternation as he waged inward conflict. "You are false. Offer me proof to hold against you in our father's eyes."

"There can be no thought of –"

"Your blood!" Tarrington fairly screamed, striding nearer. Ara withdrew in abject horror.

"My blood is sacred. I can offer it to none other than he who rules our universe."

"Your blood or your life. Hark onto me, Ara, ruler of this kingdom. I will have one or the other."

Had not the feat been impossible, the Dongal/Shepherd creature would have petrified into stone.

"Cut myself and bleed for you?" Ara whispered, visions of the ground opening up to engulf him more reality than fantasy. "I cannot perform such a deed. It is forbidden."

"Then I will accept that which has already been spilled. Soak your bleeding wounds with this."

So saying, Tarrington removed a white linen cloth from a pouch worn at his side and tossed it down. The delicately woven material fluttered, failed to achieve flight and landed ignobly at Ara's feet.

"To give you power over me is sacrilege. It will not be allowed."

"Test it and see. Take the linen and stain it with red blood. Until it drips," he added. "Then hand it to me. If it is not allowed, as you allege, I shall not be permitted to accept it. But if Satan agrees to our bargain, I will have the proof of your fealty I require."

"By all that is sacred, Tarrington, you challenge not me, but our lord."

"Then in the name of all which is evil, perform the deed. I accept the consequences."

Whimpering from shame, the fright originating in the bowels and radiating outward, Ara did as bidden. Placing the linen to his bleeding right arm, he wet it with crimson until it dripped.

"Now pass it upward."

The hand which received the troth shook as much as the one which offered it. As the pledge changed ownership, the earth shook and clouds passed over the sun, darkening the scene into preternatural night. Neither moved for fear of inciting the wrath of hell.

Three heartbeats for every second, until both were lightheaded. The trembling slowly faded and the clouds parted. Day came once more to the dominion of evil.

"We have our answer. Remember well, King Ara. I will call upon you in a month. When you are recovered from battle. Receive me as a prince, or I will make known to our disciples the power I hold over you. They will not be so kindly disposed to worship at your feet, knowing I possess Satan's tacit promise of leadership. There will be war, such as the black void has never witnessed. God's earth will be destroyed and with it, all of mortal frame. Hell will regroup but not with the likes of us. Our consciousness will continue in torment. Do you acknowledge as much?"

"I acknowledge," Ara confessed, bending his head to the inevitable.

"Then I bid your leave... your grace."

Tarrington bowed from the waist, kissed the bloodied bandage and retreated.

Two contests. Two victories. But at a cost never before extracted.

Left alone on the field of battle, Ara raised his withered limbs, holding them outward. Prayers tumbled from insensate lips.

"Heal me, my Master. Repair the damage done, so that I may grow strong in your service, to rule as your true son."

Arms extended, he exerted all his consciousness, willing the wounds to knit together and his body be restored to full vigor. As he chanted in the dungeon after sacrificing his blood to Satan, he prayed on the barren roadway, pleading for restoration.

The gashes and burns continued to seep, the pain unabated. He cried, seeking divine inspiration.

"Heal me, Master and creator. I am your servant. I walk in your path, through life everlasting."

Forgive me, Father, for I have sinned.

A sparrow flew overhead. A hawk swooped down and caught it in its talons. The struggle was brief.

Locomotion returned to they which were neither bird nor predator. The shadow-self reanimated with the substance, standing tall in the sunshine. It approached the king, walking on a man's legs.

"So," Dongal remarked, teeth bared in a rare display of might. "You have been weakened by the contest, my Lord. You have sold your soul to an unworthy. Satan rejects the call to bind your wounds. For the first time I see you... naked." Ara attempted speech, but his words were lost as the human spoke over them. "Not, for the moment, the devil's son, but a frightened, helpless boy... lying in the dirt."

Past torments filled Dongal's essence. With eyes to see, Ara cringed, fully appreciating this unexpected turn of events. He had defeated his stepfather, bought off a nobleman and been brought low by a slave.

Diffidence overcoming pride, he choked out a plea.

"Dongal, in the name of –"

"Not that!" the servant scorned, stiffening his body. "Not to me." Walking straight-legged around the figure, he absorbed the picture. "You have drained yourself beyond hope, master. I never thought to see the day."

"Remember... who you are."

Dongal's eyebrow arched. "How could I forget, master? You have reminded me every day of my pitiful service." Then, more firmly, "You have no power over me, now. You have no power over anything."

"Please," Ara implored, hands upraised, although not clasped. Were he to fail to turn the hard heart, a punishment greater than Dongal's betrayal awaited him in the regions below.

Something in the manner of the supplication halted the life-long companion. It did not take long, however, for shock to turn to scorn.

"You, who have never shown mercy, plead for yourself. Your Father would never approve of such behavior," he added with a jeer.

Responding to the truth of the assertion, Ara flinched, then attempted to crawl away, leaving an earthworm trail. He could not go fast enough, nor far enough to avoid the rest of Dongal's vituperation. Squaring his shoulders, the slave imitated his betters.

"What can you offer me, master, to make me stay my hand? What in this world can you give, which will make me pity you?" His words froze the slithering form. Hope rekindled.

"An oath... an oath never to damn your soul. In this world, or the next."

"More."

"Nor to allow any other to take that which was given you by God."

Ara backed his pledge with a quivering of lips. He asked much but offered more. Dongal hesitated, rocking slowly back and forth on the heels of his feet.

"In the name of what you hold holy?"

"By my Father's life."

He had nothing greater by which to swear.

The oath cost much, for he pledged it not only to the servant, but vouched it against the name of He who surely listened. Inside the body hosting dual spirits, the sensitivity of Shepherd Kingston reached out. He could not speak for Dongal; could not use the other man's lips to assuage the boy's hurt. But he could make his own silent vow.

I will save you if I can.

Shepherd's forgiveness could not have affected Dongal, but a barrier broke and the servant bent down, offering a hand. Mistaking his intent, Ara cringed. A beat passed before the slave scooped up the youth, wrapping him in his arms. Ara sobbed.

The moment had been won. His life spared.

The price, they understood, would be paid on a different field, among other combatants.

CHAPTER 30

The ripples of time diminished, returning the witnesses to their dungeon. Sniffing back a cry, Shepherd whimpered, "What happened?" The question had no validity inasmuch as he already knew the future, though it was already past.

"I carried him home," Dongal began after some hesitation. "After that night, Ara slowly regained his strength, and with it, his powers. He had defeated his stepfather and reigned as master. Yet his time has been a tainted rule, because of what he gave Tarrington... and his promise to me."

"Is that why you called him... a corruption?" Annoyed at the story-teller's apparent hesitation, he loudly repeated, "Is that why?"

Dongal's voice, when he did speak, sounded incredulous, causing his listener to withdraw from embarrassment.

"Why would I, of all people, call another being's weakness a corruption?"

"Where I come from," Shepherd blurted, desperately trying to make good his mistake, "the connection is obvious. I meant no –"

"Then I am glad I do not come from 'New York,'" Dongal spat, carefully pronouncing the syllables. "Weakness may be a flaw to you, but to me it is life, itself."

"I'm only trying to understand. I must know what you meant."

Shepherd could not see Dongal but felt his eyes piercing the blackness, scrutinizing his face. With mounting impatience he withstood the examination. He did not know how to interpret the outpouring of breath when it came, but somehow felt he had failed the test.

"Although Ruhvan did not win his contest with Ara, his intent to undermine him proved successful."

"Is that why Ara deprived you of your sight? Because you had seen too much?"

"More than even he dared admit. Rending me blind allowed him to overlook his transgression."

"But Tarrington did not forget."

The servant made a deprecating noise, causing Shepherd to withdraw.

"His *father* did not forget. Since that time, Ara has been made to humble himself as no other. He must offer his own blood. The ritual at the mouth of hell is prolonged... dangerous. He has no assurance his wounds will heal... or that he will not scar. To scar," he added, "is to be marked for sacrifice. Satan's ruler must be – pure. One mistake, one drop of blood spilled, and his tenure here is over."

Remembering Ericka's reaction to the spilling of champagne on the airplane and Ara's fury when Dongal's shaking hand had caused wine to drip on the carpet of the den came back with vivid memory.

"I see." Gone, the time when the guest amended ill-chosen words. He did see, but his heart served only himself. Ignoring the lack of manners, Dongal continued.

"Satan is an unforgiving parent; he will have his kingdom ruled by the strongest of his creations. He decreed that Ara must defend his title a second time – against Ruhvan, who has been granted the unprecedented opportunity of returning from the Underworld to reclaim his prize. The two will fight again."

"When?"

"Soon. Very soon."

"Within a year? A fortnight?" Dongal did not answer, which provided the answer. "Will Ara win?"

"That has not been preordained." Dongal spoke with amazing assurance, which had the opposite effect on his companion. "To defeat his stepfather, who has increased in strength during his time Below, Ara will need help."

"Me."

"My master did not find you in the two years between his nineteenth and twenty-first birthdays. After coming home to gain his crown, he was forced to return to the Outside. It has taken him three more years."

"He went back to New York, reprising his role as Ericka. On his own, without being forced," Shepherd marveled. "You knew, and did not warn me."

"By the time you arrived, it was too late. You were born to protect him. You are the fulfillment of prophesy."

"And if I refuse to intervene?"

"You have already 'intervened.' *Twice,*" Dongal added, alluding to Shepherd's unspoken vow at the conclusion of Ruhvan's earthly destruction. Shepherd flinched from the bitter accusation.

"As did you," he hissed back.

"Did I?"

"You might have left Ara to die." When Dongal did not take the bait, he added, "Let them kill one another. Let this kingdom revert to God."

A groan, and then, softly, "He will not claim what He never owned."

The blow struck heavily against Shepherd's soul, for he knew it to be true. Trent, in his tainted wisdom, had also known.

I'm very much afraid God never had Ms. Elvina.

Hanging his head, he spoke no more.

When Eldrich appeared in the dungeon, Shepherd believed his time had come. Struggling miserably against the more powerful man's strength, he spit in anger as a hand settled around his throat.

Contrary to expectations, the servant merely disentangled a lock of long hair from around a link in the chains used to restrain his wrists.

"You are to come with me," he ordered, ignoring or ignorant of the anxiety choking the youth.

"Where?"

"To your chambers. You are to dress for dinner."

Taken aback by the casualness of the statement, Shepherd turned toward where he knew Dongal to be restrained.

"And Dongal? Is he to be released, as well?"

"You ask too many questions," Eldrich complained. Despite his warning, however, he answered with a curt, "Yes."

Released from bondage, Shepherd's legs gave way. He staggered forward, knees buckling. He did not expect help, but found himself as quickly supported by another's arms. Having neither sensed nor seen the man in the darkness, he cried.

"Walk off the lethargy in your legs. We shall not carry you," came the stern rebuke.

Doing as ordered, Shepherd stomped back the circulation, then signaled his readiness. Although the newcomers had brought no light with them, they accurately transmitted his intent.

"Follow me," Eldrich instructed. "And be quiet."

Suspecting some intrigue but at a loss what it might be, Shepherd fell into line, positioned between the servants. Though he did hear Dongal being set free, he presumed he trailed behind, forced to make his own way.

After crossing the floor, a door opened from the inside, allowing a sliver of light from the tunnel to penetrate the darkness. Both drawn and repelled by this sudden intrusion, Shepherd hesitated. To remain behind meant sure death, yet to follow into the upward regions held terrors against which his mortal mind rebelled.

"Hurry. There is not much time," the unknown urged. Not a command, but rather a request, Shepherd comprehended he had not the power to order him.

"What is the urgency?"

Instead on a reply, he found himself propelled forward. Recalling that Dongal had called Eldrich a favorite, he supposed that gave him the right to use force. Pulling himself together, Shepherd plunged ahead, one hand over his eyes to shield them from the torches.

The elevated path proved difficult. Struggling vainly to lift one foot ahead of the other, he nonetheless lagged behind Eldrich's brisk pace, compelling the other to prod him along. His tardiness seemed to increase the servants' nervousness, but they remained silent until the party reached the landing.

Pausing to listen at the heavy wooden door, Eldrich finally signaled an "all safe." Inserting a key into the lock, he twisted it, exerting considerable strength before the workings responded. Looking both ways to ascertain the way was clear, the others followed into the small connecting antechamber.

"Dongal," Eldrich summoned. The servant stepped forward, head hung so low the submissive posture compelled him to view the other through upturned orbs. "You are to wash and dress Shepherd Kingston. A wardrobe has been set out. Make him presentable."

"I understand."

"Then you are to see to yourself. The master directs me to tell you ceremonial attire has been left in your room."

Exhaling air from deep within his lungs, Dongal miserably nodded.

"The nobility?" he whispered.

"They are expected momentarily, if they are not here, already." Eldrich then relayed further instructions in a guttural language Shepherd did not comprehend. Spoken hurriedly, individual sounds slurred into one another.

"Very well," came the acknowledgment. Then, to Shepherd, "Follow me. And say nothing."

Shepherd did as directed, rightly assuming any divergence from orders would mean trouble.

Crossing the room, they emerged into the main corridor, which Shepherd recognized, though much had changed. Gone were the tapestries, replaced by sheets of woven black wool. Torches blazed from every wall sconce, giving the area a festive, albeit morbid appearance. Candles, too, had been lit around the perimeters, casting flickering, uneven shadows as they passed.

A formidable stone pedestal, the height of a man's waist, had been positioned by the main entrance. Atop it perched a matching basin, the sides of which were decorated with bizarre, dancing, inhuman figures. With a shudder, Shepherd identified it as a font, of the type positioned in the foyer of a church. Although no fuel burned beneath it, the water inside boiled furiously.

Though they did not pass close by, he experienced an intense heat radiating from the burning liquid. Any human placing his hand into the basin would surely scald his flesh.

Unmoved by the additions, Dongal did not look about as they traipsed toward the staircase. With Eldrich leading the way, they climbed upward. Without pause, he guided them down the hall to Shepherd's chamber. As previously, it was unlocked. The escort held back while the pair entered, then closed the door, shutting them in. Shepherd tried the knob. It turned easily.

"I thought perhaps," he began, then cut off his sentence, noting the look of dread on Dongal's face. "Who is expected?" he queried, instead.

"Members of the ruling class. The nobility of the kingdom."

Left unspoken, the word *demons.*

"Tarrington?"

"Most surely."

"How many are there?"

"I have never counted them."

"Will he use the bloodied linen as a threat over Ara?"

An expression of concern crossed the servant's lined features.

"It is not my place to say so. You must prepare yourself. Hurry. The ceremony will take place soon."

"Ceremony?"

Dongal waved away the question as being beyond his power to answer.

"You know," Shepherd accused.

"What I know and what I am allowed to speak are two different things."

"Prepare me – warn me," Shepherd requested, crossing to the servant whom he had come to look upon as his only ally. "Tell me what I am to expect. Please. I beg you."

"Those not of the peasant class must never 'beg' those who are," the man shuddered, frightened by the consequences of Shepherd's expression.

"All right – then tell me – as a friend."

"I am not your friend. I am a slave; I belong to the master. Speak no more." Turning toward the bed, Dongal inspected the clothing, taking care not to wrinkle the fabric.

"I do not want to wear those."

As though he had not spoken, Dongal stepped away.

"I will bring water. Wash yourself and shave your face. Take care not to draw blood with the razor," he added as an afterthought.

"Why not? I thought the object was to spill blood."

"Not by your own hand."

"Why not?" he repeated, placing himself between the servant and escape. "Tell me why not. If you don't," he pursued, eyes narrowed, "I will use the razor to slit my wrists. Better to die here, than face what others have in store for me."

"Such-an-act-is-not-permitted."

"Not permitted – by whom?" Dongal's expression assured him he was prepared to hold his tongue. "By Ara?" Dongal shook his head. "By Ara's stepfather?" Again, no. "By the devil?"

This time, he hit the target bullseye.

"Is it not the same in your world?" the servant implored. "To take your own life is a sin. Be still. There are many ears listening."

Shepherd could not afford to be put off by vague insinuation. He had gone too far, suffered too much to pause on manners.

"Whose ears? Tell me, Dongal. My life is at stake – my soul, as you would have it."

"Not as *I* –"

"All right; forgive me. It's just an expression," he soothed, pulling back from his own raging fears. "But in the name of God, tell me all you know."

"You will not – cut yourself?" Shepherd's legitimate hesitation prompted Dongal to speak. "Then I will answer. Afterwards, you may decide for yourself. Do what you will, but remember: your actions will be harshly judged. But dress," he pleaded. "I must act as manservant, else he will question why I tarry."

"Very well."

Dongal, the lowly Otherworlder brought in as a gift to an infant prince, supplied the water. Shepherd went about the motions of cleaning his body. As Dongal's attention wrapped itself inside the telling, however, Shepherd's actions became slower and slower, until finally they ceased altogether.

"The appointed hour is upon us: when Ruhvan is to return. But it will not be as before. The contest is to be witnessed. By many."

"It is to be held here? At the castle? Is that why the downstairs is decorated?"

"No. Not here. At the Plain of Stones. You know the place," Dongal meaningfully interjected, "for you have been there."

"I have," came the hushed admission. "But what I saw... was in my mind. Was that past or future?"

A peculiar smile came to Dongal's lips. "Perhaps both. Or neither."

The statement held no reassurance.

"Am I to be offered to Lucifer? Sent to hell for all eternity? My soul condemned – as yours?" He meant to inflict terror and succeeded. "Does Ara have that power?"

"He does."

"Will he use it? Against both of us?"

"Hurry," Dongal admonished in uncharacteristic brashness, brushing aside that which he had no power to deflect. "The master is waiting."

"I am almost done," came the quiet, reflective reply. Then, after donning the ceremonial robe, Shepherd grabbed Dongal by the throat. "I must get out of here! Get me a horse. I will ride for the border."

"Which border?" Dongal ignorantly asked, missing the point of his complicity.

"Any border. What does it matter? Out of this kingdom. Into civilization. I want to be with people again, not devils. I don't give a damn about destiny and masters and demons. That is not my world, no matter how hard someone is trying to convince me it is." As an idea struck him, his fingers tightened around the servant's windpipe.

"You come with me. Arrange for two horses to meet us outside and we'll ride to freedom. As you once dreamed of doing."

"That cannot be."

"You don't belong here anymore than I do! You weren't born here. Join me; I am of your blood. Be a man for once. Exert your free will!"

Intrigued by the unexpected proposition, the servant wavered. Escaping alive had never occurred to him.

"They will hunt us down."

"Ordinarily, yes. But Ara has company; he will be forced to entertain – to act as though everything were normal. If he did not – if he panicked, it would make him appear weak, out of control. Imagine," Shepherd hurried, "how Tarrington would take the news that the young master's 'shepherd' had escaped his grasp. Wouldn't that prompt him to make his move – to attack Ara with the troth?"

"Yes. He would."

"So even if Ara knows we're gone, he will be powerless to stop us. It's our only chance, Dongal – yours and mine. Stay here and we die. Or worse."

"Two horses," Dongal muttered, face aflame with hope. As quickly dashed, he admitted, "I have no authority in the stables. No one will give me horses."

"Lie, for God's sake!" Shepherd screamed. "Tell them the master sent you – that he wishes you and the guest to meet him – at the Plain of Stones. They will believe you."

"At the Plain of Stones," Dongal agreed, seeing the possibility.

"Then go and dress. It would not do for you to appear unprepared. I will meet you outside."

Without thinking, Dongal slipped away. Shepherd hurriedly fashioned the gold belt around his waist, then exited the room. No one tarried in the hall. From below, he could hear the sound of festivities. A party, or what passed as one, was in progress.

Drawing up the hood to cover his face, he descended the steps, one-by-one. It would not do to hurry. While time was his enemy, it was also his betrayer.

At the foot of the stairs, he nodded noncommittally to a servant he did not recognize. The man nodded back with disinterest, then turned away. Shepherd walked to the front door which stood ajar and slipped out. No one followed.

Dongal waited for him by the stables. In his hand he held the reins of two horses, the bay Shepherd had ridden earlier and a second, shorter animal with a queer, jagged blaze down its nose.

Soundlessly both men mounted their steeds, then trotted them from the yard. Not until they were beyond the perimeter of the castle did they urge the animals to speed.

"Which way?" Shepherd demanded, attempting to guide his wayward horse. "Which is the closest border?"

Dongal pointed south. "There. But we must ride east for some time before the path diverges."

Flashing a "thumbs up," Shepherd headed east. Remarkably, the horse responded readily, as if it knew the way. Dongal trailed behind, finally slowing his pace to a crawl. Had Shepherd not glanced over his shoulder, he would have been beyond the bend in the road and lost to the servant.

Bringing the bay to a halt with considerable difficulty, he waited impatiently for his friend to catch up.

"What is keeping you? We must ride hard."

"I am afraid I will fall off."

"Hold on tight. Like this," Shepherd demonstrated, grasping the mane in his hand. "Where does the road turn?"

"I... am not certain. It has been long since I came this way."

"Try to remember. We must put as much distance as possible between us and Ara before he is free to follow."

"Beyond," Dongal faltered. "A mile. Perhaps more."

"And then we ride south? You are certain? South?"

"Yes."

"To what country does it take us?"

Dongal's mouth opened, but he made no reply. Helplessly, he shook his head. "Your names are not our names," he faltered.

"But out of this kingdom? There is a way out?"

"There is a way."

"Then we must hurry. And Dongal," Shepherd added on impulse. "When we are safe, you will be free. Truly free. No one can hurt you on the Outside."

"No one can hurt me," he repeated without emotion.

"I mean it. Once we get back to the States, I'll take care of you. I promise."

"I have heard many promises in my life."

"This one you may believe."

They rode a quarter of a mile before coming to a branch in the road. The main trail lead east; a secondary one headed north.

"You said south," Shepherd accused, nearly frantic. "Do we go on? Yes or no?"

"Yes or no," Dongal senselessly remarked.

"This is no time to play games. Which way?"

When Dongal gave no answer, Shepherd screamed in indignation, spurring his horse forward.

Away. That was the direction.

He would ride east.

CHAPTER 31

Deep below the castle in the devil's chamber, Ara stood before the open grate, arm extended. In his left hand he wielded the ceremonial knife. Pupils turned to pinpoints, he deeply bowed before the open flames, nearly scraping the stone floor with his forehead.

"In the name of the Unholy; In the name of the Evil Trinity – the Father, the Son and the God from whom this land was ceded, I offer myself, body and soul. As it was before the beginning; as it ever shall be, I join myself to the Union of Everlasting Torment. I beseech thee, who begot me, to remember thy promise. I am Ara: I am king. Protect me, as thou would thyself."

So saying, Ara dug the blade deep into his flesh, severing veins and arteries in a display of faith. Blood gushed from the wound in unexpected torrents. Startled by the magnitude of the flow, Ara hurriedly placed the sacred chalice beneath his arm, catching the tide before it spilled to the floor.

Traditionally, such a wound staunched quickly, but this time the cut had been purposely vicious. Five minutes passed, then ten without a perceivable interruption of the darkening tide. Ara waited, breathing deeply at first, then more shallowly, as his heart fluttered wildly.

"To the progenitor of my race, neither human nor beast, I commend myself."

As if he were praying to deaf ears, the wound continued to bleed. Ara's normally pale flesh whitened to the hue of distant starlight.

"To you, whom the gods worship, I avow my loyalty."

Bubbles formed across the surface of the chalice. Inside the tarnished cup, bright red mutated to scarlet, then brown, as the living fluid perished, one cell at a time.

"This night I offer you the soul of an innocent being, stolen from heaven to adorn your habitat among those of your own creation."

Blood dripped without abeyance. Sweat seeped through Ara's pores. In pained desperation, he hurried on.

"This night, I commit to your pleasure two souls stolen from God. One, a stranger from a land far outside this Kingdom. Put him to work doing your biding, as decreed by the Ancients. The other is a peasant who has served me well since the time of my birth. Take him, Master, for he is a precious gift I, your son, am loathe to part with."

Slowly, with deliberate languor, the blood from the wound began to staunch. With more relief than faith would approve, Ara made the sign of an inverted cross, then flung the overfull contents of the chalice into the fire. A flame leapt out to greet it, sizzling the fluid into atoms. Visibly shaken, Ara concluded his supplications.

"So shall it be."

Hesitating to step back from the inferno least he display fear, the servant in his own right summoned his powers of healing. Severed veins and arteries knit together, torn flesh mended. A scar formed. Increasing his devotions, the puckered skin receded, leaving no trace.

He had gained the moment. Once again, his devotions had been answered.

Returning the implements to the table, Ara fled the chamber, still clothed in the garments of Satanic rite. These he would wear at the ceremony, the only time tradition permitted him to appear outside the Devil's Chamber in demonic raiment. They marked him as Master of the Void, bestowing the right of unmitigated evil.

In his haste, the king did not notice a drop of blood staining the flowing sleeve of his garment.

As a portend of events, it boded the unexpected.

Tarrington stood by the front door, waiting for Ara to emerge. Seeing him arise from the depths, he hastily composed himself by drawing out the folds of his regal cape and resting a hand on the hilt of a dagger. Ara's reaction to his unanticipated presence was neither calm nor controlled. Frowning angrily, he pointed toward the outside.

"Why are you not with the others?"

"I awaited your emergence from prayer."

"Oh?" Ara suspiciously arched an eyebrow. Not above a confrontation, the present moment did not offer proper time or place. "You wish to escort me to the Plain of Stones? You?"

Finding himself cleverly trapped, the noble graciously nodded.

"Yes, sire. On this, a most auspicious occasion, I did not want you to go alone."

Ara hesitated, thus losing the advantage. "I... was not planning on traveling unescorted. I am going with..." A second hesitation, longer than the first, betrayed him. "With my... most trusted servant."

"I think that most unlikely."

Reacting to the sneer of sarcasm, Ara bristled. Behind his bluster, however, lay genuine concern. Dongal's life might be forfeit, but only by his hand. For any other to touch him constituted sacrilege.

"Explain."

"Console yourself, sire," Tarrington answered, holding out a hand to indicate it was innocent of bloodshed. "To the best of my knowledge, your favorite is unharmed. Although, for his act of treason, I suspect you will be more than willing to cast him into the pit this night."

"How is it you speak of sin, when I know nothing? Or, is this your way of assuming more power than is your due?"

"I have much coming to me, master, and more besides. As you are aware."

"I know only that you are fortunate to retain your life. Do not parry with me. If we have business together, speak. Tell me your information or be silent."

Issued as command, Tarrington responded by pointing outside.

"Dongal is gone; fled with the Otherworlder." Not a deflection but a thrust, Ara staggered under the blow, emotions rising. Stomping around the chamber, fists clenched, he raged with the fury of an unrequited deity.

"You lie."

"Before you, master? And transgress, myself? No. I speak truth," Tarrington confessed, waving his hand over the font in a grandiose gesture of verity. Steam floated from the bubbling cauldron, spreading around, but avoiding his fingers. This testament arrested Ara's forward movement.

Compelled to likewise perform the deed, as thus attest to his own lack of guile, the king jammed his fist into the recently vacated space. Around his flesh a cloud of condensation gathered, reddening the digits of his hand. Not until his sleeve dripped with water did he finally remove his arm. His noble vassal dropped his head in praise.

"They took two horses and rode off an hour gone by. Sire."

"Rode – where?"

"Toward the border, as I was informed. Toward freedom."

Ara dropped back, mouth agape. Raising the wet sleeve toward his face, he noted the stain of blood. A cry escaped his lips.

Shepherd's horse reared, then skittered to a stop as a voice shattered the air.

"You err, Shepherd. It is to the north you must go."

The rider reacted, turning his steed in the new direction before realizing the correction had not come from Dongal. Instantly, he identified the voice. Gritting his teeth, he glanced into the brush. His assumption proved incorrect, however, as Eldrich stepped out, not his master.

The servant, in full flush of anticipated glory, approached the animals. Grabbing the reins of Shepherd's mount, he addressed his peer.

"Get down, Dongal. You shall not ride if I may not."

Wordlessly, the servant slipped to the ground. Fortunately his knees did not buckle. Such an action was not required, however, to betray his stark terror. Notwithstanding, Shepherd lashed out.

"You betrayed me! And I believed you."

Without daring to lift his head, Dongal shifted his shoulders in the negative.

"He did not lie, human," Eldrich jeered. "He, too was deceived. An easy matter. And he knows the consequences of his act. After tonight, I will be rid of him."

"Why do you take such satisfaction, Eldrich?" the slave suddenly demanded, surprising his listener. "Why do you desire my position, when I have been the lowest of the low?"

Without breaking stride, the servant led Shepherd's horse along the northernmost trial, compelling Dongal to follow.

"Since first presented to the master, you have been the favored. No matter you were a slave. Your human blood elevated you above the rest, for Ara was fascinated by your – connection to God."

"Then you may have my 'favors.'"

"I shall take them," came the rejoinder, ignoring Dongal's implications. "You have been allowed to perform the sacred rites no human has ever been privy to. You are the master's body servant; the one to whom he confines his thoughts." Stopping so suddenly the horse nearly walked into him, Eldrich looked over his shoulder to the humble man at the rear of their small procession. "Those privileges belonged to me; they are mine by right of ancestry. Too long have you usurped me."

Sensing his unremitting hatred, the horses' ears flattened as they pranced sideways. Jerking the lead animal back in line, Eldrich waved a finger toward his enemy.

"Tonight you shall be sacrificed. Not even the master's affection can save you. He must do his duty. When your blood has been spilled and your life extinguished, I shall serve him. My power shall grow with his. I shall gain that which has been denied me."

"Then I shall see you in hell."

"Indeed you shall," Eldrich agreed. "Although our positions will not be equal ones. You will suffer eternal torment, while I will have my own corner to rule."

"There is no hell," Shepherd screamed, surprising all three. "You worship an inferior master. Good shall rule this land!"

Had Eldrich any pity in his soul, he might have expressed it by the stare he leveled at the interloper.

"You have seen and do not believe?" Shepherd made no reply. "That is, perhaps, how it should be. Cling to your faith, Otherworlder. The master and I have need of it."

"You deceive yourself," Shepherd tried, but the conversation had reached its apex. Without bothering to argue, Eldrich continued down the path.

Turning in the saddle to face Dongal, Shepherd pleaded with him.

"We are two against one. Nothing has changed. Freedom awaits us."

"There is no freedom. I was a fool to believe such could be the case. My fate is sealed."

"Fight," pleaded the rider. "Fight like a servant of God."

"There is no God... for the likes of me."

Seeing no point in arguing, Shepherd let his hands drop. The mounted man and the slave moved forward in silence, each playing out his own personal role in destiny.

Twenty-two minutes later, the group came out at a clearing marked by charred trees and burnt underbrush. Recognizing the spot as that where Ara faced his stepfather, Shepherd felt a strange lethargy steal over him. This presented his last chance to bolt, but his mind, stunned by the realization of what awaited, refused to work.

"Dismount," Eldrich commanded. "The horses will go no further. We walk from here."

Slipping off the back of the bay, Shepherd swayed unsteadily. Without waiting for him to regain balance, the servant shoved him down the blackened path.

"Hurry. We must not keep them waiting."

"Them?" Shepherd mumbled, only half curious to know who would bear witness to his death.

"The master's guests. Were you not informed the nobility of the land has been assembled?"

"No," Shepherd lied without purpose.

Casting a curious eye toward Dongal, Eldrich shrugged, yet did not see fit to further enlighten him. They proceeded in silence.

Those gathered around the Plain of Stones huddled together, identities obscured by the long overhang of hoods. Visual identification was not necessary: all assembled at the site of sacrifice knew one another well. They all sprang from the same origin; their "passports" claiming one port of entry.

The mouth of Hell.

"The time draws nigh."

The group turned as one, peering into the forest surrounding the valley. Although those expected were still far off, no one questioned the statement of the elder. An aged female, status dictated by years on earth, for strife above the Underworld claimed many before their time, stirred a gnarled finger.

"Tarrington is impatient for the confrontation," a younger companion observed. Around him a series of torches burst into flame. "It has been three years since the king ascended."

"A short reign."

"It has been three years since the king *descended*," a tall, beardless nobleman corrected, playing on his predecessor's comment. He addressed the elder. "Will Ruhvan come?"

Anticipation swept through the otherwise placid group as she gave a curt nod. All felt the coming change in power. Depending on the outcome, the nobility would either rise or fall with the new master. Choosing the wrong side equated to excommunication.

"He will."

Though not yet dark, enough celestial bodies lit the heavens to remind them of the pending sacrifice. Never before had one, much less two, of God's creations been offered to the Dark Lord. An uneasiness descended, muting their excitement. The human's acceptance by Lucifer would signify the fulfillment of prophesy.

"To your places. Prepare yourselves. Repeat the ancient invocations in anticipation of what we shall witness."

They separated. In the coming trial, places would be exchanged, favors remembered or punishments meted. A new hierarchy would emerge. None wished to be found wanting.

In the distance, a wolf howled. Death had been invited to the Plain of Stones.

Tarrington readjusted his position so that the leather pouch affixed to his belt stood out in menacing prominence.

"They have been stopped," he informed the lord.

"By whom?"

"Eldrich."

"At your bidding?" If so, it represented an act of defilement, though the cause be just.

Rather than reply, Tarrington presented his weapon, hilt forward. Are received the gesture of obedience with contempt.

"You arranged this to weaken me," he fairly screamed, blood rushing to his face. "You have allied yourself with Ruhvan. Give me the cloth," he pursued, stepping forward, but well out of the way of the dagger. "That which you obtained unfairly. It is mine, and high time I collected it from you."

"Obtained unfairly? Surely not," Tarrington demurred, slipping the knife back into the sheath with sadistic flippancy. "Obtained by fortune, perhaps. Or from a shifting of power. Satan engendered you, ordained you should rule his kingdom. But he did not bestow upon your mantle the... grace of previous rulers. I allied myself with no one," he continued, resuming his prancing around the king. "It is my belief Satan meant for the royalty of this land to rise up and assume a new position of prominence."

"You to rule? I am the direct line."

"But you forget, young master. We are all of the same blood. All 'children' of Lucifer. Your claim is no more than one of ascendancy."

"That is blasphemy, for which I shall have your head."

"Agreed, my words are profane. That does not make them untrue."

"Such an assertion to the throne is unthinkable, you insolent dog. I defeated the king; I succeeded him."

"And yet I hold Satan's warrant," Tarrington protested, touching hand to pouch. "I have waited three years. It is time I claimed my due at the altar."

Nonplused, Ara held out his hand, palm upward. "Return it! Give it back, or suffer eternal damnation on the lowest level of hell."

"Who is to damn me? You? I think not. Save your threats for Otherworlders. They tremble before your might; not I."

"You go back on your word? To me? To your earthly king?"

"What is the word of a devil? We were created to deceive. We are all masters of the evil arts. Tonight you face Ruhvan. For three years your power has remained constant, while his has been recharged by the ravages of Below. He nearly defeated you once. What could make you believe he will fail a second time?"

Visibly shaken, the young master took a step away from his adversary.

"I have powers you know nothing of." Tarrington made no reply. "How does my defeat benefit you? If, as you say, my stepfather has gained strength."

Placing a forehand to his temple, Tarrington's eyes fluttered shut. Although vulnerable, Ara dared not attack him and risk injury before his coming trial.

"I foresee a situation similar to that which occurred before your 'ordination.' One of you – and I do not care whom – will be cast into the Underworld and the survivor weakened beyond all measure. I shall slay him with the sacred knife, given me at birth. A far better weapon than the paltry human which Ruhvan bestowed upon you. Dongal's sacrifice will not be enough."

"By what right do you say?"

"By this right." Removing the blood-soaked linen, Tarrington displayed it, tantalizing close yet light years away. "This is my warrant to the kingdom. Satan permitted me to take it as his promise that when the time came, I would emerge triumphant."

Their eyes locked, each sizing up the other. Impossible to be the first to break contact, Ara remained transfixed, drilling his hatred through the other man's skull.

"Give it to me," he commanded, voice altered into a soft, yet compelling tone. Tarrington staggered from the decree, then slowly extended his hand, unable to stop himself. Reacting too greedily, Ara grabbed for the prize, inadvertently loosing eye contact. The trance snapped, effectively releasing his enemy.

Jerking back, Tarrington stumbled, cursed, then fled the room through the open door, leaving the master to savor that which he could claim as only half a victory.

CHAPTER 32

Ara's approach into the Plain of Stones befit a king. Regal cape flowing, the gold of his belt reflecting torchlight, the blood-red of his ceremonial ring pulsating with alien life, he exuded the picture of confidence. No one, including the individual who knew better, believed him anything but what he was: Satan's heir.

Gathered in the clearing of stone chairs and sacrificial altar were the nobility of the land, grown in number since the earlier conversation. While hardly legions, the sum made up in evil what they lacked in quantity. The reverse of monks, they crossed their arms left over right, tucking them beneath the generous folds of sleeves. For men of Light, this posture represented humility; for creatures begot of God's Dark Twin it symbolized wickedness personified.

Torches, burrowed into stone sconces, crackled around the perimeter, casting wildly fluctuating firelight about the interior. Writhing shadows crept in, then retreated, following the dictates of gyrating flames. Beyond, all lay in pitch blackness, merging sky to earth. No stars shone. The dark of the moon prohibited celestial rays from gracing the ceremony.

A bonfire of gigantic proportion hissed menacingly beneath the altar. Ancient gems the size of a man's fist, harvested from the depths of the earth, spat up lightning of yellow and blue. The dimmer, more humble reflections of flame off hammered metal cast beams of rust toward earth.

All parted as Ara passed, lowering their lids. Striding to the center of the circle, he swept off his outer covering, flinging the cloth into Eldrich's waiting hands. Normally Dongal's place, tonight, in the first of such transferences, it passed to another.

Reverently folding the cape in the Old Manner, the servant pressed it to his breast, then retreated, away from the revelries. Having achieved his earthly glory, the spotlight belonged to others.

In the traditional act of offering life to one's god, Ara ripped open his blouse, revealing naked flesh. Bowing his head, he counted off the seconds. When no force emerged to take it, he acknowledged thanks by silent prayer and turned to confront his coven.

"In the name of he who rules the black portions of the universe, I bid you welcome," he began, repeating ancient words, while spreading wide his arms. "Invited guests and those who watch unbidden," he added, completing a circle to the four winds, "I enjoin you to witness these proceedings."

Ending his circumference so that he faced Tarrington, Ara smiled. The fingers of his left hand rippled, beckoning the other forward. The noble accepted, striding out into the no-man's land between himself and his prince. He waited as Ara continued.

"If there are among you, whether corporeal or spirit, who wish to make objection why we should not sacrifice a living soul here tonight, let him speak, or forever hold his peace."

The moments ticked by, each an hour long. Beyond the circle, a wind stirred, twisting branches of unseen trees. Leaves rustled. Small eddies of dirt swirled around the enclave. No voice issued forth.

"Very well. Let it be noted that no one, or no thing came forward. Who will vouch his soul in testament to this fact?"

A figure crossed a beam of torchlight, temporarily obscuring a small pool of white.

"I will vouch," pledged a woman's voice, devoid of inflection.

"Who will second the testament?"

"I will vouch," agreed another, joining the faceless elder.

"So be it."

Removing a small dagger from his belt, Ara approached the witnesses. The woman held out her hand. Ara pierced the third finger of her right hand with the blade. A drop of blood formed on the tip.

After repeating the ritual with the second witness, the host performed the same act upon himself. Pressing his finger at the first joint to draw a drop of blood, he kissed the knife, then slid it beneath his belt.

"You blend your blood to mine. To retract is to suffer purgatory without honor. Do you recant?"

"I do not," the witnesses simultaneously repeated.

Satisfied, Ara raised his hand. Each, in turn, touched bleeding finger to bleeding finger, sealing the deed.

"As it was *not* in the beginning, let it be forever more," Ara concluded. The witnesses stepped back, blending into the others, like melting snow into a river. "Bring forth the sacrifice," he ordered, licking the union of bloods from his finger.

Shepherd, hearing the pronouncement, cringed in trepidation, but the summons went not to him. Twisting sharply to his left, he saw Dongal, bound and stripped, dragged into the circle. Eyes wide with unspeakable horror, he struggled vainly against his captors. When placed before his master, however, the solemnity of the moment quelled his efforts, reducing him to no more than a lamb, ignorant of its pending doom.

"Dongal," Ara began, meeting the gaze of his favorite with a stare akin to regret. "You have performed your duties faithfully. This shall be the last time you are required to serve me. Hereafter, you will hold a place in hell, serving he to whom all must ultimately subjugate themselves."

Without the aid of an assistant, though he might have had any from the coven, Ara selected a ceremonial blade from the stone table. Steel warmed by the fire, he balanced it carefully before pantomiming the thrust of a blade.

"Since the hour of my awakening, you have been my companion. You are a human, with a pure soul and a good heart. You have always pleased me," he admitted softly, almost quizzically. "No matter what torture, you have lost neither your innocence, nor that hope which kept you obedient. Inside you rages the purity of devotion to that other – lord. You have never grown accustomed to evil, though you have lived amongst devils. Satan welcomes your conversion."

Ignoring the pleading in his companion's face, Ara blinked three times, then directed his gaze downward. The power of his unholy orbs singed, then set ablaze a twig which had blown near his feet. Not until fire consumed it did he raise his eyes.

"Supreme master," he began, voice booming against the rocks, "Accept this most tender gift I offer. Of all my earthly possessions, he is the thing I hold most dear."

The hooded members of the assemblage bowed their heads, for not even they were privy to witness the emergence of majesty.

"Into the Void, ordained and sanctioned by the God you worship, I commend your immortal soul. Onto my Father, I give thee freely. Engender me, oh Lord, with your blessings, for the taste of this blood is sweet."

Using both hands, Ara raised the dagger to arm's length, then shook it to the four points, north, south, east and west. Completing the circle, he inhaled deeply, expelling air from distended nostrils as he prepared to plunge the sharpened edge across and through Dongal's heart. He was well into the action when a hand, faster than his own, grabbed his wrist, preventing the deed from being accomplished.

"What is this?" Ara hissed, unsuccessfully attempting to pull away from the viselike grip. "You dare prevent this holy sacrifice? Who denies Satan?"

"On the contrary," Tarrington, the intervener, objected with a leer of pure hatred. "I most heatedly approve. It is the object of his demise I wish to amend."

Ara shook his head in dull incomprehension. "He is my servant; I offer him —"

Maintaining his grip on the king's wrist, Tarrington addressed the coven, which had crept closer in anticipation of this contest.

"You were the witnesses: you bore testimony to my acceptance of Dongal as sacrifice. But no one," he boomed, voice rising to fever pitch, "can say I named Ara as high priest."

"Not you!" the king protested in shocked wonder. "It is not your place."

"In this Kingdom, I proclaim a new position." Spreading his arms outward, Tarrington made known his desire. "In the name of he from whom we sprang, I proclaim myself monarch." Wrenching the knife from Ara, he broke the boy's wrist by the savageness of the act. The snapping of bone shattered the preternatural stillness. "Dongal, you are mine. Prepare to meet my Maker."

Biting his lip to suppress a cry, Ara dashed at the usurper. He struck the man in the body, yet the force proved ineffective. Swatting away the annoyance, Tarrington approached the victim.

"Too long you have lived among us, human —"

Ara's roar drowned the pronouncement. Unable to stop the desecration physically, the king spun on Shepherd.

"You! Step forward!"

Whether he went of his own volition or was pushed, the Otherworlder did not know. Yet he found himself in the middle of the circle.

"Fulfill your destiny, Shepherd Kingston! Aid me in my time of need!"

Shepherd's mouth opened, then closed in mute denial. His hands hung limply at his side. He made no attempt to move, nor did he direct his gaze at Tarrington. The seconds passed.

"Act!"

A moment still, and then, with shame, "I cannot."

"You think to disobey? I will destroy you, utterly."

Not from love did Shepherd spare the servant.

"No disobedience. My... gift has deserted me."

Tarrington's eyes sparkled with complicity in acknowledgment of having achieved his supreme moment. A time decreed by the Seer of Dark Acts.

"He cannot aid you, Master. You have erred. He is not the one. You have falsely identified your savior."

A foul exhalation of air polluted the enclave as Ara pointed his one good hand at the extension of the devil.

"You lie."

The older, wiser man's eyebrows arched in supreme good humor. "From the moment of your conception, I have watched you, Little One. Overseen your development. Conspired with Ruhvan to steer you in the wrong direction. So easy," he cajoled, stroking the words as a sentient man would caress a lover.

"I do not believe you," Ara choked, his sentence nearly unintelligible as the horror of the revelation sunk into his essence, numbing colorless lips.

"I have observed and manipulated. I, who caused the death of your 'savior's' parents. Child's play for one of destiny. A landslide, perpetrated by the discovery of a golden pyramid; observed through the eyes of a stone idol."

"The pyramid." Ara swayed, nearly losing his balance. Flames from the altar rose in anticipation. The earth trembled beneath the weight of prophesy.

"Another humble gift to you on the occasion of your birth," Tarrington agreed, rubbing his hands together to ingrain the deception into his flesh. "An instrument used by you to further your ends, but one which worked for me."

"Treason —"

"To what lengths did I not go?" Tarrington soothingly pursued, speaking over Ara's impotent objection. "I nurtured the false savior; gave onto him this 'power' which so filled him with dread. I directed him to Abraham Trent, the learned one, who knew much but not enough. My familiar, who guided him on his quest from one foolish source to another, until he presented himself at your doorstop, Master. I, who arranged for *Ericka Elvina* to observe his 'power.'"

Reaching a crescendo, he added his final and most damning complicity. "The face in the painting, sire. You observed it change and believed the Master used it as a conduit of communication. To verify your discovery. Such was not the case. It was I and none other who committed that perversion. So that you would see what I wished you to see and believe you had found your secret weapon."

"No! No! I am not mistaken! I cannot be!" Beseechingly, Ara pleaded with Shepherd. "Prove him false. Reveal to them," he continued, furiously indicating the gathered demons, "your power. Augment mine for the destruction of a greater wickedness!"

Puckering his lips, Tarrington made low, deprecating noises. "A greater wickedness? But is that not what Satan seeks? You cannot win here by claiming to be the lesser of two evils."

Shocked by his own admission, Ara fell backward, the bone of his shattered wrist catching on the sleeve of his blood-stained robe. Jerking it free, he stood helplessly by as Tarrington recited the prayers of the Old Religion.

"In the Name of he who rules this void, never visited by the God of Light, I condemn you, Dongal, servant of Ara."

With the authority of ascendancy, Tarrington thrust the blade through Dongal's ribs and into his left ventricle. Instantly, a fountain of unleashed, cherry-red fluid spouted upward and outward, staining the ghostly-pale flesh of the naked sacrifice.

The once-living human plunged back, caught his balance without willful direction, gasped, then cried, his last words lost amid the bubbling of blood from his mouth.

Withdrawing the dagger past severed bone, limp tissue and dead muscle, Tarrington brought the forged steel to his lips and kissed it.

"Face me now, Ara, prince of the Kingdom, for he we worship is not yet appeased. He will have a second soul before this night is past."

The unholy witnesses moved back, retrograde movements obscured by long cloaks, conversely making it appear Tarrington had stepped forward. The contest had come to its preordained conclusion. They would not intervene.

"Kill. Kill. Kill. Kill." The chant began toward the rear, infected those nearest the source, then spread forward. "Kill. Kill. Kill. Kill." This ancient cry, a poem of everlasting intensity, arose deep within their throats and spread outward, hovering over the enclave with tangible structure.

"Kill. Kill. Kill. Kill."

Three times holy, a fourth to set the cycle in motion for all eternity.

Nowhere in their invocation did they define a subject. Left to the principals the decision on whom to destroy.

Ara needed no inspiration. Reaching for another dagger, this one of a weight requiring both his hands, he dashed forward, blade outstretched. It wavered, then held true as adrenalin replaced solid bone and muscle.

"In the name of he who rules this Kingdom! I damn you to the hottest fires of hell!"

Unthinkingly, Tarrington reached for his weapon. Not the short sword buckled beneath his tunic, but the blood-stained cloth extorted from the boy-king.

"Back!" he shouted, thrusting forward that upon which his earthly existence and unearthly afterlife depended. "Back, or I shall cast it into the sacrificial flames!"

Momentarily confused, Ara hesitated, torn between murdering his adversary and fear of ultimate retribution. While tears of indecision leaked from twin sockets, he shook with wrath.

"Fight me fairly, Tarrington, or pay the consequences."

"Fairly?" the elder sneered, contempt adding courage to his actions. "There is no such concept as 'fair' in this space ruled by Evil. Let he who wins by any means ascend the throne!" Springing forward, he raced toward the altar.

Blocking his path, Ara lunged, thrusting the dagger toward Tarrington's unprotected heart. Fending off the blow with his right hand, the enemy flung the troth in Ara's face, temporarily blinding him. The symbolism evinced a powerful reaction in one observer, whose stoical eyes were torn from Dongal's dead form to the duelists.

"Die!" Rephrasing the coven's command, Tarrington wrenched the dagger from Ara's clenched fingers. "Die by the weapon you ceded me! Die! Die! Die!"

Devils clashed, the thunderous impact of their bodies imitating heaven's rumblings, each muttering obscenities and snatches of prayer for strength. Interlocked in mortal combat, they spun around the enclosure, knocking several torches from their sconces. Fire spread over the ground, burning the dirt beneath their feet as though it were dried tinder and not the clay from which sprang God's first creations.

Insatiable, powerful, starving for fuel, the flames leapt upward, igniting the dress of the fighters. Working inward, fingers of red-hot fire tickled, singed, then ultimately consumed the flesh of legs and thighs. The odor of roasting meat permeated the arena. Clouds of grey smoke rose languidly above the contestants, then perched above their skulls in the shape of unearthly buzzards.

Still they fought, sparks flying upward as they parried, struck and drew away. Had a billion fireflies been unleashed, their light could not have equaled the spectacle of the burning remnants of cloth and skin.

A disembodied dagger flew from the conflagration, landing ten feet away. It immediately burst into flame, the steel of the blade melting like bees wax. Precious jewels of red and green popped out, rolled away, then sunk beneath the living body of ash.

"Die! Die!"

A horrific shriek pierced the enclave. A ball of flame, once housing two creatures, increased in size, then broke apart, one half flying backward, the other maintaining, for the moment, an upright position.

"Die!"

The object on the ground, once flesh and bone, writhed, transmuted, shrieked, then slowly dissipated, growing smaller and smaller as internal heat finished that which had begun. Not yet expired, the form rolled over, pitifully seeking one last chance at victory.

Before the witnesses, who had sworn a blood oath to Satan, the loser let loose one final bawl, then dissolved into nothingness. All attention turned to the victor.

The flames died down around the one left standing, though he was charred nearly beyond recognition. In place of skin, bone shone through, revealing a death's head of blenched white. Barred teeth protruded, appearing unnaturally large and pointed. With neither muscle nor ligaments, the cracked vertebrae snapped as the beast lowered its head.

"In the name of he who was created before Time, I commend my enemy," Ara, son of Satan, whispered.

Slipping gracelessly to his knees, the reigning master fell to earth. His movements were jerky, those of a puppet whose strings had been severed.

"Heal me, Father," he supplicated. "Restore my body, that I may rule your Kingdom forever."

It was more than he had a right to ask. A murmur arose around the enclosure. Ara extended his hands, no more than blackened stumps. The coven crowded nearer, their eyes, their worship to the greater master uniting them as one.

With infinitesimal slowness, fresh, vibrant marrow refilled hollow bones. Upon them grew veins and arteries, muscles and flesh, the flowers of Hades.

On Ara's scalp, a thin sheen of skin, then hair emerged, tufts of dark locks, cascading to holes where ears had not yet reformed. The sagging shoulders straightened, the back stiffened.

"By the grace of God's hidden self," Ara chanted, "restore me."

A clap of thunder shattered the Plain, then bolts of lightning, brighter than the fission of atoms, lit the scene. Rain began to fall, quenching all fire but that which continued to roar at the base of the altar. Rivulets of water flowed like blood, forming pools. The ash of the ground turned to sticky clumps of grey matter.

"Father, I have won," Ara gasped, misinterpreting the sign.

"Not yet," boomed a voice, so distorted by thunder it was comprehended by the soul and not the ears. "Not yet, my *stepson.*"

The young master shuddered, quivered, then sobbed, averting his stare from lowly ground to stately earth. A shape emerged, at first amorphous, then gradually assuming human form. Legs, torso, arms and finally head, until complete.

"Ruhvan! Oh, Lord, not now!"

"Now," the former ruler of the kingdom advised, face aglow with triumph. Strength emanated in an aura of health, muscles rippled through the veil of purple raiment. A crown of gold shimmered with glory. "Now, dear Ara. Stand and face your master."

"I worship none but he who has overseen my triumph," Ara tried, rising unsteadily to his feet. "He has sanctioned my rule once tonight; he shall do so again."

Ruhvan's face expressed a ghastly, malevolent grin.

"You have done no more than remove an... annoyance from the Kingdom. Tarrington was no match, yet he fought you as an equal. Your immolation of his soul was no great feat."

"The prophesy," Ara desperately reminded his stepfather, stalling while he concentrated shattered powers on restoring his life force. "Something you failed to heed properly while you yet ruled. As it was written, so shall it be."

"Your prophesy," the late master dismissed, "has proven false. Were you not listening? Shepherd Kingston is a creation of fantasy. His legacy, like his power, is false. Now, you must perish for that error in judgment."

"You babble incoherently," Ara countered, feeling blood pump from his newly reformed heart. "I have seen more than you know. He has saved me twice; he will do so, again."

In a desperate attempt to convince himself, Ara spun on Shepherd. "They were blinded by their own complicity. Prove to them now you are the fulfillment."

Placing a hand to his chest, Ara implored Shepherd. The human's eyes hardened. His heart, once pure and good, had metamorphosed.

"You forget your warning, Ara; that once I stepped foot in this accursed land, I lost my soul. I am no longer a... dupe... to... manipulate."

Reacting with unmitigated anger, the king spat before resuming his position before Ruhvan.

"I defeated you once; I will do so again. As was foretold," Ara repeated, retreating to the only words he knew. Strength of faith rejuvenated where physical powers failed. "I stand on prophesy. He is my chosen, as I am Satan's!"

Before the words were fairly articulated, Ruhvan raised his hand. Instantly, a flash of light erupted from his palm. Ara staggered back as the blow struck him in the neck. Had it been six inches lower, the contact would have exploded his auricles.

"Three years in hell has taught me much," the embodiment of resurrection continued, flexing his muscles until they cracked from pressure. Addressing his noble audience, he bowed before them, then spun around, fingers splayed outward. Jagged bolts of energy catapulted forward. In the reverse of a heavenly demonstration, lightning soared up, illumining the blackness. Earthquakes rolled the onlooker's feet.

"I have ruled hell," he boasted, a smile broadening deep scarlet lips. In reference to the onslaught occasioned by his command, Ruhvan continued. "How can earth be an impediment to one who commands the heavens?"

Stunned by the old one's boast of ruling more than their allotted space, Ara gasped, then seized advantage of Ruhvan's showmanship by launching an attack. A ball of fire struck the man-devil in the face, encasing him in flame. The stench of burning flesh, on a higher order than that which permeated Tarrington's demise, filled the enclosure.

To the younger's shock, however, the hellish weapon did not consume his enemy. As he watched, eyes aglow, the flames were sucked into Ruhvan's body. In a moment, they were drawn inside, replacing his outward form with an opposite aura of pulsating energy.

"You cannot defeat me by ordinary means. Fire is no longer my enemy, but my ally. What say you, now, of prophesy?"

Words failed. Heart madly fibrillating, Ara heaved another ball of fire at he, who would reclaim his place on Satan's earth. Again, a horrific conflagration engulfed the old master; a second time he absorbed the flames.

"I grow weary of your foolishness," Ruhvan sneered. "Enough." Turning his back on the boy-devil in a display of utter contempt, he addressed the other sons and daughters of Lucifer. "You came this night to bear witness to sacrifice. And so you have. Tarrington, the would-be king, presented an unworthy human to our lord. Ara, the former master, has punished him for his failing. Satan demands more. He requires *three* souls to placate his hunger."

The devil's minions dropped to their knees *en masse,* ready to worship he of superior power. Soaking in their adoration, Ruhvan spread his arms, encompassing them into his new dominion.

"No longer will an Otherworlder serve a devil; never again shall affection be permitted to thrive within this void of unmitigated evil. Hatred is our birthright. The new millennium draws near, yet the Old Ways prevail. Ruhvan has spoken."

Gesturing contemptuously toward two of the coven, he indicated they stand.

"Take this inferior – this deviling – and chain him to the altar."

"No!" Ara cried, appealing to those of no conscience. "Within my kingdom you were granted power. Worship him and you will be reduced to slaves."

His words held no effect. The chosen pair quickly subdued the youth, dragging him to the quarried stone altar. Without the ability to resist, Ara's limbs were manacled to the rock.

"Draw nearer," Ruhvan invited, throwing back the chards of his burned cowl to reveal a nearly transparent skin, still inwardly illuminated by fire. "Witness the destruction of a weakling."

The coven did as bidden, each seething with curiosity. One, a woman, handed Ruhvan the ceremonial dagger, removed from Dongal's lifeless form.

"Here, master. Use this."

The symbolism found favor. Smiling broadly, flesh twisting unnaturally as it moved over protruding bone, Ruhvan reverently kissed the instrument of mortal destruction.

"This finds favor in my eyes. It is just. Let Ara follow Dongal and Tarrington, so that they may serve as minions to the true lord of the lower regions."

While speaking, a tongue of flame erupted from his mouth, sterilizing the blade. Dried blood from the human sacrifice evaporated into the sulphuric atmosphere.

"One times one; two times two; three times three," Ruhvan chanted to the greater master. "Seven begets seven. In the names of they who forged evil; in the name of He who ceded this void to Satan, I commit a soul to hell!" Gripping the handle with an intensity ungoverned by reason, he held it over Ara's exposed breast. "Die, infant, and make penance for sins, in a place where forgiveness does not exist."

Lifting the dagger upward, points of light from the creeping firelight sparkling off his kingly ring, Ruhvan made a sweeping motion, slicing the air into halves before driving the point downward.

Ara shrieked.

CHAPTER 33

The shackled Son of Hell undulated twice more, each a pale imitation of that which had gone before. Wails disintegrated into whimpers, then sobs broke forth, rendering him, not into a level of hell, but into that childish aberration associated with babes.

Contrary to expectations; against the certainty of mortal demise, Ara lived, untouched by the blade. Stifling a sob, he raised his head by elevating his shoulders, the only locomotion allowed by the restraining wrought iron bands around wrists and ankles.

He sought an explanation for the miracle that hitherto prohibited intervention belonging solely to the realm of God's vast domain.

Were Ara or any of the witnesses disposed to laugh, they might have taken amusement in the stark disbelief etched between the eyes, nose and lips of Lucifer's elder. That devil stood, legs apart, forearms taut, knife suspended between planes of intangible dimensions, held tight by a force mightier than one being's desire for revenge.

His consciousness an erupting inferno of shock, dancing fantastically with disbelief, Ruhvan demanded explanation.

"Who – who?" he stammered, his veneer of invincibility punctured. "Who has perpetrated this sin by preventing the fulfillment of destiny?"

"Say instead prophesy," came the unknown voice. "You have misread the stars, Ruhvan. You are neither sun nor moon, but a plaything of your ungodly master."

"I –?" Stumbling away from the altar, inadvertently turning his back on the symbol of devotion and sacrifice, he challenged those assembled at the Plain of Stones, eyes distended, pupils filling the space where once there sat whiteness. "I – a plaything?"

"A fool, if you prefer. You have had your rule, once, 'master.' No one is ever allowed a second chance. You were deceived."

"How can that be? I am a devil – the living image of he who dominates the Black Regions. Show yourself!" the older man demanded, casting about like a blind man, seeking the perpetrator by ear, rather than sight. "Who dares comes between me and my father?"

"I dare," Shepherd Kingston admitted, stepping forward. The horrors of the past hour had greatly altered his countenance. Though he appeared as a knight of yore, with blond hair cast loosely about his shoulders, the sinews beneath flesh now protruded with kinetic energy, his human shape radiating with a glow reserved for those of unearthly castes.

"You?" The acknowledgement came as a gasp of escaping air, fouled by the fire consuming his interior. "You? You are false prophet."

"Granted," Shepherd agreed, raising an eyebrow in mock surprise. "For I serve neither Ara nor you."

"You are not a devil," Ruhvan persisted, the enormity of Shepherd's challenge emasculating him. "You are a human; one of... of God's creatures."

"I am... Shepherd," the youth corrected, features mobile and pulsating as the reflection of ceremonial flames reworked, reshaped his outward essence.

"Shepherd," the old master repeated, the word having no meaning. "You – are the face in the painting."

"The living embodiment of that wretched soul. But you, like Tarrington, failed to perceive the significance of that which you 'created.'"

"No," the deposed monarch demurred, refusing to believe. "You are no more than a sheep to be sacrificed to Satan."

The man created in one of God's images shook his head, a smile tantalizing his handsome features.

"That is the trouble with inspiration. There are many who divine the mysteries of the universe. A multitude who speak of events to come. Fewer who dare commit these foretellings to paper. I have seen the books," he graciously added, touching the spot near his Adam's apple where a cross once hung.

"You and your minion, Tarrington, found me. Guided my life because you thought I was not the one. You committed a most grievous mistake. I am the One."

Palms extended outward, the beneficent gesture mocked true belief. "You misunderstood; you thought Trent a fool; that his teachings were false; or that I would not believe. Yet he gave me much." Averting his eyes from Ruhvan, Shepherd approached the shackled king. "For once, you were correct, Ara. Trent, my most beloved *mentor,* erred when bidding me to evoke the names of both good and evil spirits. It is beyond the ability of either Christian or devil to enjoin these forces to fight on the same side. He should have chosen one over the other. Alas, he did not. That was his sin. For which he was duly punished."

Ara groaned, the taste of ash on his tongue mitigating the sound to a soft moan.

"He is gone and I am here. Not in the manner he anticipated, yet I survived. Let that stand as his contribution to the universe he sought so hard to know. Knowledge is worth much, old friend, but it is not an ending by itself."

"Enough!" Ruhvan choked. "You speak in tongues."

"I speak for those with ears to hear," Shepherd parodied with an admonition nearly two centuries old.

"Choose! If you have come to save Ara, then face me."

"I have 'come' to save neither of you."

"Shepherd," Ara begged, straining against his restraints. "Slay him. Free me."

As the human acknowledged the plea, the earth beneath the ceremonial Plain of Stone shook with unprecedented violence. A crack beneath the feet of Satan's witnesses hurtled rock and charred bits of wood into the depths. The coven fell back, sore afraid of impending doom.

"The time for giving orders is past, Ara. As dead as Trent. As dead as one who sought to rise above his station. As dead as Dongal, who served you faithfully. As finished as the first – and last – reign of Ruhvan, the king."

"No," Ara sobbed, straining against invisible bonds of destiny. "No! You condemn me to hell?"

"*I* condemn no one," Shepherd innocently protested. "Do not seek to place me on your own level. I am neither devil nor Satan. I am Shepherd."

"Explain," Ruhvan enjoined, the fires within him seething into coals of extinguished power.

"I am neither sacrifice, nor slave; neither ruler nor ruled. I am Shepherd of the Kingdom, destined to oversee this void until the coming of a new master. Such is the true prophesy. As regent, I shall tolerate no weakness. You, Ruhvan, have returned from hell, yet you learned nothing from your subjugation. You came back no more 'enlightened' than when you were cast down. Such... failure...is unacceptable."

Shepherd focused his concentration on the blade in Ruhvan's hand. It was a matter of no consequence to turn it inward.

"Perish," he decreed, "by your own hand. The one great impiety of heaven and hell. The single constant of both our universes."

"I will not!"

The former master of Satan's kingdom struggled against the force exerted against him, attempting to turn the dagger away.

"Die," Shepherd urged, the word spoken kindly, almost sympathetically, though the pseudo-emotion was not lost upon his listeners. "Die and return from whence you came. You have no place here."

"Lord! Master! Satan!" Ruhvan screamed, summoning he of deaf ears. "Surely this cannot be your will! Destroy the infidel!"

His pleas went unheeded. With an onslaught of unprecedented ferocity, his hands drove inward, plunging the dagger deep inside his chest. While the act was more symbolic than actual, for he had not regained his earthly form, the shade of former organs exploded. Gore erupted from the surgical incision. Molten blood spurted outward in small volcanoes of frenzy. Flowing downward, the bubbling rust-red fluid seared what was left of Ruhvan's tangible exterior, consuming it with the same sadistic delight other flames had quenched Trent's well-intentioned invocations.

"In the name of –!" But the name of he who Ruhvan evoked was never uttered, as the old master collapsed into a pool of soggy residue. The fire within him sputtered, licked at protruded bone, then put itself out in an implosion of expiration.

"Forgive him, Father, for he has sinned," Shepherd misquoted, grim satisfaction lining his otherworldly features.

A buzzing of inexpressible shock and horror swept across the coven. Male and female devils crept backwards, into the lengthening shadows cast by diminished torches.

"Return to your homes," the human commanded, approving their retreat. "Go now. Your place is not here. But beware. Much tribute will be required in this new kingdom. You have grown lax; you have worshipped falsely. There is great penance to be paid."

"We will obey, master," the elder responded, bowing deeply.

"Do not come to the castle until you are summoned. I must have time to... settle in. I anticipate many... changes. This land is stagnant; dying. There has been no improvement here in tens of thousands of years. It is time this temporal void be introduced into the 20th Century."

Not until the last disappeared down the charred trail did Shepherd turn his attention to Eldrich. Summoning the servant from his hiding place behind the tall stones, he contemplated him with disdain.

"Of all the devils I have encountered, you have been the most ambitious. Daring to rise above your station."

"As have you, sire. You are not of the blood, yet have triumphed over all."

"It is your wish to emulated me? To become a member of the nobility? I think not."

Eldrich bent at the waist in a futile gesture of nonviolence.

"You dare plead peace? After your intervention this evening?"

"If I had not, sire, you might have escaped. How different, then, your future."

"Were I a king and not a shepherd," the new master observed, running his tongue across the back of his teeth, "I would have you thrown into the sacrificial fires for such audacity."

Pointing toward the twisted, blood-stained body of Dongal, Shepherd allowed a momentary expression of sorrow to cross his sweat-streaked face.

"It was your act of treachery which caused the death of this innocent soul. Not that I condemn treachery. As you see, Ara, I have learned much in my brief sojourn in your country." Ara made a nearly unperceivable gesture, indicating he comprehended the statement. It is failure I may not condone," Shepherd resumed, addressing Eldrich. "There is no place here for miscarriage. But I am not a king. It is not my place to sacrifice life. That," he meaningfully added, "I shall leave to another. For you, I have a new position." He appeared to debate the man's fate, though the decision had already been made. "Chattel. You are too insignificant to serve me as Dongal once served Ara."

"Master –" Eldrich began, but Shepherd waved him off.

"Speak no more. Henceforth, you shall be mute. Signify you understand." Eldrich nodded, tongue cloven to the roof of his mouth. "Excellent. Now: let us consider. What shall be your first task in this new position you occupy?"

Eldrich cringed, bowing acquiesce to his new master.

"Take the body of Dongal. Wash it with fresh water and sweet herbs. Clothe it in ceremonial raiment, then set it upon a wagon, drawn by two horses. When this is done, come to me again. Go now! And do not fail to comply precisely with my orders, Eldrich, or your fate shall become a new legend in this land of mythology and mystery."

Dropping to the ground, Eldrich maintained that position a full minute before scurrying, like a rat, to gather up the body of the beloved servant. The old and the new masters observed him in silence.

With the removal of Dongal's corpse, the mist parted from the heavens. Stars shone through the night sky, illuminating the circular enclosure.

Inexplicably, a slice of moon pierced the clearing with irregularly shaped columns of light.

Sighing heavily, for he felt tired beyond description, Shepherd wrung his hands, effectively washing them of the grisly deeds he had both witnessed and performed.

"Now, Ara, stepson of Ruhvan and son of Satan, it is your turn." Crossing to the youth, Shepherd sprung him from his chains with the ease of one possessing keys at the ends of his fingers. "Come," he cajoled. "Return to the castle."

Without speaking, Ara habitually held out a hand, expecting Shepherd to wrap it around his shoulder. Instead, his former guest stepped back, denying him assistance.

"No, Ara. As you so rightly predicted, my status as guest has altered. It is no longer my place to accommodate you. I have another master, now. You shall walk on your own two legs. And be quick about it," he added, noting the sudden howling of wolves. "Were you to falter and fall, I am afraid the beasts of our country would make short work of your flesh and bones."

Shrinking from pain and humiliation, the former master of Satan's kingdom struggled to his feet. Weakened from his battles, he adopted a serf's shuffle, making small, ineffectual steps across the ash-strewn enclave, leaving behind a trail remarkably similar to that of a spineless slug.

Moving aside, Shepherd allowed the emaciated man to cross before him. Their eyes did not meet. Another moment, and Ara vanished into the charred brush.

Finally alone, Shepherd bestowed upon himself the luxury of surveying his domain. And found it good.

Gathering strength, he looked upward, first to the moon, then to the plethora of stars decorating the heavens. Sizing up the enormity of God's universe, he smiled, spread wide his arms and quoted from Trent's instructions.

"And behold, I live forever and ever; and I have the keys of death and hell."

Stooping down, he scooped a handful of ash into his palm, then slowly let it run through his fingers.

"Not exactly as you intended, old friend. But then, none of us here had the gift of reading prophesy."

Wiping his palms together, symbolically shedding himself of the old, while ingraining the new into his flesh, Shepherd addressed the universe.

"In the name of the Trinity, proceed me in our mysterious work, to accomplish that which We desire!"

Not precisely as Trent wrote, though Shepherd remembered the prayer by heart. Across the moon, a cloud appeared.

"As it was in the beginning, is now and ever shall be. Amen."

And that, too, found favor in his eyes.

Heat emanating from the flames burned immeasurably hot. Unleashed from its confines in the great fireplace, it would consume a mountain. Once, he had been afraid of such fire. The remembrance now seemed childish. There was nothing to fear in fire. Fire purified. Fire cleansed the soul.

Clutching the ceremonial robe closer around his shoulders, the wearer felt the power. While he could not come close to estimating its unquenchable strength, he appreciated its value.

Snapping his fingers, a formless shade stole close, a belt of gold within his hands. At the master's bidding, he wrapped it around the robed man's waist, clasping it with a conch of rubies and sapphires. To assert his authority, the precious stones absorbed the glory, reflecting them onto its possessor.

"The ring," commanded the earthly master. "Put it on my finger."

Extending the wedding ring finger of his left hand, he accepted the gift. It was heavy, engraved with mystic symbols, ancient lettering. Turning it one way, then the other, he admired the jewelry. He thought it beautiful; life incarnate. He smiled and his face radiated beneficently.

"The dagger."

The shade wordlessly nodded. With a gliding motion, he slipped away, returning with the sacrificial blade. He handed it to his master, hilt first.

"The chalice."

Again the shade crept forward, cradling the cup with both hands, rather than taking it by the stem. He could be forgiven his ill manners, for the position of servant in the Devil's chamber was a new one to him.

"Bare your arm."

The servant performed the act, drawing back the rough brown cloth of his peasant's garb. Fear gripped his heart, though his face betrayed no emotion. In this gateway to hell, he comprehended any expression less than total worship could cost his miserable existence.

"I am Alpha and Omega, the Beginning and the End; which is, which was, and which is to come. I am the earthly arm of the Holy Alternate. Neither the first, nor the last, I stand as guardian to he who has never lived, and shall never die.

"They are seven, they are seven. In the valley of the abyss, they are seven. In the numberless stars of heaven, they are seven. In the abyss, in the depths, they grow in power.

"They are not male, they are not female. They do not love women, they have not begotten offspring. Accept this blood ritual, as has been performed since corporeal flesh first formed in that Other's galaxy. Guide my hand, O master of this kingdom, as I spill blood for your Greater Glory."

With a quick, decisive motion, the knife-welder sliced a straight line across his companion's arm. Unchecked, blood spurted from the wound and collected in the chalice.

More. More. More. Seven times seven. Fill it to the brim.

The words came from neither participant, but from a throat of unearthly manufacture. The knife-welder complied, waiting until crimson topped the rim of the cup.

More. More. More. Seven times seven. Let it spill to the ground.

The guardian waited, content to do his master's bidding. The servant, whose life force weakened with the blood-letting, tottered unsteadily.

More. More. More. Seven times seven. Let the floor swim in blood.

Pit-pat, pit-pat, pit-pat, blood seeped from the cup and onto the floor. Pools of dark red formed, some seeping into the ageless cracks.

More. More. More. Seven times seven. No life is wasted if it is given in service to Me.

Pools transformed into small oceans. The servant cried faintly, eyes rolling back in his head. With the motion of a crippled bug, he dropped down into a clotted mass of sticky, chocolate-brown fluid.

Enough.

Bending at the waist, the cup-bearer strode to the mouth of purgatory. Grinning wildly, he tossed the contents into the roar of sulphuric flame. Sparks jumped outward, creeping along the path of that which had spilled, consuming as it went. The cup-bearer did not move; he no longer felt the heat.

After supping on that which had been fed it, the insatiable fire tickled, then seared the prone shade. The man attempted to scream, but his jaws, locked in a yawn of agony, produced no sound. Writhing, twisting, turning, stamping his feet on the stone plates, slapping his hands against the air, the living sacrifice attempted to brush back the destructive combustion.

His efforts proved desultory, pitiful. The man with the empty chalice felt like guffawing. It was too funny; a farce. The servant did not know, could not know, his life was not to be forfeit; that his flesh and bone and blood had become the eternal burnt offering. Not once, but a thousand times, they would repeat this ritual, in anticipation of a new birth, the coming of another son of Satan.

Not until the passage of Seven times Seven would his agony end, to begin anew in that black void he once hoped to rule.

"I am the Alpha. I am the Omega," the guardian repeated, watching as the fire receded. "I am he, who shall protect your flock for Seven times Seven. As it was written, so shall it be. Amen."

Standing outside the castle walls, the harsh wind blowing against his face, Shepherd stared down at the body of Dongal, wrapped in a woolen blanket. The features of the servant could not be discerned, but were well recalled.

The team of horses, a black and a bay, pranced nervously, tails swishing. Shepherd eyed them critically before addressing Eldrich.

"Take him away; far away. Across the border. Bury him in consecrated ground. Place this at his head."

So saying, Shepherd handed Eldrich a small gold cross, suspended from an intricately woven chain. The servant recoiled from the sacred relic, making wild gesticulations with his hands.

"Take it! It will not burn you. These are new times. The vampire," he added for his own amusement, "has seen his reflection in the mirror."

Comprehending only that to disobey meant death, Eldrich accepted the universally acknowledged token of the Son of God's resurrection.

"Do as I say, then return. I count the hours. There is much work to perform. You will not lack manual labor to occupy your time."

Fearful to be caught with a holy relic on his person, Eldrich clambered into the wagon. Flailing the leather reigns against the horses' backs, he drove away. Shepherd watched until he passed from sight, noting with grim satisfaction the final trail upon which Dongal progressed. It was the same he and the servant had ridden, not many nights gone by.

"In the end there is a beginning," he observed. "Fare thee well, faithful human."

Casting his head back with a jaunty air, Shepherd returned to the castle, taking the time-honed steps two at a time. The massive door opened by an unseen hand.

Inside, much had transpired. Gone were the torches lighting the entranceway; torn down and consigned to bonfires the ornate tapestries. In transition, the stark and barren walls gave comfort. They reminded him, somehow, of the Stone Gate Building, and how it must have appeared during the early stages of renovation.

In a month, perhaps two, the dreary castle would be illuminated by electricity. Generators would replace wood-burning heat. Telephones would connect Satan's world with that of God's. Newspapers from around the globe would advise on such myriad topics as wars, pestilence and famine.

It was as well, Shepherd decided, to keep in touch.

Striding into the den, once a chamber of horror and now his office, the master picked up a curled parchment. On it a signature in blood had been scrawled. He pursued it casually before consigning it to the flames.

"Good-bye, Dongal," he spoke with authority. "Your soul is free. Blessed are those who ask for little, for that is precisely what they shall receive."

Grinning impishly, Shepherd waited until it the fire rendered it into blackened ash before retrieving a small, golden pyramid from the side table by the door. Rubbing it the way a mystic would communicate with a crystal ball, he stared into one gilded side. A face appeared on the ancient, though effective communicator.

"Come to me," he commanded, settling down into a massive, hand-carved chair in front of the fire. The heat warmed him.

Moments later, a knock roused him from reverie.

"Enter."

"You summoned me?" a pleasant, diffident voice inquired.

"Yes. I wish you to review these accounts. There is much I do not know about them. And much I will know."

Craning his neck, he observed Ericka Elvina's movements as she glided toward the desk. Turning the pages of a heavy binder, she arched an alluring eyebrow at Shepherd.

"Where shall I begin?"

"With the stock market. Money is power. That much I do comprehend. Ruhvan did not understand; he sought only to punish. You did not understand. You sought only to seek for he, who would save you. And I have saved you, have I not, Ericka?"

"Yes, master. You have saved me," she agreed, in a manner suggesting nothing but devotion – tainted, perhaps by a touch of mystery. Ericka had a talent for that, he decided. She had learned from a master.

"Not in the manner you anticipated; nor in the way I perceived," Shepherd continued. "We both misjudged the... handwriting on the wall. But enough of the past. The past is dead. As dead as Tarrington. As dead as Ruhvan. As dead as Ara.

"We live for the present and the future... *for that is where you and I are going to spend the rest of our lives,*" he added with an odd quirk. That peculiar quote from a lost and unlamented horror film conversely proved that, for the moment, at least, the past remained alive.

"Wall Street," Ericka continued, oblivious to his mental digression, "is controlled by the manipulation of stocks; utilizing the powers of evil to raise and lower them at will is our advantage."

Shepherd listened attentively. In his new role, he felt acutely interested in the risings and fallings of many things.

Such being his new position as *shepherd of the kingdom.*

The End

GSFE

ALSO BY S.L.KOTAR AND J.E.GESSLER

Aside from being awarded <u>The Writers Guild of American 101Best Written TV Series</u> for our episode of **GUNSMOKE, it was also the highest rated** in the 20-year history of the series, "Kitty's Love Affair" – NOT our title, by the way; and there was no "affair")

We created, published and wrote many articles for **"The Kepi Magazine,"** an iconoclastic publication that specialized in the Civil War and 19th century life. The complete set, updated with an comprehensive index, is available again in print and electronically as : **The Kepi Volume I and II**, and **The Kepi Volumes III and IV** . These two volumes reintroduce the ground breaking Civil War research, historically accurate timelines, period photography and an eye to the life and times of this unsettled period of American history.

The next series is a character based historical 1950's courtroom based murder mystery entitled **"The Hugh Kerr Mystery Series"**..

- Book I   The Conundrum of the Decapitated Detective
- Book II   The Conundrum of the Absconded Attorney
- Book III   The Conundrum of the Sins of the Fathers
- Book IV   The Conundrum of The Two-Sided Lawyer
- Book V   The Conundrum of the Clueless Counselor
- Book VI   The Conundrum of the Loveless Marriage
- Book VII   The Conundrum of the Executed Defendant
- Book VIII   The Conundrum of the Jettisoned Jury
- Book IX   The Conundrum of the Perjured Pigeon
- Book X   The Conundrum of the Haunting Halloween Party
- Book XI   The Conundrum of the Tuneless Tunesmith
- Book XII   The Conundrum of the Meddling Motorcar
- Book XIII   The Conundrum of the Blundering Bea
- Book XIV   The Conundrum of Shooting Fish in a Barrel

  o   **To Be Continued!**

Another series is "New Beginnings" a 1950's medical drama.

- **Book I**   **The Believer**
- **Book II**   **The Heretic**
- **Book III**   **Arrow Song**
- **Book IV**   **Peas In A Pod**

"**the ReproBate saga**" is another character based series in the 1860 Civil War

- **Book I**   **Beneath the Rose**
- **Book II**   **skull and cRossBones**
- **Book III**   **Redefining Bastions**
- **Book IV**   **thickeR than Blood**

  - **To Be Continued!**

Stand-alone novels include:

- <u>**Catman**</u> *He was every man; he was no man*

- <u>**ONE**</u> Science Fiction space travel

www.ingramcontent.com/pod-product-compliance
Lightning Source LLC
Chambersburg PA
CBHW032139190626
46814CB00005BA/1762